IMPERIAL ECHOES

Ashes of Empire #4

ERIC THOMSON

Imperial Echoes
Copyright 2021 Eric Thomson
First paperback printing March 2021

All rights reserved.
This book, or parts thereof, may not be reproduced in any form without permission.

This is a work of fiction. Names, characters, places, and incidents either are the product of the author's imagination or are used fictitiously. Any resemblance to actual persons, living, or dead, business establishments, events, or locales is entirely coincidental.

Published in Canada
By Sanddiver Books Inc.
ISBN: 978-1-989314-35-7

PART I – A FADING ECHO

—1—

Agonized screams echoed off the interrogation room's slick, plasticized walls as the prisoner, strapped to a metal table, bucked and spasmed, an expression of utter horror on his haggard face. A black-clad Sister of the Void Reborn stood beside the table, hands joined in front of her, eyes closed, head bowed, as she focused on her victim's mind. The Sister, a truth-sayer and interrogator, was skilled at releasing a subject's own inner demons from the darkest corners of the soul, where he'd tucked them away.

Crevan Torma, a muscular, short-haired man in his early forties, watching from the observer's gallery, fought to suppress shivers of fear in sympathy with the man he'd arrested on charges of subversion, a capital offense in the Wyvern Hegemony. Like every other senior Guards State Security Commission officer, he'd endured a mere hint of the horrors the Sisters could liberate from a subconscious mind's deepest recesses as part of his training and understood the power of their talent. He fought to keep his square, angular face, dominated by hooded eyes framing a hooked nose, from showing any hint of emotion.

His prisoner, a starship captain who'd sailed beyond Hegemony space without permission to engage in illegal trading on former imperial worlds devastated by the Retribution Fleet generations earlier, would see the edge of madness. And then he would understand cooperation meant a clean death. He'd tell Torma everything — who chartered his expeditions, who furnished him with trade goods, who purchased the things he brought back, his deepest desires, and his family's most closely guarded secrets.

Torma wasn't exactly comfortable with the State Security Commission's classified interrogation procedures, the ones only a small cadre knew about. But interrogation drugs sometimes caused idiosyncratic reactions, to the point of damaging a subject's mind if they didn't kill him or her outright. They also often caused the consciousness to drift, making the process a lengthy chore for the questioner with no guarantee of obtaining correct answers.

Yet the Sisters were human lie detectors, and the psychic torture he routinely witnessed wasn't necessary with ninety-nine out of every one hundred prisoners. However, the Commission wanted absolute certainty when it concerned crimes against the state. That meant those arrested on such charges suffered a Sister's intrusions. Afterward, even those few capable of outfoxing truth-sayers wouldn't dare think about lies or obfuscation.

The prisoner, seized at New Draconis' cargo spaceport after the Commission received an anonymous tip, let out one last shriek and went limp, panting like an overheated dog. The Sister, a tall, lean woman whose short red hair framed a pale, narrow face dominated by sharp cheekbones, raised her head and looked at Torma with icy blue eyes.

"He is ready, Colonel."

Torma inclined his head as much in thanks as to avoid the Sister's unnervingly direct gaze at this intensely uncomfortable moment. Even now, he still didn't understand how a human capable of touching other minds could use that talent to cause such anguish. Surely the Almighty in the Infinite Void would disapprove, but what did Torma know? He was neither a religious nor a particularly spiritual man. Few in his position could afford belief in a higher power.

Yet the Order of the Void Reborn had served the Wyvern Hegemony almost since the latter's founding in return for being the sole religious authority recognized by the government. The Order's supreme leaders, who'd taken on the title Archimandrite, considered themselves second only to the Regents who ruled over the tiny remnant of the once vast human empire and inspired enough reverence that no one would dare gainsay them.

"Thank you, Sister."

"Shall I stay and monitor his feelings?"

Much as Torma would prefer she left after what he'd witnessed, interrogating someone accused of subversion without a lie-detecting Sister present would raise eyebrows. And that was the last thing he wanted in such an unusual case. The answers he obtained must be irrefutable.

"If you would."

Torma entered the interrogation room via a connecting door and approached the table. Jan Keter, erstwhile master and sole crew member of the starship *Callisto*, seemed lost in a trance-like state, his gaze empty though his breathing remained heavy. A tall man, craggy, dark-haired, with a lean, yet powerful physique, Keter bore more than a passing resemblance to his captor. Yet strapped to the interrogation table, he seemed the furthest thing from an all powerful senior Commission officer.

"He is conscious," Sister Ardrix said, laying a hand on Keter's forehead. "Though still struggling to send his demons back whence they came."

The merchant spacer spasmed at her touch, though whether it was because of another mental intrusion or out of revulsion at physical contact with her, Torma couldn't tell. He activated a control, and the table swung up so that Keter was vertical.

"Jan Keter, you stand accused of subversion, contrary to the laws of the Wyvern Hegemony. The penalty for this crime is death. How you die depends on your cooperation. The Sister offered you a foretaste of hell. Answer my questions honestly, and I shall make your execution painless so you can merge with the Infinite Void. Lie, and you will suffer in this life and for all eternity."

How many times did Crevan Torma speak these words to doomed men and women who thought they could escape the Hegemony's retribution for violating its laws? The galaxy was a harsh place, more so since the empire self-immolated on the pyre of the Ruggero Dynasty's overweening conceit. Only four star systems inhabited by humans capable of navigating the wormhole network and crossing space at faster-than-light speeds remained.

They were holding off a long night of barbarism that might otherwise drive their species to extinction. It was a task with no margin for error and no tolerance for anything that might threaten Wyvern and her three companions, Arcadia, Dordogne, and Torrinos. The Barbarian Plague, long ago, remained the most potent proof that Hegemony laws and their ruthless enforcement were an unquestionable necessity. No one left Hegemony space without permission. No one.

Torma fished a cylindrical device from a tunic pocket, a shiny metallic tube that fit comfortably in his hand. He held it in front of Keter's eyes and, with a flick of the thumb, extruded a blade so sharp it could cut through base metals.

"Where did you get this medical instrument? It isn't of Hegemony manufacture, though clearly made by humans. Analysis tells us its manufacture is as advanced, if not more, than anything we produce. Yet, no human worlds beyond our own are capable of anything more than pre-industrial technology, if that."

Keter, shivering, licked his lips nervously. When he spoke, his voice came out as a broken croak.

"Hatshepsut. Thirty-one wormhole transits beyond Torrinos. Traded railguns, solar power pack chargers, slugs, and plenty of household items for the instruments and finer tools than I've ever seen. Old imperial artifacts too. They can't produce power weapons on Hatshepsut. At best, they use chemical propellant stuff. Crude and inaccurate as hell, so I got good trading value from the guns."

If Keter wasn't a dead man because he smuggled tech beyond Hegemony space, the admission of gun-running would have sealed his fate. Torma glanced at Sister Ardrix, who nodded once.

"Well, the instruments clearly weren't manufactured there. Where did they come from?"

"No idea. The seller didn't say, and I didn't ask."

Ardrix nodded again. Keter was telling the truth.

"What about the other advanced tech items you bought on Hatshepsut?"

"Same."

"Why were they selling tech they presumably bought at great expense from other traders?"

A faint smile creased Keter's face.

"Power weapons, packs, and ammo are more useful than medical instruments when you fear barbarian intrusions. They'd sell me their firstborn in exchange for crew-served plasma guns and a year's worth supply of ammo. That's how nasty it is out there."

Another nod from the Sister with the expressionless eyes.

"Other than Hatshepsut, what worlds beyond the Hegemony did you visit?"

Keter rattled off half a dozen names, then said, "Don't worry. None of them showed a trace of this mythical Barbarian Plague. Didn't even remember what it was. I found a few antimatter cracking stations still operational after all this time. Enough to re-establish trade routes. The old empire built tough stuff."

That attitude was precisely why the Hegemony strictly controlled traffic. Historical records indicated the plague, one hundred percent deadly, had emerged from the far frontiers and spread through the wormhole network like wildfire until it died out short of what was now the Hegemony just as mysteriously as it appeared.

Yet, no one knew whether the pathogen still lay dormant on nearby worlds decimated by the Retribution Fleet. But a determined trader with a ship capable of crossing interstellar space at faster-than-light speeds to a wormhole junction that was not under the Guards Navy control could sail across the former empire at will. If they had a sponsor or an owner with sufficiently deep pockets, connections in the government, and access to an antimatter fueling station whose staff wouldn't ask questions of a ship taking on five or six times the standard fuel load. And if Keter found automated stations still in working order, generations after they were abandoned…

"Who paid for your expedition?"

"I don't know."

Torma looked up at Sister Ardrix, who nodded. Keter was telling the truth.

"How was your ship chartered?"

"Anonymous contact. In certain circles, I'm known as someone who takes risks if the money is right. They gave me funds and trade goods, an itinerary, access to refueling stations in the Hegemony and told me they wanted intelligence about the worlds I visited, not just profits."

"Did those trade goods include the weapons?"

"Yes."

"Did you sell them on other worlds?"

"Only Hatshepsut. The others either didn't have the minimal industrial base to produce ammunition or didn't even know what ranged weapons were. Chemical propellant slug throwers, on the other hand? Any pre-industrial place can handle them."

Except the Hegemony didn't manufacture that sort of ordnance. And since the government tightly controlled the weapons industry, the guns traded by Keter were likely stolen from a Guards depot. Or sold by a corrupt official. Torma would eventually find out and ensure more subversives merged with the Infinite Void, along with the manager of whichever fueling station supplied Keter and forgot to log it as required by law.

"How did the anonymous shipper contact you?"

"Darknet."

Keter's reply didn't surprise Torma. No matter how hard the State Security Commission tried to kill it, the darknet remained indestructible. New nodes sprang up whenever existing ones died, and new administrators appeared whenever previous ones went into hiding or into the Commission's cells. The darknet's decentralized nature just made matters more complicated, not only among the Hegemony's star systems but within them.

"Any identifying markers?"

"The usual letter and number string. Sorry. Can't remember it now, no matter how hard the Sister tries."

Torma glanced at Ardrix, who shrugged. She was an experienced Commission auxiliary and knew better than to speak during an interrogation.

"Where did you take on antimatter?"

"Torrinos Eight."

Torma's eyes narrowed. The State Security Commission Groups in each of the systems operated almost independently, though their commanders answered to the Chief Commissioner, Guards General Cameron Bucco. It ensured cross-jurisdictional investigations became politicized. Few in the three subordinate star systems enjoyed doing the bidding of the Wyvern Group, which technically oversaw the entire Commission as well as the Hegemony's homeworld. But the Consuls governing Arcadia, Dordogne, and Torrinos, every one of them retired four-star flag officers, liked it that way. It allowed them more control over the Commission units operating in what they considered their private satrapies.

However, Torma had no choice but to see that the Torrinos Group arrest Antimatter Fueling Station Eight's manager and determine how he was bribed or coerced into topping off Keter's magnetic reservoirs. He questioned Keter for a while longer until it became clear the man knew nothing more. Whoever chartered the expedition made sure they would stay anonymous.

At Torma's orders, a pair of uniformed Guards privates assigned as jailers dragged Keter off to a cell in the basement of the Commission's brooding stone headquarters, where he would remain until his trial, in case Torma thought of more questions.

With Keter gone, he bowed his head at Ardrix, repressing once more the urge to ask how she could meddle with another's mind and not seem affected by her acts.

"Thank you, Sister."

She returned the gesture. "We serve the Hegemony."

"Indeed."

— 2 —

Major General Ishani Robbins, head of the Wyvern Group's Anti-Subversion Unit, which dealt with political and criminal matters affecting Hegemony security, put on a thoughtful air after Torma related what he heard from the unfortunate and now doomed Captain Keter. In her mid-fifties, fit, with a narrow, angular face framed by short dark hair, Robbins studied her subordinate with deeply set brown eyes that conveyed less emotion than the two silver stars on the collar of her black uniform tunic.

"Are you saying the rumors that reached us long ago about another human star system retaining advanced technology might be grounded in reality? Our historians are convinced they belong to the realm of myth."

Torma, wearing a black uniform like his superior but with a colonel's crossed swords and three diamonds on the collar, ran splayed fingers over his skull, ruffling black hair tinged by the first hints of gray, and shrugged.

"It's the only way I can explain the items Keter brought back from Hatshepsut. They're clearly meant for human hands and weren't manufactured in the Hegemony. Our analysis proved they were made of alloys devised far from our home stars."

"The records tell of non-humans with hands very similar to ours." Robbins sounded dubious.

"They also tell us that non-humans capable of faster-than-light travel in this part of the galaxy fared badly even well before the empire's collapse. Besides, we've not heard of any coming through the wormhole network in a long time. No, General. Humans with advanced tech capabilities made those items, which means the rumors are true. And they evidently roam the network or perhaps even cross interstellar space faster than light."

She grimaced.

"The Regent will not be happy with this news."

"Understandably. Another human polity with the same capabilities as the Hegemony will almost inevitably present a threat. Perhaps not at once, but in the future, when we reunite humanity under our banner." Torma paused for a moment. "Maybe we should track down the source of those rumors and see for ourselves."

He looked up at Robbins again.

"I'll raise the matter with General Bucco. He can decide whether it's worth the Regent's time."

Even as she spoke, Torma realized the Chief Commissioner wouldn't mention this development to Vigdis Mandus. She wasn't the sort who would welcome news that might disturb her nine-year term as ruler of the Hegemony. As far as Torma could tell, Mandus, like her immediate predecessors, paid only lip service to the ideal of reuniting humanity under Wyvern's leadership. She seemed just as uninterested by the idea of sending expeditions to conquer the closest of the fallen worlds and slowly spread a new civilization, one purged of the defects that destroyed the empire. But what did he know? Mandus was even more of a cipher than the previous Regents, one who reached the pinnacle of power ahead of four-star flag officers with a greater claim to it.

Yet Torma didn't dare show his skepticism. Officers who disparaged the Hegemony's ruling class saw their careers drastically cut short. His purpose, and that of every other State Security Commission member, was to make sure nothing ever threatened the current order. Yet his private study of the past proved that unchanging, stratified societies eventually perished, often violently, when conditions shifted.

The regime's reluctance to expand when nearby star systems were theirs for the taking showed how stagnant it was. No Regent wanted to be the first threatened with removal from power for upsetting the elites. And they would be annoyed at whoever sent military forces beyond the Hegemony's sphere on a mission of conquest because it would make the home systems more vulnerable to unrest.

Robbins stood and walked toward the bank of windows overlooking the HQ courtyard. Her third-floor office, one of the more spacious ones in the headquarters building at the heart of New Draconis, seemed austere, but it was an accurate reflection of her character. If it weren't for wood paneling, the obligatory stand of flags, and the windows, it might pass for a storage room.

Torma watched her movements and was struck again at how much menace she projected, though it had to be unconscious. Perhaps the Almighty had blessed her with a touch of the Sisters' talent. Some of them, such as Ardrix, could put the fear of the Almighty into ordinary people with a simple glance if they so wished.

"Shall I inform the Navy of my findings, General? Their intelligence analysts will probably consider the appearance of advanced tech items on Hatshepsut worthy of further inquiry. Perhaps the Chief of Naval Operations might even send a reconnaissance mission, in case there is a threat brewing beyond our sphere."

Though he didn't see her face, Torma knew Robbins was frowning as she parsed the implications of his suggestion. She always frowned when facing delicate decisions. The two fighting branches of the Armed Services, the Navy and the Ground Forces, didn't play well with the State Security Commission at the best of times. And this was despite the Chief Commissioner sitting on the Ruling Council alongside the other two service heads, the Regent, the Chancellor, and the four Consuls.

Politics. Torma mentally shrugged. He was aware of a faction in the military that would gleefully embark on a campaign of expansion, as did General Robbins. But because successive Chief Commissioners remained opaque about their views on the matter, Torma and his colleagues left the Expansionists to seethe in silence at their leaders' lack of energy. What ordinary citizens thought didn't matter. They had no say in the affairs of state. Provided they obeyed the law, paid their taxes, and weren't a burden on the public purse, the Commission didn't bother them. And they understood attracting the Commission's attention was a bad idea.

Robbins turned and faced him. "Pass the details to Naval Intelligence personally, outside normal channels."

Torma kept his eyebrows from creeping up in surprise. He'd never figured Robbins was an Expansionist, or at the very least, sympathized with them.

"In fact," she continued, "I think you should speak with Rear Admiral Godfrey himself."

"Yes, General."

Johannes Godfrey, Chief of Naval Intelligence, favored the Hegemony's expansion, though he kept his views well hidden. Torma only found out because of a chance remark by one of Godfrey's subordinates. He'd filed the information away for future use, should an occasion arise. It was what Commission officers did for a living. Data hoarding, one of his juniors called it. They stored unguarded words for a rainy day or an interrogation. Did that prove Robbins was on the Expansionist side? If so, it was another tidbit he would add to the rest.

Torma himself was agnostic on whether the Hegemony should pursue its stated and sacred mission of reuniting humanity across the stars. He would obey his superiors and protect the state to the best of his abilities, no matter what they decided.

"I'll tell him you'll be in touch."

"Thank you."

Torma wondered what her words meant. Did Godfrey and Robbins enjoy a friendly relationship? Was she feeding him information collected by her investigators, thereby breaching the wall between the Commission and the Navy? Did Chief Commissioner Bucco know, or Robbins' immediate superior, Commissioner Cabreras? And what was the quid pro quo from the Navy? There must be one. It was how the various parts of the Hegemony government worked with each other. Games within games within games. Some days, he needed a program to keep the network of quiet connections and backchannels straight.

"You may go."

Torma stood, briefly came to attention, and nodded once instead of saluting since he didn't wear a headdress.

"General."

As he returned to his office, Torma idly wondered whether the long-gone Imperial Constabulary's inner workings had been as complex and twisted as those of the Commission. Unfortunately, he might never know. Most of the Constabulary's records perished in the orbital bombardment of old Draconis, the former imperial capital. It had been unleashed by admirals of the 1st Fleet tired of watching the last empress destroy humanity. In the aftermath, they'd established the Hegemony and saved what little was left after the Retribution Fleet's depredations.

When he entered, he saw Sister Ardrix sitting on her meditation mat in the lotus position by her small desk. She opened one eye and speared him with her intense gaze, then glanced at the far end of the mat, her usual signal he should join her and unburden his soul. The difference between her usual persona and that in the interrogation chamber never failed to surprise him. Where he'd sensed nothing earlier, in the basement, he now perceived an aura of calm, as if she'd never unleashed the demons hiding behind Keter's soul.

Could Ardrix throw a switch and shut off the part of her that reached into the unwilling minds of others? Perhaps. Though she'd been his unit's chief truth-sayer for over a year, he still knew little about the woman behind the always serene facade. It was as if she lived both in this world and another he couldn't perceive.

Torma obeyed her unvoiced command and adopted the lotus position facing her. He closed his eyes and regulated his breathing pattern as she'd taught him while he let his thoughts roam freely. Ardrix was a strange woman. Ageless, like all those of her kind, she might be older than his mother, yet her unlined face would lead a casual observer to assume she was his junior.

If Ardrix had ever spied on his innermost feelings, she'd never let on, though Torma was paranoid enough to believe she would mercilessly denounce him the moment she sensed disloyalty. Too many senior officers had taken abrupt retirement and vanished not long afterward for no apparent reasons during Torma's career with the State Security Commission.

However, the meditation sessions after difficult interrogations helped him regain his mental balance, and for that, he felt grateful. But Torma never asked his colleagues whether the Sisters assigned to the Commission did the same with their commanding officers or whether Ardrix was going above and beyond her duties for reasons only she understood. And if so, why?

"How did the general react?" She asked the moment both opened their eyes after surfacing from a deep dive into the Infinite Void.

Torma thought about it for a moment, then said, "Interested, curious, but somehow aware our superiors might not welcome the news. She asked I pass our findings on to the head of Naval Intelligence in person and that she would open the lines of communication for me."

A copper-tinted eyebrow crept up Ardrix's pale forehead.

"Fascinating."

"Strange more like."

Torma rose and waited until Ardrix did the same before bowing.

"This could be our first actual evidence someone else survived Dendera's holocaust. But I fear we might never find out who they are, how they survived the Retribution Fleet, and where they've been hiding if our betters suppress the evidence in the name of avoiding social unrest. The myth of being the last survivors is too deeply ingrained in our people."

"Those who command the Navy's fighting formations still have fire in their bellies. Once news reaches them, they will do everything in their power to track the origin of the items Keter brought back from Hatshepsut." Ardrix's soft alto voice seemed wrapped around a core of absolute certainty.

"And you know this how?"

Instead of answering, she gave him a mysterious smile.

"If you have no more tasks for me, I shall bid you a good day and rejoin my Brethren at the abbey."

"Right. The Order has its own grapevine. Enjoy your evening, Sister."

3

Once back in the New Draconis Abbey, the Order of the Void Reborn's Mother House, Ardrix sought Archimandrite Bolack, the Order's *Summus Abbas*. Though he led the Hegemony's only official religious organization, Bolack, like his predecessors, lived as simply as any Sister or Friar. At this time of day, he would be engaged in a walking meditation among the abbey's extensive orchards, and so she made her way through the quadrangle, around the Void Reborn Orb dominating its center, and past the main buildings.

Set on New Draconis' southern outskirts, the abbey had been built as a precise copy of the one destroyed during the empire's final collapse. It even looked as old as Wyvern's earliest settlements, those established during humanity's quasi-mythical first age of expansion when an almost forgotten Earth still ruled. But it was endowed with a much larger tract of land than its earlier incarnation, one the Brethren farmed intensively.

When she found Bolack's usual path, she composed herself and stood on one side, hands folded in front of her. If he was ready to speak, the Archimandrite would stop. If not, he would continue walking, and Ardrix would continue waiting.

Within a few minutes, a dark-complexioned, heavy-set, bald man in his late sixties came into view. His intense, hooded eyes beneath bushy eyebrows framed a flattened nose set at the center of a square face outlined by a short salt and pepper beard. Bolack's sole concession to the display of rank was the small Void Reborn Orb hanging around his neck from a simple silver chain. Otherwise, he wore the same practical monastic robes as any Friar.

Acceding to Ardrix's silent request, Bolack stopped a few paces distant, and she bowed her head with the amount of respect due to the head of her Order.

"Yes, Sister?"

The Archimandrite's basso profundo bounced off the pear trees surrounding them.

"My day has been most eventful, and there are things you should know."

Bolack tilted his head to one side, a sign she should speak freely, and Ardrix recounted Keter's interrogation, with emphasis on the goods Keter brought back from Hatshepsut.

"And you saw those items?"

"I did. Crevan allowed me to inspect them."

A faint smile split Bolack's beard.

"He trusts you to that extent? Excellent."

"Crevan accepted my tutelage in matters spiritual and meditates with me regularly, especially after we deal with subversives. From there, I built a closer rapport than my fellow Commission Sisters enjoy with their assigned officers."

"Then matters are unfolding better than I'd hoped. And the objects?"

"I recognized several of them as high-quality alloy surgical instruments. Items of recent manufacture, better than what the healing Sisters use. They most certainly weren't produced on Hatshepsut, nor were they relics of the empire." She pulled a small notepad from one of her robe's inner pockets. "The instruments bore small markings in hidden spots. I reproduced them from memory."

Ardrix activated the pad and held it up so Bolack could see. Surprise creased the Archimandrite's broad forehead when he recognized part of the marking, three nine-pointed stars inside an orb.

"That looks suspiciously like an imperial-era Void abbey imprint. But I'm not familiar with the initials. From memory, there was no abbey whose name started with an L on a world whose name also started with an L during imperial times. Even the Mother House on Lindisfarne used AL, for Aidan/Lindisfarne, if I recall correctly."

"You do. That is indeed the former Order of the Void mark. I verified the records while Crevan was with Admiral Godfrey. As far as we can tell, there was no abbey using L/L at any time in our history before the Great Scouring."

Bolack's eyes narrowed as he contemplated Ardrix's drawing. The Order of the Void Reborn used a different imprint, a phoenix rising from the flames within a circle representing the Infinite Void's Orb.

"Then it can only mean there's a new abbey out there, one founded after the empire's collapse and not part of the Order Reborn."

She nodded.

"An abbey which manufactures higher quality surgical instruments than we or anyone else in the Hegemony. Or someone is using the old Order's markings for unknown reasons. Sure, the stars and orb were once a sign of quality, but it's unlikely anyone remembers those days."

Bolack scratched his beard and grimaced.

"The simplest explanation is usually correct. There is another on a world with which Wyvern lost contact. But where? There are at least half a dozen worlds I can think of whose names begin with L. And that's without contemplating the possibility this L was colonized after the fall or disappeared from the astrogation records because of data integrity issues caused by the Great Scouring's battles." He glanced at Ardrix. "Did you discuss the markings with Colonel Torma?"

"No. I wanted to speak with you first and confirm my conclusions by perusing our archives." She paused for a moment. "If you're wondering whether the Ruling Council will be more likely to order a reconnaissance expedition based on the inscriptions, I can't say."

"Are you reading my mind now?"

He gave her a mischievous glance. As head of the Order, he possessed a powerful male mind, and no Sister dare probe it without his knowledge. She knew he was teasing her and ignored his question.

"If I tell Crevan, I'm sure he'll inform the Chief of Naval Intelligence, and from what I hear, it will stir things up. Intelligence has been quietly militating for expeditions into the former empire in recent times. But proof some part of it beyond our star systems retained FTL space travel and the ability to manufacture advanced artifacts might trigger a political crisis."

He contemplated Ardrix for a few seconds, eyes searching hers.

"A valid warning. You've learned well from your time with the Commission. What do you suggest?"

"I'll show Crevan the markings tomorrow morning and explain what we just discussed. If I don't, he will eventually find out the stars and orb were imperial-era abbey manufacturing marks and wonder why I said nothing about them. That might affect his trust in me."

"Indeed. And with things going so well, any setback would be a shame..." Bolack left his words hanging between them. "I give you my blessing. Tell Colonel Torma about the markings. Perhaps he or Naval Intelligence can make an educated guess as to what L/L might mean. I confess I'm curious about answers to this mystery. If Brethren from the old Order are prospering out there, it will make life interesting."

"You're afraid they might consider us schismatics?" Amusement danced in Ardrix's pale eyes. "Or an evolutionary step too far?"

Bolack let out a bark of laughter, proving she'd hit the mark.

"You may go. Search the records and speak with Torma tomorrow. Then tell me how he reacts."

She bowed her head.

"As you wish."

Ardrix turned on her heels and retraced her steps through the orchard and back to the abbey's building cluster. Throughout, she felt the Archimandrite's thoughtful eyes following her. Evidence that a house of the old Order was engaging in the trade of advanced items could only mean it enjoyed the protection of a faster-than-light fleet, or at least had access to one. That fleet would be perceived by the Hegemony as a rival, if not an enemy, and Bolack knew it, though he'd not raised the matter. It revived the specter of warfare between human factions, a final war that might end the species once and for all.

**

"Show me." Torma stood and headed for his office lockup, where he kept evidence during an investigation, in this case, samples from Captain Keter's confiscated cargo. He placed his palm on the door's reader, and a soft snick announced the latches had retracted. Torma reached in and retrieved the box marked surgical instruments.

After returning to his desk, he withdrew bagged items one by one and placed them in front of Ardrix, who had her notes ready with the records she'd retrieved from the abbey's database. She carefully took a set of shiny surgical scissors from one bag and turned them over until she found the tiny engraving. Using her notepad, she magnified it and nodded.

"Three nine-pointed stars inside an orb, with the notation L/L. I'm no expert, but these don't look like they were manufactured in Dendera's day." She carefully ran her thumbnail over the edge of one blade, then studied it. "Sharp. Perhaps even unused."

Ardrix let Torma compare the engraving with the old Order records on her pad, then returned the scissors to their bag before examining a pair of forceps.

"The same marks." She looked up at Torma. "According to the records, abbeys would commission the manufacture of surgical instruments, both for their healers and as gifts for non-Order infirmaries, and have the maker engrave the abbey's mark. That way, everyone knew the provenance. The instruments would be simple, so even the most rustic colonial health care providers could use them in the absence of power sources. And they'd be made to last a lifetime without sharpening, oxidizing, or falling apart."

"Then they might be artifacts from the imperial era." Torma perched on a corner of the desk and watched Ardrix go through the samples.

"That is always a possibility. Unfortunately, the metallurgical analysis didn't offer enough clues linking them to know imperial manufacturers. But here is the most important indication." Ardrix pointed at the L/L inscription on a scalpel whose blade was sheathed in hard plastic. "Based on our records, no old Order abbey used this particular letter combination."

"Perhaps the data was lost during the ultimate attack on Dendera's capital. A lot of records vanished during that time."

She inclined her head.

"A definite possibility. But think of it this way. Pre-industrial healers can use those instruments, making them perfect trading goods on fallen worlds, yet their manufacture is beyond any of them. Coupled with the other items Keter brought back, I think we're not looking at leftovers from the distant past. This is fine work, finer than anything we've saved from imperial days."

Torma stood. "I'll see if the lab can deduce anything from those engravings."

"Will you bring this to Admiral Godfrey's attention?"

"You better believe it, Sister. If you're correct, this is momentous news. Why not bring the matter up yesterday, so I could inform General Robbins?"

"I had to be sure and needed a few hours in our records hall." She gave him an amused smile. "You taught me I should always confirm before speaking, lest we make the sort of mistakes that might damage investigations beyond all repair."

"So I did. Glad we can teach each other new tricks. Will you prepare a full report on your findings? I'm sure Admiral Godfrey would like something his analysts can work with."

"Of course. Give me an hour. I'm not due in interrogation until ten."

Torma settled behind his desk.

"Which case is on the menu?"

"Administrator Kai Ornelas. Charges of perverting the course of justice."

He nodded.

"Right. Centurion Yau's investigation. A nasty customer, that Ornelas."

Since official corruption came under the subversion umbrella, Major General Robbins' division investigated those accused of taking bribes. But Torma found such cases more annoying than satisfying, grubby rather than cleansing. He rarely took them on himself unless the quarry was of sufficient stature that nothing less than a full colonel heading a central Anti-Subversion section would do.

But the Hegemony didn't lack for corrupt officials, no matter how severe the penalties because — and no one in his or her right mind would ever say so openly — many, if not most, got away with it thanks to political patronage.

4

Torma returned the two sentries' crisp present-arms with an equally precise salute as he climbed the Navy Headquarters' front steps the next morning. Though they were there more for ceremonial purposes than actual security, both wore black battledress uniforms, the Guards Corps black beret with the Navy's phoenix, sword, and crossed anchors badge, and carried well-used plasma carbines.

Navy HQ, along with Ground Forces HQ and Commission HQ, occupied one corner of the Hegemony Government Precinct at the heart of New Draconis. An inner security perimeter separated the three from the other ministries, one that only visitors whose names appeared on the approved list could cross. As a result, the Guards Corps sector was a forbidden city within the capital for all intents and purposes, a distinction it shared with the nearby Regent's Wyvern Palace and its counterpart, the Chancellery.

Armored glass doors slid aside at his approach, and he entered a spacious foyer whose granite floor was decorated with the Hegemony coat of arms. He knew an invisible sensor would scan his credentials and match them to the biometrics on record in the expansive Hegemony database, maintained by the Commission itself. If there was a mismatch, armed duty personnel would appear out of nowhere and arrest him. But nothing stirred.

Torma looked around to orient himself and check if anything had changed since his last visit. The huge, metallic representation of the Guards Navy insignia still hung from the far wall, between a pair of grandiose staircases curling away toward the building's wings, above the flags of the Hegemony, the Guards Corps, and the Navy.

Various display cases lined the remaining sides, each holding relics from the empire's downfall, including a piece of the Retribution Fleet's flagship, the battleship *Ruggero*, destroyed by the combined might of the 1st Fleet on the day of Empress Dendera's death. Although tempted, Torma didn't walk around the foyer to see if the Navy added anything new to its collection. Instead, he took the left-hand ground-floor corridor toward the Naval Intelligence offices.

Because he wore the Commission's phoenix, sword, and scales of justice insignia on his beret, he received curious looks from naval officers and noncoms along the way. Still, no one dared ask him about his business with one of the fighting branches. The appearance of a senior State Security officer never boded well. Torma found Rear Admiral Godfrey's office suite at the far end of the wing and entered the antechamber without announcing his presence.

Godfrey's clerk, a grizzled senior petty officer, wearing a high-collared black service uniform with silver rank insignia on the sleeves, stood the moment he spied Torma's crossed swords and diamonds. The aide-de-camp's desk was vacant, though a metallic plate in a wooden holder said 'Krennek.'

"Please come in, Colonel. Admiral Godfrey is expecting you."

He waved toward the inner door, which opened silently at Torma's approach.

Mindful of his manners, Torma marched up to Godfrey's desk, halted a regulation three paces, and saluted, fingertips brushing his right temple, just below the band of his black beret.

"Thank you for making time to see me, sir."

Godfrey, tall, lean, with thick white hair and the intelligent features of a man who missed nothing, gave his visitor a formal nod in return.

"At ease, Colonel. Please sit. From what Ishani said, I'll be the one thanking you."

Torma didn't react at hearing a Navy flag officer casually use his superior's first name. Still, it reinforced his suspicions that there were more connections between the Commission and the Navy than anyone let on.

"Sir."

Torma took one of the chairs facing Godfrey's cluttered desk.

"Ishani says you found evidence there could be another remnant of the empire that didn't sink into pre-spaceflight barbarism."

"Yes, sir. We seized trade goods from a merchant ship that traveled beyond Hegemony star systems without permission after an anonymous tipoff. Unknown parties chartered him, and he brought advanced technology artifacts back from Hatshepsut, the sort we'd be hard-pressed to copy without diminishing quality. It means they were made by someone who not only didn't lose knowledge after the collapse but kept progressing. And some of those items, surgical instruments, bear the manufacturing mark of an old Order of the Void abbey, one whose initials don't appear in what remains of imperial records. That means it was probably established after the Great Scouring."

Godfrey cocked a surprised eyebrow at Torma.

"I was about to ask whether those artifacts could be of non-human origin, but it seems you've just given me the answer. Instead, please tell me about those abbey markings."

"There's not much I can tell, sir. The Void Reborn Sister assigned to my unit recognized the engraving as an old Order mark — three nine-pointed stars inside an orb rather than a rising phoenix — and the initials L/L, which indicate the abbey name and the name of its home planet. According to the New Draconis Abbey's database, there was no L/L at the time of the empire's collapse. But as with most records from that time, the Void Reborn's are not one hundred percent complete."

"And that trader knows nothing about the items' origins?"

Torma shook his head.

"No. Although he asked for provenance, the vendor on Hatshepsut couldn't tell him anything beyond the fact they were given in barter by locals, part of a seafaring society heavily involved in trade, who got them from off-worlders. I gather the vendor wasn't keen on revealing too much. And since Keter — that's my prisoner's name — was alone, he didn't press the issue, lest he finds himself a target far from any sort of help." Torma fished a memory chip from his tunic pocket and placed it on Godfrey's desk. "This holds everything we know, sir. I made sure the chip and the data can't be traced to the Commission."

A cold smile briefly twisted the Admiral's lips.

"Ishani said you were a shrewd man, Colonel. Good. Anyone who's attuned to Hegemony politics can go far, so long as he takes care where he steps. In return for your discretion, I'll discourage my analysts from speculating about the source of this information. That way, we keep the firewall between the Navy and the Commission intact. And the parties unknown who chartered him?"

"They used the usual cutouts on the darknet, so they're effectively untraceable, but Keter submitted a report before we arrested him, so they know about what he found and brought home. No doubt, by now, they're also aware he's in our hands and told us everything he knows, meaning they'll make sure there is nothing left that could connect them."

"No doubt." Godfrey studied Torma for a few seconds. "You're probably wondering what I'll do with your information."

"Yes, sir."

"But you won't ask."

"No, sir. Mainly because of that firewall you mentioned. My job is rooting out the state's enemies, not following up on intelligence that is, at best, extraneous to my investigation. I have Keter dead to rights. He'll face a trial in due course, and if found guilty, he'll be executed."

"If?" A mischievous smile appeared on Godfrey's lips. "Don't you mean when? No need to answer that, Colonel. But you're still curious, admit it."

"Certainly. Evidence that one or more star systems survived the collapse and are sending starships through the wormhole network without our knowledge is the biggest news in living memory. Until now, we believed ourselves the sole heirs of humanity's accumulated knowledge and history."

"Which is precisely why many would suppress your discovery. Overturning the belief that kept the Hegemony as it is for almost two centuries might not end well for our people, especially those whose power and wealth are intimately woven into our founding myth. They'll not look kindly on any chance of upsetting the status quo."

Torma grimaced.

"Sadly." Then a thought struck him. "Is this why General Robbins had me brief you personally, sir? So that word gets out no matter what?"

Godfrey nodded.

"Reality will unfold as it does, no matter what humans want, and you can't stop a signal if it's repeated over many channels. I'll see that Ground Forces Intelligence receives a copy of your report, again unattributed, and I'm sure Ishani will do her part. That covers the three services. What happens afterward will happen. Thank you, Colonel."

Torma, hearing dismissal in Godfrey's tone, stood and came to attention.

"With your permission, sir?"

"Dismissed."

Torma saluted, pivoted on his heels, and marched out, wondering whether he'd just been co-opted by a cabal of senior officers working to rouse the Hegemony's senior leadership from its complacent torpor. If so, he would take part willingly because he knew from his lifelong study of humanity's history, including parts the regime would rather keep buried, that societies in stasis eventually decayed.

And if the rising number of corruption cases was any sign, the rot was already setting in. Left untended, it could just as surely end the last spark of star-faring civilization as the long-ago Retribution Fleet's orbital bombardments almost did. Only it would take years, if not decades, leaving most unaware the end was nigh.

Torma crossed the broad parade square separating the three HQs from each other at a steady pace, absently returning salutes as he brooded on the idea of not only stopping the rot he saw in every sector of society but reversing it.

A message to see General Robbins at once upon his return from Navy HQ sat on his desk. As per schedule, Ardrix was helping with another interrogation in the basement. Therefore, after dropping his beret on his desk, Torma took the stairs up to his superior's office. Her door stood open, so he tapped on the jamb with his knuckles to gain her attention.

"You asked for me, General?"

"Come in. Close the door and sit."

Torma did as he was bidden and settled into a chair across from her, waiting for the inevitable questions.

"How did Admiral Godfrey react?"

"With great interest. I believe he'll pursue the matter via intelligence channels within his organization and that of his Ground Forces counterpart. He said words to the effect that one cannot suppress a signal if it's spread through multiple channels."

By the cast of her eyes, Torma guessed Godfrey and Robbins spoke over a secure channel while he was on his way back. In other words, Robbins was testing him.

"And what do you think he meant?"

Torma thought for a few seconds, choosing his words carefully.

"Admiral Godfrey believes the news of another world or star system cluster not only surviving the Great Scouring but advancing technologically would be quashed. It proves the Hegemony is not the sole custodian of humanity's long history and its best hope of reviving an interstellar civilization."

She cocked an ironic eyebrow at him.

"Thereby going against the state's founding narrative."

Torma gave her a helpless shrug.

"Inevitably, and it will invalidate a system of government built on existential preservation at any cost, one which cannot be questioned without committing treason against humanity itself. It's the sort of paradigm shift many will resist, especially those whose whole existence is tied to said narrative."

She contemplated him for a few moments.

"Did you ever hear the saying about hard times making hard people?"

"Yes. Hard times bring forth hard people, hard people create soft times, soft times make soft people, and soft people lead to hard times, correct?"

"Indeed. And where are we in this cycle?"

He thought for a moment.

"We're frozen halfway between hard times making hard people and hard people making soft times."

"Correct. Stasis. And what do you think will happen now that the signal is being dispersed over several channels, to use Johannes Godfrey's words?"

"I truly couldn't say, General."

"But you're okay with it?"

He looked Robbins in the eyes.

"I have devoted my life to the pursuit of truth in service of the Hegemony and its citizens. If there are others like us out there, they could be either a threat or an opportunity, and suppressing the reality of their existence won't serve anyone."

If she faulted his brush with heresy, then so be it. Fate, or the Almighty, or an impish universe, take your pick, put narrative-shattering evidence in his care. The moment he opted against suppressing it in the name of truth and duty, even though he'd done so unconsciously, he'd embarked on a path of no return.

"Then we understand each other, Crevan. Keep your prisoner alive and well. He might be of further use. And do not discuss the matter with anyone other than Sister Ardrix and me, not even if Commissioner Cabreras presses you."

"As you command, General." A faint sense of relief coursed through his veins as he stood. "With your permission."

"Dismissed."

— 5 —

As Torma expected, the Commission's Torrinos Group was lukewarm about investigating the Torrinos Eight antimatter refueling station manager. Whether it stemmed from the usual truculence at doing Wyvern HQ's bidding or because of a coverup, he couldn't tell. Even the State Security Commission, especially its groups in the three subordinate star systems, occasionally suffered from bouts of official corruption and needed cleansing from one of Major General Robbins' teams.

Torma had done his share of those over the years. But short of traveling to Torrinos and making himself even more unpopular with his colleagues there, he couldn't do much but wait for the inevitable inconclusive report. That meant his efforts to find the people who chartered Keter and his ship were likely doomed.

However, Torma's unit didn't lack for cases, and many days passed without a further word about the possibility of another advanced tech-producing human entity capable of faster-than-light and wormhole travel. It was as if his superiors had consigned the news to the nearest black hole. As instructed, he didn't discuss the matter with anyone, not even Ardrix or Robbins. The subject never came up, and Torma wasn't the type who indulged in idle conversation. After all, he was known as 'Torma the Taciturn' by his colleagues for a reason.

Unattached and with no living relatives, Torma occupied a senior officer's suite in Guards Joint Forces Base New Draconis's accommodations section and took his evening meals in the officer's mess where he usually ate alone. None of the Navy or Ground Forces officers of comparable rank were keen on socializing with a State Security Commission member. Moreover, the few Commission officers living on the base were junior to him. They thus kept their distance, not only because of Torma's seniority but a reputation for ruthlessness few wished to test.

Rumors of his using the Void Sisters' dark talents didn't help, not when everyone in State Security HQ knew Sister Ardrix shared his office, although none dared whisper that she might also share his bed. That would be a step too far, one which could end promising careers, if not lives. Ardrix never set foot on Guards Joint Forces Base New Draconis, nor did Torma ever visit the abbey.

Thus, it came as a surprise when a Navy captain Torma never met before sat at his table in the dining room one evening without so much as a by your leave. Dark-haired, stocky, with deep-set brown eyes and a square face hewn from granite, he wore little more on his black uniform than gold rank insignia at the collar and a diamond-shaped device on his right chest marking him as a Navy Headquarters staffer. He carefully placed a full coffee cup on the linen-covered table and fixed an astonished Torma with emotionless eyes.

"My name is Ewing Saleh, Colonel. Apologies for intruding on your meal. I'm told you prefer solitude."

"Whoever told you that was right." Torma pushed his empty plate aside and pulled a steaming tea mug closer. "What is it you want, Captain? No offense, but only folks with a specific goal in mind accost me in public. It comes with being a State Security officer."

His tone wasn't unfriendly, but he kept a wary expression.

Saleh let a brief, wintry smile cross his face. "Hatshepsut."

"If I recall correctly, that's the name of a star system halfway between Wyvern and the old Coalsack Sector, which suffered the tender mercies of Dendera's Retribution Fleet almost two centuries ago. What about it?"

"Perhaps I should have told you straight away I work for Admiral Godfrey on particularly sensitive files." Saleh shrugged. "Chalk it up to habit. We rarely broadcast our branch affiliation. I'm sure you understand."

Torma's gaze never wavered, nor did his expression. He kept his eyes on Saleh and remained silent. It was an old interrogation technique. Some people felt a compulsion to speak, and, in their haste, they might let a tidbit slip. Saleh's icy smile returned.

"Let's just establish we're fellow professionals who know a thing or two about digging up intelligence and leave it at that, shall we? I'm here at the admiral's behest."

Torma nodded once, then raised his cup for a sip of tea.

"And in that vein," Saleh continued, "between your isolation in this corner of the mess, my field distorter and the one you surely carry as a matter of course, no one can hear us speak or read our lips. We're as secure, if not more so, than in the Commission's deepest dungeons."

"Probably. We professional paranoids enjoy spying on each other. It keeps us honest. Or rather it keeps us more honest than most." Torma's eyes never left Saleh. "So, speak. If you know I'm a loner, you'll also know I like taking a walk around the base before retiring to my quarters, and my need for fresh air is peaking. It stems from spending too much time in those deepest dungeons dealing with the enemies of the Hegemony and taking care I don't trigger my colleagues' paranoia."

"Alongside the mysteriously terrifying Sister Ardrix." He raised a restraining hand when it seemed as if Torma might protest at his characterization of her. "I'll come to the point, Colonel. Admiral Godfrey is in discussions with senior officers about a covert naval expedition to Hatshepsut. The Ruling Council has little interest in matters beyond our sphere, but many within the Guards Corps feel otherwise. Something is out there, and we must know who and what that is. It comes under our oath to protect the Hegemony against all threats."

Torma shrugged. "It concerns me how, exactly?"

"Word of this expedition will eventually find its way to the Regent's ear, hopefully after it leaves Hegemony space."

"And I'll receive orders to arrest everyone the moment it returns. Thanks for the warning. Giving me the names of the starships involved would help even more. They'll be quarantined when they come back, and I'll need time to set that up. Then there are interrogations, followed by executions. General Robbins will go on a hiring spree, I suppose." Torma took another sip of tea. "But if you work for Admiral Godfrey, you already know that. The Ruling Council forbids expeditions beyond the Hegemony's star systems without its permission. And it hasn't given permission in over a hundred years."

Saleh's faint smile returned. "That you know of."

Torma inclined his head by way of acknowledgment.

"Granted." The Hegemony government operated on a strict need to know and had done so since its creation atop the former empire's ruins. "Even though we of the Commission feign omniscience, our eyes can't peer into every corner, nor do our ears pick up every little tidbit of treason."

Saleh let out a brief bark of laughter.

"I never thought I'd see the day when a State Security officer admits his service is as flawed as the other two and not a present-day incarnation of the legendary Argus who saw everything. But you're correct about our betters preferring the status quo to an uncertain outcome if we head into the unknown before the Hegemony Navy is unbeatable. And it will never become so, stasis being preferable to the socio-political turmoil that would result from expanding our horizons, the sort that might realign Wyvern's power structure."

Torma scoffed.

"And yet they forget history is replete with stories of societies in stasis collapsing the moment factors beyond their control disturb the balance."

A broad grin spread across Saleh's face.

"I was reliably informed you were clear-eyed enough to understand the wider implications of your findings, and you've proved my sources correct."

"Sources being Major General Robbins and Rear Admiral Godfrey, no doubt." Torma drained his mug. "Very well. Why don't we cut the persiflage? You've made your point. I won't entertain Chief Commissioner Bucco with this story. Tell me what you want."

"The factions in the Navy putting together the covert expedition think it would be good insurance if a senior, respected

Commission officer and his assigned Void Sister go with it. Our respective superiors agree as General Robbins will no doubt confirm in the morning."

"You think that with the expedition under my and Sister Ardrix's gimlet eyes and us confirming no subversive or treasonous intent could blunt the Ruling Council's wrath? I doubt our word would carry much weight, seeing as how we'd be on the side of the accused."

Saleh chuckled.

"How far do you think the Regent would go in antagonizing Archimandrite Bolack by turning one of his precious mind-meddlers over to the Commission's most psychopathic torturers? I'm sure you're aware Grand Admiral Mandus and Bolack enjoy an unusually close relationship."

"You mean Bolack is in favor of the expedition?"

A nod.

"He also understands the implications, especially if Sister Ardrix is right about the markings and there are still old order Void abbeys out there capable of challenging the legitimacy of the Void Reborn and its leadership."

"I see. So Ardrix and I are designated hostages of sorts, so the Ruling Council won't lash out in blind rage at disobedience in the Navy's senior ranks. Are the Ground Forces in on this?"

"Yes. The expedition will bring a company-sized security contingent from the 1st Guards Special Operations Regiment."

Torma's eyebrows shot up.

"Why not a company from the Wyvern Regiment while you're at it? The Specials are rabidly loyal."

"To the Hegemony, Colonel, not to the office of Regent, as is the Wyvern Regiment. The Specials' commander sees the same potential problems facing us if there is another space-faring human polity slowly expanding its reach out there, and people listen to him because he's slated for higher command."

"That's quite the little conspiracy you have going there."

"Not me, Colonel. I'm merely the messenger. But I speak for a long list of open-minded, intelligent people with stars on their collars, officers from every service whose loyalty to the Wyvern Hegemony and its people transcends politics."

"And what about the wishes of the Ruling Council?"

"Its choices might not be in the Hegemony's best long-term interests."

Torma sat back and studied Saleh.

"What if I say no? What if Ardrix and I say no?"

"The good Sister will obey her superiors as per the vows she made upon entering the Order." Saleh gave him a sardonic look. "And you won't say no not only because you understand what's at stake but because you possess every talented investigator's defining character trait."

"Which is?"

"Unquenchable curiosity."

"Perhaps."

Torma glanced away, knowing he'd accept even though it meant he would deserve every second of the same suffering inflicted on Jan Keter at his orders. The idea of one law for the powerful and connected and one law for the rest always stuck in his craw. It was what made him so relentless at rooting out subversion and corruption, no matter whose toes he stomped on. No guilty parties escaped his long arm.

"Cheer up, Colonel. It's not like you have a choice in any case. This brief conversation is merely to decide whether you're right for the job or would serve better as the guest of honor at your own funeral. General Robbins vouches for you, but since your work makes her shine, she's not what I would call the most disinterested of flag officers."

A bitter chuckle rumbled up Torma's throat.

"You'd have killed me if I decided it was best the Regent heard of this?"

"Me?" Saleh placed his hand over his heart. "No. We use specialists for that sort of thing, the kind who can operate inside this base with complete impunity. But it would have been a shame. Officers who combine ruthlessness in pursuit of duty with an inquisitive, open mind aren't common in the Guards Corps. I can't even say the former trait is common on its own, period, let alone the latter."

Torma shrugged wearily as he turned his eyes back on Saleh.

"Societies in stasis do their best to suppress inquisitiveness, which in turn, generates disaffection."

"A political police officer with a talent for philosophy. The universe is truly a wondrous place." Saleh climbed to his feet. "You'll receive instructions in due course. Until then, carry on as if this discussion never happened."

— 6 —

The next morning, when Sister Ardrix reported for duty, Torma indicated she should shut the office door and take a chair across from him. He made sure his field dampener worked because every office in the State Security Commission HQ was under surveillance by an AI looking for words that could be construed as treasonous. But like every other senior officer, Torma got away with using dampeners designed to frustrate the AI because it was understood they sometimes conducted business that should not be recorded. Such as interrogations skirting even the Commission's broad parameters, for example.

"Did your Archimandrite give you a new, confidential mission yesterday, Sister?" Torma asked once Ardrix sat across from him, eyes searching his face in that unnerving manner of hers.

"You know I cannot speak—"

"Of the secret expedition to Hatshepsut?"

Ardrix nodded once after a pause that seemed to go on forever.

"You were approached as well."

"By an officer from Naval Intelligence who claimed he worked for Rear Admiral Godfrey."

Her eyes widened slightly, but one not used to her ways would miss her reaction.

"Was it Captain Ewing Saleh, perchance? He visited the Archimandrite yesterday in the afternoon, shortly before I returned to the abbey. I did not meet him but was told the gist of their conversation after vespers. You and I will accompany the covert expedition to discover more about the unknown humans trading advanced artifacts bearing old Order markings."

Torma cocked an eyebrow in question. "Does the prospect please you?"

"Of course. Though the Archimandrite would not give me a choice either way. Secrecy means I alone, among the Brethren, am the right choice."

"And I alone among Commission officers, it seems." Torma let out a soft sigh. "So be it. Neither of us has a choice."

"You seem displeased?"

"We will violate the law in the same way Jan Keter did, along with hundreds, if not thousands, of Guards Corps Navy and Ground Forces members and one Void Reborn Sister. Yet my presence and yours will somehow make sure we don't suffer Keter's fate. It doesn't seem right or particularly realistic."

"Keter is still alive and healthy, and chances are good he will go with us. We can release him on Hatshepsut before returning home. That should salve your conscience."

Torma let out a strangled laugh.

"A Sister of the Void Reborn thinking in utilitarian terms? To quote our charming Captain Saleh, the universe is truly a wondrous place. No. The inner demons you released to torment him at my orders will always be on my conscience, along with the souls of those I directly or indirectly dispatched."

"Then take comfort in knowing you can spare Keter's soul. Was there anything else?"

Torma knew Ardrix no longer wished to discuss the matter, and there was no use insisting. Besides, he'd merely sought confirmation she and Archimandrite Bolack were part of the scheme. Somehow knowing the Hegemony's chief religious figure sided with those favoring an expedition lifted just a smidgen of the weight he'd felt draped over his shoulders since the previous evening. Supposing a conflict emerged between Regent Vigdis Mandus and Archimandrite Bolack, unimaginable as that might be, Torma couldn't call a likely winner.

Mandus needed Bolack if only as a sign the Almighty still smiled on the Wyvern Hegemony. Did Bolack need her? Probably not. His most devout faithful outnumbered the entire Guard Corps — Navy, Ground Forces, and Commission — by a factor of over twenty to one. If not more. Those who survived the empire's collapse almost two hundred years earlier had embraced the Void Reborn teachings as their sole salvation, like men and women stumbling upon an oasis in the desert moments before dying of thirst.

Those thoughts crossed his mind while Ardrix waited, a patient expression on her face as if she heard his internal dialog.

"Please carry on, Sister. Knowing we've both accepted our destiny and will travel the same path is enough at the moment."

Ardrix stood and bowed her head respectfully before turning on her heels and leaving the office, bound for the interrogation rooms where one of Torma's investigators waited with the newest prisoner. No sooner had she left than his communicator buzzed insistently. General Robbins. Torma knew what awaited him upstairs and stood with reluctance.

She was the last of three checkpoints. When Torma agreed one last time to this secret expedition, his fate would be sealed. Neither he nor his late father, who retired as a Commission general, ever overstepped the bounds set by the Ruling Council. Today, he would be the first Torma who did so.

Saleh was right, though, at the moment, Torma didn't consider his natural curiosity an investigator's greatest asset. He saw it as his biggest downfall. Ardrix's serene acceptance of this unexpected path seemed equally strange, despite her vows of obedience. He stood, tugged at his waist-length tunic's hem, and headed for the stairs at a measured yet determined pace.

Robbins was staring out the window at the quadrangle when Torma stomped to attention in the open doorway. Upon hearing the sound, she turned and gestured at a chair in front of her desk.

"Close the door, will you?"

"General."

"My distortion field is active. Is yours?" She asked once both sat facing each other.

"Always."

"Good. You had a visitor last night?"

Torma nodded once. "One of Admiral Godfrey's messengers."

"And?"

"He proved an excellent judge of character."

"So, you'll go?"

He nodded again.

"Yes, since the alternative is the sort of trip that I'm not ready for just yet. I spoke with Ardrix a few minutes ago, and she's ready as well."

"I'm glad you accepted. It would pain me to lose you, Crevan. You'll no doubt be sitting in my chair a few years from now, and perhaps even in one on the top floor. I'm sure I need not emphasize how important this matter is for the Hegemony. You knew from the moment you searched Keter's ship."

"Yes, General. It's greater than politics or anything else in the Hegemony's history."

"I'm glad we agree."

Torma hesitated for a few heartbeats. "What about Chief Commissioner Bucco?"

She locked eyes with him.

"You may return to your duties, Colonel."

Knowing it was the only answer he would hear, Torma climbed to his feet.

"With your permission?"

"Dismissed."

When he returned to his office, Torma felt a strange sense of dislocation, as if he'd suddenly lost control over his destiny and was now only a pawn in a power play whose genesis predated his interrogation of Jan Keter. Perhaps by more years than he could imagine. Did that make him a catalyst?

He shrugged off his unease and, seated once more behind the bare desk that served as his barrier against the grubbiness of official corruption, Torma plunged into his unit's latest investigation reports. Part of him, repressed but still present, hoped he would find nothing that meant more souls on his conscience, individuals he'd send to certain death for defying a regime whose legitimacy seemed more tarnished some days than others. Such as when he faced evidence its commitment to the Oath of Reunification was nothing more than a masque that forced loyal servants of the state into action despite the Ruling Council.

Like most Commission officers, Torma had an almost instinctive ability to compartmentalize his thoughts, and he shoved those he considered quasi-treasonous to the very back of his mind so he could focus on his duties. And so, over the following days and weeks, he forgot about Captain Ewing Saleh, the secret expedition to Hatshepsut, and what it meant for the Hegemony's future. He and his people had enough corrupt officials lined up for investigation, trial, and in many cases, execution to keep them busy.

Sadly, he hit dead end after dead end in his pursuit of Jan Keter's backers, meaning they were either among the Hegemony's quasi-untouchable elite or its secretive, violent criminal underground. Those categories were by no means entirely distinct from each other, as his colleagues in the organized crime units discovered when their investigations were derailed by unnamed senior government officials with enough power and connections to escape their clutches.

It left him with nothing more than speculation about why said backers were interested in both trade and intelligence gathering on human worlds struggling to support a modicum of industrialization, be it ever so primitive. Were those who chartered Keter also straining under the Ruling Council's inertia?

Equally puzzling and no less frustrating was the lack of progress in identifying the location of an old Order house using an L/L mark on its products. Hatshepsut was home to an abbey and numerous priories before the Great Scouring, but Keter saw no traces of them, nor did he pick up any indications they might still be operating on that world.

What happened to the Brethren, no one knew. They'd lost countless historical records during the ultimate battles between the Retribution Fleet and rebellious admirals, and parts of human history seemed like a patchwork. Torma doubted anyone in the Hegemony could name every single star system colonized by humanity over the millennia, let alone the habitats, stations, and other settlements. If ever the Hegemony sallied forth, they would surely find hundreds of forgotten worlds. If.

When the long-awaited summons finally came, it caught Torma by surprise. One morning, shortly after arriving at Commission HQ, General Robbins summoned him and Sister Ardrix to her office. That alone told Torma something was up. Robbins never called a unit's Sister along with the commanding officer for whom she worked.

When he and Ardrix were sitting across from Robbins, the latter said, "Colonel, Sister, the Navy requested a senior Commission officer and a Commission Sister to accompany Task Force Kruzenshtern on extended naval maneuvers along the Hegemony's outer borders. I chose you two for the mission as you are the most experienced team available."

Torma found his superior's choice of words interesting. Interservice requests usually filtered down from the Wyvern Group commander, Commissioner Cabreras, who often chose senior assignments himself rather than let his divisional commanders make the call. Did that mean Cabreras was in on it? Surely Robbins couldn't hide Torma and Ardrix's secondment to the Navy for what would likely be several months. He mentally shrugged. Did it matter? Dealing with Cabreras was Robbins' problem.

"You have forty-eight hours to brief your second-in-command, make the arrangements for an orderly handover, and pack. The abbey will send a temporary replacement for you, Sister. I copied Archimandrite Bolack on the Navy's request."

Ardrix inclined her head.

"I will make sure she knows the full extent of her duties."

"I don't doubt that. You're both expected at the Joint Base spaceport terminal the day after tomorrow, at oh-eight-hundred. A shuttle will take you to Task Force Kruzenshtern's flagship, the light cruiser *Repulse*, in orbit. There, you will report to Commodore Gatam Watanabe, the flag officer commanding. A list of required and forbidden items will be in your message queue shortly, along with weight and volume limitations."

"How many ships besides *Repulse*, General?"

"Four. The light cruiser *Reprisal*, the frigates *Dominator*, and *Devastation*, and the armed transport *Terror*. Not the Navy's newest and best ships, by any measure, but their prolonged absence will be less noticeable, especially since the warships were drawn from all four fleets and *Terror* is freshly out of her latest life-extension refit. She'll carry a company from the 1st Special Forces Regiment along with an air wing."

Torma's heart sank just a bit. He recalled that the youngest of the five, *Repulse*, was launched before his birth, and even she was built based on an imperial design that was outdated when the empire collapsed, albeit improved. Robbins must have read his thought because she let out a humorless chuckle.

"Task Force Kruzenshtern can deal with anything it might meet, considering we've not encountered anyone with more powerful starships since the Hegemony's founding."

"Only because we've not gone looking, General. But I get the point. Old ships won't be missed as much as newer ones, though I'd rather we come back in one piece."

"I share your sentiments, but perhaps a good scare out there might convince the Ruling Council it should place more emphasis on advancing our shipbuilding program rather than let it languish through lack of vision."

Torma allowed himself a derisive snort.

"With all due respect, General, visions of greatness interfere with the sort of grubby graft that keeps the Hegemony trapped. It'll take more than running across a mighty interstellar fleet gobbling up star systems to wake the Council from its slumber and consider long-overdue changes."

"True. But one step at a time. If you have no other questions, you're dismissed. Good luck. Task Force Kruzenshtern's expedition may be the catalyst that sets us back on track to reclaim humanity's heritage."

— 7 —

Crevan Torma entered the spaceport terminal's departure room at the appointed time, a heavy bag in each hand, and found Sister Ardrix already there, staring out the window at an empty tarmac. But instead of the usual monastic robes, she wore a black Guards Corps Navy uniform — hip-length, high-collared tunic over trousers tucked into calf-high black boots and a beret not unlike the one on Torma's head, minus a branch of service insignia. The uniform was devoid of any adornment other than the Order's metallic Phoenix Orb on her right breast. Ardrix turned the moment she heard his footsteps and smiled at the obvious air of surprise on his face.

"This is how Brethren serving in naval vessels as healers, chaplains, and counselors dress these days. The Navy prefers we don't appear overly different from its crews. Besides, when we're aboard, we come under the same code of discipline as anyone in the Wyvern Hegemony Guard Corps and hold assimilated warrant officer rank." An air of mischief crossed her face. "I suppose I should salute you, Colonel."

"Don't," Torma growled as he dropped his bags beside hers. "My vanity does not need stroking this morning."

"No worries. Even though we sometimes wear Guard Corps uniforms, the Brethren stay civilians and are exempt from the usual military protocols. We simply obey military commanders in certain situations, provided doing so doesn't contravene our vows or our obligations to the Almighty."

Momentary discomfort overtook Torma, and he needed a few seconds to realize why. She'd just openly stated, for the first time in their acquaintanceship, that entering the minds of prisoners and making them face their worst fears in preparation for questioning didn't contravene the Order of the Void Reborn's vows. Did donning a uniform bring on such honesty, or was she simply making it clear she would do whatever was necessary to ensure their safe return? One thing was sure, said uniform's close-fitting, severe cut and its accompanying beret turned her narrow, angular face into a more intimidating alabaster sculpture than ever.

"Is something wrong, Crevan?"

He shook his head, banishing the thought, and smiled in return.

"I just find you strangely transformed."

"Yet I'm still the same person."

Torma was saved from a response by two Commission noncoms escorting a manacled Jan Keter wearing regular spacer clothes and carrying a backpack into the waiting room. The one who was senior saluted Torma.

"Sergeant Onofri and Corporal Leduc reporting with the prisoner, sir."

Torma returned the compliment.

"At ease. Our shuttle isn't here yet."

"Yes, sir."

As they adopted the parade rest position, he studied a visibly confused Keter in silence. The latter's eyes were all over the place while his lips twitched nervously, as if he wanted to ask a question but feared his captors' reaction. Since Torma couldn't give a truthful answer within earshot of escorts who were surely just as puzzled about delivering a subversive to the spaceport and whatever surveillance devices monitored the departure room, he turned away and stared out the window. Ardrix imitated him moments later.

"Fear consumes him," she murmured in a voice pitched for his ears only.

"Now there's a surprise."

The minutes ticked by in tense silence until Torma spotted a small, boxy shuttle banking toward Joint Base New Draconis' landing strip as it shed altitude and speed. When it was near enough to read markings, he knew it was their ride.

The inelegant, rectangular hull, heavily covered in black streaks from too many re-entries and not enough time in drydock, bore the Hegemony sigil, a registration number, and the name *Repulse*. It deployed landing struts from the four pods festooning its flanks, two per side, and gently settled on the cracked tarmac a few dozen meters from the terminal. A side door dropped, forming a ramp, and two spacers wearing the Guards naval uniform emerged.

Torma glanced over his shoulder at the prisoner escort.

"That would be for us."

"Sir." The sergeant snapped to attention and nodded at his colleague.

Torma and Ardrix picked up their bags, and the former led their little procession through the sliding doors. As they neared the shuttle, both spacers straightened and saluted. Torma, hands full, gave them a grave nod.

"I'm Colonel Torma. With me are Sister Ardrix and Detainee Keter. Please take charge of Keter while the Sister and I settle in."

"Yes, sir. Just drop your luggage on the right at the top of the ramp. We'll stow it when the detainee is secure."

The handover was brief since, by design, Keter's transfer into naval custody wouldn't be recorded. Within minutes of the shuttle's arrival, they and the spacers were strapped in, their bags stowed in an aft compartment. The ramp lifted, cutting off their view of the low-slung concrete terminal.

Moments later, Torma felt thrusters come to life. After countless days of wondering and waiting, the moment was finally here. He wouldn't officially violate the laws against unauthorized travel until Task Force Kruzenshtern left Hegemony space. Still, it seemed as if they were crossing the line by merely leaving Wyvern's surface.

The notion passed as quickly as it came on when his inner ear told him the shuttle was rising. Without windows in the passenger compartment, or a display mimicking one, they couldn't tell how fast they were moving. After one glance at Ardrix, who sat still, eyes closed, breathing regulated, he slipped into a similar, light meditative trance.

Torma roused himself when the shuttle switched to artificial gravity, indicating they'd reached orbit and were likely approaching *Repulse*. He wasn't a frequent space traveler, although he'd visited each of the Hegemony's other three star systems at least once during his career. However, he still knew what to expect and understood his behavior aboard *Repulse* would determine his effectiveness.

The Navy nurtured a deep distrust for members of his branch, one exacerbated by the Chief Commissioner's so far unsuccessful attempts at stationing political officers aboard each warship. Torma privately disagreed with the idea, as did most experienced Commission members, but couldn't say so aloud.

A little over ten minutes later, he sensed a slight shift in the artificial gravity field and understood they'd passed through the hangar deck space doors. He received confirmation shortly afterward when he heard the shuttle's landing struts connect with the metal decking.

The spacers guarding Keter unfastened their seat restraints and stood, stretching. After exchanging silent glances, Torma and Ardrix did the same. Before the latter could ask how long they would wait, the portside door unlatched and transformed into a ramp again. The older of the two spacers gestured at the opening, indicating Torma, the most senior officer aboard, should disembark first.

As he walked down the ramp, Torma saw a compact, black-haired man with a Navy captain's rank insignia on the collar approach the shuttle while watching him with deep-set, dark, emotionless eyes. Jason Park, *Repulse*'s commanding officer, coming to greet his no doubt unwanted guests in person. Torma stopped at the ramp's bottom edge.

"Permission to come aboard, Captain?"

There was a slight but noticeable pause before Park replied, "Granted and welcome."

Torma took a single step and saluted the ship.

"Colonel Crevan Torma and Sister Ardrix reporting for duty."

"Commodore Watanabe is expecting you, Colonel. I understand you brought a detainee for my brig?"

"Yes, Captain. A merchant officer who went where this task force is headed and can give helpful advice."

"I see." Park glanced over Torma's shoulder at a manacled Keter, standing behind Ardrix with a spacer on each side. "And you're sure he won't cause mischief by lying?"

"Detainee Keter knows better after spending time with Sister Ardrix and me. Anything he says is what he believes to be the truth."

Torma saw Park's eyes narrow for a second or two as he processed the implications of his statement. But instead of dwelling on the subject, Park nodded at his men.

"Take him to the brig." Then he turned his attention back on Torma. "My people will see that your luggage reaches your quarters while I take you to Commodore Watanabe. I've given you the spare VIP suite which consists of two sleeping compartments separated by a common day cabin with workstations."

Torma inclined his head. "Thank you."

"If you'll follow me." Park turned on his heels and led them toward the open inner airlock while hangar deck maintenance personnel swarmed the shuttle.

Though Torma didn't get a chance to inspect the cruiser's outer hull during their approach, he somehow sensed *Repulse*'s advanced age as they walked along clean passageways, each door and intersection clearly labeled. There was something about her atmosphere that spoke of more light-years and wormholes transits than any human could travel in a single lifetime.

Park stopped at a door bearing a dark blue rectangle with a single gold star in the center. He glanced at Torma and Ardrix, then pointed at the door across from it.

"Your quarters are in there." Then he touched the call panel.

A disembodied voice answered, "Enter."

The door slid aside with a tired sigh, and Park waved them through. Torma marched in, stopped a regulation three paces in front of Watanabe's desk, and snapped off a crisp salute. He sensed, rather than saw Ardrix stop beside him, back straight, head held high.

"Colonel Torma and Sister Ardrix reporting as ordered, sir."

"At ease and welcome to Task Force Kruzenshtern."

Torma adopted the parade rest position and looked at Watanabe, a tall, lean man in his late fifties with short, iron-gray hair topping a craggy, olive complexioned face. Brown eyes beneath beetling brows stared back at him for a few seconds, then Watanabe gestured at the chairs in front of his desk.

"Please sit." A glance told Torma that Park was standing by an inner doorway marked 'Flag Conference Room,' instead of taking the third chair. "I won't dance around the issue, Colonel. You and the Sister are aware of your role on this expedition, correct?"

"Yes, sir. We're an alibi of sorts, something that gives this task force greater legitimacy if the Ruling Council decides it's unhappy with our unauthorized voyage."

"Good. Then you understand I won't look kindly upon either of you acting as State Security Commission officers looking for crimes and criminals in this command unless I give you specific permission."

"Yes, sir." Torma allowed himself a small, albeit ironic smile. "Technically, by volunteering for this mission, Sister Ardrix and I can be credibly accused of crimes against the state, and the Commission does not allow its officers to investigate themselves."

Torma thought he saw a glint of amusement in Watanabe's eyes, though the commodore's expression remained impassive.

"A wise practice, no doubt. Now tell me about those findings of yours that triggered this unprecedented mission and about the man now sitting in Captain Park's brig."

When both Torma and Ardrix finished relating what they knew, Watanabe sat back and exhaled.

"Fascinating. I now understand why flag officers of the three services devised such a risky scheme behind the Council's back. And do you suggest we follow this Keter's original route to Hatshepsut?"

Torma shrugged.

"That's not for me to say, sir. But if I were retracing his movements in the course of my investigation, it is what I would do." He reached into his tunic's left breast pocket and retrieved a thin wafer. "This holds a copy of Keter's logs, with the navigation data we retrieved when we seized his ship's computer core. Our analysts found no signs of tampering."

"Then why bring Keter along?"

"Because I think we should speak with his trading contacts on Hatshepsut and find out who sold them the items we seized, and that is not recorded in his logs."

"Excellent point, Colonel." Watanabe gestured at Park, who took the proffered data wafer. "Does that mean you'll place what I understand are superlative investigative skills at our disposal in tracking these mysterious others?"

"Absolutely, sir. If a potential threat to the Hegemony travels the wormhole network without our knowledge, finding it is our duty."

"Then you and I should enjoy a pleasant expedition."

8

"Nice." Ardrix emerged from her private cabin. "A porthole would improve things, but since this section is deep within the ship's hull, the display will have to do."

Torma stuck his head through the door connecting his quarters with the day cabin.

"It's better than anything the Navy ever assigned me before now. I can live without a porthole."

She gave him an amused look.

"I grouse, but in jest. None of the Brethren, not even Archimandrite Bolack himself, enjoys this sort of luxury. I shall pray to the Almighty I don't get used to it. Believing we're aboard a warship seems rather difficult at the moment."

"You've never left the surface before today?"

Ardrix shook her head.

"No. My talent is not the sort desired by the Navy. Our trek is my first time away from Wyvern." She wandered around the day cabin, examining every nook and cranny, opening and closing cupboards, then sat at one of the workstations and brought it to life. "I suppose I should track down my Brethren serving aboard *Repulse* in more traditional roles. Taking the ship's pulse via my Sisters could tell us much, no?"

A slow smile relaxed Torma's face.

"Indeed. But purely for reasons known only to the Void Reborn and not in service of the State Security Commission."

She dipped her head. "As you say."

"You're free to do what you wish with your time, Sister. Do you know the Brethren serving in *Repulse*?"

"No. This is a 3rd Fleet ship, remember? They would come from the Arcadia Abbey. While senior Order members routinely visit Wyvern for special events at the Mother House, we ordinary Sisters from different abbeys don't interact much. Most of us stay with the same house for our entire lives."

Torma nodded. "Of course."

"And you?"

"I'll do my own reconnaissance when I join the ship's officers in the wardroom for the midday meal. Their reaction should be instructive."

"Perhaps we should enter together, so I can taste said reaction."

"Even better." Torma glanced at the day cabin's display. "From what I read just now, they serve the midday meal in one and a half hours, at what the Navy insists on calling eight bells in the forenoon watch."

"I'll return a few minutes before that time, and we can make our grand entrance. I confess I'm curious about their feelings."

"As am I."

She gave him a sly look.

"About what? Our presence aboard or the mission?"

"Our presence. Only Commodore Watanabe and his captains should know where we're headed. If others are aware, they violated orders, something I will report on our return."

"Then I shall see if my colleagues caught wind of the mission. We Sisters often know things ahead of time."

Torma let out a soft snort. "So I noticed. Go take the pulse of the ship's Brethren."

Ardrix quickly found her way to the senior Sister's quarters aboard and touched the door panel's call screen. A few seconds passed, then the door slid open.

"Enter and be welcomed, Sister. I am Beata."

Ardrix stepped across the threshold and found herself facing a small, silver-haired woman in naval uniform with the Phoenix Orb above her breast pocket. She bowed her head respectfully.

"I am Ardrix of the Wyvern Abbey, assigned to the State Security Commission."

"And now on Commodore Watanabe's staff."

Beata smiled, revealing small, white teeth set in a face with such smooth features that Ardrix wondered about her actual age. She was surely much older than she appeared. Only the most experienced Sisters were appointed as ship's counselor and chaplain.

Beata would certainly be senior to the Sister appointed as chief medical officer, and the latter were seasoned physicians.

"Along with your Commission superior, Colonel Crevan Torma. Yes, word gets around, my child. Though no one has yet informed me or anyone else why you're among us and for how long, which is clearly by design. And that can only mean something unusual is afoot with a task force whose ships come from each of the four fleets."

"I suppose rumors are rampant."

Beata let out a delighted peal of laughter.

"The Navy lives on rumors, child. They entertain crews during what are almost always boring patrols. Right now, the rumors are such that everyone expects something so out of the ordinary, they can barely wait for it to begin. Shall I take you to meet the other Sisters serving in *Repulse*?"

"Yes, please."

Ardrix had studied the names, images, and biographical thumbnails of her Brethren in Task Force Kruzenshtern, along with those of the senior Navy officers, as had Torma. She was curious about these Sisters trained in a different abbey in another star system. And she wondered whether Beata would see her as another of the flock she tended rather than independent of the ship's Void Reborn contingent.

"Then please follow me. We shall visit sickbay where most work."

Beata led Ardrix out of the cabin and down the passageway. After a few paces, she glanced over her shoulder.

"Just so we're clear on lines of command, child, you answer entirely to your colonel, not me. Not even for spiritual matters, though you're welcome among us for worship, meditation, and discussion. But it's not because of your assignment as a State Security Commission interrogator and truth-sayer. As someone personally selected by Archimandrite Bolack for this cruise, you stand apart from the other Brethren, me included. And no, I didn't touch your mind to know you were wondering about that very same subject. Anyone in your position would."

Beata let out a throaty chuckle.

"Besides, I'd be a fool to dare intrude on a truth-sayer's thoughts. My mind isn't nearly as strong as yours."

**

"How are the Brethren?" Torma asked when Ardrix entered their common day cabin a little over an hour later.

"Curious, like everyone else. Only Sisters, no Friars, not even among the medical orderlies. Reserved in my presence, though whether it's because I come from a different abbey or because I work for the Commission, I couldn't say. They're my Sisters in the Almighty, but I sensed little sisterly feeling." She shrugged. "It was probably just so in the old Order when abbeys dotted most of the known galaxy, and each developed a slightly different culture because of particular environmental and social pressures, and there was little intermixing between them."

"What's the general mood?"

"If Sister Beata is right, the crew hopes for something that will break the boredom of endless patrols. Considering the level of anticipation I sensed in the crew members I crossed during my brief tour, she's probably right."

"I suppose that makes sense. They'll find out when we jump to hyperspace on our first leg beyond Hegemony space. Then we'll really see if excitement at being on a proper mission in the Hegemony's defense will trump realization that this expedition might not be sanctioned, thereby exposing everyone to retribution when we return."

Ardrix chuckled.

"That's where we come in, Crevan. How can this be unsanctioned if a senior Commission officer and a Commission Sister are aboard, advising Commodore Watanabe? Whoever thought of using us in this way is a genius."

"My money's on Admiral Godfrey. He has a reputation for being highly imaginative and ruthlessly devious."

"One could say the same about General Robbins. Did you do anything interesting while I was gone?"

He pointed at the display.

"I watched us break out of orbit."

"Oh. Too bad I missed it. In any case, it's time for the midday meal. Shall we cause consternation among the ship's officers?"

"You say that as if the thought entertains you."

She made a face.

"A Sister's life isn't exactly filled with base amusements, let alone the more sophisticated ones."

"Then perhaps dining in the wardroom will offer at least a modicum of fun." Torma gestured toward the door.

They walked aft until the next spiral staircase and descended a deck to where the ship's officers had their quarters, then headed forward, lured by the soft buzz of many voices drifting through an open door. As they entered a half-full wardroom, a few heads turned in their direction, but the conversations went on unabated.

A woman wearing the rank insignia of a commander stood and stepped toward them. Torma recognized her as Laetitia Julianus, the ship's first officer, based on the dossiers he'd read the previous day. Tall, lean, and pale, she was her commanding officer's physical opposite in almost every way.

"Colonel, Sister, welcome to the wardroom. Consider it your home while you're serving in *Repulse*."

Both Torma and Ardrix inclined their heads.

"Thank you."

"We're informal most of the time, and other than during official dinners, it's self serve." Julianus gestured toward the buffet. "I'd consider it an honor if you joined me at my table."

"Very gracious of you, Commander. We accept."

"Then I'll let you help yourselves."

As they crossed the compartment, Torma and Ardrix briefly glanced at each other, and he figured they were thinking the same thing. Julianus probably told *Repulse*'s officers they should treat their guests as they would any others and ignore that he and Ardrix worked for the fearsome State Security Commission. It was the only thing that explained the lack of evident curiosity on their part.

Tray in hand, Torma led them to where a smiling Commander Julianus waited. As they sat across from her, he said, "The food certainly has a delightful aroma."

"We eat well in this ship. Is this your first time aboard a Navy vessel, Colonel?"

"No. I've traveled in a few different naval transports and corvettes, but never in a ship of this size."

"How about you, Sister?"

"This is my first time off-planet."

"Then welcome to the wonders of outer space. Would either of you be interested in touring *Repulse* this afternoon?"

Torma nodded.

"With pleasure. How about you, Sister?"

"Please, yes."

"We'll do it after going FTL, then. I'll pick you up at your quarters. Now please dig in."

Julianus, who'd already eaten, kept them company while enjoying a cup of rich, aromatic coffee and answered questions about life in *Repulse*. Her ease with the two State Security Commission officers made Torma suspect Park told her about their purpose, which meant she knew where Task Force Kruzenshtern was headed.

However, he mentally shrugged the thought away. A commanding officer who didn't confide in his deputy wouldn't gain much trust or loyalty. His own second-in-command knew everything Torma did, and now, he ran the unit under General Robbins' direct supervision, a good career move, and proof she trusted the man, which in turn meant he was on their side. If there were such a thing as political sides within the Wyvern Hegemony Guards Corps.

Once back in their quarters, Torma asked, "What did you pick up?"

"Curiosity. A lot of it. More than any apprehension at our presence."

"Isn't that interesting? We must be losing our touch."

"I think it's more because of our unexplained presence under the circumstances, along with Commander Julianus' hospitality. Both are a clear sign something unusual is afoot."

"And speaking of Julianus, what about her?"

"What we saw was the real deal."

"That was my impression as well." Torma rubbed his chin. "As I said, interesting."

He dropped into one of the workstation chairs and stretched his long legs.

"Remember, we usually deal with those who have a guilty conscience and fear our presence. Navy personnel who aren't engaged in subversion are hardly our usual customers."

Torma let out a bark of laughter.

"We're all engaged in subversion at the moment. Or it will be so once we leave the Torrinos system and enter interstellar space. But I get your meaning. Being around criminals most of the time warps one's perception of humanity."

Before Ardrix could reply, the public address system came to life, startling both of them.

"Now hear this. Transition to hyperspace in five minutes. All hands to jump stations." They recognized Julianus' voice even before she repeated the message.

Torma gave Ardrix a crooked grin. "Your first time leaving this universe. I'm interested in how your body will react."

She grimaced back at him.

"Based on what I've read and heard from those who traveled through hyperspace, it likely won't be pleasant."

"But it will be mercifully short."

"How do you perceive it?"

"Similar to a nauseating light show, although I've never lost my lunch as a result."

"I look forward to the experience."

— 9 —

"They crossed the hyperlimit and went FTL for Wormhole Three," Rear Admiral Godfrey announced the moment Major General Robbins dropped into a chair across from his desk. "In just under eleven hours, they'll transit to the Torrinos system, an eight-hour run."

"Any danger of the wormhole fort stopping them?"

"No." Godfrey shook his head. "Not unless the Regent gets word of Task Force Kruzenshtern's destination and finds a way to give the fort's commanding officer orders without going through the regular lines of communication. Even though Vigdis Mandus still wears a Guards uniform and holds the rank of Grand Admiral, she can't plow her way through the Navy without raising a ruckus, and she knows it. None of the Council members enjoy the idea of Regents reaching deep down into their chains of command. Besides, she wasn't overly popular as the Navy's Supreme Commander because she spent too much time playing politics. So I doubt she has that many backchannels who'll do her bidding without question."

Robbins chuckled.

"Those elevated to the most senior ranks were rarely popular as three or four stars, Johannes. It comes with being politicians in uniform running roughshod over others in pursuit of promotions and power most of their careers."

"Which is why you and I won't go any higher."

She smirked.

"You flatter me, however I can be as slippery and devious a politician as any flag officer."

"But not in pursuit of personal gain. Otherwise, you'd be whispering sweet nothings in Vigdis' shell-like ear before telling her the dastardly Navy is heading into the galaxy without her permission. That might be good for a third star and command of the Commission's Wyvern Group."

"Keep it up, and I'll open an investigation into your private affairs. Perhaps your effusive praise is a cover for subversive activities."

This time, Godfrey laughed.

"The only subversive activity I'm pursuing is the same as yours, which means if found out, we will surely hang together."

"Then I shan't investigate. How long do you think until someone realizes Task Force Kruzenshtern isn't actually patrolling the Hegemony sphere?"

Godfrey shrugged.

"Who knows? They'll be seen by the wormhole fort on the Torrinos end and one of the fueling stations, then they'll vanish from the sensor grid when they go interstellar using the same route as the smuggler. Officially, they've not taken one of the wormholes leading out of Hegemony space, and if anyone asks,

Commodore Watanabe is carrying out a stealth patrol to test new tactics. How did Colonel Torma's people catch that smuggler, by the way?"

"Jan Keter? Torma received an anonymous tipoff. We figure whoever called it in did so out of good old-fashioned greed. Keter held a chunk of the inbound trade goods back from the folks who chartered his ship and looked for buyers on the darknet. They, in turn, probably found out and punished him in the worst way possible by ensuring we'd become involved."

"Great things are born of minor errors committed by insignificant, greedy little people."

Robbins cocked an eyebrow at Godfrey.

"Did you just make that up?"

"No. It was uttered by Lexa Mundie, an imperial historian circa eight hundred years ago. She commented on how the empire rose from the Commonwealth's decaying corpse through a series of relatively small errors born from naked greed. You should look up her works. Some of what she wrote is germane to our current situation, in a slightly twisted, roundabout way, if you consider our dear Hegemony will eventually become a decaying corpse itself unless we change course."

"Noted. Now, why am I here? Surely not for a discussion on long-dead historians."

"Ah." A smile crossed the intelligence officer's face. "The Chief of Naval Operations wants to meet you in person."

"Admiral Benes? Why?"

The smile became both mischievous and mysterious.

"Your sending Colonel Torma to me with his findings put in motion events certain senior people in the Guards Corps see as an answer to their prayers concerning the Hegemony's future. That makes you a potential ally in rousing our people and especially our government from their torpor."

She returned his smile. "Or a potential infiltrator seeking to bust the lot of you on behalf of Regent Mandus. One who merely used Crevan Torma as bait."

"Doubtful. We had you vetted by our own assets shortly after Colonel Torma shared his findings with me. And if you prove a better dissembler than we thought, well… I'm sure you can figure out the rest yourself. It won't be a story with a happy ending for your career."

Robbins arched an eyebrow.

"Or my life? I thought we were friends as well as Academy classmates."

"Some things transcend both. It depends on how close your lips end up against Vigdis Mandus' ear."

Robbins let out a humorless laugh.

"She's not my type."

"That's what we concluded. Though I understand your own Chief Commissioner works hard at ingratiating himself with the Regent."

"Perhaps, but we 'manage' Cameron Bucco, if you get my meaning."

Godfrey snorted.

"There's a lot of that going around these days. I daresay the three services manage their supreme commanders in the same fashion, seeing as how they spend more time playing politics than dealing with their commands."

"Too big a span of control, too rigid a system, and never enough trustworthy people. The curse of every authoritarian regime. It would probably be a different story if they weren't members of the Ruling Council."

"No doubt.." Godfrey climbed to his feet. "Admiral Benes is expecting us."

He led her through a warren of corridors to the glass and concrete HQ building's other side. Navy personnel stepped out of their way with alacrity the moment they saw the stars on their collars.

A few nodded politely, and Godfrey greeted many by name, wishing them a good day. Robbins got her fair share of curious stares once people noticed the State Security Commission scales of justice on her insignia.

Admiral Benes' aide jumped up the moment Godfrey led them into the corner office suite.

"Sirs." He indicated the open door behind him. "Please enter. The CNO is waiting for you."

Robbins had never visited this part of Navy Headquarters, and her eyes were everywhere as she followed Godfrey into a wood-paneled room lit by broad windows on two of its four walls. The usual plaques, souvenirs, portraits, and naval art decorated the other two walls, while a stand of flags formed a backdrop behind an expansive glass and steel desk.

Benes stood when they entered and watched their approach with intelligent brown eyes deeply set in a craggy face framed by short, silver-shot hair and a well-groomed beard. A compact man, he seemed as broad in the shoulders as he was tall, although Robbins knew it couldn't be so.

They halted a regulation three paces in front of the desk and saluted in unison. Benes returned the compliment with a formal nod since he wasn't wearing a headdress.

"At ease and welcome, Ishani." He glanced over their shoulders at the door where his aide stood. "We'll be fine, Arturo. You can carry on with your duties. I'm not available to anyone other than the Supreme Commander or the Regent, short of an emergency."

"Yes, sir."

As the door closed behind the departing aide, Benes' gaze settled on his visitors again. He gestured at chairs around a low table in one corner.

"We'll be more comfortable there."

Once they were seated, he studied Robbins in silence for what seemed like a long time. Unfazed, she returned the favor.

"What has Johannes told you so far?" Benes finally asked.

"That there are senior officers in the Guards Corps who seek a way of rousing the Hegemony from its torpor; that my peoples' findings gave them a perfect excuse to deploy a task force beyond our sphere, and that you see me as an ally."

He nodded once.

"Our first in the Commission."

"And you're considering me for membership in your group."

"It isn't so much a group as a network of like-minded individuals who fear the Hegemony will wither away if it keeps paying mere lip service to its founding principle, the reunification of human star systems under a single government. We can already see the effects of stagnation through the lack of technological innovation, the loss of our forebears' pioneering spirit, and the increasing amount of corruption, as more and more activities our betters dislike are carried out illegally. Such as the expedition your people uncovered, and which resulted in us speaking this morning while Task Force Kruzenshtern is outbound with senior representatives of the three Guards Corps branches aboard."

"So, what does this network call itself?"

A cold smile briefly lit up his face.

"Nothing. It grew organically over the past few years, starting with the previous Regent throttling innovation more than ever for fear our leaders might lose their absolute control over Hegemony affairs."

"An illusory control at best, in my estimation, sir." Robbins grimaced. "The Commission would need four times the people at least, and even then, the biggest threat to our future comes from within. Sadly, there's nothing we can do about it because of the glass ceiling preventing my people from investigating our elites. They were probably behind the smuggler's expedition to Hatshepsut and points in between, to begin with."

"And many other outrages, no doubt."

The smile returned, this time with a more predatory cast, and she returned it measure for measure.

"You'd be amazed how they keep each other and their minions in check with various bits of blackmail. But since they're off-limits, the only thing we can do is watch, take notes, and wait for a slip-up. And before you ask, there are people within the Guards Corps vulnerable to said blackmail because, as some in the Commission whisper among themselves, they traded their immortal souls for power, wealth, and the pursuit of illicit pleasures."

Godfrey nodded wisely. "They took a ticket to eternal damnation, as our friends in the Order of the Void Reborn would say. We know of some within the Navy. There are probably more."

"Would you like a list of those we know about?"

Benes let out a bark of laughter.

"This is getting more interesting by the minute. Yes, please, do tell us. Johannes can share what we know about Commission members who, to use his expression, took the ticket. But let me discuss a few ground rules everyone within the network observes."

She inclined her head by way of acknowledgment.

"First, none of us know everyone involved. We use the old cell system for security. I could meet a general from the Ground Forces and not know they are part of the network and vice versa. You are now part of a cell that includes Johannes and me. Don't ask if there are others in this cell. Neither of us will answer. Second, you can form a cell within the Commission involving trusted personnel, such as your colonel in *Repulse* and his assigned Void Sister. However, mention the network as little as possible. In fact, it would be better if you said nothing more than you know kindred spirits with the same goal of securing the Hegemony's future and seeing that the Oath of Reunification is implemented."

"Understood. I assume I can form more than one cell so long as each isn't aware of the others?"

"Yes. Third, we don't mention the network nor give it code or cover names. Outsiders cannot perceive what is nameless. And four, we hold discussions in secure locations, covered by field dampeners, and never over any communications devices whatsoever. Your service is much too adept at intercepting everything and anything."

"Sensible rules, sir. Would you like my services in case you need to vet someone? We can access resources beyond your reach, and my people never ask why any given individual is under scrutiny by the Commission's senior leadership. They fear the tender mercies of our Void Sisters."

"Johannes was hoping you'd make that offer. Yes, we accept with pleasure." Benes sat back, indicating he'd said his piece. "From here on, communications will remain solely between you and him. It wouldn't do if our betters found out one of the Wyvern Group's leading generals was getting overly friendly with the Chief of Naval Operations."

"Agreed, sir." She imitated Benes when the latter stood.

"Johannes and I still have a few matters to discuss." He held out his hand. "A pleasure meeting you, Ishani."

"Likewise, sir."

On her way back to Commission Headquarters, Robbins didn't quite know how she should interpret the meeting with Vice Admiral Benes. But part of her felt strangely elated at the thought there were others concerned about the Hegemony's future and eager to implement the Oath of Reunification sworn by its founder as he surveyed the ashes of humanity's first interstellar empire.

— 10 —

Commissioner Nero Cabreras, the three-star commanding the State Security Commission's Wyvern Group, strolled into Major General Robbins' office unannounced several days later, shortly after lunch. A tall, lean, narrow-faced man with a prominent nose and equally prominent Adam's apple, he always reminded Robbins of nothing so much as a human version of the Wyvern Long Bird. The native avian was known for standing in marshy ponds on one leg while watching their surroundings through eerily shimmering compound eyes.

Cabreras perched himself on a corner of her desk, crossed his arms, and stared at her.

"A little lizard told me you're rather chummy with Johannes Godfrey of Naval Intelligence these days, Ishani. Is that related to the cruise Crevan Torma and Sister Ardrix are taking?"

"As a matter of fact, it does. Johannes gives me regular updates on their status. So far, so good. Both are integrating well with the task force commander's staff. I'm optimistic the concept will work."

Robbins had sold the temporary assignment of Torma and Ardrix to Watanabe's staff as a way of getting Commission people aboard Navy ships. It was ostensibly so they could step up the fight against smuggling by interrogating suspected merchant captains on the spot rather than weeks later after they disposed of their cargoes.

Since starships engaged in illegal activities were seized as prizes, it made sense the Navy would enjoy being in on the action rather than let the Commission pocket the prize money. Godfrey had dreamed up the cover story, more proof if any was necessary, that his mind worked in twisted ways.

"The same little lizard told me the task force fueled up in the Torrinos system and vanished from the sensor grid. Any idea what that's about?"

She shrugged.

"Search me. The Navy doesn't discuss its ship movements with anyone. We'll find out when Crevan and Ardrix are back."

Her gaze never wavered, but she wondered about the talkative reptile whispering in Cabreras' ear. Her superior gave no sign of having high-level contacts in the Navy, nor did he ever hint at being among those who wanted a more vigorous Ruling Council, one ready to reclaim lost worlds.

It was well known around HQ that he wanted to become Chief Commissioner when Cameron Bucco retired, which meant convincing the Council of his utmost loyalty and showing an almost religious adherence to the policies it proclaimed. If it entailed embracing stagnation with all his heart, he would do so. Not that Cabreras would call it so. No, he would use terms such as preserving harmony and balance, security and stability, that sort of thing.

"Why do I get the impression you're not telling me everything, Ishani?"

"I couldn't say. You know as much as I do about what goes on around here, sir."

He scoffed. "Are you forgetting I once sat in that chair and carefully managed the flow of information to the Group Commander's office?"

"No, sir."

Cabreras stood. "Then do try to remember you're a State Security Commission flag officer first and foremost. We might be one big, happy Guards Corps, but we owe our primary loyalty to our branch."

With that, he left a thoughtful Robbins staring out the window. Cabreras rarely came down from his aerie, and then only for urgent matters. Otherwise, he summoned his divisional commanders. Something was bothering him, that much she could sense without the help of a Void Sister. Could he suspect Task Force Kruzenshtern, with two of his officers among the crew, was going rogue because of Jan Keter and his illegal expedition? But why should he?

Torma had closed the Keter smuggling case weeks earlier due to lack of evidence. Though very much alive in *Repulse*'s brig, Keter was listed as having died of natural causes while in custody, a common occurrence. She'd never specifically reported the items of advanced manufacture bearing mysterious old order abbey markings, lumping them in with the rest of the illegal trade goods Keter brought back when she wrote up the summary for Cabreras.

Could one of the network's cells involved with the reconnaissance mission be leaking information? She should tell

Godfrey as soon as possible but make sure their meeting wouldn't come to Cabreras' attention. Otherwise, he'd know something was up. Her superior might consider ambition a virtue, yet he was no fool, and he'd surely be monitoring her every move for the next day or two.

Robbins pushed the thought from her mind and concentrated on the case file in front of her. She always came up with her best ideas while doing something else. Besides, if that's all Cabreras heard, then his informant didn't know the truth. Nothing said he or she was part of the network in any case.

She looked up at the windows again after a few minutes when another thought struck her. They wouldn't hear from the task force until its return. There were no functioning subspace radio relays beyond the Hegemony sphere because Dendera's Retribution Fleet had destroyed every last one long ago. It meant that if the task force ran into something dire, she might never hear from them again.

The idea came shortly before quitting time. Robbins pulled up the file the Commission kept on Rear Admiral Johannes Godfrey. All senior officers were scrutinized, and their lives dissected before promotion beyond lieutenant colonel or commander, even those wearing the Commission's insignia. Yes, her accessing it would leave a trace, but her name would be only one among many who read up on the Chief of Naval Intelligence in the last year, Commissioner Cabreras among them, and his last time was only the previous day.

And there it was, her solution. Godfrey attended religious services at the abbey every Friday evening. As part of the deal between the Order and the Hegemony, surveillance of any Void Reborn house and those who visited them was strictly forbidden. It was the price the Ruling Council and its enforcer, the State

Security Commission, paid in return for the services of truth-saying Sisters, the ones who could plunge into another's mind and see what it contained.

Now Robbins had to show renewed faith in the Almighty and make it believable. Like most Commission officers, she paid little attention to spiritual matters. However, a Void Reborn Orb sat on her office's sole bookshelf, a reminder of the Hegemony's symbiotic relationship with the monastic order that made her service branch so terrifyingly effective.

Thus, two evenings later, after an early supper, Robbins headed for the abbey in her private ground car, which, contrary to most in New Draconis and indeed most on Wyvern, wasn't equipped with a tracking device that betrayed its owner's every move. A major general, especially one of the Commission's divisional commanders, enjoyed that particular perk along with most of the planet's elite.

She parked in the assigned lot beyond the main gates and walked the rest of the way to the large, vaulted yet simple stone building where the Brethren held services for the public. Its pinkish granite cladding seemed to glow as it reflected the last rays of the setting sun while soft light seeped through tall, stained glass windows.

A gentle murmur of voices escaping through open doors reached her ears when she joined the flow of silent worshipers. Like them, Robbins was dressed simply — dark trousers, a loose, long-sleeved white blouse beneath an equally dark jacket, and comfortable, flat-heeled shoes.

In deference to the abbey's sanctity, she'd left her sidearm in the car and felt strangely naked without its comforting heft. Technically, a Commission officer going about in public unarmed was against policy, especially if she wore civilian clothes, but this was the sacred abbey.

It wasn't the first time Robbins entered the Hegemony's premier place of worship, but it was the first time she would join a service. Finding the cathedral-like hall bursting at the seams well before the appointed time gave her pause. One of the few aspects of Hegemony society to which the Commission paid little attention was the Order of the Void Reborn's influence, mostly because of the mutual interest compact between the secular and the religious.

That so many would attend a regular Friday night service within the abbey walls surprised her, although perhaps it shouldn't. The abbey ran regular services in outlying houses of worship scattered around New Draconis, as did priories elsewhere across the planet, and those were always well attended.

Her eyes searched for Godfrey's familiar face among the crowd but in vain. And yet, shortly after she found room on a densely packed pew in one of the higher tiers lining three of the house's four walls, a hand tapped on her shoulder. She turned her head and found herself face-to-face with a smiling Godfrey. Like her, he wore sober civilian clothes, the sort favored by the rest of the congregation.

"Did you suddenly find religion, my dear Ishani?"

"No, but I suddenly found you just now, which means my prayers were answered. We must talk."

"In that case, after the service, I suggest we take a stroll through the abbey orchard, where the Brethren engage in walking meditation exercises. That makes it one of the most private places in New Draconis."

"Sure."

Robbins turned her attention back on the altar where a bald, gray-bearded Friar and an equally aged Sister were uncovering the sacred Void Orb. That done, both turned toward the congregation and raised their arms. Almost at once, the soft buzz of conversation died away.

They dropped their arms, and the Friar intoned, "The Void giveth."

His voice echoed off the walls, as did hers when she said, "The Void taketh away."

To which those present replied, "Blessed be the Void."

Though Robbins hadn't attended a service since graduating from the Guards Academy, she quickly fell into the familiar rhythms and found herself eerily at ease among so many strangers. It ran counter to her instincts as one of the state's guardians, feared by most and hated by many, but she wasn't fazed.

When she stood as the officiants raised their arms and invoked the Almighty's blessing one last time, ending the service, it was as if a weight had been lifted from her shoulders, one she hadn't been aware of until that very moment.

Robbins followed the flow of people down the tiers and through the door, then stepped aside and waited for Godfrey, who showed up moments later wearing an air of contentment she'd never seen before, even though they'd known each other since their Academy days.

"What did you think?" He asked as they fell into step side-by-side on the path leading to the orchard.

She thought about the question for a few moments.

"It was more powerful than I remember. Mind you, I've not attended a service since graduation."

Godfrey chuckled.

"You're on the right track. The form hasn't changed since our younger days, but this place gives it a more profound meaning. Or perhaps the great number of devoutly faithful in this sacred house amplifies everything. Many of us didn't enjoy attending the Academy services, and that attitude permeated the congregation back then. In contrast, everyone comes here by choice."

"An interesting way of looking at it."

"If you ever have a few moments with Archimandrite Bolack, ask him. Or better yet, ask one of the Sisters he assigned as Commission auxiliaries. They're the sort who really understand the human mind from the inside out."

"Don't I know it," she replied in a dry tone. "What I wonder is how you know about that."

"Come now. The Commission has been using Sisters with a particular talent as truth-sayers and interrogators for decades. Even if you don't publicize your practices and eliminate many of those subjected to their full extent, the word is bound to reach ears such as mine. Although I have difficulties reconciling the beauty of the service that we just witnessed with the darkness that Sisters who work for the Commission encounter daily."

"I do as well. Perhaps those with the strongest talent no longer feel empathy for others or at least for those subject to their tender mercies. Or they have other coping mechanisms we can't begin to understand." She shrugged. "None besides the Brethren know, and they certainly won't tell."

Entering the orchard after sunset was like stepping into another world, lit only by the stars and Wyvern's two moons. The trees, green and lush, absorbed not only New Draconis' nighttime glow but its constant background noise so that one might never suspect they were on the outskirts of the Hegemony's capital. Pleasant, flowery scents tickled Robbins' nostrils, and an unusual sense of peace enveloped her.

"I can see why the Brethren practice walking meditation in this place," she said in a subdued tone.

"It's quite something, isn't it? Finishing my week here always leaves me content with life. Now, what brings you to the abbey, my friend?"

—11—

When Robbins finished relating her encounter with Nero Cabreras, Godfrey glanced sideways at her, never breaking stride.

"You're right. It could be no more than gossip. I'm sure he has friends or informants inside Navy HQ. Many Commission officers do, you being a case in point. But the fact he went out of his way to let you know is another matter. A warning, perhaps?"

She grimaced.

"Could be. Cabreras believes he's on a fast boat to the Chief Commissioner's office, and woe betides anyone who rocks it, no matter how noble the cause. He would consider flag officers of the three branches conspiring to ignore the Council's policies, something capable of ending his ride up the greasy pole. Especially since officers from his own group are actively participating in the conspiracy. The fact we suspect that someone with at least our level of technology is out there based solely on a few crates of innocuous if illegally obtained trade items would strike him as ludicrous." She let out an exasperated sigh. "Although he's a skillful administrator and a loyal servant of the state, no one ever mentioned sound strategic thinking as one of his more notable characteristics."

Godfrey nodded.

"I'd heard Cabreras' vision stops with his own career goals. Do you think he has a chance at the Commission's top job?"

"With the current Regent and Ruling Council in office? Yes. He's been cultivating them for years. But if their terms expire before Chief Commissioner Bucco retires, it's anyone's guess."

"And will he retire after Vigdis and the rest of the rogue's gallery?"

"Not a clue. We don't speak much, and then only in passing. Besides, Bucco would make the sphinx of legend seem loquacious."

"And if Cabreras becomes the chief, will you become the Wyvern Group's commander?"

She allowed herself a few grim chuckles.

"Fat chance of that. Naming group commanders is the chief's prerogative, and I'm not part of Cabreras' little clique. That, and he doesn't like me much because he suspects, with reason, that I'm much smarter than he is."

Godfrey let out a soft snort.

"I don't doubt it."

They walked on for a few more paces, then Godfrey stopped.

"I'll get a few trusted people on the trail of his little lizard inside Navy HQ, and then we'll see. Thank you for taking the trouble to cover your steps in contacting me about the matter. Since you enjoyed the service — don't deny it, I can see the light in your eyes and the spring in your step — perhaps we could do this every Friday. I can't think of a better cover for our discussions on certain matters, and I enjoy this orchard. Wait until harvest time rolls around. The scent of ripe fruit is intoxicating, almost as much as the schnapps the Friars distill from them."

"I thought you were a whiskey connoisseur."

"And I am. But there's nothing like a fruit schnapps for digestion after a rich meal." He patted his still flat stomach. "Eating well is one of my many vices, as are the products of the abbey's distillery. Plus, buying their products supports the good works they do."

"I'll keep that in mind the next time I need fruity firewater. But back to your suggestion, yes. I'll attend Friday evening services. We can walk the orchard afterward and discuss business. That way, the office gossips won't see me haunt Navy HQ anymore. It'll keep Cabreras guessing, something I enjoy, if you're interested in my particular vices."

"Keeping the Cabreras of the galaxy in the dark is a virtue, my friend, not a vice. And yes, between Sandor Benes and me, we do the same thing with our own supremo from time to time, and not only because VanReeth suspects Benes of ogling his seat at the Council table with undue avarice." They turned around and headed back toward the abbey proper. "We probably shouldn't be leaving simultaneously, just in case. If you'd like more time here, I can go first. Otherwise, I'd be happy for another ten or fifteen minutes in this magical place."

"Then enjoy your extra time here, Johannes. I'll be off. See you next Friday."

Robbins picked up the pace and soon vanished in the gloom. When she reached the parking lot, Godfrey's was among the few remaining cars. None of them screamed Commission stakeout team, and she hoped it would stay that way at least until Task Force Kruzenshtern's return.

At that point, its findings would blow apart secrecy, or the whole matter might be quashed because there was no one capable of challenging the Hegemony out there. Robbins fervently hoped the former would materialize because the latter meant no impetus to rouse from a long slumber, one which might turn into the big sleep as the last human bastion of star-faring civilization merged with the Infinite Void.

**

The following Monday, Sister Sankari, one of the Commission auxiliaries working for the Anti-Corruption Division and in Ardrix's absence, the senior of the Sisters under Robbin's command, appeared at the latter's open office door. She rapped her knuckles lightly on the door jamb and waited, hands joined in front of her, an air of indefatigable patience on her round, puckish face.

Robbins looked up from her reader and smiled, as she always did when seeing Sankari.

"Please come in and sit, Sister. What can I do for you?"

Sankari bowed her head and obeyed Robbins, taking a chair facing the desk.

"I noticed you at the abbey's Friday evening service, General."

"I was there, yes," Robbins replied in an even tone, though she wondered what this was about. "And I found it most uplifting. Surprisingly so."

"One such as you who returns to the faith after a long absence often does." The Sister studied Robbins with her piercing gaze, then asked, "Would you like a spiritual guide who might help you along the path of rebirth?"

The question stunned Robbins for a few heartbeats, then she remembered Crevan Torma taking lessons from Ardrix and becoming calmer, more perceptive, and more efficient because of the mental disciplines he learned. At the same time, a paranoid little voice wondered whether the Void Sisters worked on their own hidden agenda, and this offer of guidance wasn't just the selfless act of a monastic devoted to a life of service but a way of gaining influence over the Commission's inner workings.

Robbins pushed the thought away. Considering Sisters had been serving the Commission for decades, they would have every bit of influence the Order needed by now. And perhaps studying under Sankari might give Commissioner Cabreras something more he could worry about. That alone made the offer attractive.

Robbins inclined her head.

"I accept in all humility, Sister."

"May I suggest we start with half an hour first thing in the morning, say seven-thirty?"

Was Sankari's suggested time fortuitous, or had she studied Robbins long enough to know that meetings in general and especially those called before oh-eight-hundred were anathema to the head of the Wyvern Anti-Corruption Division?

"Done."

"In that case, we will begin tomorrow." Sankari rose in the graceful motion common to Sisters and bowed her head. "Enjoy the rest of your day, General."

"You as well."

While watching Sankari vanish into the corridor, Robbins wondered how many of the Wyvern Group's senior officers were taking lessons from the Sisters. And how many from the State Security Commission's HQ staff. She knew Crevan Torma had been for months, if not longer. Perhaps ever since Ardrix came to work for his unit.

Later that day, Commissioner Cabreras poked his head through her office door and smirked. "I hear you found religion, Ishani."

Robbins swallowed an exasperated sigh, placed her reader on the desk, and speared him with emotionless eyes.

"You can't find what you never lost, sir. I merely thought it was time I rekindled my faith in the Almighty." She kept her tone conversational, knowing he'd like nothing more than see her rise to the bait.

"I can think of better things to do on a Friday evening."

Contempt mixed with derision glimmered in his eyes. Although he'd never dare say so out loud, Robbins knew Cabreras considered religions utterly useless. Even worse, he saw the Void Sisters working for the Commission as mere mercenaries who wielded an eldritch talent best kept under wraps.

"No doubt, sir. Is there anything I can do for you?"

Instead of replying, Cabreras gave her a small wave before vanishing down the corridor. That told Robbins he'd just delivered another warning. Either one of his minions saw her at the abbey on Friday, or she'd been tailed there.

Curious he didn't mention Godfrey. Perhaps whoever spotted her missed him, but then, Godfrey looked remarkably different in civilian clothing, something he probably cultivated. Or the tail, conscious of the agreement that Commission personnel on duty will stay off the Order's abbey and priory grounds, didn't dare go further than the main entrance for fear one of the Sisters might detect him or her.

But why was Cabreras playing games? She was hardly on the fast track to glory, let alone the sort of politician in uniform that might interfere with his plans, and knew the two stars on her collar were it. Robbins mentally shrugged. Time she checked for increased surveillance and a convenient side door in the house of worship that might allow her and Godfrey to reach the orchard unseen by the regular Friday night crowd out front. Other than that, it would be best if she made herself forget about the covert expedition in favor of pretending Crevan Torma and Ardrix were truly testing a new anti-smuggling concept with the Navy. Perhaps Sister Sankari's teachings might help.

**

Captain Ewing Saleh, Hegemony Guards Corps Navy, entered Rear Admiral Godfrey's office and shut the door behind him. The latter gestured at a chair and said, "We may have a problem."

Saleh's eyebrows crept up in question as he sat. "What kind?"

"The whispering lizard sort. Commissioner Nero Cabreras has a friend inside this HQ, one who told him I've been seeing a lot of Ishani Robbins lately. Find out who that is and put him or her under surveillance."

"You think this whisperer is one of us?"

Godfrey shook his head.

"No. Otherwise, Cabreras wouldn't play coy. He's not the type. Someone isn't buying Task Force Kruzenshtern's stated mission but doesn't know why."

"I trust General Robbins and you are using other means to communicate."

"We'll be meeting at the abbey after the Friday evening services. The crowd provides suitable cover, and the orchard is a sacred place where we can talk without being overheard. Even the Commission's most rabid atheists wouldn't dare go against the compact between the Order and the Ruling Council on matters of trespass and covert surveillance."

"For now."

Godfrey smiled at his subordinate. "Always the optimist, aren't you?"

"Someone must be, so why not me?" Saleh replied, deadpan. "It helps bring balance to the galaxy. Was there anything else, Admiral?"

"No. Happy hunting."

With Saleh gone, Godfrey turned back to the overnighters, top-secret reports from his various sections on events of the last twenty-four hours. The only item of note was yet one more meeting between Archimandrite Bolack and the Regent the previous evening in the Wyvern Palace. Godfrey tapped his chin with an outstretched index finger, eyes narrowed. Bolack and Mandus were spending a lot of time together in the last little while, and that made him wonder why. But short of asking either, he'd find no straightforward answers and filed the information where his subconscious could retrieve it should any further clues cross his desk.

— 12 —

Torma's eyes fluttered open seconds after his stomach returned to its accustomed place. He glanced at Ardrix, slowly unfolding her limbs from the lotus position she'd adopted on her meditation mat when the five-minute warning to transition sounded.

"I've never been in hyperspace for such a lengthy duration."

"Neither has anyone else aboard this ship or the entire task force." She rose in a graceful motion. "My theory was correct. Entering a light trace dampens the effects. I felt no nausea whatsoever this time. You should join me next time."

"I believe I will." Torma reached out to stroke his workstation's screen, which lit up with the bridge data feed anyone in *Repulse* could access. "It seems navigation brought us to the heliopause of a star system beyond the Hegemony. Whether it's the right one is still up in the air."

The day cabin's primary display came to life with the image of a starfield. A blue circle surrounded one of them, slightly brighter than the others, marking the target.

"If we're in the right spot, this is a system without habitable planets but five wormhole termini. Perhaps we'll find the remains of old imperial wormhole forts, fueling stations, or automated mineral mining complexes." He paused for a moment. "If Commodore Watanabe is willing to explore instead of heading directly for our exit wormhole. We are under something of a time constraint, our records of this place are sparse, and Jan Keter didn't search for artifacts dating back to the old empire."

"I'm sure the commodore will order long-range scans, the sort that our enterprising smuggler couldn't carry out with his little ship. With any luck, they'll pick up something that might show how our ancestors used this wormhole node." Ardrix shrugged on the robes she wore in the privacy of their quarters, covering her exercise clothes.

"Indeed—" The public address system came to life, startling both.

"Now hear this. We arrived at the target system's heliopause. Before proceeding on our next hyperspace jump, we will assume survey stations. Report any discrepancies or suspected issues to your divisional chiefs. That is all."

Ardrix gave Torma a questioning glance. He touched his workstation's screen and called up the lexicon.

"Survey stations means checking the ship bit by bit to make sure our lengthy FTL run didn't cause undue stress on the hull or systems."

"Is there a human equivalent, something that might detect undue stress on crew and passengers?"

He snorted with amusement.

"I think that's called a Void Sister scan. Ask your colleagues if they need help. In any case, at least we know we hit the right star system, so that's progress, though I can't help but feel like the explorers of old. You know, the ones who left Mother Earth in the first faster-than-light starships almost two thousand years ago, not knowing what they would find at the end of an impossible journey." A pause. "I wonder if we'll ever find her again."

"Who? Mother Earth?"

Torma nodded.

"Legend has it she was mostly abandoned shortly following the empire's formation after vast swaths were scoured by civil war."

Ardrix gave him an amused smile.

"Legend? I daresay the fate of our species' original homeworld is mostly myth in an age when the fall of the empire has become in large part a fairy tale where fact cannot be separated from fiction." A pause. "Is it true the navigation records that survived the collapse don't give coordinates for Earth?"

"I couldn't say. Perhaps *Repulse*'s sailing master knows." Torma stood. "Now that my stomach has settled, it realized the midday meal should be ready. If we're lucky, she'll be there, and you can ask her."

Lieutenant Commander Prince, the cruiser's second officer and one of those who regularly ate with Torma and Ardrix, chuckled when the latter asked her about Earth.

"We know her galactic coordinates and spectral signature. But according to our files, Earth only has two wormhole termini which lead nowhere useful without several transits through uninhabited systems. As a result, she became a backwater once the empire's entire shipping network shifted to wormhole travel. I'm afraid Earth withered on the vine, as one would say, well before the Retribution Fleet scoured rebellious worlds. In fact, she may have escaped that fate entirely because she no longer mattered."

Ardrix put on a disconsolate expression.

"Quite a sad epitaph for our original home."

Prince raised her coffee mug.

"Here's hoping a functioning civilization flourishes on her surface, perhaps even a space-faring one, keeping the memory of bygone glories alive."

Torma raised his own cup and smiled.

"I'll second that motion."

Once more, Ardrix marveled at his curious and unaccustomed lack of introspection. Did he not wonder how both made friends with the ship's key officers so quickly? The thought of asking her obviously never crossed his mind.

He'd simply accepted the idea that his presence, and hers, as members of the commodore's staff while he led his task force on a secret mission, was a good omen as far as the rank and file were concerned. After all, spacers loved their strange notions, the sort that most of humanity considered little short of superstition.

Ardrix gave him a sideways glance before concentrating on the simple meal before her. Fortunately, keeping the friends she'd helped him make took less and less effort with time as they grew accustomed to his presence. That he had a reasonably pleasant personality, despite being somewhat taciturn, when not hunting subversives helped, of course. Then there was the matter of them counting among the subversives, now that they'd left the Hegemony sphere without permission from the Council.

"How much time will we spend in this system?" She asked.

Prince swallowed a sip of coffee.

"We can't make for the exit wormhole directly, so the plan is two jumps, with a pause between them so we can run a detailed scan, in case there are imperial remains that might be of interest."

"And if we find some?"

"We'll make a note for any follow-on mission."

Torma nodded.

"Wise."

Prince studied him with a thoughtful gaze.

"I hear you're the ones who made this expedition possible."

"We found intriguing evidence and passed it along to Naval Intelligence."

"I didn't know inter-service cooperation was that good on Wyvern."

He cocked an eyebrow.

"It's not on Arcadia?"

Prince grimaced.

"We can't be called a happy Hegemony Guards Corps family there, unfortunately. The rivalry between Navy, Ground Forces, and Commission is rather fierce. Neither trusts the other, though the two combatant services trust each other more than either trusts the Commission."

"In truth, it would be just as bad in our star system if it weren't for the Regent's unblinking eye staring at us directly. That and the fact we share space with the Navy and Ground Forces HQs."

Torma, ever the cautious Commission officer, wasn't about to mention the personal relationships between flag officers of the three services who made this expedition possible. But they were no doubt a strong influence pushing back against mistrust and internecine conflicts.

A smile lit up Prince's round face.

"Got it. Bickering and backstabbing where the top brass can overhear isn't a career-enhancing move."

"It depends on how, where, and who. Infighting still happens, just not as visibly." Torma took a sip of coffee. "But back to your original question. The evidence we discovered in the course of our investigation hinted at a possible external threat to the Hegemony, hence our informing Naval Intelligence. Once I did my duty and briefed the CNI, events proceeded without my or Sister Ardrix's intervention. We're merely on this expedition as mission specialists of a sort."

"And not what my fellow crew members and I expected."

"You mean we don't come across as dour, unfriendly political officers who spend their waking hours sniffing for subversion and treason?" Ardrix asked in a mischievous tone.

Prince nodded. "Something like that."

"Many of us have hobbies and a sense of humor, Commander," Torma replied, deadpan. "The good Sister here builds scale models of ancient torture instruments in her spare time, and I'm part of a group re-enacting Empress Dendera's 1st Bodyguard Regiment during the Great Purge."

When Prince gave him a startled look, not knowing whether he was joking, Torma winked. She let out a burst of laughter which stopped suddenly seconds later, and a faint air of embarrassment replaced her mirth.

"You are definitely not what we expected from a Commission colonel, sir. But no complaints on anyone's part."

"Good. Otherwise, we'd be forced to investigate. Any complaints that is."

"Noted." Prince drained her coffee and stood. "No rest for the wicked. It's time I checked the navigation plots our sailing master and those in the other ships prepared."

When she saw the question in both Torma's and Ardrix's eyes, Prince added, "It's a way of making sure we're not committing errors. If the five sailing masters come up with the same solution, then it's either the right one, or we're beyond hope. Should one or more of them differ from the rest, then they go back and re-run their calculations."

"Ah. Added safety. Good. I'd hate for us to roam the galaxy, lost without hope of returning home."

Prince chuckled.

"An error would hardly be that dramatic, but it might cost us precious fuel and even more precious time. Wormhole transit errors, on the other hand? Our charts are old, and termini do shift over time."

She wiggled her fingers by way of goodbye and walked away.

"I think Commander Prince meant that last comment as a joke, Crevan," Ardrix said in a low tone.

He gave the Sister a stern look.

"Why would you think it worried me?"

"Because I know you."

They finished their meal and returned to their quarters. That evening, just before twenty-two hundred hours, Task Force Kruzenshtern went FTL again, its ships having shown no sign of undue stress from the long interstellar jump, and they crossed the system's heliopause on the first leg. By the time breakfast rolled around, *Repulse* and her companions dropped out of hyperspace deep within the star system identified only by an old Imperial Catalog number.

They were enjoying a second cup of coffee in the mostly empty wardroom when Torma's ship-issued communicator chimed. He retrieved it from his tunic pocket.

"Torma."

"Flag CIC duty officer, sir. Our scans picked up something unusual, and the commodore wondered whether you and Sister Ardrix were free to join him in the CIC."

They glanced at each other in surprise. Watanabe granted them the freedom of the CIC at the beginning of the voyage, but it was a privilege neither used without invitation, and this was the first one.

"A flag officer wondering if we're free means he expects us there forthwith," Torma murmured before draining his half-empty mug. "Besides, I'm curious about what they discovered."

Watanabe didn't stand on ceremony, and they entered the CIC without breaking step when the armored door slid aside silently. Once inside, both took seats at unoccupied stations and waited until the commodore, deep in conversation with his chief of staff, acknowledged them. After less than a minute, Watanabe's chief of staff stepped away from the command chair, and the commodore turned to face them.

"I'm sure this will interest students of history such as yourselves. We picked up several faint distress beacon signals from this system's second planet, an airless rock. We can't decipher the data stream. It's too degraded at this distance. But according to our records, the frequency is that used by the Navy during the empire's final years."

"Survivors?" The moment the question left Torma's lips, he felt foolish. "Surviving ships, I mean."

"Or wreckage. The signals are so faint we can barely make them out against the background static, indicating their power sources are almost depleted. That they survived this long is nothing short of amazing, however."

"Will you check out the source close in, sir?"

"That's why you're here, Colonel. This may prolong our expedition by a few days, and as the closest thing to a political authority in the task force, I'd like your opinion."

Torma immediately understood Watanabe was keen on examining the signals' source and asking him if this side trip would come under the same political cover as the primary mission.

"I think it would be in the Hegemony's interest if we investigated what might be still-functioning remains of the old Imperial Navy, sir."

Watanabe glanced at his chief of staff.

"Please enter Colonel Torma's advice into the task force mission log."

"Sir."

"And then get us there."

— 13 —

Shortly after Task Force Kruzenshtern emerged at the rocky, airless planet's hyperlimit, Commodore Watanabe invited Torma and Ardrix to join him in the flag CIC once more.

"Since you're as curious as the rest of us, it seems only fair," he said, indicating vacant workstations when the pair entered. "Without you, we wouldn't be here."

This time, Torma resisted glancing at Ardrix. Part of him was beyond tired at his status as the perceived catalyst for the first naval expedition beyond Hegemony space in living memory. If the Regent ever decided on a scapegoat once they returned and faced her wrath, he might well be forced into the role. And should that happen, he would face execution in the State Security Commission Headquarters' basement.

Ardrix would likely be safe, although cloistered at the abbey for the rest of her life. Suddenly, his role as alibi or safeguard didn't look quite as rosy anymore. Were General Robbins and Admiral Godfrey planning on his acting as the sacrificial offering all along?

He mentally shook himself. "You give me too much credit, sir."

"Be that as it may. Yet even the smallest pebble can trigger the most devastating landslide."

Torma's lips uncharacteristically ran away from him.

"I'll try not to take that personally, sir."

Instead of rebuking him for his less than deferential tone, Watanabe chuckled.

"None of us in your situation would feel any different, Colonel."

Before Torma could debate whether the commodore's comment merited a response, he felt Ardrix's hand on his forearm, and the urge to reply vanished.

Instead, he asked, "Can we make out who or what they were, sir?"

Watanabe pointed at a side display.

"Definitely Imperial Navy ship emergency beacons, five of them, but we're still decrypting the data they're transmitting."

"Why would an emergency beacon be using code, sir?" Ardrix asked in a soft tone.

"Operational security, so potential threats can't tell what sort of ship is in distress, or whether it's in distress, period. We use the same protocols, Sister."

"Sir." One of the duty officers raised her hand. "The sensors pinpointed the signals' source. Visuals coming up on the primary display now."

When the image swam into focus, centering on a dark starship hull, Torma let out a low whistle.

"That's no wreck."

"Indeed not," Watanabe replied without glancing at him. "A heavy cruiser, I should think."

"There are three of them, sir. Along with two smaller frigate-sized ships. They appear to be in the same general condition."

The heavy cruiser shrank as four more images joined it on the display, each showing what seemed like an intact starship.

"And after so long," the duty officer added, wonderment in her voice.

"They built solid ships back in those days," Watanabe's chief of staff said. "Not that we don't, but still."

"Sir, we found a tentative ID. The larger ships are Conqueror class heavy cruisers, and the smaller, Byzance class frigates, the two most common imperial types used during the Ruggero Dynasty. We can't detect any emissions other than the beacons at this range, not even faint traces of heat from the hulls."

Watanabe turned his chair to face Torma once more.

"What do you say, Colonel? Shall we join them in orbit and send boarding parties?"

"That is entirely up to you, sir. But why five seemingly intact ships are orbiting this dead world almost two centuries after the empire they served was destroyed intrigues me as much as anyone else. Were their crews perhaps decimated by the so-called Barbarian Plague that supposedly ran through the former empire's outer sectors like wildfire during that era?"

Watanabe furrowed his brow.

"Hard to say. Most records about this plague date from at least three decades after the empire fell, which could mean it didn't emerge until a generation later. Still, I suppose we should send remotely operated probes aboard first, nonetheless. Good of you to bring it up."

When Task Force Kruzenshtern entered orbit a few hundred kilometers ahead of the ghost squadron, closeup imagery revealed scarred and pitted hulls, damaged by decades of micro-meteorite strikes. Some even looked like through and through punctures.

"What in the Almighty's name happened aboard those ships?" The duty officer whispered as she studied the images.

"Whatever that might be, it surely wasn't in the Almighty's name," Ardrix said in a gentle voice. "There's a dark aura surrounding them as if something horrible happened long ago. Or I should say the echo of a dark aura that is even now fading back into the Infinite Void. Time erases just about everything except the worst evils, which can last until the end of all things, defying even entropy."

Watanabe glanced over his shoulder and gave her a strange look. When his eyes shifted to Torma, the latter made a small, helpless shrug that said don't try to understand a Void Sister's mystic side.

"But it should be safe for a remotely operated probe?" Watanabe asked.

"It should be safe for flesh and blood, sir. An echo carries no actual power. However, I can't speak for a virus surviving almost two centuries without a living host. I'm not trained as a healer."

Watanabe visibly hesitated for a moment, as if wondering whether he should ask about her training, then simply dipped his head by way of acknowledgment.

"I'll speak with the ship's chief medical officer in that case, Sister." Watanabe gestured at his chief of staff. "*Repulse* and *Reprisal* will send boarding parties to the furthest two heavy cruisers. *Dominator* and *Devastation* will take the two frigates. *Terror* gets the leading cruiser. Boarding parties shall stay on the outer hull and send remotely operated probes through the airlocks. Once we know what we're facing, I'll issue further direction."

"Yes, sir."

**

After a few hours in their quarters and a meal, while the various boarding parties prepared for their sorties, Torma and Ardrix returned to the flag CIC and took their by now accustomed seats behind Commodore Watanabe.

"Just in time," the latter said without turning around. "Boarding parties are leaving their ships now."

The primary display was once more split into five, each segment showing a standard Navy shuttlecraft nosing its way through open space doors, including that from *Repulse*.

"If I may inquire, how will they get aboard?"

"Ask any question you like, Sister. It's quite simple. Our basic starship design principles haven't changed since imperial days and include certain fail-safes. For instance, should a ship lose power, manual access to door and hatch locking mechanisms is automatically enabled. The boarding parties will simply look for a given airlock's access panel, open it, and unlatch that airlock. Then, it becomes a matter of brute force. But if necessary, they'll use laser cutters. I doubt those ships are salvageable, even for parts, after so long since it's unlikely in the extreme that they used proper storage procedures, as a result, some creative destruction won't matter."

"I see." Ardrix sat back, eyes on the display as silence settled over the CIC.

One by one, the shuttles circled their target ships, studied it from up close until the officer in charge chose the best ingress point. Then they settled on the hull. Several minutes later, space-suited figures emerged from the crafts' airlocks, a spacer in each boarding party carrying a spherical remotely operated probe roughly the size of a human head.

Ardrix watched with fascination as hidden access hatches popped open beside the designated airlocks and armored arms reached inside to release the mechanical latches. Airlock after airlock opened, three of the five venting a brief burst of atmosphere, proving they'd been under pressure.

One boarding party member per team, carrying a probe, entered. The outer doors closed, and the primary display's video feeds switched over to five helmet cameras showing the claustrophobic confines of pressurization compartments. According to the labels, the three larger ones were those of the cruisers while the rest belong to the frigates.

New telemetry appeared on side displays, showing ambient temperature, pressure, or lack thereof beyond the inner doors, emission levels, and, surprising no one, the lack of artificial gravity aboard. The latter would make it easier for the probes to move about. But it would be more challenging for the follow-on humans.

Those who'd entered quickly found the inner latch releases and opened the doors, three to a brief rush of air filling the small compartment; the other two, a cruiser and a frigate, were unpressurized beyond the airlock, though to what extent wasn't immediately apparent. One by one, the globular probes floated out the airlocks and into darkened passageways, their lights catching details here and there. Then…

Ardrix let out a soft gasp. The form on the deck of a pressurized cruiser had clearly been human, long ago, but was now nothing more than a desiccated mummy with wisps of hair still clinging to a mostly bare scalp. And so it went, ship by ship as the probes found mummified bodies, many showing signs of injury. They saw charred clothing, blackened holes, in a few cases split skulls and limbs twisted at odd angles, when they weren't missing altogether. Nearby black stains on decks and bulkheads could only have been made by human blood.

"It looks like they fought each other," she said in a subdued tone. "Perhaps that was the dark aura's echo I sensed."

"A battle group, or the remains of one whose crews mutinied during Dendera's downfall, perhaps?" Torma asked. "Some wanted to head for Wyvern and either attack or defend the seat of empire while the rest were opposed?"

Watanabe shrugged.

"Possible. Without recovering the logs, provided their computer cores haven't decayed, we'll likely never know." He tapped the arm of his command chair with his fingertips, then turned to his chief of staff. "Boarding parties shall enter, make full recordings, and see if they can retrieve the computer cores. The configuration shouldn't differ greatly from ours. At this point, we might as well take the time to investigate what occurred here. Do you concur, Colonel?"

He tossed the last sentence over his shoulder at Torma.

"I do, sir."

"Excellent. Then I suggest we leave our people to do their thing and reconvene in four hours?"

"As you wish, sir." Torma and Ardrix stood.

Once back in their quarters, Torma dropped into his by now accustomed chair and exhaled.

"Can you imagine? A crew divided against itself, locked in mortal combat until no one remained standing. I'll bet the two ships without an atmosphere were depressurized on purpose. Murder on a grand scale, as it were."

"When passions are roused to a fever pitch, be they because of political, religious, or social disagreements, our species acts without a shred of humanity against those it perceives as being on the opposite side. We consider them not simply wrong but fundamentally evil."

He nodded.

"Dendera's Retribution Fleet being the most glaring example."

"There were equally horrifying instances during our long history. For example, formerly healthy nations self-immolating due to irreconcilable visions of what their societies should be."

Torma let out an indelicate snort.

"Considering what we know of the divide between our ruling caste and those of us who believe in the Oath of Reunification, do you think the Hegemony could head along that path?"

"Certainly." She studied him for a few moments. "Many among us believe the Wyvern Hegemony as it stands has no future. It is merely a last and rapidly fading remnant of the long-dead empire, one slowly dying from its own internal contradictions."

Torma gave her a wry grin.

"Thanks for cheering me up, Sister." Then he frowned. "Wait a minute. Just many rather than all? I thought the Void Reborn was of one mind."

"Hardly. The Order is as split along philosophical lines as any large organization. However, those of us who find no future along the current path are considered by a few as heretics of a sort, seeing as how the Void pledged itself to support the Hegemony's government and its policies."

He exhaled loudly.

"So, you see no future along the current path. Wonderful."

"Nothing is set in stone, Crevan. But steering the Hegemony on an alternate course, one which might give it a real future will need courage, vision, and faith. And boldness."

Her words, as well as her almost ethereal voice, sent involuntary shivers down Torma's spine as if she'd given him a glance of what could be. Not an echo of the imperial past but a rebirth.

PART II – FALSE DAWN

— 14 —

A short, deeply tanned teenager wearing a fisher's breeches and vest hopped off a rusty bike and carefully leaned it against the priory's granite walls before racing into the courtyard fronting the infirmary, his calloused, bare feet slapping against worn flagstones. Though partly ruined during the empire's collapse long ago, the ancient, solemn complex built with black basalt carved from the island's cliffs had housed the Order of the Void's mission to the Republic of Thebes for the last three years and still awed the youngster.

He poked his head through the open door and blinked a few times as his pupils, shrunk by the dazzling tropical sun, adapted to the cool, dark interior. Spotting the Sister on duty, he stepped in and bowed at the neck.

"Pardon the intrusion. *Aswan Trader* just passed the end of the mole, and she raised the signal for severely wounded crew aboard. The harbormaster asks if you can send a medic team."

"Certainly." The lean, equally tanned woman with a narrow angular face framed by black hair climbed to her feet and shook out her loose, khaki tropical robes. "Let me gather my people. You may tell the harbor master we'll be there when she docks."

He bowed again.

"Yes, Sister. Thank you."

The boy vanished, leaving Sister Gwen to call for her fellow healer, Sister Renelle, and the two Friars trained as physician's assistants, Basam and Achar. She warned Prioress Hermina so the locally hired medical staff and trainees could prepare their small hospital. Then, Gwen gathered her field kit, a backpack containing medical equipment and drugs more advanced than the sort last produced on Hatshepsut almost two centuries earlier, before the Mad Empress' Retribution Fleet destroyed the local abbey and its dependencies.

The Thebes Priory, now home to the Void's missionary team from Lyonesse, was the least damaged of the old Order's houses, just as the Thebes archipelago, a minor district of Hatshepsut, was the least damaged of the planet's subdivisions. That made both eminently suitable as Lyonesse's beachhead in this star system.

Sister Renelle, dark-complexioned, gray-haired, and stocky, appeared in the infirmary seconds before the Friars, who seemed cast from the same mold. Both were square-faced, muscular, and middle-aged, with short silver-shot hair and beards. They too wore loose khaki clothes suitable for the torrid climate rather than their Order's standard black.

The four Brethren, along with three more Sisters and an equal number of Friars, were volunteers from the Lyonesse Abbey.

They'd left the only home they knew aboard one of the Republic's newest Void Ships three years earlier and settled on Hatshepsut with the understanding that it might be for the rest of their lives. However, since their work would be for the greater glory of the Almighty and humanity's reunification, none of them felt any regrets at leaving everything behind. In time, more Brethren would join them as the mission expanded beyond Thebes. Then, eventually, the Lyonesse Defense Force would establish an outpost that would grow into a full garrison with the amenities of home. But that might not happen in their lifetimes.

Gwen made sure her three companions carried sealed packs, then led them into the glare of an equatorial mid-afternoon. The priory sat on a hilltop above the town of Thebes, a major seaport spread out along the three sides of a broad bay. From that vantage point, they could see the nearest of the republic's over one hundred islands and the countless dun-colored, single-masted sailboats of the fishing fleet bobbing on the calm, shimmering waters just beyond the harbor.

One ship, however, caught their attention as they hurried along the gravel road leading into town, a three-masted merchant barquentine slowly shedding forward momentum as its crew hauled in the sails. One of dozens operated by Theban traders, the ship carried an auxiliary Stirling engine which took over, propelling her at a stately pace toward one of the long wooden piers jutting out from a stone quay.

"Anyone know where *Aswan Trader* went on this trip?" Renelle asked, her voice steady even though they moved at a half walking, half running pace.

"I believe she planned on circumnavigating Aksum," Basam replied, naming the medium-sized, oddly shaped continent fifteen hundred kilometers west of the Thebes Archipelago, parts of which largely escaped the worst of the Retribution Fleet's wrath.

Friar Achar let out a grunt. "Pirate waters."

"Nothing that can outrun or outgun one of the trader barquentines. But let's hope their people weren't hurt during an engagement with Aksumite or Saqqaran pirates because it would mean the ship's medic has been dealing with them alone for a week or more, if not longer."

"It would have been worse before we equipped the merchant fleet's sick bays properly," Gwen said. "But let's not borrow trouble. Sailors sometimes fall from masts in a gale and break sundry bones, and there was a storm out over the ocean to the southwest yesterday."

The four entered Thebes proper at the base of the hill, hurrying past a mix of sagging imperial-era buildings and more recent construction. They took one of the broad avenues connecting the port with the large island's interior, where farms produced much of the republic's primary food exports.

By now, whenever the locals saw one or more Brethren moving at speed while carrying an easily identifiable medic pack, they stepped out of the way, just as their ancestors would have yielded to ambulances equipped with flashing lights and sirens back when ground cars still existed. Nowadays, all that remained were animal-drawn carts and the odd Stirling engine-equipped carriages, and the Brethren yielded to them rather than risk being run over by an inattentive driver.

They reached the quay just as *Aswan Trader*'s crew tossed her mooring lines to the stevedores waiting on Pier Two. By the time they were alongside, both a gangway and the ship's captain had appeared. The latter waved the Brethren aboard with urgent gestures. After three years, Gwen knew the merchant shipmasters by their first names and dispensed with formality as she stepped onto the wooden deck.

"What happened, Lars?"

"We were attacked by pirates aboard a swarm of small, fast boats in the Central Passage five days ago, just before we could clear the last of those infernal islands. Buggers are upping their game, if you ask me. Had to fight them off because wouldn't you know it? Someone sold them slug throwers. Not accurate at a distance and on the water by any means, not like ours. But put enough of them into action, and the odd shot will find a target. Three of mine took hits before we sank the bastards and their damned weapons. No survivors that we could see, thankfully, so they won't try that again. Doc extracted the slugs, but they're doing poorly."

"Call for a Stirling engine carriage and prepare stretchers. We'll examine them, perform any necessary first aid, but if they're doing poorly, it'll be a hospital bed at the priory."

"That's my thought as well." Captain Lars Fenrir, a man whose tanned, weather-worn features surrounded by sun-bleached hair and a short beard screamed master mariner, gestured at a sailor hovering behind him. "Take the Brethren to sickbay, Matty."

"Aye, aye, Skipper."

"While you check them over, I'll make the arrangements."

Gwen and her colleagues followed Matty below decks and forward to *Aswan Trader*'s sickbay, a tiny compartment that would be overcrowded with three injured. The barquentine's medic, whose primary responsibilities were as a master's mate — in a ship with a crew of fewer than forty souls, most men shouldered more than one job — met them at the sickbay's door. He was in his early twenties, barely out of apprenticeship, and one of those trained by the priory. The Brethren knew him as a steady man, conscientious and hard-working.

He bowed his head.

"Sisters, Friars. I'm overjoyed to see you. I fear my patients are on the decline even though I tried my best."

"Penetrating wounds can get tricky, especially abdominal ones."

"And that's the case with two of them. I removed the slugs, stitched them up as well as I could, and gave them antibiotics, but I fear sepsis might set in, nonetheless. They're sedated and have been since they were hit, but I've run out of sedative and most medical supplies."

Friar Basam let out a grunt.

"Gut shots are always bad. Now stand aside, lad, and let us be at it."

"Of course."

Gwen and Renelle headed straight for the two abdominal cases, squeezing in between cots, while Basam took the leg wound. All three pulled medical sensors produced by Lyonesse's finest supplier from their packs and scanned the victims. In the meantime, Achar rifled through the sickbay cabinets and inventoried the remaining stocks so *Aswan Trader* could be resupplied before she headed out again. The ship's medic stayed in the passageway, there being no room left for anything larger than a cat.

"You did as well as possible," Gwen tossed over her shoulder after examining her patient's injuries. "He's in a rough shape, but the odds favor him. Once we get him in our hospital and I reopen the wound, we'll know for sure."

"Ditto with this one," Renelle said.

Basam looked up from his patient.

"Mine will limp for a while, but he's lucky. A millimeter further left, and the slug would have nicked this boy's femoral artery.

Unless someone receives immediate medical attention, that sort of wound is usually fatal."

"Then I shall offer a prayer of thanks to the Almighty," the ship's medic said in a subdued tone.

Fenrir's voice came from behind him. "Stretchers are ready, and a Stirling engine carriage is on the way, Sister Gwen. What's your assessment?"

"The leg shot should pull through without complications," Gwen replied. "But both gut shots will need further surgery, so I make no guarantees, but your men are strong, Lars. Their will to live might make the difference."

"From your lips to the Almighty's ears, Sister. We are at your command."

"Let's bring them up one at a time, but slowly and carefully."

Once the injured lay on the deck near the gangplank, Gwen thanked those who produced the sedatives back home on Lyonesse. Maneuvering stretchers through narrow passageways and up steep ladders wasn't for the faint of heart or those who could still feel their serious injuries even though they were unconscious.

Thankfully, the crew had erected a midship awning that provided vital shade, so neither patients nor healers suffered under a harsh sun waiting for one of the rare self-propelled conveyances with sprung axles and rubber tires. They alone among ground vehicles wouldn't add to the unconscious men's suffering by bouncing over every bump and pothole between the port and the priory.

When the carriage, a box on four wheels with an open aft deck covered by a striped canopy, finally trundled down the pier under the impulse of its primitive engine, Gwen felt an unaccustomed longing for the air ambulances of a home hundreds of light-years away. They could whisk dangerously injured patients to the nearest hospital swiftly and in absolute comfort, cared for by the best trauma healers in the known galaxy. Here? It was no different from bringing sick livestock to the nearest veterinarian, one who didn't make house calls.

Would that she lived long enough to see this place regain its ancient birthright, so the good people of Thebes and elsewhere on Hatshepsut enjoyed the same existence as those on Lyonesse and the first few worlds it had reclaimed.

But once they were aboard the conveyance and moving through the town, Achar leaned toward Gwen after making sure the driver couldn't overhear.

"Sister, there may be a problem with *Aswan Trader*'s sickbay stocks. Not the consumables, but the instruments. Half of the inventory is gone. The medic must have constantly been cycling his remaining pieces through the autoclave without a break, or not sterilizing, period."

Basam gave his colleague a knowing look.

"Bartered them for trade goods on the side, eh? It wouldn't be the first or the last. Besides, Lyonesse goods finding their way into every corner of this world via regular trade routes is part of the plan."

"So long as we don't run out of stock before the next Void Ship shows up."

Gwen looked up from her patient.

"Make sure you tell Metrobius once we've taken care of these men. He can discuss it with Hermina if he so wishes. Still, Basam is right; replaceable medical instruments going walkabout can only help our mission by spreading the word we're here to help the planet prepare for reunification."

— 15 —

"Captain Fenrir. Welcome to the priory." Sister Hermina formally bowed her head as *Aswan Trader*'s master entered the infirmary the following morning. A thin, gray-haired woman of middling height, with sharp features and deep-set eyes, Hermina had the typical ageless face of a Void Sister. She'd been expecting him thanks to word from her informal intelligence service, a network of watchers in and around Thebes. Many of them were youngsters keen for an apprenticeship with off-worlders who were bringing back technology. Most of the rest were grateful patients healed of injuries or illnesses that were often fatal a few years earlier.

"Sister." He returned her bow with proper courtesy. "I'm here to see how my men are doing and offer my thanks for your devoted care."

"The man with the leg wound, Tobias, will fully recover. Your medic did a good job cleaning the wound, and we found no signs of infection. He'll go home in a day or two, but it'll be a few weeks before he's fit for duty. The other two, with abdominal injuries, are still in the intensive care unit. Sister Gwen operated on both yesterday and redid your medic's field surgery. It was outstanding work under the circumstances and kept them alive until they reached us, but both are fighting off serious infections, Jiang more so than Okano. The intensive antibiotic treatment should work, but it'll be a day or two before we can release them from the ICU."

"Good news, then, Sister. Thank you."

"Come. You can speak with Tobias, but the others are sedated, though you can see them through the ICU window." Hermina turned on her heels and led him through the waiting room and along a corridor with white walls, pierced by equally white, numbered doors. A clean, almost antiseptic tang permeated the air, and Fenrir felt his anxiety ease a bit.

Although they called it an infirmary, the building was, in every respect, a fully-equipped field hospital, one of countless such put together on Lyonesse and sent off with missionary teams aboard Void Ships crewed by the Lyonesse Navy. The merchant mariner's awe at his surroundings, something even the least talented Friar would sense, pleased Hermina.

When the Lyonesse government decided, long ago, it would reclaim human star systems patiently and through peaceful means, many scoffed at the idea. The republic's armed forces were the most powerful in the known galaxy, or at least, they'd not met anyone capable of fielding anything comparable. As a result, taking star systems by might and imposing colonial governments would have been simple in the short term.

But judging at how avidly the Thebans absorbed the missionaries' teachings, in part because of vague yet persistent generational memories of better times, the wise men and women of the day were right. By the time Lyonesse offered a rebuilt Hatshepsut a seat on the republic's council of state, years, if not decades, of accumulated goodwill would ensure the best outcome.

And the people of this world would be ready to rejoin humanity at large without needless trauma. At least that was the theory, and though Void Sisters were long-lived, Hermina might not witness the eventual result. This was the work of generations. By the time that blessed day rolled around, a new Hatshepsut Abbey, supported by dozens of outlying priories, would be entirely composed of locals whose abbess answered to the *Summus Abbatissa* on far away Lyonesse.

Hermina ushered Fenrir into a brightly lit, cheerfully decorated recovery room with beds lining opposite walls. Patients sleeping, reading, or otherwise keeping themselves busy occupied most of them. One, a young man with the deeply tanned face of a sailor, sat up and waved when he spied his captain. The smile on his face seemed genuine, though his features were still marked by his ordeal.

"Tobias. How are you?"

"Feeling great, thanks to the good Sisters, Captain. Whatever they're giving me for the pain, it beats rum halfway across the galaxy, and at hyperspeed, if you'll believe that."

Fenrir chuckled.

"And it has you talking like a galactic instead of a mariner." He glanced at Hermina. "Any chance I could taste this marvelous elixir? Tobias normally swears by rum."

"Only if you're in pain." She smiled at him. "Not something I recommend seeking out on purpose."

"You mean like—" Tobias' mirth-filled voice died away when confronted by Captain Fenrir's hard stare. "Never mind."

"Take care of yourself, lad. I'll see that the Sailor's Union makes sure you receive the shore pay you're owed while you heal."

Tobias bobbed his head in gratitude. "Thank you kindly, Captain."

"You'd best thank Sister Hermina. It was her and the other Brethren who proposed the Sailor's Union scheme, and a fine idea it's turning out to be." Fenrir glanced at Hermina, who replied with a faint nod.

"Yes, Captain." Tobias turned his gaze on the prioress and lowered his head. "Thank you for everything, Sister."

"You should direct your praise at the Almighty, Tobias. The Void giveth."

Without missing a beat, the young sailor replied, "The Void Taketh Away."

"Blessed be the Void," both intoned in perfect harmony, drawing an astonished look from Captain Fenrir.

"I didn't know you were a believer, Tobias," the latter said.

"Many of us in *Aswan Trader* and most other ships are, Captain. Thinking of the Almighty helps us pass the dark hours of the night watch in pirate waters."

Hermina suppressed a pleased expression. The spiritual mission was progressing just as well as the worldly one.

Fenrir shrugged. "If it helps, then I suppose it's good. But don't let the Sisters recruit you. I need able sailors for our next voyage."

"I'll be there, Captain. Guaranteed. The damned pirates in the Central Passage owe me one." As soon as the words left his mouth, Tobias reddened with embarrassment. "Sorry, Sister."

She waved away his apologies and smiled.

"Those who prey on others because they're both lazy and depraved are indeed damned, Tobias. Considering this planet's natural riches and its small population, there's enough for anyone who'll put in the effort."

"Is there anything you need?" Fenrir asked.

"Not a thing, Skipper, but thanks. When are you heading back to sea?"

"In a few days, provided I can find replacements for you, Jiang, and Okano. Can't sail with three experienced deckhands missing. At least not beyond the Theban Isles."

"Nothing wrong with short-haul contracts, even in a barquentine."

"Provided they're for settlements with deep enough harbors. Rowing bulk supplies ashore in our boats just isn't my idea of a good time."

Tobias grimaced. "Roger that, Skipper."

"Well… Glad you're on the mend, lad. I'll pop my head in once a day while we're alongside, and if there's anything you want, I'm sure the Brethren can send a messenger to the ship."

"Thank you. Tell the lads I said hi."

"Will do." Fenrir glanced at Hermina. "Can I see Jiang and Okano now, please, Sister?"

"Certainly. Follow me."

She gave Tobias a little wave, then led Fenrir out of the ward and further down the bright, sterile corridor. They passed through doors marked 'Intensive Care' before stopping in front of a large window made from off-world plastic, judging by its clarity. Beyond it, he could see beds with display panels at one end. Two were occupied by men asleep beneath silvery blankets, their panels lit.

"Your men are doing as well as we can hope, Lars. If anything changes for the worst, the duty physician's assistant will receive a warning from the medical sensors and intervene."

Fenrir shook his head in awe.

"All this technology is beyond anything we can make or sometimes even imagine."

"For now. You and I should live long enough to see Hatshepsut regain a lot of what she lost, but it will take time. Our starships can only carry so much and must supply dozens of missions."

"Provided President Granat's successor keeps his policies in place. I hear grumblings that several among those who would replace him don't like off-worlders with your tech level operating at will rather than under government control and plan on making drastic changes. And a president who would impose controls on you will find plenty of support in the senate. Many of our esteemed representatives covet your technology for themselves and aren't pleased with your generosity, independence, and the fact you're above anyone's self-interested influence. We who hear such things fear you might leave rather than continue serving our community under political duress."

Hermina, whose private and unofficial intelligence service had already reported as much, turned a reassuring smile on Fenrir.

"Then the citizens of the republic must make their voices heard and elect a president and senators who will work with us."

He grimaced.

"You've not yet witnessed our elections, Sister. The republic's ordinary citizens have little real influence on who governs us. And that's everything I'll say on the subject, even in this sanctified place."

"Fair enough. Can I offer you iced tea in my office before you walk back to your ship?"

He inclined his head.

"With pleasure, thank you."

Iced drinks were a rare luxury on a planet that was still years away from re-establishing mechanical refrigeration and whose tiny ice caps could only be harvested a few times per year. However, the priory's field hospital came equipped with a miniature fusion unit which powered, among many other things, a bank of refrigerators.

Hermina used iced tea invitations whenever she wanted more from a Theban than he or she would likely give without feeling an obligation after being treated to something so rare. So far, none declined the invitation, and only a few repaid her hospitality by evading questions.

She led him out of the infirmary and across the broad quadrangle to the main house, which was equally cool, though not as brightly antiseptic. They took winding stairs to the second story and walked along a wood-paneled corridor whose only lighting came from a tall window at the far end.

Fenrir had never visited Hermina's inner sanctum and was impressed by the view when he entered on her heels. Broad windows overlooked the town and harbor and the shallow inner sea surrounded by the republic's many islands, most of which were mere shadows in the mist. He noted with amusement that the priory sat on a taller hill than the republic's senate building and presidential palace, large but unprepossessing stone buildings erected long after the Retribution Fleet scoured Hatshepsut and destroyed most of its cities.

Her office furniture was simple but well crafted by local cabinetmakers, and the glassware on the sideboard was also clearly of Theban manufacture. At her gesture, he sat in one of the chairs facing a wooden desk whose only adornment was a small orb filled with tiny stars floating in a black medium.

No sooner had she settled in across from him that a young man, a local postulating to become a Friar in the Order, entered, carrying an insulated jug of the sort the off-worlders were teaching Thebans to make. He bowed his head at Hermina, then at Fenrir before heading toward the sideboard and filling two glasses. The postulant offered Fenrir one and Hermina the other, then withdrew, closing the door behind him.

"Your health, Lars."

"And yours, Sister."

He raised his glass to his lips and took a tentative sip. The surprisingly cold, sweet liquid felt like a balm on his parched tongue and burned an icy path down his throat. A second sip followed the first, and he sighed.

"Here's hoping the day when ordinary people enjoy access to refrigeration will come soon."

"In our lifetimes, Lars. In our lifetimes." Hermina sat back and let a faint smile play on her lips. "So, tell me, did you get interesting merchandise in exchange for your ship's medical instruments?"

— 16 —

A fleeting air of guilt crossed Fenrir's seamed features, and he grimaced. "I should have known you'd find out quickly, Sister."

"Whenever a ship brings back injured, the emergency medical team inventories the sickbay, so we can replace items consumed in treating those injuries. What we don't normally see are several non-consumable instruments missing and definitely not half of them." She took another sip of iced tea. "Please indulge my curiosity. What happened?"

Fenrir let out a long sigh.

"Sister, me and the other merchant ship captains, we're traders at heart. We've been bartering off our surplus for a long time, and for the last three years, that includes the things you give us freely. I figure since your mission here is to help Hatshepsut regain its lost technology, you wouldn't mind if we spread our off-world wealth among the heathens. Usually, we exchange a few items at a time so that you wouldn't notice or write it off to normal losses.

It's amazing how small instruments can vanish into the bilge of a ship during a storm, never to be found until the day she's broken up, or better yet, wash overboard. If you check every ship's sickbay in the merchant fleet, you'll not find two complete instrument sets. One complete set, yes, but the second set will miss items. The same goes for tools and other things you've gifted us."

"I see." She took a sip of tea, eyes studying Fenrir over the rim of her glass. "And in your case, the full medical instrument backup set is now in the hands of, as you call them, heathens on Aksum. Did you trade it all at once or in bits over the last few voyages?"

Another grimace.

"Could we possibly change the subject, Sister? I'm deeply grateful for everything you Brethren do for us, but…"

"Rest assured, anything we discuss in this room will remain confidential, and I do need to know about happenings beyond the Republic of Thebes, Lars. This may be our sole base of operations right now, yet at some point, we'll be sending out missions of our own so we can help the rest of this world rise again."

Hermina's steady gaze and the quasi-hypnotic quality of her tone slowly but surely pushed aside Fenrir's reluctance.

"We traded the second set as a whole this time."

"What did you take in return? It must be rather unusual."

"You might say that. The trade cost me my two spare boat Stirling engines and a few other items as well."

She smiled at him.

"And?"

Fenrir's jaw muscles worked in silence for several heartbeats as he chose his words, knowing Hermina's questions would only multiply.

"You promise what we discuss here is confidential?"

"Depending on the nature of your answer, I might need to inform the Brethren who came with me from Lyonesse, but no one else. Certainly not the Theban authorities."

"Railguns. We obtained four working railguns. New, by all appearances."

Hermina's eyes widened slightly at his answer, though Fenrir didn't notice.

"From an ancient arms depot recently uncovered on Aksum?"

He shook his head.

"No. From off-world. They bear manufacture markings we can't identify, but they're certainly not from old imperial stocks. The guns came with solar power pack chargers, spare power packs, and two thousand slugs apiece." His jaw muscles worked again. "Those weapons saved our hides when the pirates attacked, but not before they put my three in our sickbay, mind you. When we finally fired back, their boats became sieves and sank right quickly. However, if the government finds out, they'll confiscate the guns and charge me with the illegal weapons trade. Our beloved leaders don't like us citizens being better armed than their henchmen are."

"The government won't hear about them from me, but they present a mystery we must investigate. May Friar Metrobius and I come aboard your ship and examine the items in question? If off-world traders are visiting Hatshepsut, then they're either from Lyonesse and in violation of our laws, or there are others out there who retained spaceflight and the capacity to produce advanced technology. The latter might represent an opportunity or a threat, and we must know which it is for our safety and that of this world."

"I have no answers for you, Sister. The one who does is a merchant named Dave Crimple in Mazaber, a seaport on Aksum's east coast. A true blackguard if there ever was one and the sharpest trader on the entire continent. He dealt with the off-worlders in question or someone who works for him in Aksum's interior will. I couldn't say for sure since we heard no rumors of a spaceship landing in Mazaber."

Hermina nodded slowly.

"It would make sense if they landed away from any settlement and approached on the ground."

A guffaw escaped Fenrir's serious countenance.

"You would say that, seeing as how you showed up on foot coming out of nowhere three years ago. We didn't see any of your spaceships land until much later."

She gave him a sly smile.

"We didn't want to spook the heathens before they found out we were harmless monastics interested in reclaiming the priory on the hill."

This time, Fenrir laughed uproariously.

"You got me there, Sister."

"Back to this Crimple. Would he speak with one of us?"

He shrugged.

"If you make it worth his while, I'd say so. The man sells everything and anything, information included. But you can't just wander over and knock on his door. It's at least a two-week trip in a ship like mine with a better than even chance of sighting pirates in the Central Passage. If you'd rather avoid the Passage, it means going around the Saqqara Islands the long way. And at this time of the year, the seas are rough in both the northern and the southern latitudes. Even more so when you're headed into the prevailing winds down south. There's a reason we call them the Roaring Forties. As we mariners say, there's no law below forty and no God below fifty, so it's best we stick closer to the equator or go around to the north. A shame you don't keep one of those spaceship shuttles for your own use."

She put on a resigned air.

"Indeed, but we must be practical. Who'd maintain them? And where would we obtain fuel? One day, yes. In the meantime, travel across this world is by sail and Stirling engine, even for missionaries from Lyonesse."

Fenrir took a sip of iced tea while studying Hermina with a calculating look she knew only too well from interacting with Theban merchant captains.

"If the priory can charter *Aswan Trader*, I'll take you to Mazaber. My expenses, plus a small profit, perhaps paid in Lyonesse-manufactured goods I can use for barter at the other end. Say a five-week round trip."

"And what would your expenses plus a small profit look like?"

"Nothing a fountain of modern wonders such as your priory can't afford, Sister."

Her smile returned.

"We don't as yet manufacture those modern wonders. They come in via supply ships, which means finite quantities, especially since Hatshepsut is at the far end of Lyonesse's network. But perhaps we can figure something out. In fact, if I turn the trip into a reconnaissance and see whether Mazaber might suit for a new mission in a few years—"

Fenrir's snort cut her short.

"I can already tell you the answer is no. What's the old expression for places like that? A cesspool of scum and villainy?"

"Something of the sort, but that's where the Almighty is most needed, don't you think? However, as I said, the trip could be a reconnaissance as well as finding out what this Dave Crimple knows about the provenance of your railguns." She drained her glass. "But first, I'd like to examine the weapons along with Friar Metrobius, who served in the Lyonesse Defense Force as a young man and therefore knows more about them than anyone else here."

"Metrobius, a soldier? He looks like everyone's favorite uncle."

"Spacer, actually. He was a petty officer back in the day, a boatswain's mate trained in small arms handling. His time aboard starships gave him a deeper appreciation of the Void, and when his contract was up, he postulated with the Order." Her eyes crinkled with amusement. "You and he have more in common than you may think. I'm sure you spend night watches staring at a clear, star-lit sky on occasion, no?"

Fenrir bowed his head in acknowledgment.

"Some of my best memories are of reclining on the deck after full dark and looking up at a universe that once teemed with my fellow humans. It's both awe-inspiring and depressing. So many dead."

She made a sad face.

"Up to ninety percent of our species, most historians say. I'm not sure it was that dire, but the imperial records we collected on Lyonesse tell us Hatshepsut had upwards of five hundred million inhabitants in the final years. When our survey ship scanned this world five years ago, it picked up maybe fifty million distinct life signs. One-tenth of the original population, which means only one-tenth of that likely survived the Retribution Fleet after it scoured the major population centers. Five million out of five hundred million. Ninety-nine percent dead at Dendera's hands. There is no hell deep enough for her rancid soul."

"And yet we prevail." Fenrir raised his glass before draining it. "While Dendera and her empire are gone. So, what'll it be, Sister? A charter to Mazaber for a few of your Brethren?"

"Yes. You, me, and Metrobius will discuss the modalities after we examine your weapons."

"Are you busy this afternoon?"

"What time?"

"Would fourteen-hundred suit?"

"It would. Thank you for trusting me with this, Lars. If the railguns didn't come from Lyonesse but from another world that either survived the collapse or rebuilt at breakneck speed, it would mean a significant realignment of our efforts to rebuild a human community across the stars."

"You make that sound ominous, Sister. Should I be worried?"

Hermina gave him a reassuring smile as she stood.

"No. Metrobius and I will see you this afternoon."

Fenrir imitated her and bowed his head at the neck.

"Always a pleasure, Sister."

"Likewise, and don't worry. You brought us a mystery worth solving, and I thank you for it and for your honesty."

— 17 —

At the appointed time, Hermina and Metrobius, a stocky, white-haired, kindly-faced man with an equally white beard and twinkling blue eyes beneath thick brows, walked up *Aswan Trader*'s gangplank. The first mate met them with due courtesy under the side-to-side awning, which provided the only bit of shade beneath shimmering white masts and spars, the latter hugged by tightly furled sails.

Even over Thebe's expansive harbor, the still afternoon air felt like it had escaped from an open furnace. But low, dark clouds over the ocean racing toward them promised relief in the form of a rainstorm, provided it came over the archipelago instead of skirting it like so many this year. Upon spying the distant squall as she and the chief administrator headed downhill toward town, Hermina had prayed the Almighty would grant them relief, not just because of the stifling heat but because the ripening crops inland desperately needed rain.

Though Theban agricultural practices were about as good as they got in societies on the verge of industrializing, irrigation remained a constant issue, as did fertilization and land use. Hermina hoped a new contingent of Brethren, agronomists, and civil engineers among them, would show up within the next year or two. It wasn't enough that Thebes could export foodstuffs; it would soon become imperative they also export know-how under the Brethren's gentle prodding, so the more primitive parts of Hatshepsut embarked on the long climb back up the industrialization ladder.

They followed the first mate down a flight of stairs and aft along a narrow passageway to the captain's quarters above the three-master's giant rudder. The man knocked twice on a wooden door at the end of the corridor and, upon hearing a gruff 'enter,' opened it and led them into a brightly lit cabin that spanned the width of the deck.

A cot hung from thick deckhead beams on the starboard side, while a desk occupied space beneath open windows on the port side. A table surrounded by chairs dominated the center, and on it sat a long, narrow carrying case made of a material that assuredly did not originate on Hatshepsut. Lars Fenrir, who stood behind it, nodded politely.

"Welcome." He swept his arm over the case. "You may inspect it as you wish."

Hermina and Metrobius inclined their heads as the former said, "Thank you."

Under his superior's watchful eyes, the Friar approached the table and ran his fingertips over the case.

"A plastic compound of sorts, no doubt. A hard shell impervious to anything but a direct hit, I'd say. It resembles nothing we use on Lyonesse for weaponry storage and transport."

He found the latches and popped them open, then raised the lid and examined the case's contents.

"That's a railgun, no doubt about it. Twelve or fifteen millimeters. I see four power packs and a high-efficiency solar collector array to charge them. None of these look like anything made by Lyonesse Arsenals, which equips the Defense Force or any manufacturers serving the civilian market. Granted, I've been out of the Service for a while now, but the basic design and basic look and feel changes little over the generations. If it works well, don't modify things just for the sake of it, I always say."

Metrobius looked up at Fenrir and chuckled.

"As my old divisional chief used to say, overthinking design doesn't necessarily mean better, but it could easily mean clogging the drains, and on a starship, that's the last thing you want. May I handle the weapon and see an example of the slugs you bought?"

"Sure." Fenrir pulled a dull gray, tapered cylinder from his pocket and placed it on the table. "You're right, fifteen millimeters. We checked. Makes nasty holes in wooden boat hulls. Nastier ones in human flesh."

"Aye, it would. The hydrostatic shock from the transfer of kinetic energy when it enters a body is hard on human tissue. I doubt any of the pirates you hit survived, even if they didn't drown." Metrobius reached into the case and lifted out the gun. "Heavier than ours. Not a dismounted infantry weapon, let alone any good for boarding parties. However, I'll wager it would do for long-distance sniper work, what with its large caliber and the flat trajectory you get from the energy discharge of a barrel this long."

He turned the weapon over in his hands, studying every nook and cranny until he found proof marks on the barrel's underside.

"Definitely not made on Lyonesse. I don't recognize those marks. Ours always include a representation of a Vanger's

Condor." Metrobius glanced at Fenrir again. "Our national symbol, a large, double-headed bird of prey with its wings outstretched. Except the real version, flying high above our mountains only has one head. This mark includes a sort of avian as well, but vastly different from ours. If I were a fanciful type, I'd almost think it was a phoenix rising from the flames. I also see the letters W and H and three digits, seven, one, four, so we know it's of human provenance."

Metrobius carefully worked the action to make sure the firing chamber held no ammunition, then inserted a powerpack into a slot on one side of the butt. He watched as electricity awakened the gun's small control screen, confirming the electromagnets that would propel slugs were charging. A few seconds later, the Friar let out a soft grunt.

"Not as smooth or as quick to go live as the ones I trained on with the Marines, to be sure. But well balanced and likely as accurate as any railgun in existence. Mind you, that's just my gut feel. Whoever manufactured this must be at almost the same technological level as Lyonesse. Perhaps a little behind, considering the quality isn't what our Navy would accept back when I served." Metrobius powered down the weapon, released the powerpack, and returned both to their place.

Then he picked up the solar charger and studied it intently.

"Our ground forces also use the like. The thing doesn't seem as well machined, nor are its marks anything I can recognize, but it'll no doubt charge packs if you can't access a power source which is pretty much everywhere on Hatshepsut beyond the priory walls. Did you try, Captain?"

Fenrir nodded.

"Aye. The moment we left Mazaber, and a good thing too. Thankfully, the instructions that come with it are easily decipherable even by heathens like us."

"Ah yes, instructions." Metrobius opened a pocket under the lid and retrieved a plasticized booklet. He scanned each page carefully, then glanced up at Hermina. "Written in Anglic, the same as our version, using soldier-proof language your slowest trooper can understand. Nothing else that identifies provenance, except for a larger version of the proof mark. That's definitely a phoenix."

He turned his eyes on Fenrir. "How long did it take to charge the power packs?"

"From what I could tell, they were at half when we bought them, and it was at least three hours exposed to the equatorial sun before they reached full."

The Friar nodded knowingly.

"Meaning a full charge would take most of the afternoon. That's slow compared with ours, even those we use to keep the priory's emergency power banks full. It might indicate they're a bit behind us. Perhaps a generation or so." He eyed Fenrir again. "Wait until you folks manufacture your own solar collectors based on our designs. Your power packs won't need more than an hour, ninety minutes tops, for a complete charge from empty. Heck, even the powerpack designs will be better and give you more shots before dying, pun intended."

He turned to Hermina.

"We must find out more about these off-worlders who sell railguns on planets without large-scale power generation. This is huge. The folks back home will want answers, which makes a quick trip to Mazaber imperative before the next supply ship arrives."

"When is it due?" Fenrir asked.

"If they keep the schedule, in four or five weeks, perhaps even less."

"And a round trip with seven days in port at the other end means five weeks, but we can't tarry. The winds are uncertain at this time of year and relying on engine power alone means a much slower trip. She fairly flies under full sail. Until we use something better than Stirling engines and can build larger screws, sail means speed, and yes, that was a hint." He winked at the prioress.

Hermina gave him a resigned look. "Name your price, Lars."

"Let me see the priory's high-tech storeroom, and I'll tell you what I want."

She glanced at Metrobius, who shrugged.

"We don't have gemstones or precious metals, and I doubt Captain Fenrir plans on bartering his services for those of our healers and teachers."

"Very well. How about you come to the priory in the morning, say around oh-nine-hundred, and Metrobius will show you what we can offer?"

Fenrir nodded once, a pleased expression on his deeply tanned face.

"Done."

Metrobius picked up the slug. "May I keep this? When our ship arrives, I'll hand it to the crew, and they'll take it home for analysis."

"Of course, but I'll be looking for a little extra tomorrow morning since we can't yet manufacture railgun ammunition, and every round is precious."

Both Brethren exchanged amused glances.

"Fair enough, though Lyonesse might advance a few things on Hatshepsut's timetable now that another player has introduced electromagnetic weaponry. And if your metal smiths are open to new ideas, we might show them ways of producing replacement slugs, though they won't be as finely machined nor as high density as these."

Fenrir escorted them back to the gangway and watched them amble down the pier until they vanished behind one of the warehouses, wondering how he could squeeze the most from this unexpected development. Getting in the Brethren's good graces was, of course, step one.

**

When Hermina and Metrobius were halfway up the hill, and well beyond anyone's earshot, the latter allowed himself a brief chuckle.

"You know our friend Lars will see that he gets the better part of the bargain, right? None of us have even the remotest idea what chartering a barquentine for five weeks might cost."

"Oh, I know. I could sense his glee at the chance of inspecting our little supply depot. He dreams of becoming the wealthiest, most powerful shipowner in the Republic of Thebes, that's clear. Having us as his best friends will only help if the government puts obstacles in his way. And yet, finding out about those mysterious others is worth every expense. Hatshepsut might quickly become a buffer system between two human polities capable of traveling the wormhole network, and our leadership will want to know everything we can discover."

"No arguments here. But who will we send? Certainly not you or me. But it should include a Sister with a powerful talent since this Mazaber merchant might not be free with his knowledge.

However, losing even one healer for weeks at a time isn't a good option."

"Rianne. She's stronger than the rest of us. We can spare a counselor more than a surgeon. A Friar with technical knowledge should go with her."

"Horam, then. As a bonus, he can fight like a berserker should they meet with trouble. That railgun would be a plaything in his hands, a precise and lethal toy."

"Which he will hopefully never use, but I agree. Rianne and Horam it is. Should we add a pair of locals to the team, one of the new Sisters and Friars?"

He nodded.

"Yes. I think Friar Alcide would be an asset. He's smart, fearless, and almost as big as Horam. May I suggest Sister Lilith as the fourth member?"

She turned her head and glanced at him through narrowed eyes without breaking step.

"Why?"

"Something tells me an adventure of this sort will help her talent flourish, especially under Rianne's tutelage."

"Oh?"

"Yes, oh. And you know I'm right."

This time it was her turn to chuckle.

"How is it you can read my mind as well as I can read yours? Lilith was my choice even before you spoke her name."

"Our Mother House matches its missionary teams carefully, particularly the Sisters named prioresses and the Friars who would be their administrators. It's almost as if they deliberately engineer a true meeting of the minds. A match made in the Almighty's Infinite and Heavenly Void, if I may use that ancient, albeit trite expression."

"Hah!" She let out a bark of laughter. "The miracles of modern psychology. The sort that relies on actually knowing what's going on in a person's head rather than guessing based on the practitioner's own prejudgments and coming to utterly incorrect conclusions."

"So I read in the ancient texts during my postulant period. Then we agree. Rianne, Horam, Alcide, and Lilith. I'll see they're equipped for a long voyage into the wild, weapons, rations, and shortwave radios included. After Lars' attempt at plundering my stores."

"Lars may be a shrewd negotiator, but I think one of the Order's shrewder administrators will make sure he gets precisely what he deserves."

"You can count on it, Prioress."

— 18 —

"Good morning, Captain Fenrir. I trust you slept well." Metrobius waved his visitor through the priory's main gate the following day. "Especially after I confirmed your newly acquired tools were worth their price."

"And a good day to you, Friar." Fenrir inclined his head by way of greeting. "I enjoyed a peaceful night indeed, but not because of the items in question. Simply knowing I would enjoy a profitable cruise after visiting your stores is what allowed me to sleep like a man without sin."

Metrobius let out a hearty burst of laughter as he patted the mariner on the shoulder.

"That man has yet to be born, but I'm sure we'll both feel satisfied by our upcoming arrangement, my friend. In fact, I guarantee it."

"Is that a promise or a threat?" Fenrir gave the Friar an amused grin.

"Neither." Metrobius turned on his heels and led Fenrir toward the low-roofed storehouse, with its steel window shutters and a door that couldn't be opened by thieves unless they came equipped with a high-powered laser. "But I can offer a glass of iced tea once we shake hands on our deal."

"Considering how Sister Hermina's iced tea made me reveal the secret of the railguns, I'm not sure I should accept the offer. You might make me reveal more secrets best kept within the confines of my ship."

Metrobius touched a small gray panel set into the ancient stone wall beside the door. It, along with the shutters and roof, was newly constructed. The rest of the building, its surface smoothed by centuries of rain and wind, was from early imperial times, a solid landmark that seemed as if it could survive another dozen centuries. He gave the door a gentle push, letting it swing inward on silent hinges, and ushered Fenrir into a blessedly cool, though dark space.

"Our revered prioress has a way of making an honest man even more honest, my friend. I wouldn't worry about it. My iced tea comes without her special touch. And if we were doing this at the end of the day instead of halfway before noon, I would offer a cold ale in its stead."

"Now there's a thought." Fenrir stopped in his tracks and looked over his shoulder. "How about I come back in six hours?"

"Time is of the essence." The Friar entered behind his guest and closed the door. He reached for a switch, and pale globes came to life, bathing the storehouse in a pleasant light, not quite subdued but not aggressive either. Row upon row of wooden racks filled it from wall to wall, each laden with items packed in boxes of various sizes, shapes, and colors.

Fenrir let out a low whistle.

"Impressive, even without knowing what those crates contain. What would you do if the people of Thebes lost their minds and raided the priory, seizing this wealth for themselves instead of waiting while you distribute it in measured doses, as per your quasi-mystical plan aimed at elevating Hatshepsut to galactic citizenship again?"

"First, they would have to get in here. Did you think we wouldn't protect this place?"

When Fenrir looked around with an air of alarm at having missed signs the storeroom might be impregnable, an amused sound escaped Metrobius' prominent nose.

"Then, there's the matter of Thebes losing the Mandate of the Void. I'm sure the government and those citizens with more than two functioning brain cells understand attacking this priory means the end of our mission here, whether the Brethren, be they Hatshepsut natives or from Lyonesse, survive an attack or not. Whoever comes after us would set up a new mission elsewhere, and Thebes would find itself lagging behind another city-state in the race to become first among equals on this world. And whoever is first will represent this star system within humanity reunited."

Fenrir nodded in understanding.

"I get that. But does everyone around here?"

"The current government certainly does, and I suspect its successors will as well. Politicians, by their nature, often aren't capable of seeing the long game, but in this case, they know what losing the Mandate of the Void would mean if we vanished. And with us, any hope Thebes might be the first who rises again and leads Hatshepsut. Because being first means power, and even the most short-sighted, most corrupt, most venal politician is attracted to power like a bee to nectar, or a fly to manure."

Fenrir contemplated his host for a few seconds, then burst out laughing.

"For a monastic, your worldview is surprising and refreshingly secular. Count me among those who will do their utmost to keep you here, if only so I can eventually launch a fleet of ships that don't need sails and can outrun any pirates they can't outgun. And I'm already on the path of outgunning the motherless bastards because of wonderfully lethal off-world tech."

Metrobius thumped him on the arm in a comradely gesture.

"That's the spirit, my seafaring friend. Come. Let me show you our wares, and you can tell me what suits as payment for the charter. We'll start by replacing the items you sold on your last trip and count that toward the total."

Metrobius gave Fenrir a sideways glance and smiled when he saw a faint air of annoyance cross the latter's face. The mariner could hardly argue since he'd already profited from the Order's generosity by becoming the best-armed man in the Republic of Thebes. Or at least the one with the deadliest weaponry, considering the Theban police and military forces were equipped with chemical propellant slug throwers whose range was only a fraction of a railgun's.

The Friar quickly tagged a medical instrument kit and a tool kit of the same sort Fenrir had bartered away in Mazaber.

"And what value do you place on them?" The latter asked. When Metrobius gave him the estimated production cost translated into Theban marks, Fenrir blanched beneath his deep tan. "I did not know that. And you're simply giving these away?"

"To help Thebes and through it, Hatshepsut recover, yes. Our leadership on Lyonesse decided long ago the best way of reviving a civilization destroyed by Dendera, such as yours, is first through improvements in health care and economic productivity. Only then can it absorb new technological advancements at a higher rate without causing social fractures."

"I should have demanded another pair of railguns from Crimple for what I gave."

"How many of those weapons did he own?"

Fenrir shrugged.

"No idea. But back to our negotiation. How many will you send with me?"

"Four. Two Sisters and two Friars."

"Then the replacement kits cover their cabins and food. Agreed?"

The mariner stuck out his hand. Metrobius grasped it, and they shook.

"Agreed."

"Now, let's discuss my expenses, meaning food and pay for the crew, wear and tear on the ship, and say ten percent profit."

"Five percent. And that's being generous considering how tight a shipowner's margins are. I'll include a captain's pay among the expenses, though."

Fenrir gave the Friar a look that was half amused, half exasperated.

"You drive a hard bargain."

Butter couldn't melt in Metrobius' mouth as he smiled back.

"We chief administrators running abbeys and priories are among the toughest negotiators in the known galaxy, my friend. Our job is squeezing the last bit of revenue from every item we produce to fund our good works without relying on charity. Ask the food sellers in town."

"And enjoy an extra earful of complaints over and above the ones I hear whenever my purser shaves a fraction of a percent off their profits? No thanks. Now, what can you offer that would cover my operating expenses and a five percent profit if I sell it in Mazaber or in the Thebes bazaar, for that matter? I might actually earn more here since folks know what they're buying."

"Do multi-function tools with solar power pack chargers interest you? Sell a kit to a carpenter and watch him raise a house in one-tenth of the time at a much lower cost than his competitors."

"How many?"

Metrobius studied Fenrir with a calculating gaze.

"For you, three kits."

"Show me."

The Friar took him across the storeroom and pulled a crate off a metal shelf. He cracked it open and pulled out the power unit.

"Attach any of the heads to this, and you can drill, cut, grind, or drive any screw or bolt."

"Why didn't you release these into the general population?"

A mischievous smile appeared on the Friar's round face.

"Who says we didn't? At a price in supplies, of course. Food and other perishables don't travel that well from Lyonesse and take up space better suited for goods useful in rebuilding Hatshepsut."

A smirk tugged at Fenrir's lips. "You keep it nicely under wraps."

"Not so much us as the buyers, happy at a temporary advantage over their competition, small as it may be. As I said, we pay for what we need, and our currency is advanced technology. Filtering it into the general population a bit at a time is better than a massive wave that will knock down many who need longer to adapt and literally wipe out those whose livelihood relies on current technology and processes."

Fenrir let out a soft snort.

"You people really do work according to a plan, don't you?"

"Yes, although things sometimes seem chaotic, to say the least. But it's working on other worlds, and it'll work here. Three kits. Yours to keep and use aboard your ship or sell wherever you like. That covers your expenses and profit."

"Four kits."

"No. Three. And I'm being generous."

When Fenrir glowered at him, Metrobius said, "Three and a small bottle of Glen Carhaix."

"What's that?"

"Possibly the best single malt whiskey in the known galaxy, distilled in my hometown on Lyonesse. Out here, hundreds of light-years and countless wormhole transits away, it's worth more than the richest man in Thebes can pay, except no one on this world remembers the taste of the good stuff." The Friar smiled as Fenrir's eyes narrowed with suspicion.

"Now you're just playing with me."

"What have you got to lose? It's better than the hooch you folks make. That stuff will kill you in due course, or even instantly if you're not careful who you buy it from."

"Okay. Three kits and your wonder booze."

As they shook on it, Metrobius said, "If you enjoy the whiskey, I can give you instructions on setting up your own distillery, but a word of warning, it takes at least three years of aging in barrels before it's drinkable. The longer, the better. But if you nail it, customers will line up to pay healthy sums for the privilege of sipping a nectar unknown on Hatshepsut for at least two centuries."

"Three years, eh? Heck of an investment."

"As I said, the plans are yours for the asking."

When Fenrir noticed the twinkle in Metrobius' eyes, he chuckled.

"You just want a supplier for your favorite tipple on this planet."

"True. All too true. Come. Let's crack open your bottle and share a sip to celebrate our deal."

"I should have known."

After watching Fenrir head back to the harbor aboard a hired Stirling engine cart with his kits, the bottle of Glen Carhaix nestled in a padded tunic pocket, Metrobius intercepted Hermina as she crossed the forecourt.

"It's done, Sister."

"Good."

"And we may have a whiskey distillery in Thebes shortly. I gave Fenrir a small bottle of the Carhaix. One sip was enough. He asked for a copy of the plans, and I expect he'll form a consortium with his fellow captain-owners to finance the construction and babysit the initial batch through the first three years of maturing."

Her eyes crinkled as she smiled at him.

"And another bit of progress unleashed on an unsuspecting population. Did he mention when *Aswan Trader* could set sail?"

"In two days."

— 19 —

Two mornings later, while enjoying a cup of tea beneath the quarterdeck awning, Captain Lars Fenrir spotted four Brethren, two tall, slender women and two burly, bearded men, emerging from a shaded alley and head for *Aswan Trader*'s berth. They caught sight of him staring at them, and the larger of the Friars nodded once, indicating he knew they'd been seen. Each carried a thick duffel bag in one hand, and a smaller pack slung over the opposite shoulder. From a distance, they seemed fit, their backs erect and their pace vigorous. The two younger Brethren with the deeper tans were undoubtedly the locally recruited Friar and Sister, while the older pair must be off-worlders.

Not for the first time, Fenrir marveled at the subtle changes wrought upon Theban society by the Brethren from Lyonesse over the last three years. At the advanced yet straightforward knowledge, they unobtrusively spread throughout the republic, allowing its citizens to rediscover industrial techniques just as they rediscovered faith in the Almighty through the works of the Order of the Void.

Part of him admired their oblique approach rather than risk overwhelming the descendants of those who survived the Retribution Fleet's scouring. But an increasingly larger part wished they would simply get on with things more directly so Thebes could take a gigantic leap forward and claim the rest of Hatshepsut while it built starships of its own.

Some nights, when he lay awake in his bunk, unable to sleep because of the harbor's stifling heat, he imagined owning a fleet of small, faster-than-light traders crisscrossing the wormhole network. Ships with climate-controlled environments, rather than a primitive barquentine whose only concession to modernity was its auxiliary Stirling engine, a technology the Thebans rediscovered well before the Brethren arrived with their books of knowledge and secretive smiles.

But by this time next year, that same engine would provide electricity to *Aswan Trader* while she was under sail, and could radio be far behind, perhaps even long-dreamed-of air conditioning? Space, however, would likely remain beyond Fenrir's reach. Part of him resented the idea he would never enjoy the same experiences as the Brethren because their plan was generational, beyond the lifetimes of those who grew up on Hatshepsut clawing their way out of the pre-industrial mire.

The group stopped at the foot of the gangway, and the big off-world Friar asked, in a deep, well-modulated voice pitched to reach Fenrir's ears, "Permission to come aboard, Captain?"

His respectful tone hinted at a man who, just like Friar Metrobius, had a military or naval past in the Lyonesse Defense Force. Perhaps the Order of the Void chose veterans from among the Brethren for their missions, men and women who knew their way around weapons and small unit tactics. Warrior monastics, perhaps? If so, they would be useful should the increasingly bold and restive Central Passage pirates try again.

"Granted." Fenrir drained his tea and put the cup on the binnacle before heading toward the entry port to greet his passengers properly.

As the dark-haired, dark-eyed lead Friar came up the gangway, *Aswan Trader*'s master realized he wasn't just a big man, but one whose height, square shoulders, and broad, angular face could intimidate anyone bent on mischief. The equally tall but slimmer Sister on his heels moved as if she hid a lean, muscular physique beneath her loose khaki clothes. Her intelligent blue eyes, set in a narrow, sharp-featured face beneath short, bleached blond hair, seemed to miss nothing. The other two were more compact, darker of hair and complexion, but no less fit or alert, though Fenrir recognized fellow Thebans. They carried themselves with a shade more familiarity with their surroundings. He couldn't have explained it in words, but he just knew.

To his surprise, the leading Sister spoke first, even though the Friar seemingly led the group.

"Thank you for allowing us aboard, Captain. I am Rianne." She gestured at the man beside her. "This is Horam. And behind us are Lilith and Alcide. We're the Order's delegation to Mazaber."

Fenrir bowed his head.

"Welcome."

As instructed earlier that morning, *Aswan Trader*'s purser appeared, and Fenrir gestured toward him.

"This is Uri. He'll show you to your quarters and give you a rundown on how we do things. We're casting off lines in sixty minutes so we can take the outgoing tide. If you've forgotten anything on shore, best retrieve it now."

"Thank you, Captain, but we are in every respect ready for sea."

Sister Rianne's choice of words both surprised and amused him. She looked like the furthest thing from an old salt, yet she had the lingo down pat.

"In that case, go ahead and settle in. If you'd like to observe our departure, then please join me at the taffrail in an hour but be careful you don't stumble on my sailors along the way."

"Captain." The four Brethren bowed their heads in unison, like a well-trained drill team.

Fenrir watched them take the stairs and vanish into the barquentine's depths, then retrieved his mug from the binnacle and headed for the galley to drop it off.

Friar Horam found the tiny inboard cabin immediately forward of the saloon a little tight for comfort, but he knew the outboard cabins, though they were equipped with portholes, wouldn't be any better. In fact, they'd be worse because of the space taken up by the hull's thick members. He quickly unpacked his duffel bag and stowed the contents in the dresser affixed to one bulkhead and gingerly tried the swinging cot, but its ropes didn't so much as groan under his weight.

Satisfied, he then pulled a large bore needler from his backpack and checked it meticulously to be ready in case of danger. Congruent with Horam's status as a servant of the Almighty, his needler's magazines were filled with non-lethal ammunition, though Horam knew he could kill if there was no other choice.

Though Rianne led their small team, Horam handled its physical security. He visited the other three cabins set aside for the Brethren, in turn, inspecting them and making sure his colleagues checked their personal weapons. No sooner did he finish that the trill of a whistle, followed by the sound of stomping feet on the deck, reached his ears. They were preparing to cast off.

Conscious they might be in the way, but curious nonetheless, Horam, followed by the others, cautiously climbed the aft steps. He poked his head above the coaming just in time to see the main deck awning flutter down as smoke came out of the Stirling engine's stack, sitting halfway between the main and mizzen masts.

"Come on up, my friends. There's plenty of room on the quarterdeck."

They emerged one by one and joined Fenrir aft of the mizzenmast. The latter, eyes on his men as they prepared the sails, asked, "First time in a sea-going vessel?"

"Yes, Captain," Rianne replied on the group's behalf, "though we've sailed between the islands on water taxis."

"While spreading the word of the Almighty, modern medicine and knowledge lost to us, no doubt." He glanced at her over his shoulder.

Rianne inclined her head.

"Indeed. We don't just work in Thebes, and soon, I expect we'll set up small priories on the republic's other main islands."

"I suppose you're finding new recruits every day?"

"The lure of learning what their ancestors once knew is powerful. Mind you, we're also training people who won't take vows, such as teachers, engineers, and technicians."

Fenrir chuckled.

"The Thebes University must be overjoyed at a competitor teaching for free."

An amused smile lit up Rianne's face.

"We're working closely with the University, Captain. It is fast becoming a force multiplier in disseminating knowledge."

"I look forward to a bit of new technology, something that will make a sailor's life safer and more comfortable. Perhaps ships that don't need sails and can travel in any direction, regardless of current and wind."

"It's in the research and development pipeline now, Captain, along with radio and mobile power generation beyond what Stirling engines can offer. But remember, your fellow Thebans working on such things using the information we gave them can only do so much at any given time. I believe you have fire hoses on board?"

"Yes. Hand-pumped, to wash the decks, clear the bilges, and, the Almighty forbid, if needed, fight fires."

"Then imagine the researchers, designers, and engineers drinking from such a hose when it's at maximum output."

Fenrir nodded wisely.

"Point taken."

He turned his attention on the ship again, eyes missing nothing as his first mate made one last round before declaring them ready. The latter finally approached Fenrir.

"Engine is warmed up and ready, sir, lines but one fore and one aft hauled in and dock personnel standing by to cast us off."

Fenrir nodded by way of acknowledgment and walked over to the binnacle where a quartermaster stood by the wheel, eyes on the simple control panel with its engine levers. *Aswan Trader*'s master studied the various dials and, apparently satisfied with what he saw, raised his right fist above his head.

"Cast off forward and aft."

Moments later, lines snaked aboard, and at a muttered instruction, the quartermaster pulled on one of the levers. The Brethren felt a thud run through the ship as the propeller shaft gearbox engaged. Moments later, they could see the pier slip away as the barquentine backed into the harbor, clearing the port proper.

At Fenrir's further order, the quartermaster released the first lever, and *Aswan Trader* quickly lost way as he grasped the wheel and turned the rudder to port. The barquentine pivoted neatly until she faced the open sea, all backward motion gone. Another lever and another thud, and the ship began moving forward, aimed at the passage between Thebes and Raqote, the republic's next largest island, still under engine power.

Soon, the Brethren saw whitecaps dance over the deep blue waters as they came out from under Thebes' lee. A few orders, another rush, and the foremast sails dropped from their spars. Sailors on deck tightened the sheets, and, at Fenrir's command, the quartermaster disengaged the engine. Then, fore-and-aft rigged sails bloomed on the main and mizzen mast, and the barquentine picked up speed, her prow cutting through the wavelets with authority.

Friar Horam felt a smile split his face at the sensation of racing before the wind, one unlike any other he'd experienced in his long career. *Aswan Trader* might move at an infinitesimal fraction of even a starship's lowest sublight speed, but it felt as if she was outracing the elements under a deep blue sky dotted by small, white puffs of cloud.

Some days, his choice to become a Friar of the Void instead of continuing as a Marine noncom in the fabled 21st Pathfinder Regiment seemed inspired, but none more so than at this very moment.

20

Horam and Lilith found their sea legs in a matter of hours after leaving the calmer waters surrounded by the Theban Islands, but the open ocean didn't agree with Rianne and Alcide. Ironically, the locally recruited Friar came from a fishing family. But they worked the shallower waters at the archipelago's heart rather than venture beyond the isles looking for Hatshepsut's large pelagic animals. The latter's size meant they could feed several families for over a week and command handsome prices at the Thebes dockside market. However, their strength made them a challenge for most fishers whose boats were simply too small.

Horam joined them at the leeward railing, where they commiserated while the archipelago dwindled beyond the horizon.

"You seem disgustingly cheerful," Rianne grumbled as she glanced at Horam sideways.

"Fresh sea air, a nice cleansing wind, and no priory responsibilities waiting for me, what's not to like?" He found a place at the rail, upwind from his green-tinged colleagues, and sighed. "If I wasn't a Friar, then on this world, I'd be a sailor. Tell me, how does motion sickness feel?"

"A bit like the transition to and from hyperspace, but less intense and a lot more permanent. Fortunately, meditation helps dampen the worst of it. We'll be fine once we master the skill of suppressing the feeling without conscious effort."

Friar Alcide let out a soft groan.

"Speak for yourself, Sister."

"Once I've mastered the process, I can teach you."

"Then please master it quickly. I'd rather the crew not find out a fisher's son can't stomach the waves out here."

Horam patted him on the shoulder.

"Just be happy this isn't the stormy season, my friend."

"I'd be happier if we brought motion sickness medication."

"Consider this a learning opportunity. Friars and Sisters of the Void must be in control of their bodies and minds, so they don't need medication for minor inconveniences."

Alcide grimaced at his colleague.

"It doesn't feel minor right now."

Rianne abruptly straightened her back and smiled.

"Done. I figured it wouldn't take long." She turned toward Alcide and touched his temples with her fingertips. "Open your mind and let me show you how I did it."

After a few seconds, Alcide's face muscles relaxed, and a faint smile replaced his earlier misery.

"There." Rianne released him. "Consider this a special occasion. Normally, we expect that Brethren learn these things on their own since it's the best way of making them second nature. But seeing as how the evening meal is approaching, and I'd rather see you eat with your accustomed appetite, I decided an exception was in order."

"Thank you, Sister."

The immense relief in the young Friar's voice drew chuckles from both Horam and Lilith. The former said, grinning at Rianne, "She can be a veritable paragon of mercy when she deems it appropriate, which isn't often. And that means this is your lucky day, lad."

Alcide bowed at the waist.

"In that case, I'm doubly grateful, Sister."

"Call my mercy enlightened self-interest. Shall we take a stroll around the deck and work on our appetites?"

**

The days succeeded each other in a monotonous rhythm as *Aswan Trader* sliced through the Equatorial Ocean under a burning sun, tacking twice a day, no more. For Rianne and Horam, the sensation of solitude in this watery vastness was a novel experience. Both were born on a world where suborbital shuttles connected distant settlements in ninety minutes or less, meaning the average Lyonesse citizens rarely found themselves isolated from the planet's advanced, thirty-seventh-century civilization. Finally, one morning, the lookout's cry of 'land ho' saw everyone scurrying up on deck.

The four Brethren joined Fenrir aft and waited as he scanned the western horizon with his telescope. Soon, they could make out indistinct bumps rising from the water, not just straight ahead but marching both north and south until they faded from sight.

"The Saqqara Isles," *Aswan Trader*'s master said without looking back at the monastics. "They run well over a thousand kilometers in either direction. Most of the channels are impassable by ships of our size, except for a very few. We're headed for the Central Passage, the most direct route to Mazaber and the deepest, widest, and until the pirates came along, safest of them. Using either the North or South Passages would add a week to our trip and be a beast if the wind turns. On the other hand, considering how the Saqqara barbarian tribes are becoming more aggressive, they're probably no safer from a sneak attack by small boat swarms unless we stand well out, and that means fighting beastly currents that circle the globe."

"What's driving the surge in piracy?" Rianne asked.

"Who knows? Their gods driving them; humors in the blood; unscrupulous Aksumite merchants looking for cheap profits or chieftains with delusions of grandeur. Take your pick, Sister. They're just as fanatical and deadly, no matter what reason. Two or three years ago, this was just as safe as Theban waters. Now? We'll be hauling our guns up on deck within the hour and posting sentries night and day. If you've come armed yourselves, keep your weapons handy. We could always use a few more pairs of hands, especially since we're short three men because of the last time we navigated these waters."

Rianne and Horam exchanged a quick glance. Better to reveal they carried needlers than spring the surprise during a night attack. Besides, Horam could handle one of the ship's railguns as if it were a mere pistol.

"We carry personal weapons, Captain," she said. "And Horam can handle a railgun better than any of your crew. He learned how during his service in the Lyonesse Defense Force."

Fenrir studied the big Friar.

"No doubt. Size helps as well with something that long and heavy. I'll see you're issued one of our off-world slug throwers the moment we stand to."

"Could I familiarize myself with one now?" Horam asked in a respectful tone.

"Sure."

Fenrir sought out his first mate, standing amidship and waved. The man trotted over, an air of curiosity on his round face.

"Captain?"

"Friar Horam has volunteered to man one of the railguns if we encounter pirates. He's used them before and will manage better than our people in a pinch. Show him the armory and let him practice."

A nod.

"As you wish." The first mate turned to Horam. "Please follow me, Friar."

While watching both men head for the stairs, Rianne asked, "Do you think we'll meet any when we cross the Passage?"

"Perhaps. If their chieftain is hungry enough and the wind is against us. Or the Aksumites backing the pirates want another try at capturing this ship and using it for their own purposes. Aksum shipwrights can't yet build barquentines capable of sailing as close to the wind as *Aswan Trader*, let alone equip them with Stirling engines." He gave Rianne a quick smile. "But never fear. Our engine is warm and ready if the winds play us foul, and we need a few extra knots to escape."

"Does it push your ship faster than the pirates can row?"

"It depends on how much qash they've been chewing," Fenrir replied, naming a native plant species with wildly varying, idiosyncratic effects on the human nervous system. "Get enough of the bastards in any given boat feeling good, and they'll row themselves to death. Too bad it doesn't affect their aim that much."

"It will, in time. We studied qash because we were curious if the plant had medicinal properties. The republic's government is right in banning its cultivation, import, and consumption. Continued use will eventually end in irreversible nerve damage, including loss of all five senses, with insanity finally taking over after the drug destroys enough brain cells and rewires neural connections. Premature death is inevitable."

Fenrir cocked an astonished eyebrow at Rianne.

"Really? And how much use will trigger this?"

She shrugged.

"It depends on the individual, but on average, we estimate a few years of daily use, perhaps as little as two or three. Once the decline begins, we figure users die in a matter of months."

"That might explain the last attack. They seemed a tad rabid."

"Any idea how long since someone introduced qash in the Saqqara Islands?"

"Two or three years is my guess. The islanders only began attacking our ships recently." Fenrir paused and wrinkled his brow as an idea struck him. "Do you think Aksumite commercial interests are feeding them qash deliberately and inciting them to commit acts of piracy? Perhaps as a way of eliminating us as competition now that we're advancing beyond their technological level with your help?"

"They wouldn't be the first who introduced deadly addictive substances into a vulnerable population to debauch and destabilize opponents. It's a trick as old as humanity. Considering Thebes is rapidly becoming a dominant force on Hatshepsut, I wouldn't be surprised the leading Aksumite city-states are using Saqqarans to erode the Theban trade advantage."

Fenrir scowled.

"Nasty. Mind you, the islanders were always more savage than the rest of us for as long as anyone can remember. Something happened to them in the years after the Great Scouring that changed their nature."

"A not uncommon occurrence on worlds devastated by Dendera," Rianne replied in a soft, sad voice. "Many couldn't deal with witnessing so many lives and the future of an entire civilization erased in a matter of moments and went mad as a result. Their descendants, especially those living in isolated societies cut off from the rest of the planet, still experience a form of that madness caused by intergenerational trauma."

A grim chuckle escaped Fenrir's throat.

"So, the Saqqarans are crazy. Figures. You hear rumors of folks landing on the islands, looking for adventure or to seize territory and vanishing without a trace. Just like *Cimarron*'s crew."

When Rianne cocked a questioning eyebrow, a mysterious grin twisted Fenrir's lips.

"I'll tell you the story in a few hours when we're in the Passage, where you can feel the menace emanating from the thick jungle on both sides. It makes for a better atmosphere."

Over the following hours, the bumps on the horizon grew into hundreds of mountainous, presumably volcanic, vegetation-covered islands, with gigantic trees marching out into the narrow channels on massive root tangles. Even this close, the Brethren, standing by the aft starboard railing, couldn't make out the Central Passage's entrance. It seemed as if a massive living barrier stood between *Aswan Trader* and her destination.

Then, the barquentine tacked to port, and the scenery shifted, at first subtly, then more dramatically, and they saw a broad channel cutting through the brooding, dark green mass. Moments later, Fenrir called his ship to action stations, and sailors from both watches took observation and firing positions in the tops and around the deck. Horam, one of the long railguns in hand, joined them aft, from where he could act as a sniper and cover either side if needed.

As they rounded the first island to starboard, Rianne saw a dark outline lying on a shingle beach, deep within a narrow inlet.

"*Cimarron*, schooner. Or what's left of her," Fenrir said.

"Pirates?" Horam asked.

"No, Friar. Her disaster predates the era of Saqqaran depredations."

"What happened?"

"No one knows. I was an apprentice at the time, a junior master's mate learning his craft, about twenty years ago. *Cimarron* was headed for Mazaber with a cargo of wine and grain on what would be her last voyage. The captain had a reputation as a hard man, who feared little in this life, not even the Almighty. My ship back then, the schooner *Morningstar*, traveled through this very passage on our way to Mazaber as well, weeks after *Cimarron* was due back in Thebes. Naturally, her owner asked Theban ships to keep a lookout." Fenrir paused and squinted at the shadowy inlet. "That wreck wasn't there during our outbound leg. Three weeks later, on our return home, we inexplicably found her as she is now, beached, her masts down, her spars and ropes a complete mess."

"Was she driven ashore by a storm?"

Fenrir turned his eyes on Sister Lilith.

"There were no storms during the time between *Cimarron*'s departure from Thebes and us finding her wreck. She simply vanished after leaving Mazaber, her business concluded, only to reappear here days after we passed through. The captain sent me with a landing party to investigate. We found her cargo holds full, her crew's personal possessions stowed away normally, the ship's log and books in the captain's desk. Even the purser's money chest was still there, intact. The captain's last log entry placed her at anchor overnight on the other side of the Passage, waiting for daylight before crossing. Even without pirates, a sane sailor doesn't try it in the dark."

Friar Alcide let out a low whistle.

"Spooky. Now that you mention it, I vaguely recall the tale of *Cimarron*'s strange fate."

"As do I," Lilith added.

"No one ever found out what happened. We brought the sailors' dunnage bags, the log and books, the purser's chest, and anything else we could carry and handed it to the ship's owner when we got home. Ever since, Theban mariners consider the wreck cursed and therefore out of bounds. The Saqqarans might have plundered the cargo after we left. They might even have helped drive her aground and killed the crew. But if so, why didn't they take anything at the time? And more importantly, where was she between her last log entry and when we spotted her on our return trip, some time later?"

Horam gave Fenrir a skeptical look.

"Quite the ghost ship story, Captain. Is any of it true?"

Fenrir placed his hand over his heart.

"I swear by the Almighty. Hatshepsut hides more inexplicable mysteries than anyone knows. Perhaps this planet has been out of sync with the universe since the Great Scouring."

"Possibly," Rianne mused. "The Infinite Void is unknowable, though it influences what we are and what we do and resonates with both the good and the evil our species is capable of, and the Scouring was one of the worst evils in our history."

— 21 —

All afternoon, *Aswan Trader*'s Stirling engine propelled the barquentine through the sinuous passage aided by the foremast's topsails. On deck, a thick, heavy blanket of noxiously aromatic air enveloped crew and passengers. Each breath was like swallowing a lungful of warm water, and the native insects, though incapable of digesting human blood and flesh, multiplied with each kilometer deeper into what Horam privately dubbed a green hell. If ever his old unit wanted a new training area that would challenge its troopers, the Saqqara Islands might well do the trick.

He and the other three Brethren felt the sailors' heightened awareness like a living entity enveloping the ship. It was evident in Captain Fenrir's demeanor, the way his eyes were never at rest, and his fingers never stopped touching the shotgun hanging from his right shoulder on a leather sling. Primitive by Lyonesse standards, the twin-barrel weapons firing chemically propelled ball bearings could be more devastating at short range than even a plasma rifle. But beyond a dozen meters, perhaps even less, they were well-nigh useless.

Other than the four railguns of unknown origin, *Aswan Trader*'s only longer-range weapons were smooth-barreled muskets firing a fifteen-millimeter ball. More accurate and with greater range than the shotguns, they would still be hard-pressed to hit a pirate boat at fifty meters from the deck of a moving ship. And their rate of fire was desperately slow when faced with a hundred screaming savages intent on murder.

Horam knew this before coming aboard the barquentine, both from reading about primitive firearms and spending time at the range in Thebes with the local militia. He understood his and the other three railguns would be instrumental in case of a pirate raid. Their first line of defense was distance.

If they were reduced to shotguns against a drugged swarm climbing over the gunwales, the battle was as good as lost. Would that a squad of his former comrades was backing him up. Nothing on this world would win against a half-dozen armored and armed Lyonesse Marines. Unexpectedly, a deep longing for his former vocation threatened to overwhelm the Friar, even though he'd taken off the uniform almost fifteen years earlier. Until now, the bond among Brethren of the Void had been enough, but as he faced his first real peril since donning a cassock, Horam missed the rough comradeship among Marines ready for anything.

As the sun kissed the sharp hilltops, throwing long shadows across the Central Passage, the dark shores took on a more menacing aspect. Try as he might, the Friar couldn't make out the far end where the risk of a pirate swarm vanished. As a result, he wondered whether they might be forced to anchor in this narrow channel, exposed to shore-based predators capable of launching an overwhelming attack against a tired, anxious crew.

Another bend in the broad channel, another tack while the engine kept chugging along. The shadows now reached the deck, and the Brethren, clustered at the taffrail, felt a collective chill seize their bodies. Lilith caught Rianne's attention and made a face.

"I sense evil," she murmured.

"Likewise." A pause. "In fact, I've sensed evil since we saw *Cimarron*'s wreck. As if pirate scouts were watching us."

Lilith gave her superior a startled glance, then thought back, wondering if she'd missed anything. The Friars, privy to the conversation, exchanged looks. They knew about the Sisters' fey talent and respected it. They also possessed enough extrasensory awareness of their own to be more on edge than usual.

"Now that you mention it, I've been uneasy ever since but didn't consider my feelings worthy of mention since I thought they might stem from the story Captain Fenrir told."

"Never dismiss your feelings. They might be the only thing standing between you and the Infinite Void."

Lilith bowed her head.

"Yes, Sister."

"Are we in danger?" Alcide asked in a whisper.

Rianne didn't immediately reply. Instead, she leaned over the starboard railing and studied the next bend in the channel.

"Perhaps. Feral energies stir beneath the trees now that the shadows are growing longer. Lilith, please reach out."

The younger Sister, who'd been a mere novice only a few months earlier, inclined her head, knowing this was part of her ongoing development. She faced the shore, closed her eyes, and opened her mind. After a few seconds of silence, Lilith physically recoiled as if something had slammed against her.

"I've never touched something so demonic, so inhuman," she said in a hoarse voice pitched for her companions' ears only. "They're of our species but not like us."

"How many?" Rianne asked.

"Countless dozens."

"Try to be more precise, my child."

"Yes, Sister." Lilith let her mind float for much longer this time. "I can make out approximately a hundred separate souls, but I suspect there are probably many more whose weaker minds are drowned out by the insane aggression of their fellow tribesmen. Perhaps another fifty or so."

Rianne turned toward Fenrir.

"How much longer before we leave the Passage, Captain?"

He glanced at his surroundings and grimaced.

"Hopefully, and if nothing slows us down, we'll be clear by last light."

"Can you increase our speed?"

Fenrir frowned.

"Why?"

"We're picking up signs that Saqqaran pirates are massing in the woods ahead of us, perhaps just around the next bend."

The frown turned into an air of worry.

"Did you spot any boats?"

"Not yet."

Fenrir, voice raised, called out, "Stand by, lads. We'll be under attack shortly."

Neither of the two newly minted Brethren wondered aloud why Fenrir didn't inquire about the signs Rianne mentioned. They knew better than to ask. When a Void Sister, especially one of Hatshepsut Priory's strongest, used her powers of conviction, normal humans took everything she said as the unquestionable truth.

Horam hefted his railgun and headed for the mizzenmast's starboard ratlines, which would give the weapon's long barrel some added stability. The three sailors with the remaining railguns had already taken up their firing positions.

Rianne gave Lilith and Alcide a significant look, then drew her personal weapon from the holster hidden beneath her loose robes. Both followed suit.

"Can you sense a change in the pirates' mood?"

Lilith closed her eyes again, then nodded.

"Excitement rising to a fever pitch. It's almost obscene in a manner I cannot explain with mere words."

"It likely means they'll attack while we're coming around the bend. We should say a prayer now, so the Almighty ends the torment those tortured souls endure every day of their lives."

"Yes, Sister."

An ominous silence settled over *Aswan Trader*, broken only by the regular, dull rumble of the Stirling engine's pistons going back and forth, propelling the ship on its own. Harnessing the faint, constantly shifting breeze was too tricky with the entire crew standing by to repel boarders, and all sails were furled.

The first high-pitched yelp echoing across the channel's dark waters caught everyone by surprise. Several among the crew almost jumped out of their skins. Dozens of more voices joined in an incomprehensible, rhythmic war cry intended to enhance aggression and suppress any hesitation. Moments later, the first boats appeared, each crammed with rowers and men holding spears, bows, and even weapons that seemed not much different from *Aswan Trader*'s shotguns.

And the boats kept coming from beyond the bend, filling the channel until the surface teemed with a single unbroken carpet of wood and flesh reaching out for the far shore.

The men in the boats hardly seemed human. Shoulder-length hair of various shades, from light blond to coal black, braided or hanging in thick mats, along with scraggly beards, framed thin, surprisingly pale, unhealthy faces disfigured by ritual scars. Eyes burning with the fires of hell almost seemed to glow in the late afternoon gloom. They wore little more than leather loincloths and vests, the latter decorated with bone shards, some of which might even be human. And the voices…

Horam's voice rang out unexpectedly.

"Railgun snipers, aim for the hulls just below the waterline. On my command, Yost, first boat on the far left; Chiang, the second boat from the far left; I'll take the first boat on the far right and T'kana, you'll take the second from the far right. One round, then first switches to third and second to fourth, and so on. We sink them at three hundred meters, and they won't be boarding when we crash through." The Friar gave an astonished Captain Fenrir a vaguely apologetic smile. "Sorry, sir. Force of habit. You can get the man out of the Marines and make him a servant of the Almighty. But you can't erase years' worth of reflexes."

"No, no." Fenrir waved the apology away. "You understand best how one uses those weapons. Consider yourself *Aswan Trader*'s acting gunner and do what is necessary, so we may pass through unharmed."

"Roger that, Skipper." Horam turned his eyes back on the growing and rapidly nearing flotilla. "Railgunners take aim. Call out your names when ready."

In rapid succession, the three sailors answered while the Friar pointed his weapon at his own target.

"FIRE."

Four subdued twangs rang out almost simultaneously, and within an instant, four little waterspouts erupted centimeters from the pirate boat hulls.

"Reload and fire at will."

While the long-range weapons carried out their work, Rianne and Lilith studied the pirates through narrowed eyes, looking for souls beneath the contorted faces. But all they saw were gaping mouths spewing the vilest kind of hate as they waved their weapons while the oarsmen pulled with frightening vigor.

The boats soon filled the channel from shore to shore, and while none could stop a three-masted barquentine under engine power in its tracks, it didn't matter. The pirates were preparing to abandon them and swarm *Aswan Trader*, as evidenced by one man in each hoisting a grappling hook tied to a rope.

Rianne carried out a quick headcount of the Saqqaran pirates and came up with approximately one-hundred-and-fifty, which matched Lilith's estimate. The young woman would go far in the Order if her talent was already this strong after not even a year as a consecrated Sister. Would that they found more like her so the Theban priory might quickly become an abbey with dependencies in each of Hatshepsut's centers of civilization. The planet's rebirth would only speed up as a result.

"Railgunners — target the men with grappling hooks and firearms," Horam called out. He turned his head toward Fenrir and said, in the same loud tone, one that cut through the Saqqaran pirates' shouting, "Sir, we'll be switching power packs in a moment. Might I suggest getting our muskets ready for a volley?"

"Aye." Fenrir let his eyes roam over the line of boats and shouted, "Musketeers, take aim."

Lilith leaned toward Alcide, her eyes fixed on the rapidly nearing boats.

"Is it just me, or are they lower in the water than a minute ago?"

"No, it's not just you. They're sinking thanks to the railguns, and I don't see anyone bailing just yet."

"That's because they plan on taking this ship," Rianne said.

"Good—"

Fenrir's roar cut off Alcide's reply. "Muskets, FIRE!"

A deafening crash rang out, accompanied by the acrid smell of gunpowder, then, "Reload and prepare to repel boarders."

"Railgunners, swap power packs and reload."

Rianne, Lilith, and Alcide, needlers in hand, watched everyone save Horam fumble with their weapons, even though the Friar put them through their paces earlier. One dropped his spare pack while another spilled slugs on the deck. The elder Sister closed her eyes and poured out her energy to stiffen the sailors.

She knew it would leave her exhausted within minutes, but minutes were all they had to make it through or die under the pirates' savage assault. The latter still outnumbered *Aswan Trader*'s crew and passengers over two to one.

The railguns resumed firing, and at this close range, the Brethren saw chests and heads exploding in a red spray as the fifteen-millimeter slugs tore through human flesh and bone. But the pirates simply kept rowing, oblivious to the carnage. Rianne absently noticed Alcide and Lilith fighting off nausea by subvocalizing their meditation mantras.

"Here they come," the forward lookout shouted, hoisting his shotgun.

— 22 —

"Don't let any of the bastards climb over the gunwales, or we're done." Fenrir hoisted his weapon. "Steady now, lads, steady."

Shots from the few remaining pirate muskets whined past the crew's heads as the first grappling hook came sailing over the side just aft of the starboard cathead.

The nearest sailor leaned over and fired his shotgun. An upthrust spear tip almost caught him before he could take cover again.

Another grappling hook caught on to the port gunwale, a little further aft than the first one, but the sailor who exposed himself and fired into the boat wasn't quite as lucky as his mate. An arrow caught him in the left shoulder, though mercifully, he held on to his shotgun as he dropped behind the railing with a loud groan. *Aswan Trader*'s medic scurried over to the man and examined the wound while more grappling hooks sailed through the air. Horam and the other railgunners were now firing as fast as possible from their positions on either beam. At this range, each slug tore through wooden hulls and countless bodies, birthing fountains of blood that fell back upon the boats and the water like a horrible red rain.

A pair of hooks appeared level with the quarterdeck, and Rianne braced herself back-to-back with Lilith and Alcide. When the first head appeared on either side, the Brethren fired their needlers, and the pirates disappeared.

Throughout the brief engagement, the barquentine kept moving westward at the same speed, her quartermaster's eyes on the waters ahead, ignoring everything else as best he could. More shotguns fired, one barrel after the other, drawing howls of agony from unseen Saqqarans in their sinking boats, then the first of them came into sight astern, their gunwales awash, surrounded by reddish stains.

Around the ship, sailors ripped grappling hooks from the railing and tossed them overboard while dodging upthrust spears, and the odd arrow fired at too short a range for both power and precision.

A fight that seemed eternal to Rianne's hyper-sensitive awareness ended abruptly, and she felt fatigue envelop her while the railgunners took parting shots over *Aswan Trader*'s stern.

She touched Lilith's arm.

"How many are left?"

The younger woman closed her eyes and reached out with her mind.

"I can make out approximately forty souls."

"Meaning we killed over a hundred."

"It would appear so."

"Any injuries other than Paolo?"

Lilith took a quick look around the deck but saw only the medic tending to the man with the arrow wound.

"No."

"Good. Take Alcide and help with Paolo. They have smeared the arrowhead with a noxious substance, perhaps human excrement, and his wound could fester quickly if it isn't cleaned with care."

Lilith knew an order when she heard one and bowed her head.

"Yes, Sister."

The two hurried off while Rianne leaned against the mizzenmast, exhausted. When Horam finally stopped sniping at the increasingly distant pirates, he slipped his gun's sling over a shoulder and joined her, an air of worry on his plain, square face.

"Are you okay?" He asked in a low-pitched voice.

"I reinforced the crew's courage and determination, and it took every bit of energy I could muster."

"Ah." Understanding lit up his eyes. "I wondered why they fought with more resolve and less fear than I expected, even under the circumstances. Maybe ships using the Central Passage should take Lyonesse-trained Sisters as part of the crew."

"Or the Thebans can take the Northern or Southern Passage and count themselves lucky using either only adds a week or so one way to a given trip."

"What was that?" Fenrir asked as he joined them behind the wheel while his first mate secured the ship from action stations.

"I was telling Horam you and your fellow captains might consider trading distance for safety by using the other passages until the Saqqaran pirate problem is sorted."

Fenrir rubbed his chin, the shotgun in his left hand forgotten.

"Well," he drawled, "this one was worse than the attack that put three of my crew in your hospital, Sister. Much worse. Without your warning, our railguns, and Friar Horam's military training, things wouldn't have ended well."

"And the pirates will adapt. Today's survivors will make sure their people use different tactics the next time a Theban ship enters these waters."

"They lost a lot of men."

She nodded once.

"True. But we don't know how many of them salivate at the idea of capturing an ocean-going vessel crammed with trade goods and, for Hatshepsut, modern technology such as it is. I would feel happier if our return voyage was through another channel, one without a recent history of pirate attacks."

"That'll cost extra on the charter."

"The priory would rather pay for another week at sea than for the burial of four Brethren."

Fenrir inclined his head.

"Point taken, Sister."

"And," Horam said, "if it weren't for our ability to snipe at their boats from a distance with your railguns, they'd have made it over our gunnels. Thankfully, those boats were rather low in the water by the time they reached us, and their crews were more than a little damaged."

"Aye. Point taken as well, Friar. It's a shame we can't yet talk with our home port and warn other ships headed for Aksum that the Central Passage has become too dangerous. Unless…" He gave Rianne a speculative look.

"Yes. We brought a pair of shortwave radios so we can contact the priory in case of an emergency. I think this qualifies. Let me warn Sister Hermina, and she'll speak with the shipping authority."

"Tell me, Sister, would you have thought of doing so if I hadn't brought it up?"

"Yes. Perhaps not at once, but within the hour. You must excuse me. I'm still a little out of sorts."

"Understandable. If you'll excuse me in turn, I must see that we leave this place pronto." Fenrir nodded once, then headed for his first mate, who was re-organizing the watches so they could hoist as much canvas as possible.

"You'd have called home without his suggestion, all right." A sly smile crept across Horam's face. "But you wouldn't have told Lars, would you?"

She shrugged.

"At this point, I'm not sure I can answer that question honestly, but yes, I would most certainly have warned Hermina on my own."

"Do you need help getting below deck?"

Rianne took a few tentative steps, then shook her head.

"I'm fine, but after the evening meal, it's to bed until morning. I never boosted forty minds at once before today."

"And this one thanks you for the effort. Calmer spirits are more apt to hit the target. If not for our engaging them at extreme range, we would have suffered more than just one casualty. Though they're solid men, my fellow railgunners aren't Marines, capable of keeping their wits about them while facing three times our number in drugged-up savages screaming like the souls of the damned. This channel must be placed out of bounds until someone cleans up the pirate problem. And with no nation on Hatshepsut fielding a Navy, it'll probably wait until our people set up a military outpost here."

"Which will take a decade or two. I'll warn Hermina now. There's nothing we can do for ships already at sea, but it might offer the Thebans added impetus to move ahead with building a radio network and equipping their ships. The government hasn't been overly enthusiastic at diverting the resources."

Horam winked at her.

"Not enough potential for graft."

"Cynic."

"Realist. The Thebans are no worse or better than any other politicians and bureaucrats throughout the ages. Besides, graft has always been omnipresent in one form or another. Even back home on Lyonesse."

"Sadly."

She gave him a vague wave and vanished down the aft stairs.

Horam rounded up the railgunners and checked their weapons, power packs, and ammunition stocks before chatting with them informally about the battle. It was a habit he'd picked up when he wore the Republic of Lyonesse Marine Corps uniform with command sergeant stripes on the sleeves and led a Pathfinder troop. All three were still keyed-up, their synapses firing at high speed, but Horam knew they would hit a sudden wall within the next hour or two, certainly the moment *Aswan Trader* left the Central Passage.

After ensuring the weapons were back in their cases and the used power packs rigged to their solar chargers, Horam knocked on Rianne's cabin door.

"Enter."

He pushed the wooden panel aside and stuck his head in. She was sitting on the bunk, one of their shortwave radios in her lap, a tired expression lining her face.

"Any luck."

She shook her head.

"No. Either no one's listening back home, or I'm not getting through."

"Try again after sunset. Shortwave radios work better at night, and if nothing else, it'll be late enough in Thebes that the duty Friar will be in the main office and capable of hearing your call."

Rianne put the radio on the bunk and stood.

"Is the end of the channel in sight?"

"Not yet, but it's widening, or at least that was my impression just before I came below deck."

"The sooner we're away from this evil place, the better. The effort of dealing with its oppressive aura is becoming increasingly difficult in my weakened state."

"Since I also feel it in an attenuated fashion, for once, I can imagine what it's doing to you."

She grimaced at him.

"In which case, it must affect the crew as well, though they know it not."

Later, when the sun was kissing the western horizon, all four Brethren stood at the stern and watched the last Saqqaran islands drop away on either beam. The barquentine, a full suit of sails aloft, had entered the Aksum Sea and turned her prow several degrees to starboard.

Rianne let out a soft sigh and smiled at Horam.

"The evil aura is fading away; praise the Almighty." Then, a frown crossed her tired features. "Now that it's not blotting out everything else, I can sense the crew's dismay. Slaughtering so many Saqqarans will leave a mark on their psyches. Whether it heals is up to each individual."

"The Void giveth," Horam intoned, his right index finger raised up.

"The Void taketh away."

A new voice joined them at that moment, Captain Fenrir, who'd heard them reciting the Order's overriding mantra and stepped over from his side of the binnacle.

"Blessed be the Void." He inclined his head. "And its servants. Without Friar Horam directing the railguns, we surely would have fought on this deck and perhaps lost lives of our own."

The former Lyonesse Marine grinned.

"I'm always happy if I can send blackened souls into the Infinite Void where they can no longer harm the righteous, sir."

A smirk appeared on Fenrir's tired-looking face.

"Remind me to never piss you off, Friar. But am I mistaken in believing the Order's Rule forbids taking another's life? I thought you religious types were pretty scrupulous about the sanctity of life."

"Usually," Sister Rianne replied. "But the Almighty allows exceptions, such as when we face evil, especially one trying to kill the innocents around us."

"Then I should take a closer look at this faith of yours that so many of my sailors are embracing."

"I would be glad to teach you, Captain. But right now, I'd be even gladder for a warm meal and a comfortable cot."

At that moment, the galley bell sounded, and Fenrir chuckled.

"Your first wish is granted, and the timing for your second is entirely up to you. But the Aksum Sea is usually calm at this time of year, so the night should be peaceful."

"When will we arrive in Mazaber?"

"The day after tomorrow." He waved at the aft stairway. "I won't stand between you and supper. Enjoy."

— 23 —

"This is Hatshepsut's star, alright, sir." The flag combat information center's officer of the watch glanced over his shoulder at Commodore Gatam Watanabe. "*Repulse*'s navigator is one hundred percent sure. It matches what we found in the old imperial star catalog and what Colonel Torma's prisoner recorded in his log. Now to find the planet itself. The information in the navigation database is just as spotty and out of date as that on the previous star systems."

"Thank you." Watanabe swiveled his command chair to face Torma and Ardrix, sitting at their accustomed stations behind him. "I hope this star system isn't as depressingly wrecked as the others we crossed. Whatever did your man — Keter, was it? Whatever did he find to trade with those poor wretches?"

Task Force Kruzenshtern had stopped at almost a dozen inhabited planets on its way, brief tours in orbit so they could scan the surface and search for traces of human activity. They also visited another two dozen airless worlds that, according to the records, once boasted artificial habitats. Of the latter, they found nothing more than faint traces.

The visits added a couple of weeks to the outbound journey. But neither Watanabe, nor Torma, nor anyone else in the formation could resist the allure of checking on how the rest of the former empire fared two centuries after the Great Scouring. It left them wondering why the Hegemony hadn't sallied forth and reclaimed those star systems yet.

"Artifacts from imperial times, precious alloys, books which survived the Great Scouring, things of that nature. Items mainly of interest to collectors who no doubt paid well for both the items and Keter's silence."

A frown creased Watanabe's forehead.

"Isn't collecting imperial artifacts without a government license illegal?"

Torma nodded.

"It is, but those wealthy enough for such a hobby can buy their way around licenses, sir."

"I see. And what happened to the things your man brought back?"

A grimace.

"I ordered them warehoused until a judge rules on their disposal once Jan Keter has been tried."

"And found guilty?"

"That's a foregone conclusion, I'm afraid." The grimace widened. "Though I suspect many of the items will go walkabout while we're out here, with the inventory list adjusted accordingly, and I'll be informed I should ignore any discrepancies. Not by my superior, mind you, but via backchannels. Should I not comply, I would quickly become ineffective as an investigator with doors slammed in my face and resources quietly withdrawn."

Watanabe's frown became a scowl.

"Does that happen a lot?"

"More than those of us who hold our duty to the Hegemony sacred would like. We play a delicate balancing game in the Commission and either quickly find the uncrossable lines in the sand or perish."

"And here I thought you folks were omnipotent, capable of bringing anyone who violates Hegemony laws to a swift and merciless justice."

A bitter smile replaced Torma's earlier grimace. "You'd be surprised how many are above those laws, sir."

Watanabe scoffed. "Because they're for the little people, right?"

Ardrix inclined her head. "Sadly. But that's been true in most societies throughout history. If I may ask, how long until we arrive?"

"However long we take to find Hatshepsut. If you'll recall, we spent anywhere from six to twelve hours finding the other inhabited planets. Add to that our jump inward, on average twelve hours, give or take two, depending on the planet's position, and another three or so from the hyperlimit. We'll likely enter orbit sometime tomorrow morning."

The Sister exchanged a glance with Torma, who rose to his feet.

"Thank you for letting us witness our arrival at Hatshepsut's heliopause, sir."

"Enjoy your last day of peace, Colonel, Sister. Once we get there, it's your show. You'll be busier than the rest of us then."

"Indeed, sir. But we shall rely on *Repulse* to find the city Jan Keter's log calls Mazaber, so we can land there and interrogate the man who sold him the abbey-made medical instruments, a David Crimple."

**

Horam found Sister Rianne standing by the port side rail staring at the Aksum coastline the next morning shortly after sunrise, a steaming cup of tea in hand.

"Did you enjoy a good night's sleep?"

She glanced at him and took a sip.

"Restful. You?"

"Once the adrenaline bled off, I slept like a newborn in his mother's embrace." He nodded at the broken landscape bathed by the reddish light of dawn, a raw, damaged mess that bled into the Aksum Sea. "Isn't that where New Aden stood before the Scouring?"

"Yes. Millions died in a matter of minutes on that unfortunate shore. I can still pick up a faint echo of their fear, anchored as it is to the very granite."

"Another of those places that give one the shivers," Fenrir's voice reached their ears from the aft stairway. "No one has landed there since. We merchant captains keep offshore as much as possible, but there's little choice along this part of the coast between the reefs and the sunken starship. The Aksum Sea is not only narrow but shallow around here."

He waved toward the east.

"As you might notice, we can still see the summits of the tallest leeward Saqqara Isles."

"Sunken starship?" Horam turned around and gave *Aswan Trader*'s master a questioning glance.

"No one knows the name, but we'll be passing her within the hour. Look over the starboard side. In these waters, you'll see her clear as day. Her topsides are shallow enough to present a risk for ships such as mine at low tide."

"Crashed during the Retribution Fleet's attack, I suppose?"

Fenrir shrugged.

"No one knows what she is, who operated her, and when she came down."

"A shame we don't have any sort of independent air supply system. I'd check her out from up close in an instant. Maybe I could free dive since she's shallow enough to be considered a navigational hazard."

Rianne gave her colleague an amused smile.

"Let's leave the archeology for another time. I'm sure Captain Fenrir isn't keen on anchoring around here anyhow. Not with what happened over where New Aden once stood. We'll provide the supply ship with the coordinates, and they can at least give this mystery wreck an intensive scan from low orbit."

He inclined his head.

"Of course, Sister. But a man can dream. Imagine. A perfectly preserved imperial-era starship almost right beneath our feet."

"Content yourself with a passing glimpse from above."

"You may join the lookout on the foremast top if you wish, Friar." Fenrir gestured at the small platform above the foremast's mainsail. "It's the best view I can offer. See the bosun and ask for a safety harness."

"Thank you, Captain. I will."

Less than an hour later, warned by the lookout, Horam scrambled up the starboard ratlines and through the lubber's hole. The sailor who'd called him up made sure he fastened his harness properly, then pointed at a patch of sea off their starboard bow.

"You can just make out a bit of shiny stuff below the surface about a hundred meters away, Friar. That would be her."

The Lyonesse Marine turned monastic squinted as he sought out what the sailor saw and found it almost at once, a faint shimmer reflecting the early morning sunlight beneath a dappled surface. As they neared, he could trace more of its shape and let out a low whistle. He looked down at the other three Brethren and Captain Fenrir, now leaning over the rail beneath him.

"It's a big one," Horam said in a voice that carried. "I figure easily as large as one of our corvettes. Local marine life must not like the hull's alloy. It's as spotless as the day she was launched. Probably tried lifting from the New Aden spaceport when the Retribution Fleet came overhead and took a disabling hit. If so, she's probably the crew's final resting place."

"In that case," Rianne replied, "we should offer the Almighty a prayer on behalf of their souls so that if they've been restless in their watery grave since the crash, they might ultimately merge with the Infinite Void."

The Brethren lowered their heads, imitated by those sailors within earshot who didn't have immediate duties. When they raised them again, Fenrir let out a soft grunt.

"I guess that's why this place always feels eerie." When Rianne gave him a searching glance, he shrugged as if embarrassed by his comment. "I don't believe in immortal souls or the Infinite Void, but I've encountered enough strangeness on this world to wonder whether your lot might be right about certain things."

"The offer to learn about our beliefs remains open, Lars. We know there are such things as souls because the most talented among my Sisters can feel them. Not me, mind you, at least not yet. I'm still young and relatively inexperienced in comparison with our greatest teachers. Think of what we call a soul, the intangible essence of a living being, if you like, as something which animates our bodies. Every faith throughout human history has that belief in common."

When he opened his mouth to speak, she held up a hand.

"You wonder why such essences might stay at the site of the body's death instead of merging into the Void, correct?" When he nodded, she made a dubious face. "I don't know. Nobody does, but it's the only explanation for some phenomena we encounter. Unfinished business, perhaps? Or the trauma of death, especially if caused by something as fundamentally evil as Dendera's Great Scouring, somehow bound the soul to a physical place? We of the Void, who are more sensitive than most humans, know that the universe is stranger than our species can possibly imagine. Our interaction with said strangeness remains largely indecipherable. What you experience as eeriness stems from this interaction."

Fenrir chuckled.

"Aren't religions based on interpreting that which is undecipherable?"

"Certainly. Humans crave comforting beliefs, whether they acknowledge it, even those who reject any form of religious faith for whatever reason. The latter simply find something else, political ideology or a militant if not zealous opposition to all religions being the most common substitutes."

"Funny. I neither believe in an Almighty nor politics or opposition to religion. Where does that leave me?"

A knowing smile lit up Rianne's face.

"With a plurality of human beings, those who've not yet examined themselves or won't do so lest it upsets long-held preconceptions."

"And what if I told you my fundamental belief is in profit?"

"Then I'd say you were both lying to and cheating yourself." She turned her eyes back on the vast, submerged starship hull and reached out. "This is definitely a tomb."

"One of those interactions, Sister?"

She looked at him once more.

"Yes. I daresay this planet is littered with places where souls were seared by the Retribution Fleet, like so many other worlds once teeming with human beings."

**

"Found it," *Repulse*'s navigator announced when Captain Park answered his communicator.

"Are you sure?"

"A sweet little pea-like ball of blue and white hanging in this star's habitable zone. Ten and a half hours FTL to its hyperlimit. I've advised the flag CIC and synced the task force for hyperspace at the commodore's command."

"Well done."

"Thank you, sir."

"Park, out."

He finished reading Chapter Ten of Rutan's *History of the Great Scouring*, a not quite Hegemony-approved tome, but one the current government hadn't yet suppressed, then placed his reader on the side table and let out a sigh. Once Task Force Kruzenshtern entered Hatshepsut orbit, events might no longer be under their control.

24

Aswan Trader rounded one last headland the following morning, and Mazaber, the leading city-state on Aksum's east coast, appeared before the Brethren's eyes. A sprawling port stuck on a narrow strip of flat ground between the shoreline and a curtain of craggy, volcanic hills, it sat across a broad bay opposite the ruins of the Mazaber that existed before the Great Scouring.

Dozens of ships either sat at anchor or were tied up alongside rickety, partially rotten wooden piers jutting out into the muddy water. Most were single-masted, with a few two-masted schooners among them, but none matched *Aswan Trader* for sheer size, even though the smallest faster-than-light starship in the Lyonesse Navy would dwarf her.

As they neared, the Brethren could make out more detail and what they saw left them wondering. The one and two-story buildings, for there were none taller, seemed only a step above wood and stone shantytown shacks, a far cry from Thebes' solid architecture with its clean lines. Where the latter seemed poised on the verge of progress, Mazaber gave off the appearance of ongoing decay which would soon see it slip further down the civilizational ladder.

"Doesn't look too impressive, right?" Fenrir asked as if he'd read Rianne's mind. "Wait until you're ashore. It gets worse. I wouldn't live here, and neither would any of my sailors, but they offer good barter items for the things we bring — precious metals, imperial artifacts, cured and preserved meats we can't obtain at home, grains, and wine. Surprisingly good stuff."

"Will you dock?"

"And pay their extortionate fees when I'm not carrying much as cargo? No. We'll anchor away from the rest and go ashore by boat."

"Why well away?" Horam asked.

"Discourages the bumboats and lets us see and hear thugs coming if they have a mind to plunder my ship. The Saqqarans aren't the only pirates in this part of the world. A few of those at anchor out there are merely part-time merchants who do more or less honest work when there's no easy Theban prey around." Fenrir spat over the rail. "Tried me once, they did. I made them understand *Aswan Trader* has teeth."

"I gather there's no government authority around here with the job of preventing piracy?"

A bitter laugh.

"There's no real government, period. Mazaber is run by the strongest criminal boss in the region, just like the other cities on Aksum's coasts. The Almighty only knows what happens inland because none of us do. The way I hear it, the moment the boss running things shows weakness, it's a free for all until the next boss takes charge. Can't rightly say it's any worse than our system.

We both throw out the bastards when their corruption becomes too noticeable. Around here, they simply make sure the former rulers can't stage a comeback." Fenrir ran an extended index finger across his throat. "If you'll excuse me, I need to get the sails furled just about now. I'd rather glide to our anchorage instead of using the engine because saving fuel can save lives. Sure, there's plenty available here, but it's muck that'll gum up our engines and no mistake. Stinks like a fish that's been dead two weeks."

Standing on one side, out of the sailors' way, the Brethren watched as the remaining spread was hauled in and furled, leaving *Aswan Trader* to shed her forward momentum until the shore no longer seemed to move by. At a shout from Fenrir, one of the bow anchors splashed into the water. A few tense moments passed as they waited for confirmation it had set correctly. The ship gently turned toward the mouth of the river entering Mazaber Bay beyond the town, pushed by the current into the same orientation as the other vessels. Then, all apparent movement ceased.

"Anchor set, Captain," the first officer called from his post by the anchor chains.

"Place the ship at harbor stations and prepare the launch." Fenrir rejoined the Brethren aft of the binnacle. "I trust you'll be armed because my people and I certainly will. Mazaber's current boss knows mugging traders is bad for business and thus bad for tax collection. But his uniformed goons sometimes keep their eyes closed in return for a cut of the take."

Horam let out an indelicate snort.

"How charming."

"It's that kind of place, Friar. I'm glad the Republic of Thebes is an island group in the middle of the ocean, more or less inaccessible to the Aksumites. With their sort as neighbors, we wouldn't be rebuilding industrial society. There's a reason the

Sterling engine isn't in widespread use, for example. Whenever we sell any around here, those engines are quickly stolen and eventually end up in the hands of a thug who can't figure out how they work and who ends up dismantling them for scrap metal."

He nodded at the Stirling engine-equipped launch, stowed on the deck, amidships. There, sailors were busily rigging the necessary tackles to hoist it overboard.

"Another thing you should know. We never leave our boats at the dock or pulled up on shore. My men will drop us off, then head out into deeper water and wait or return to the ship, depending on how the coxswain feels. A little beauty like our launch is just too tempting for a pirate who dreams of closing in on his prey independent of the wind." He turned and stared at the town and its dilapidated port. "You can be certain there are dozens of eyes watching us right now, wondering whether they can squeeze an extra few percent out of a rich, arrogant Theban or whether they can send a flotilla of boats in the middle of the night and help themselves."

Fenrir glanced back at them.

"Yes, my friends. This is a place the Almighty forgot. If your intention is sending a mission to civilize them, take a battalion of Lyonesse troopers with you, men like Friar Horam, who can kill pirates with a railgun at half a kilometer."

The latter scoffed.

"It would hardly take a battalion. A company, maybe, and of trained Friars, no more. It'll be a while before my old comrades show up to knock sense into the primitives."

"But they will show up." It was a statement, not a question.

"Yes, eventually," Rianne replied in a resigned tone.

"Good. Hatshepsut won't be fit for galactic life until Aksum learns the basics of civilized behavior."

Fenrir let his eye roam over his ship before watching the launch as his men gently swayed it over the port side rail and lowered it on *Aswan Trader*'s lee side, one sailor holding the bow rope and one the stern. Shortly after the launch vanished, a faint puff of smoke shot up from where she was last seen as her engine lit.

"If you're not ready to go ashore yet, may I suggest you prepare now and don't forget personal weapons?"

**

"Colonel, Sister, thank you for joining us."

Watanabe, sitting at the head of the conference room's oval table, waved at two empty chairs on his right when Torma and Ardrix entered. *Repulse*'s captain sat on the commodore's left while holographic representations of the task force's remaining captains, as well as the senior Ground Forces officer, Major Enzo Vinh, C Company, 1st Special Forces Regiment, took up the remaining spaces. Lieutenant Commander Yee, the cruiser's combat systems officer, stood by the wall-sized screen covering the forward bulkhead, waiting patiently to begin his briefing. When the Commission officers were seated, Watanabe nodded at Yee.

"Please go ahead, Commander."

"Thank you, sir." The primary display came to life with the image of a planet mostly covered by water. "This is Hatshepsut. What you're seeing is a composite of the ongoing scans performed by Task Force Kruzenshtern's five ships and what's in the historical database."

Torma and Ardrix exchanged a brief glance. Watanabe's people weren't wasting any time, considering the task force entered orbit only a few hours earlier.

"The roundish continent almost entirely in the northern hemisphere is called Sylt, where most of the planet's major settlements, including its capital, flourished back during imperial times. Our first orbital run shows nothing where cities once stood and no lights indicating human presence. The second continent, spread across the equator, is Aksum, where our target lies. Nothing remains of the major cities there either, but we can see settlements that aren't in the historical records." Yee turned his eyes on Torma. "For instance, the port your prisoner named as Mazaber sits across a broad bay from the long-vanished original city of the same name."

"Besides those two continents, we've identified several dense island groups." Pointers appeared on the display. "The Saqqara Islands are here, off Aksum's east coast. They once boasted several smaller settlements, which vanished with no visible replacements. The Western Isles, off Sylt's west coast, also appear depopulated. The biggest by square kilometers of surface, at the center of the planet's largest ocean, are the Theban Islands.

"Interestingly, they not only bear few visible scars, but the current settlements appear to be thriving. Where the historical records show minor fishing villages, we now see rather large towns, each with its own port and plenty of sailing vessels. The other major groups, the Hades Islands and the Lost Islands, never had a permanent human presence, which hasn't changed.

"As you can see, the ice caps are rather small, meaning the planet could be almost at the end of an ice age or beginning one. I suspect that if Hatshepsut's ice caps were like Wyvern's or Dordogne's, many, if not most of those islands would be mountain tops of small continents or single large islands, and the barrier islands around Aksum and Sylt part of their respective parent landmasses. That is the high-level overview. Did you want me to focus on something specific at this point, Commodore?"

Watanabe turned toward Torma. "It's your mission, Colonel."

"Understood, sir. With your permission, I'd like to focus visuals on Mazaber and the surroundings, so we can find the landing zone Jan Keter used, as well as the best route into town. I'm also curious about the Theban archipelago. If its development seems so different from the rest of the planet, we should investigate why."

"You're thinking outside intervention?"

"It is one possibility, sir. Due to the apparent lack of industrialization on Hatshepsut, the items we seized surely weren't manufactured in this star system. And that means someone other than Keter landed here in the recent past. Perhaps near Mazaber as well, but if our initial scans are correct and that isolated island group is prospering compared with other settlements, then it merits examining."

Watanabe nodded. "Anomalies attract attention."

"That's pretty much the core tenet of investigative procedures, sir. Besides, if I were looking for a secure foothold on a primitive world, nothing beats islands far from major landmasses."

"Then I think everyone here will pay closer attention to our anomalies, Colonel," the commodore replied in a dry yet amused tone. "Very well. Mazaber and Thebes will be the focus of our scans. Any thoughts about a landing party?"

"Sister Ardrix and I, along with Jan Keter, of course. And anyone you'd like to name, sir. Based on Keter's description of conditions in the Mazaber area, a troop of Special Forces soldiers should suffice. One or two teams will go with us. The rest will serve as force protection around our landing site. But I'll leave the final decision to their commanding officer." He nodded at the hologram of the Ground Forces commander.

"I'd prefer two troops in two shuttles, sir," the latter responded. "No one has ever complained of excessive protection, just as no one ever survived to complain about insufficient security in a potentially dangerous area."

"Point taken. Two troops it is."

"Then I'd like us ready for departure once we know all we can learn about Mazaber."

"Which won't take much longer, Colonel," Commander Yee said.

Watanabe stood.

"Then I'll leave you to it. Colonel Torma, I'd like a back brief once you've settled on a course of action everyone agrees with."

"Yes, sir."

With that, the commodore swept out of the conference room.

— 25 —

Mazaber stank. Badly. Even the gentle offshore breeze helping propel *Aswan Trader*'s motor launch toward the shingle beach couldn't keep a nauseating symphony composed of rotting seaweed, dead fish, animal and human feces, and much more from reaching the Brethrens' nostrils. Alcide and Lilith, raised in a city that never entirely lost basic sanitation, grimaced in horror.

"The Almighty must have forgotten this spot," the latter said in a hoarse voice, struggling to keep the miasma from polluting her airways.

Horam gave Lilith an amused smile.

"The Almighty forgets nothing. Those who live here, on the other hand, forgot more than simply basic technology, it seems."

Alcide turned to Rianne with an imploring air.

"On the day Prioress Hermina decides who will set up a new priory here, please let my name be at the bottom of the list."

"Your name will be where the Almighty wills it. Besides, in ten minutes, you won't notice the aroma anymore. It's amazing how humans can become inured to the worst things."

Horam clapped the younger man on the shoulder.

"Especially those who benefit from our sort of training, right?"

Before Alcide could reply, Fenrir asked, "Do you mind risking wet feet? Only, I'm looking at the pier, and I don't like the greedy little bastards ogling us as if we were a Sunday ham. It's harder to swarm us from the beach, and the launch will be away much faster."

Rianne gave him a shrug.

"Whatever you think is best, though I sense no danger."

"The beach it is then." Fenrir turned to his coxswain and gestured at a clear patch of shale a hundred meters east of the piers. "That should do."

"Aye, aye, Captain."

The small crowd that worried Fenrir began moving toward the beach when it became clear the launch would ground itself there. However, by the time it backed away from the murky shallows, having disgorged the Brethren, Fenrir, and two armed sailors with no more than damp shoe soles, the locals were still a good fifty meters distant. Once they noticed the seven newcomers were visibly armed, the group dispersed back into dark alleys between the waterfront godowns and taverns.

What little the Brethren glimpsed of them spoke of poverty and malnutrition — ragged clothes, bare feet, spindly limbs, matted hair. They could have been any age beneath the grime.

"Local urchins?" Horam asked.

"Don't let their small stature fool you, Friar. Those are vicious, albeit stunted adolescents and young adults, the result of awful food, worse hygiene, and either absent or uncaring parents. Allow them within arm's reach, and those shoulder bags of yours would be gone, cut off."

"Unfortunate children with no real chance at a decent life," Rianne said.

"Save your compassion for those they prey on, Sister. Maybe in a few years, or more likely decades, your Order can rescue the ones who remain after you've established a priory and convinced what passes for the local government it should cooperate with you rather than bleed you dry. But the current set of thugs in charge are more likely to enslave those they catch and shoot those they can't. The ones who end up as forced labor merely take longer to die."

Fenrir led them along a gravel road separating the town from the beach, eyed by idle citizens sitting in the shade of warehouse doors and tavern awnings. Of the urchins, no trace remained.

They eventually reached a warehouse larger and better maintained than the rest. The most significant difference between it and the others was the location. This godown sat squarely in front of the piers, at the corner of the shoreline road and a cobbled avenue cutting through the heart of Mazaber like a giant slash. The dark, sharp-ridged hills surrounding the town loomed beyond the avenue's far end and above the many buildings lining it on both sides.

"This is it, David Crimple's house of trade."

Horam looked for a sign, something naming the company or proprietor, but saw nothing above or beside any of the wooden doors, both small and large. Fenrir, who noticed his inspection, chuckled.

"Everyone who counts knows where Crimple holds court. His is one of the few mostly stone buildings, with a nice tile roof and real glass windows. You could say he's the commercial king of the town. Successive Mazaber bosses keep old Dave sweet because he can make or break even the biggest politically motivated criminal organization in these parts." Fenrir jerked a thumb over his shoulder. "This is where the richest man in town makes his profits."

The merchant captain pivoted on his heels and headed for a wooden door giving onto the street. He pushed it open and vanished, swallowed by the shadows, his sailors hard on his heels. After one quick glance at each other, Horam and Rianne followed suit, the two junior Brethren behind them.

The dry, earthy scent of old leather tickled Horam's nostrils as he entered the twilight of a space that was part office, part showroom, part museum. A broad counter cut off the back third of the high-ceilinged room. Filled with dusty desks, cabinets, and shelving, it felt more like an abandoned counting house than the customer-facing facet of Mazaber's biggest merchant lord.

Display cases lining the public two-thirds held books, artifacts that could only date back to imperial days, including relics none of the Brethren could identify at first glance. And they saw items that came from Lyonesse, almost assuredly via Theban ship masters looking for a bit of extra profit.

But what struck Horam and Rianne almost at once were other pieces of equally advanced manufacture which they knew had not passed through the Thebes Priory. Among them were gleaming metal hand tools, bladed weapons, cooking implements, and more. They saw no railguns, but neither was surprised. On a world where ordnance was primitive, anyone with power weapons could overthrow entire governments and advertising that fact didn't end well.

A wizened man, short, slight, and wrinkled, with wispy hair fringing his bald dome, appeared as if by magic behind the counter. His deep-set eyes took in the new arrivals, then he bowed.

"Captain Fenrir and party. Welcome. You're back in Mazaber much earlier than expected. I trust you bring interesting trade goods once more."

Fenrir returned the formal gesture.

"Mister Crimple. You honor us by your personal welcome. With me are four Brethren serving the Order of the Void, Sisters Rianne and Lilith as well as Friars Horam and Alcide."

Crimple turned his intense gaze on the Brethren as if looking for souls behind their stoic facades.

"I've heard legends about the Order of the Void. They say its votaries fled Hatshepsut during the catastrophe that made us the fallen race we are today, abandoning the faithful to Empress Dendera's genocidal retribution. I'm not sure I should welcome you. No offense, but around here, memories are long, even if lives aren't."

Rianne reached out with her mind to taste Crimple's emotions and see whether he was serious or merely looking for a reaction, perhaps as a form of opening move, the sort a shrewd trader would make out of instinct. But she couldn't sense much, if anything. Either Crimple exercised almost perfect control over his feelings, or he possessed none and was among that small percentage of humans who stood apart from the rest of the species, such as some of the worst criminals exiled to Lyonesse's Windy Isles prison complex. Like every Sister with a sensitive talent, Rianne spent a season in the Windies, working as a counselor and ministering to the republic's irredeemable so that she might experience humanity's most depraved minds and souls firsthand and develop ways of dealing with them.

"Members of the Order were being hunted and murdered in those days, Mister Crimple," she replied in an even tone. "Both sides in the rebellion scapegoated our predecessors and sought their deaths. Millions of Void Brethren perished through no fault of their own, while only a few found sanctuary far from imperial worlds. But we are back and once more working for the betterment of humanity."

Crimple squinted at her. "Perhaps. I suppose since Lars Fenrir is bringing me visitors instead of Theban goods that might fetch a good price, I should assume you come for answers rather than items for sale or barter. I'm a busy man, Sister, so speak your mind and leave."

She inclined her head.

"I shall. The advanced technology items Lars and his fellow captains are selling you these days were either manufactured by my people or by Thebans under our supervision."

Crimple let out a bark of laughter so dry it sounded like sandpaper on wood.

"You're star people, aren't you? Just like the one who came here with a load of items no one alive ever saw before and exchanged them for Theban goods and ancient imperial artifacts. He clearly didn't appreciate his merchandise's value, but that's not my problem, now is it? Let the buyer beware lest the seller plunders his pockets."

"What can you tell us about him?"

More laughter, but soft, almost mocking this time.

"What can you give me in exchange? Information has value."

"It certainly does." Rianne gave him a mysterious smile. Did she sense a glimmer of curiosity? Or even cupidity. Perhaps Crimple was merely one of the rare humans who could instinctively mask his feelings, a useful talent for a merchant or a gambler. She reached into her satchel and retrieved a fist-sized plastic cylinder.

"I offer you antibiotic pills, a true rarity on Hatshepsut beyond the Republic of Thebes."

"Antibiotics?" Crimple rolled the word around his mouth as if savoring it. "And what are those good for?"

"They cure routine bacterial infections often in one or two doses, and by the looks of Mazaber, such infections are probably quite common."

Horam grinned at the merchant.

"Bacterial infections cause gangrene in septic wounds, are at the origin of most sexually transmitted diseases, stomach problems, and all sorts of other nasty things. Considering folks probably fight and fornicate a lot around here, not to mention eat stuff that's well past its best before date, that little bottle in Sister Rianne's hand is worth more than the railguns you bought from the other star man."

Crimple cocked a skeptical eyebrow at the Friar.

"And how do I know that stuff really works?"

"Ask Captain Fenrir."

Without further prompting, the latter said, "This medicine has saved many a life and limb in Thebes, Mister Crimple. A lot of sailors injured at sea survived nasty infections thanks to its properties. And that included a few of mine who were wounded by pirates on the way back from Mazaber the last time."

The merchant let out a dismissive snort.

"You could be telling me a tall tale as well."

"We've been trading for how many years now? And in that time, did I ever try to cheat you?"

"If you've tried, I neither noticed, nor did you succeed," Crimple replied in a grudging tone, eyes narrowed as if he was evaluating Fenrir's past truthfulness.

"Besides, this is information we're talking about, not valuable goods. You have nothing to lose and everything to gain."

While Fenrir and Crimple debated the merits of her offer, Rianne gently nudged the latter's mind with thoughts of trust and friendship until he let out a long, exasperated sigh.

"Very well. How many doses are in that container?"

"Two hundred. Only the most advanced and most stubborn cases need more than one. But be warned, the medication does not confer immunity; it merely heals existing infections."

Rianne placed the container on the counter in front of Crimple, who snatched it up with surprising speed. She watched him figure out how it opened it with equal swiftness, then he peered inside.

"Please count them if you wish. You will find 200 capsules. We of the Void cheat no one and nothing, not even death."

Crimple glanced up at her through narrowed eyes as he replaced the lid.

"If you can't trust a Sister of the Void to deal honestly, then I suppose humanity is truly screwed. Very well." Crimple tucked the medication into one of his vest's capacious pockets and licked his lips. "My star man, then."

— 26 —

"He calls himself Jan Keter and is the captain of a faster-than-light merchant starship from something called the Hegemony. I tried to get him talking about it, but he was cagey. Wouldn't give me any place names, but from his answers, it sounded like something run by folks not much different from our rulers here in Mazaber, despots who control every damn thing and shoot those who dare disagree. Speaks understandable Anglic, by the way, not like the Saqqarans do nowadays. Said he was traveling through the old imperial wormhole network, whatever that is, looking for trade opportunities. I got the feeling he wasn't exactly on a trip approved by his government."

"Why?"

"Search me. He was nervous, sure. Alone on a fallen world, far from home, but there was something else bothering him."

Rianne mentally nodded at herself. Crimple must have a bit of the talent that allowed Friars, and especially Sisters, to keep their feelings hidden behind impenetrable walls, which was why she sensed little. Perhaps his abilities were strong enough that he might be a sort of minor truth-sayer, someone with an innate instinct for people. He wouldn't be the first wild talent she'd encountered. It would certainly explain how he became the most successful and feared merchant in Mazaber.

"One fine day," Crimple continued, "this Keter shows up in town riding a large, powered ground car, something no one ever saw before. Though I didn't manage a close enough inspection, I'd wager it was both armored and armed. Otherwise, a lone visitor wouldn't dare show up unannounced in what could be hostile territory."

"What did this car look like?"

He shrugged.

"A big black box on eight wheels, say four meters long, over two meters wide, and about the same in height. Made little noise. He stopped right outside my door, climbed through a side hatch that slammed shut behind him, and came in wearing a weapon somewhat like the town sentries' pistols on his hip."

"How did he figure you were the one to see instead of your competitors?"

An amused snort.

"He may come from off-planet, but he's a trader and knows the same tricks as Captain Fenrir and me. A port's most powerful merchant will always own the largest, best maintained, and most strongly built godown right by the main pier. There's a hierarchy, you see, and I'm the number one Mazaber merchant."

His tone was sufficiently matter-of-fact that Rianne knew he was making a simple statement, not boasting.

"Fair enough. What happened then?"

"He introduced himself, said he carried samples of advanced technology wares he was selling in his ground car, and would I like to examine them. So I followed him out, and he opened one side of his vehicle. It had a very fancy protection system, a sort of transparent, shimmering curtain. He could reach in and take stuff out. I couldn't. A lot of it wouldn't do much good around here without a power source. But what came with solar chargers interested me, especially the railguns.

"We dickered around for a long time. He'd ask so much for a dozen of that or that, and I'd counteroffer until we agreed. I'm sure you can imagine how it is. He was really interested in the items I bought from Theban merchants like my friend Lars Fenrir, medical instruments and tools that presumably come from your homeworld, so I sold him my entire stock. That, and a lot of ancient imperial artifacts. Keter left town in his wheeled monster and returned the next day with the trade goods. We exchanged, and that was it."

Rianne studied Crimple with an air that was half amused, half skeptical.

"Surely you sent someone to follow Keter out of town."

Another snort, this time resigned.

"Both times. The first day and when we concluded the deal. Keter landed a spacecraft in a valley about ten klicks south of town, where there are ancient ruins. Plenty of those around, most big enough for something like Captain Fenrir's ship and more. The craft was approximately six or seven times the size of his vehicle, and on both occasions, he drove it up a rear ramp. Both times as well, the thing jumped straight up into the sky with an eerie whine and vanished from sight within moments."

"You didn't try to seize it?"

A bark of laughter echoed across the room.

"Are you crazy, Sister? A visitor from the stars with advanced tech who goes around armed won't neglect his security. It would have been more than my men's life was worth. Besides, I figure I snagged the better part of the bargain, and if he's of a mind to return, I'll gladly deal with him again. Made a mint off his wares, I did, not least from Captain Fenrir."

"Can your men show us where he landed his shuttle?"

Crimple's wispy right eyebrow crept up.

"Is that what you call it? A shuttle? Yes, my men can do so, but they don't enjoy walking, and that means you're on the hook for renting transport."

"Which would be?"

"Argvags," Crimple replied, naming native, equine-equivalents with often nasty tempers and even more offensive odors. Thebans used them as plow animals on farms and not much else. "I figure taking an argvag cart is uncomfortable, and the round trip will take the rest of the day. Riding argvags is a lot faster, but even more uncomfortable. Your choice."

Rianne turned to Fenrir with a questioning glance.

"We ride," he replied without hesitation. "The beasts aren't as bad as that. I'm sure Mister Crimple will gladly rent us a herd for a price."

The latter nodded.

"One hundred gold Theban marks."

Fenrir winced theatrically but reached into his pocket and pulled out a purse from which he withdrew five coins.

"This goes on your tab, Sister."

"Naturally."

He placed the twenty mark pieces on the counter.

"There, you old pirate."

The coins vanished in the blink of an eye, swept up by Crimple.

"Can you show us the items you bought from Keter you've not sold yet?"

Crimple squinted at Rianne as if evaluating her request. Then he nodded and flipped up a section of the countertop.

"Follow me." He led them to a heavily barred door at the back of the room, where he fiddled with several locks before pushing it open. "My secure storeroom. I don't let just anyone in, but as I said if you can't trust Void Brethren…"

Sunlight streaming through several barred windows high up on two walls lit a grimy room lined with rickety wooden shelves. As they entered on Crimple's heels, the musty odor of partially decayed organic material assaulted their nostrils.

"There's not much left, you understand. Sitting on inventory won't make me rich."

"Any more railguns?" Fenrir asked. "Because if you're selling, I'm buying."

"Are you kidding me?" Crimple grimaced at him over one shoulder. "I couldn't get rid of the things fast enough once I realized my mistake. For one thing, the town's boss would have confiscated them if he'd found out. Ordinary citizens better armed than the government always ends in revolution. And for another, no one in his right mind wants the local enforcers equipped with off-world advanced weapons. Balance of power, right? So I sold them to you and your fellow Theban captains. Let your lovely republic deal with the problem."

Crimple walked over to a tarpaulin-covered pile of what looked like small crates, and Rianne realized the rotting canvas was responsible for the storeroom's unpleasant miasma. He flipped the tarp up, exposing slick, plasticized oblong boxes with Anglic letters and numbers printed on the sides.

"What are those?" Rianne asked.

"You tell me." Crimple lifted one of the boxes up onto a nearby shelf and stepped back. "Since I can't find a buyer, I'll make you a good price."

Rianne gestured at Horam, and the Friar stepped forward to examine it.

"May I open the container?"

"Sure."

Horam studied the box for a few seconds.

"Packaging doesn't seem much different from what we use back home. Simple but solid, proof against even the nastiest environments." He unlatched the cover, opened it, and peered inside. "No wonder you can't find a buyer, Mister Crimple. That looks like a portable fabricator."

"Which is what Keter called the damned device. Except it doesn't fabricate a thing."

"Of course not. You need a power source and input materials." Horam extracted a rectangular metal object from the packing materials and turned it in his hands, examining the various sides. He peered into the box once more. "Neither of which are included."

"And for that, Jan Keter owes me a good discount on his next offerings. If he ever darkens my door again, I'll be having a few words with him."

"How many of these did you buy?" Rianne asked.

"Three. Make me an offer for them, and maybe I won't rip your fellow off-worlder another orifice."

She and Horam exchanged a brief glance. Then Rianne reached into her bag and withdrew two plastic cylinders, each a different color but of the same shape as the antibiotic container now sitting in Crimple's vest pocket.

"The red jar contains two hundred doses of a powerful analgesic. If you suffer from joint pain, are hungover, or suffer from clogged sinuses, among other bodily aches, it'll do wonders. The blue jar contains medication that cures insomnia, also two hundred doses. One of those pills, and you sleep like a baby."

"That buys you two of the — what did he call them, fabricators?"

"And you'll sit on the third one forever? Consider that you can make a huge profit on the antibiotics, seeing as how you exchanged mere information for them."

Rianne concentrated another wave of positive emotions on Crimple's mind, and he nodded, scowling.

"Done. Take those things out of here, and I'll be happy. Any other off-world wonders you'd care to trade?"

She gave him a pleasant smile.

"Not now, but if you find the medication you bought useful, let one of the Theban captains know. Given the right conditions, we might set up an Order of the Void house in Mazaber, and you could enjoy direct access to those off-world wonders."

"I shall take it under advisement. So long as I enjoy a measure of exclusivity."

"Can we leave our purchases here while we scout out the location where Jan Keter landed his shuttle?" Horam asked.

Crimple shrugged.

"Sure. And I won't charge you extra. I suppose you'd like me to round up a herd of argvags and the men who followed Keter?"

Rianne beamed at him again.

"If you'd be so kind."

Less than an hour later, the landing party found itself bouncing in hard saddles strapped to four-legged creatures whose gait reminded the Brethren of nothing so much as a ship in a storm.

The argvags — whose long rubbery faces, floppy ears, and large, sparkly compound eyes made them resemble horses designed by a madman suffering from hallucinations — did have a distinct odor. But the Brethren no longer noticed it by the time they crossed Mazaber city limits.

Both of Crimple's men, wiry street toughs with mean, narrow faces, were taciturn to the point of mutism. One rode point while the other trailed the group. They were clearly used to argvags and sat easily in the high saddle, undismayed by the constant swaying.

Horam noted their watchful eyes and the way they held short-barreled shotguns across the saddle horn. When he'd asked the point man if they were expecting trouble, the latter merely grunted and said, "Can't be too careful out in the hills. If you carry weapons, keep them clear and ready."

As the sun rose higher in the sky, it became much warmer but no less humid, increasing their discomfort. After two weeks with a constant sea breeze keeping them cool, they'd almost forgotten Mazaber was near Hatshepsut's equator, just like Thebes, but didn't enjoy the latter's constant trade winds. The stifling heat eased a little when the ancient imperial road, still in excellent condition, took them into the tree-covered hill country.

Shortly after the midday hour, they emerged in a narrow valley whose center was curiously devoid of vegetation. As they moved forward, the cracked road became a broad, smooth surface, untouched by both war and time. Familiar markings etched into the tarmac caught their eyes, and a slow grin split Horam's face.

"Figures. That's an old landing strip. Those overgrown humps over on the far side must be ruins that were once part of a commercial or private complex. Dendera's killers probably decided it wasn't worth the ammunition expenditure, and this Keter character saw it clearly from orbit."

Rianne nodded in agreement.

"We really should do better surveys before landing on a fallen world. Otherwise, we'd know there was an intact strip south of Mazaber."

A shrug.

"Until the government authorizes satellite constellations for places without a Lyonesse security presence, there's only so much the Void Ships can do. How about we check out the ruins before heading back into town?"

— 27 —

"Crap." The sensor chief swung around and faced his captain, seated in the combat information center's command chair. "I'm picking up ships in Hatshepsut orbit, sir. Five of them, and they sure aren't merchants or Lyonesse Navy. No evidence they spotted us yet."

"We're as tight as a drum," the first officer said from his post on the bridge. "There's no way they can detect us, even at this range."

"I expected no less," Commander Al Jecks, captain of the Republic of Lyonesse Starship *Serenity*, replied in a dry tone. "But do you think now would be a good time to thank the Chief of the Naval Staff for ordering that Lyonesse ships exit hyperspace rigged for silent running at all times?"

The directive, issued a few years earlier, when Lyonesse ships began venturing beyond the Coalsack Sector, wasn't popular, mostly because no starships other than those bearing the double-headed Vanger's Condor emblem of the republic traveled that part of the galaxy. Going silent every time a ship dropped out of FTL seemed excessive for most spacers, officers, petty officers, and ratings alike.

"Consider me suitably chastised, Skipper," the first officer replied. "What's our plan?"

"Cruise in silent running at Hatshepsut's hyperlimit and watch until they leave. Heading back with the mission's supplies undelivered isn't an option until we've run out of loiter time."

"Which won't be for months."

"And we keep our passive sensors on them. Suppose there's another human civilization out there that recovered from the empire's collapse to the point of fielding FTL warships, or even worse, non-humans expanding into former imperial space. In that case, we should find out everything we can. Otherwise, HQ will scold us for being lackadaisical." Jecks paused for a few seconds. "And if anyone thinks it might be a good idea, no, we won't make contact. Not without permission from the CNS, and we're too far from the nearest subspace relay for a quick call home."

"I don't think we need to worry about non-humans, sir." The ship's combat systems officer pointed at a side display. "Those hulls are clearly based on imperial-era cruiser and frigate designs, though with enough differences to indicate they're not two-hundred-year-old survivors. The fifth is probably an armed transport, though it shares design characteristics with the others. The only markings I can make out are hull numbers, names, and a symbol that resembles nothing so much as a bird of sorts."

Jecks studied the side-by-side comparison of the intruders with images drawn from *Serenity*'s database, then checked the markings visible on the primary display.

"Definitely cousins of ours, and I'll venture that bird is a phoenix rising from the ashes. But what's their origin? And why are they here?" He turned his chair to the right. "Signals, see if you can pick up any radio chatter on the old imperial frequencies. Chances are good they're still in use, considering those ships look very much like pre-collapse technology."

The first officer let out a soft snort.

"At least our starship designs have advanced enough that the folks over in Hatshepsut orbit won't immediately identify us as human, and boy, will they get a shock if they ever try us on."

"Best if they don't identify us, period, Number One."

Serenity and the rest of her class were colloquially known as Void Ships because of their solitary voyages reconnoitering fallen star systems and linking the Order's scattered missions. But they bore little resemblance with the originals that sought refuge on Lyonesse long ago and were drafted into the nascent republic's tiny Navy. The size of a light cruiser, with advanced weaponry beyond anything the empire once fielded, the Lyonesse Navy armed transport *Serenity* was a match for any of the ships in orbit. But Lyonesse's best defense, despite her growing fleet of warships, was still anonymity, as decreed by the Defense Force's first chief of staff and subsequently the republic's second president, Admiral Jonas Morane.

"Roger that, Skipper, but do we at least warn the priory?"

Jecks shook his head.

"No. Neither we nor the priory can risk the intruders picking up a transmission. The Brethren will have to cope with any surprises on their own. I'm sure Sister Hermina has contingency plans in place and will hide the Lyonesse folks if ever off-worlders land in Thebes."

"I gotta say, Skipper, I don't enjoy feeling helpless like this. Those could be enemy ships between our people and us."

Serenity's captain knew the first officer spoke for the entire crew. Spacers crisscrossing the former imperial sectors in Void Ships quickly developed a protective attitude toward the Brethren who volunteered for mission duty on primitive worlds from which they might never return.

"Understood, but they knew what they were signing up for, and our primary obligation is protecting Lyonesse. As a wise man once said, the needs of the many outweigh the needs of the few."

The first officer snorted.

"That saying should be the Navy's motto."

"True." Jecks tapped his command chair's arm with his fingertips. "But who says they're enemy ships? We're all the descendants of those who survived the Retribution Fleet's wrath. Surely that makes us kin?"

"I don't know, Skipper. But the names on those hulls aren't friendly like ours or that of the other Void Ships. *Repulse*, *Reprisal*, *Dominator*, *Devastation*, and *Terror*? Kind of nasty sounding, like the old imperial nomenclature I read about in the history books. If nothing else, it makes me wonder what sort of Navy they serve."

"Either an aggressive one or a Navy wanting to seem so, I suppose."

**

"That's the place, Colonel." Jan Keter, Adam's apple bouncing nervously, nodded as he studied the image on the conference room's primary display. "An old imperial-era private landing strip. I didn't meet another soul in that area, but it's hot as Hades in the middle of the day."

"Why there?" Major Vinh asked.

Keter gave him a curious look.

"Because it's the only landing strip near a large settlement I could see from orbit, and because it's far enough from human habitation to see threats coming."

"And was it? Far enough?"

The former merchant spacer nodded.

"The only thing they did was follow me back from town, but since the creatures they rode couldn't keep up with my ground car, I was aboard my shuttle and secure by the time they arrived."

"How's the road?"

"Easily passable. Also from the imperial era. Mazaber itself, however." Keter screwed his face into an expression of sheer disgust. Something on the display attracted his gaze and he pointed at it. "Is that live?"

"Yes."

"Then the landing strip has visitors."

Everyone in the conference room turned to watch the video feed. Nine humans riding four-legged equine analogs were emerging from the shadows of a tree-covered pass between two jagged hills and were making their way toward the landing strip.

Vinh let out a soft grunt.

"Seems we're not the only ones interested in that particular spot."

"Perhaps they're just passing through," Ardrix suggested. "Isn't that another road headed south at the tarmac's far end?"

"It is. I guess we'll see soon enough, Sister."

The answer came quickly when the small caravan busied itself around ruins smothered by vegetation before heading back toward Mazaber.

"Why would those people be interested in the spot you chose as landing site?" Torma asked his prisoner.

Keter replied with a twitchy shrug. "I couldn't say, Colonel."

"Did this Crimple who sold you the items mention their provenance?"

"No. He called it a trade secret."

"Then we'll ask, and not quite as nicely as you," Vinh growled. "Anything else you can tell us about the area?"

"No, sir. Everything I know you know."

"Then if you don't mind, Colonel, I suggest we land at daybreak, local time, tomorrow morning."

Torma inclined his head.

"Agreed." He gestured at the bosun's mates guarding Keter. "Take the prisoner back to his cell."

Both snapped to attention and the senior of the two barked out, "Aye, aye, sir."

**

"Did you want to see Crimple again?" Fenrir asked once they dismissed the two men and their herd of argvags at the livery stable close to the town pier.

The late afternoon shadows of a sun reaching for the western horizon were painting Mazaber's streets with dark stripes. At the same time, a curious hush hung over the settlement, as if it went into suspended animation during the worst of the afternoon heat. Almost no one seemed up and about, not even the thieving urchins.

Rianne grimaced.

"No. We've uncovered everything we can, but Alcide and Lilith should pick up our purchases."

"Then I'll recall the boat while they do so, and we can be quit of this place." Fenrir looked around them as they walked down the cobblestone avenue toward the pier. "And not a moment too soon."

"Will you sail on the evening tide?"

Something about the Sister's tone caught Fenrir's attention.

"Why do you ask?"

"If I suggested we raise anchor the moment we're aboard, what would you say?"

"That for a mystic, you're remarkably sensible. I'd rather spend the night at sea than in this harbor, don't fear. And on a heading for the North Passage. The waters in between are safe enough for a ship sailing under moonlight only. No hidden reefs reach out far from shore in these parts." He gave her a searching glance. "May I ask why?"

"I can't tell you, and that's because I don't know myself. But the sooner we're away from here and just one more ship at sea, the better."

Horam gave Fenrir a pat on the shoulder.

"You can trust a Sister's intuition more than a politician's promises or a weather prognosticator's forecast, my friend. For what it's worth, I agree with her. Let's set sail for where the air is clear and healthy."

"You're paying for this charter, which makes you the boss."

He stepped out on the pier, facing his ship, and raised both arms over his head to make a large circle. Moments later, the launch appeared around the barquentine's hull, stack emitting puffs of smoke as it headed for shore.

With a nod of satisfaction, Fenrir pointed at the rocky beach to their right.

"Let's leave the same way we came, just in case."

They were aboard *Aswan Trader* within the hour, her launch back in its accustomed place amidships beneath a rapidly darkening tropical sky. By the time the last rays of the sun vanished behind purple hills marching in staggered rows across the western horizon, the barquentine was beating out of Mazaber Bay using her engine. Once clear of the headland, Fenrir aimed her prow north-north-east on a course that would take them to the North Passage.

That night, Rianne contacted the priory on the shortwave radio and told Sister Hermina what they learned.

**

Colonel Torma and Sister Ardrix — both wearing battledress with combat harness, visored helmets, and in the former's case, a holstered blaster at the hip — entered *Repulse*'s hangar deck. There Jan Keter, flanked by two of the cruiser's Marines in combat armor, waited by the aft ramp of a dropship prepared for departure. Both troopers snapped to attention and saluted while the shuttle's pilot, a Navy noncom in battledress, appeared at the top of the ramp.

"Petty Officer Klaasen, sir. Everything is ready. The dropships with Marines from the 1st Special Forces have just launched from *Terror* and are trailing *Repulse*, waiting for us."

"Then let's get to it."

After making sure his passengers were strapped in correctly, Klassen vanished through the door to the flight deck, and moments later, the ramp lifted, cutting them off. Torma could see red warning lights strobe through the portholes on each side as the hangar deck's inner airlocks slammed shut. Then, the space doors opened, leaving a shimmering force field in their wake to keep the deck pressurized, and their shuttle began moving.

Once they were free of the cruiser, the two dropships carrying Major Vinh's Marines flanked them, and the flight began its lazy spiral down into Hatshepsut's atmosphere, bound for the abandoned landing strip south of Mazaber. Meanwhile, dawn spread across the Saqqara Islands and over the Aksum Sea, where a three-masted ship sailed north at best speed.

—28—

Shortly after sunrise, Friar Horam came on deck and greeted the quartermaster at the wheel before taking his usual spot by the taffrail so he could watch the coast of Aksum slide by. Mazaber was already well beyond the horizon after a night under full sail, and this part of the coast had no settlements, leaving him with a view of ragged shorelines and rough beaches.

As he lazily scanned the western sky, a trio of dots caught his eye, and he studied them intently. After a few moments, the former Marine decided their movements were too regular and too much in unison for native avian species, and he walked over to the binnacle.

"Can I borrow the bring them near, Padraig?"

The quartermaster nodded.

"Knock yourself out, Friar."

Horam fished the collapsible telescope from its slot and pulled it to full length as he walked over to the portside mizzenmast shrouds and used the taut rope to steady the burnished copper and glass instrument as he searched. After zeroing in on one of the dots, he studied it intently, and though it was too far for details, he recognized it as a shuttlecraft of some sort.

"Good morning, Horam. Are you looking at something interesting?" Rianne, who'd emerged from the aft stairs, joined him.

"Good morning to you as well, Sister, and yes, your premonition last night was spot on. See those three tiny dots a hand-span above the horizon?"

A few seconds later, "Seen."

"I make them as three unidentified shuttles, and I give you one guess where they're headed."

"Mazaber, or rather the landing strip south of town."

"It's the only plausible explanation. They can't be ours since ours wouldn't land anywhere other than Thebes until we set up new houses elsewhere on the planet. Nor can I think of a reason why they might be looking for us, not when we have shortwave radios for contact with the priory."

Rianne nodded.

"Could they belong to this mysterious Hegemony with the hard-nosed, autocratic regime? I'll bet the Lyonesse Abbey-manufactured items Keter brought home sent them on the same mission as us. Like us, they're here to discover who else in the galaxy travels the former imperial wormhole network aboard FTL-capable starships two hundred years after the Retribution Fleet scoured civilization from most human worlds."

Horam lowered the telescope and carefully slid its tubes back into each other.

"Did we leave in time to avoid complications, or should we have stayed and greeted them as long-lost cousins?" He sounded dubious about the latter option.

"Definitely the first, though if they interrogate Crimple, they'll know off-worlders are on a ship that left yesterday, headed for an island archipelago where they've established a beachhead of sorts."

The Friar grimaced.

"I suggest you switch on one of the shortwave radio sets and warn Hermina that we have company from who knows where."

"I'll do so right away."

While Horam returned the scope to its place, Rianne hurried below deck. She returned a few minutes later wearing a grim expression.

"I can't raise the priory." She glanced at the distant shoreline. "Did they land yet?"

"Probably, or if not, they're on final approach."

"Should I keep on with the radio?"

Horam nodded.

"Let's try every thirty minutes, alternating between the sets. We might get lucky. Otherwise, it'll have to wait until after sunset when conditions are more favorable."

"By then, it could be too late."

"For whom? Us, or the priory?"

"Either? Both? If Crimple talks, he'll surely describe *Aswan Trader* and tell them about our last known heading. There can't be many three-masted ships in this area. We certainly didn't see any in Mazaber Bay. Let's warn Fenrir and see if he has any ideas on how we could disappear from view in the next few hours." Rianne saw movement behind the Friar. "And here he is."

They quickly brought Fenrir up to date, and when Horam fell silent, he asked, "Why do you automatically assume these visitors present a danger?"

Rianne let a quick grimace flit across her face.

"Gut feeling based on what Crimple told us. Something calling itself a hegemony isn't interested in anything else than dominating and ruling others. Besides, there's the description of it from Keter. It doesn't sound like a nice place."

Fenrir cocked an eyebrow.

"And your Lyonesse is different? Aren't you here to pave the way for your own interstellar hegemony?"

"Certainly not. The Republic of Lyonesse is founded on the principle of free association. Each member star system has equal representation on the councils of state and an equal voice in matters affecting them. If a united, rebuilt Hatshepsut declines membership, we will leave her to govern herself freely and without interference from Lyonesse, though we will offer alliances and trade treaties."

Aswan Trader's master let out a soft grunt.

"Lofty ideals. The old empire was founded on lofty ideals as well, or so I heard. We know how that turned out. But fine, you think we should avoid contact with whoever is now orbiting this planet," he pointed a finger at the clear blue sky, "and has sent a landing party to Mazaber. Why would they look for us in particular?"

"Because Crimple will tell them about the Brethren who visited yesterday. Were I in their position, I would search for these other off-worlders traveling in a slow, waterborne ship."

"Would it be so bad if they found you?"

"That depends on who and what they are. However, I have a bad feeling about this situation, and my instincts tell me we should do everything possible to evade any search."

Fenrir gestured at the open water surrounding the ship.

"As you can see, hiding a three-masted barquentine from shuttles flying over this sea is rather impossible."

Horam jerked his chin toward the small bumps rising above the eastern horizon.

"How about a nice little inlet over there?"

"The Saqqara Islands? Are you mad?" When Horam replied with a half shrug, Fenrir said, "Our charts of the islands anywhere other than extensively used passages are dangerously blank. Plus, there's the minor matter of half-crazed barbarian tribes like those we met in the Central Passage. Besides, hiding a big girl like *Aswan Trader* can't be done by simply sailing her into a small inlet and hoping she won't be noticed."

"In that case, put us ashore with the launch. If the off-worlders catch up with you, give them false coordinates. We'll figure things out."

"The Almighty help me, a mad Friar. That's the last thing I need." Fenrir raised his eyes to the heavens and sighed. "If I leave you on one of the Saqqaras, your prioress will turn my guts into banjo strings, and I rather like my digestive system as it is. It may not seem so, but she scares most of us sea captains. Very well. Let me look at my charts and see if I can find a way of assuaging your fears while keeping my hull intact."

With that, Fenrir vanished below deck, headed for his cabin, where he carried out most of his navigational calculations.

**

Torma watched Major Vinh's troopers, armed and armored, secure the landing strip before driving a pair of sleek, menacing black combat cars down their dropship ramps. The vehicles, propelled by eight wheels almost Torma's height, were the Ground Forces' standard armored personnel carriers and would protect passengers against anything the inhabitants of this planet might throw at them.

Equally, the remote weapons station, inside a low turret on top of the car's sloped hull, was built around a twenty-five-millimeter plasma gun, which could lay waste to Mazaber in a matter of minutes. And both vehicles, like the Marines, carried nothing but live ammunition.

Moments after the cars vanished from view, Petty Officer Klaasen, at an unheard signal, dropped his craft's ramp as well. He poked his head through the flight deck door.

"You're clear to exit, Colonel."

Ardrix and Torma unfastened their safety harnesses and stood, the latter nodding at Keter and his armored escort.

"Let's go."

When they emerged into the morning sunshine, Major Vinh, trailed by his wingman, walked over from where he'd been speaking with his company sergeant major.

"The area is secure, sir. If you climb aboard the combat car on the right, we can head into Mazaber straightaway." He pointed at the vehicles waiting on the cracked roadway, facing north, partially hidden by long grasses gently swaying in the morning breeze.

"Thank you."

One of Vinh's men helped them settle into the troop compartment, aft of the turret shaft, and the remaining seats filled with Marines from the platoon tasked with close protection.

Moments later, ramps and hatches slammed shut, and the little convoy moved off, leaving the other platoon to guard their shuttles under the sergeant major's gimlet eye.

Torma, eyes glued to the displays feeding real-time views of the surroundings to those in the troop compartment, watched the hill country zip by and was impressed with the speed at which they reached the city's outskirts. There, they slowed to almost a walking pace, in case their approach startled the inhabitants enough to cause an unfortunate road accident. Torma was pleased when he recognized the principal buildings they'd mapped out from Task Force Kruzenshtern's orbital scans and soon spotted the pier at the end of the central avenue a few hundred meters ahead.

Keter saw it as well, and he pointed at a corner building on the forward display.

"That there is David Crimple's godown, Colonel."

"Seen."

Within moments, the two cars parked in front of the place and disgorged a dozen Marines who formed a security perimeter under the astonished eyes of a dozen or so Mazaberites. Some of them were no doubt wondering whether they were still drunk from the night before and hallucinating. Onlookers kept a healthy distance, instinctively knowing these strange creatures were heavily armed and dangerous.

When Vinh was satisfied there weren't facing any dangers, he allowed Torma, Ardrix, and Keter with his escort to disembark and sent a pair of Marines through the godown's front door. Moments later, a loud raspy voice, half-outraged, half-shocked, and speaking easily understood Anglic, reached Torma's ears, demanding they tell him who they were and what they were playing at.

"Crimple," Keter murmured. "I'd recognize that snarl anywhere."

"How about you introduce us." Torma glanced at Vinh, who gave them the go-ahead with a nod.

A few steps took them into a sizeable musty space with dust motes dancing in the sunbeams coming through high, barred windows.

"What is this?" A wizened man with a surly expression stared at them from behind a counter bisecting the room. "Off-worlder week or something?"

Then he recognized Keter.

"You. How dare you come back here with an armed escort? Will your toughs rob me clean of everything I own this time?"

"Mister Crimple, I presume?" Torma stopped three paces in front of the counter. "We're here for information, not to steal your possessions."

A surly look crossed the merchant's face.

"And another one. This really isn't my day, week, or month. And what will you offer me for that information?"

"Let me introduce myself. My name is Crevan Torma, and I'm a senior official in the Hegemony government. This is my aide, Sister Ardrix of the Order of the Void. Mister Keter is in my custody and helping us solve a minor mystery. The Marines here and outside are merely there for our safety, nothing more."

Crimple's eyes narrowed, and Ardrix knew, without touching his mind, that he'd made the connection.

"You want to know about the provenance of the items I sold to Keter, right?"

Torma nodded. "Indeed."

"Funny, the last bunch of off-worlders that came through here wanted to know about the provenance of the items I bought from

Keter. You folks should get together and compare notes rather than bother honest merchants making a lousy living in a rotten seaport."

"And these off-worlders were?"

Crimple's eyes gleamed with cunning, and he smiled.

"People who paid for information, and they did so handsomely, with off-world items that'll fetch a good price. Make me an offer."

— 29 —

The demand caught Torma, with whom no one ever dared negotiate, by surprise and Crimple's smile widened at his blank expression.

"What I know is obviously of great value to you, Mister Torma, otherwise you wouldn't have come all the way from your homeworld to speak with me. I'm a trader. I trade items of value for other items of value."

"What did the others offer you?" Ardrix asked, mental fingers brushing Crimple's mind with thoughts of trust and friendship.

"That too is information, Sister. But let me tell you this for free. You sure as hell don't dress like the Brethren who were here yesterday. They didn't look like soldiers."

"Brethren? From the old Order of the Void?"

For the first time in as long as he could remember, Torma heard genuine surprise in Ardrix's voice.

Crimple tapped the side of his nose with an extended index finger and winked at her.

"They didn't seem old to me. And if your boss makes me a friendly offer, I can tell you more."

"You might want to back off on that, Crimple," Keter said in a somewhat strangled tone. "These two know ways of making people talk no one should experience. Tell Colonel Torma what he wants, and he'll leave without giving you an indelible memory of things that should stay deeply buried."

"Are you speaking from firsthand knowledge?"

Keter nodded nervously.

"The Colonel's people arrested and interrogated me not long after I landed back home. They do things to your mind in his organization, terrible things, the sort that make sure you tell him everything."

Crimple turned his eyes back on Torma and Ardrix, and the latter nodded.

"We'd rather not use those techniques, but if you won't cooperate…"

After a moment of thought, Torma reached into one of his combat harness pouches, pulled out a pair of compact ration packs, the sort landing parties carry in case, and placed them on the counter.

"Food that will last for years. The only thing you need is water, and not even potable at that. It includes a filter capable of removing any contaminant. They're convenient in an emergency." He glanced at Ardrix and eyed her pouch. She retrieved her ration packs and placed them next to Torma's. "Four packs. That should buy us answers."

Crimple picked one up and turned it in his hand, studying the markings.

"I guess it's like what the others gave me, something I need to take on trust. What else can you offer?"

Ardrix reached into his mind and projected an image of Crimple writhing in agony. The man took a step back, fear writ large on his face.

"What the—"

"I suggest you accept our offer, Mister Crimple. This is as good as it gets."

Her voice was so soft, so gentle, so at odds with her words that Crimple's confusion grew. She reached in again and smoothed the ripples of his disturbed thoughts, leaving him with nothing but the faint echo of a sensation he might have imagined.

"Besides, you're giving something intangible, which has no value for anyone other than us, and receiving items you can use or sell. I see no downside for you."

"Okay, okay. That's what the other Void Brethren said as well. You must learn the same negotiating techniques in school," he replied in a querulous tone to cover his confusion and recounted everything he'd told Rianne and Horam the previous day.

When he fell silent, Ardrix said, in a tone of wonder, "So there's an old Order priory in Thebes, Brethren we'd thought lost these two hundred years. And they come from a world called Lyonesse?"

Crimple nodded. "That's what the Theban ship captains say."

She turned to Torma. "The name Lyonesse would explain the second letter L in the abbey mark on the surgical instruments, but I've never heard of the planet."

"I'll tell you what, though," Crimple said, "that Order mission in the Thebes archipelago has to be a beachhead. The Brethren are spreading advanced medicines and technology for free, to the point where merchant captains simply sell it off in Aksum ports, knowing they'll get more. The Sister in charge of yesterday's delegation gave me antibiotics in exchange for information and several medicines for the merchandise from Keter I couldn't sell. Anyone with a bit of cunning will tell you that's what sneaky invaders do. Make you dependent on them. As they say in the back alleys, the first taste is free."

"And this delegation you saw yesterday, where did it go?"

He shrugged.

"I presume they went home, back to Thebes. Captain Fenrir didn't offer trade goods, which means he likely came here in ballast, for the Brethrens' sake."

"In an ocean-going ship, I presume?" Torma asked.

"Yes. A three-masted barquentine by the name *Aswan Trader*. She's a fine ship, with a Stirling engine to power and propel her as necessary. The damn Thebans will end up owning the planet thanks to those off-world Void people."

"Can you show us the medication they traded?"

A scowl briefly darkened Crimple's face.

"You'll not steal them, will you?"

Ardrix reached into a harness pouch and pulled out a small case.

"These are field tools. I offer the kit for one dose of each medication."

She placed the case on the counter and waited as Crimple picked it up, figured out the opening mechanism, and examined the contents.

"Done." He produced the vials, opened them one at a time, and placed a single capsule in front of the Sister. "We'll make a trader out of you yet. Your colonel, maybe not so much."

"What direction did their ship take?" Torma asked after Ardrix retrieved the medication samples.

"They were heading north-north-east at sunset, but that doesn't signify. Theban ships use the Central Passage through the Saqqara

Islands, and it's slightly to the south of here. Using the North Passage adds at least five days. If you're after *Aswan Trader*, the Central Passage is your best bet."

"Can you show us on a map?"

Crimple let out a bark of laughter.

"I can't read a damn map to save my life. The only thing I know is that you'll find the Central Passage approximately two days' sailing from here. More than that, you'll need to see for yourself."

Torma turned his head toward Ardrix.

"Anything else we should ask Mister Crimple?"

"No. He told us what we needed. The old Order Brethren should be the subjects of our next investigation."

"In that case, Mister Crimple, enjoy the rest of your day and thank you." Torma inclined his head, then turned on his heels and headed for the door.

Major Vinh, waiting just outside, asked, "What's next, sir?"

"Back to the shuttles. I need a secure link with the commodore. We face a few hard and probably delicate decisions."

"Yes, sir. In that case, please climb back into your car." Once they'd done so, he raised his right arm, index finger extended, and twirled it in a circular motion. "Mount up."

Thirty minutes later, Torma sat in the dropship flight deck's jump seat and waited as Petty Officer Klaasen established a link with *Repulse*. He faced a situation beyond his experience and training and was far from sure of what should happen next. That his mission succeeded beyond anyone's wildest dreams didn't even register. The biggest question concerned next steps, both to deal with the information that a star system called Lyonesse established an old Order of the Void priory on Hatshepsut and what might happen once this Lyonesse discovers the existence of the Wyvern Hegemony.

When Watanabe's face finally materialized on the flight deck's primary display, Torma steeled himself.

"What's the word, Colonel?"

"We face a problem, sir. One that could transcend both our best and worst expectations." Torma recounted the conversation with Crimple almost word for word before laying bare the issue that faced them both. "At this point, we can be reasonably confident that these people from Lyonesse know about the Hegemony's existence thanks to Jan Keter—"

Watanabe turned his head to one side and raised a hand.

"Keep that thought for the moment, Colonel. We found a single mention of Lyonesse in the database. It was, apparently, a little imperial colony, part of the Coalsack Viceroyalty, though so distant from the sector capital, Yotai, it existed apart from the empire for all intents and purposes, at the far end of a wormhole cul-de-sac."

"Which means it could have survived the collapse more or less intact."

"And is now carrying out its own version of the Oath of Reunification. Please continue."

"As I was saying, agents of Lyonesse on Hatshepsut, members of the old Order of the Void, now know about the Hegemony. But chances are good that knowledge hasn't left the planet, meaning their superiors remain unaware. We can either allow them to inform what is probably a technologically superior polity with expansionist goals of our existence or make sure the results of Keter's unfortunate visit are quashed. But I do not consider myself competent to make such a decision."

Watanabe studied Torma for a few seconds.

"You mean we either leave with what we gleaned so far and hope for the best or erase the traces of our and Keter's passage. The latter implies razing Mazaber, sinking the ship that carried the Lyonesse Brethren there, and seizing or killing the entire Lyonesse mission. Perhaps even destroying this Republic of Thebes, which is hosting said mission. That's a lot of dead humans, Colonel. And if Thebes is the center of Hatshepsut's rebirth as part of a long-term plan, then liquidating it will arrest progress, if not send the planet spiraling backward. Either will leave the Hegemony with a greater mess to clean up in the future, if we finally expand and absorb this star system."

"In a nutshell, yes, sir. I'm no fan of mass murder, but my oath to protect the Hegemony is absolute."

"As is mine." Watanabe's jaw muscles worked as he chewed on the dilemma Torma placed at his feet. "How about a compromise? We don't engage in wholesale slaughter, but we round up everyone from Lyonesse and bring them home with us for questioning and to wake up our Ruling Council. Perhaps the Regent will reaffirm the Oath of Reunification and put some teeth behind it."

Torma gave him a rueful look.

"I was hoping you'd consider something of the sort, sir. I'm not an advocate for mass murder, no matter what people might think of us Commission officers."

"And I'm glad you didn't disappoint me by proposing our own small-scale version of the Great Scouring. It would have been a foul way of laying the foundations for our rebirth."

"That it would."

"Let me see if we can track down this surface ship you mentioned, based on the last twenty-four hours of sensor scans. I assume you'd prefer leading the raid on the priory in Thebes?"

"Yes, sir."

"Then we'll intensify our scans of the area and see if we can figure where it's located."

"Scan for low-level power source emissions, Commodore. I doubt this mission will have gone fully native, not if the goal is elevating Thebes as the center of a new planetary government beholden to Lyonesse."

"What will you do in the meantime? Rejoin us in orbit?"

Torma shook his head.

"There's no point. Once we're sure of our targets, we'll go there directly from here. This disused landing strip will do fine as a temporary operating base."

"All right, if there's nothing else?" Watanabe cocked a questioning eyebrow at Torma.

"No, sir."

"*Repulse*, out."

Torma found Ardrix chatting with Major Vinh in the command dropship's shade and informed them of his intentions. Vinh gave him a quick nod, then left to tell his people.

"What will you do with Keter?" Ardrix asked in a low tone so their prisoner, sitting inside the shuttle with his escort, couldn't overhear. "Leave him on this strip or near Mazaber and let him find his own way?"

Torma allowed himself a grimace.

"Considering his only crime is one we're committing ourselves, I think it's too harsh a punishment. You saw Mazaber. I wouldn't wish life there on anyone."

"Thebes, then?"

"A better place, no doubt, if they have access to more advanced technology, but that would mean people from Lyonesse will eventually question Keter about everything he knows. I'm afraid he's coming home with us. I'll see that he's spared execution, and perhaps once the Ruling Council learns of our expedition, I can quietly release him in what will probably be a brouhaha of epic proportions."

She smiled at her superior.

"You're showing surprising compassion, Crevan."

"Perhaps this trek has opened my eyes and thus my mind to possibilities few back home even dream of. That's bound to change someone's outlook on things, including what they've done to support a state actively rejecting those same possibilities." He gave her a crooked grin. "And to be honest, spending weeks aboard a Navy ship, taking my meals with *Repulse*'s officers, sitting at Commodore Watanabe's table, socializing with his command team, and living among the crew has changed my outlook. They would deeply disapprove of my stranding a Hegemony citizen on this primitive planet instead of ensuring his safety back home, and for a reason I can't quite explain, their good opinion of me matters."

"You're experiencing a spurt of spiritual awakening, my friend, and from that comes personal growth. It pleases me more than you might imagine."

— 30 —

The tension aboard *Aswan Trader* seemed like a living entity hovering over them as Fenrir steered her into a narrow fjord-like inlet between two jagged islands covered in dense vegetation. Everyone aboard stood to.

Fenrir had stationed half a dozen sailors in the bow and foremast top looking for signs of shoals that could puncture the barquentine's hull while the rest, Brethren included, scanned the shores for Saqqaran pirates. Everyone was armed with Horam and his sharpshooters carrying the precious railguns.

They'd been moving under engine power only since Fenrir decided on a hiding place, the topmasts and sails stricken below, leaving her strangely bare. But as he'd remarked when his first mate made a comment, they might as well get used to it. The days of sail would eventually end as Thebes refined engine technology with Lyonesse's help.

The surrounding air was still and the heat more stifling than ever. Yet, the sounds of countless native life forms trilling, snapping, chuckling, and otherwise communicating with each other provided a measure of reassurance that no humans waited in ambush.

Finally, Fenrir disengaged the propeller and signaled his first mate he should stand by with the anchor. The instant forward motion ceased, he raised his balled fist.

A loud splash silenced the wildlife, though the crew and passengers remained watchful until the usual sounds of a busy jungle reached their ears once more.

"This is as good as it gets," Fenrir said in a soft tone pitched for Rianne's ears. "I don't think we'll find any true overhead cover, but they'll only see us if they pass directly above this inlet."

"Make sure you dampen the Stirling engine, so it doesn't look like a big heat flare on any infrared sensors." When Fenrir gave her a blank stare, she smiled. "If the Hegemony has starships, it certainly can detect heat signatures that differ from background emissions. Perhaps Horam can explain in greater detail once we're settled in."

Fenrir let out a sigh, shaking his head.

"All this technology. It's enough to give an honest sailor a brain cramp. Now, please excuse me while I discuss the guard roster with my first mate."

"Make sure everyone understands if off-worlders show up, we surrender without firing a shot," Horam warned. "They'll be better armed, likely armored, and supported by their dropships' heavy weapons."

"No worries. We're not suicidal."

**

Petty Officer Klaasen stuck his head out of the shuttle, eyes searching for Torma. One of the troopers noticed him and ambled over, raising his helmet visor.

"Are you looking for someone, PO?"

"The colonel. *Repulse* is on the secure link with our search results, and I'd rather not break radio silence by using the company push."

"Hang on. Last I saw, he, my boss, and Sister Ardrix were together." The trooper jogged across the landing zone and vanished behind one of the two other dropships.

Less than a minute later, Torma, Ardrix, and Vinh appeared and hurried over.

"I understand *Repulse* is calling?" Torma asked when they were within earshot.

"Flag CIC, Colonel. They have data on our next two targets."

Klaasen led them through the passenger compartment and into the flight deck, which felt a bit crowded with four, but both Ardrix and Vinh needed to hear this. He slipped into his seat and touched the controls.

"*Repulse,* this is command ship Fury. I have the Niner."

Moments later, the flight deck's primary display lit up with the Task Force Kruzenshtern chief of staff's face.

"Colonel, I'm sending you the results of our latest scans. Once you've digested it, the commodore would like a back brief. If you're ready, I'll give you a quick verbal report."

"Ready."

"First, the surface vessel. We found a last known position based on scans of the area taken earlier today but cannot detect it anymore. We suspect the people aboard saw us when we were on final approach this morning and made for the shore where they found shelter. They can only be along a limited stretch of coast, either on the Aksum side or among the Saqqara Islands. The latter is more likely because of its numerous fjords and inlets. Our sensors are still looking. You should see the latest results and our estimate of where she could be hiding in the command ship's database by now."

Torma inclined his head.

"Thank you."

"We're much clearer on the situation in Thebes." An aerial view of a port city replaced the chief of staff. "There's a strong power emissions source coming from the structure south of town, on a relatively tall hill. We think it could be where the old Order established a priory during the imperial rule. It is the strongest source on the planet and indicates someone is operating at an advanced level of technology."

"The Lyonesse Mission," Ardrix said.

"That's what we figure, Sister. A high-tech node on a low-tech planet is the sort of anomaly we're looking for. Since they aren't taking much care to hide their emissions, we think their people on the ship we seek can't communicate with them, which means they likely have no inkling of our presence on this planet."

Major Vinh let out a soft grunt.

"An unsuspecting target means perfect conditions for a quick in-and-out raid."

"Indeed," the chief of staff replied. "It's late afternoon there at the moment, which means you can easily arrange for a strike after dark."

A grin played on the Special Forces officer's lips.

"Even better."

"It still gets better than that, Major. There's a cleared area behind the priory, which I'm marking in red." A red square appeared on the aerial image. "It is of a size and shape that suggests they use this as a shuttle pad. An outpost requires regular resupply of those items that can't be procured locally, and I daresay the list of such items is probably quite long. Based on our calculations, there's room for at least two dropships, perhaps even three. The intelligence on this target is now in the command ship's database as well. Any questions?"

Torma glanced at Ardrix and Vinh in turn, but both shook their heads.

"Let us study what you sent and figure out a plan of action. If we need more information, I'll call. Otherwise, the next time you hear from us will be to brief the commodore."

"And the surface ship?"

"Unless the commodore decides otherwise, I think we should keep looking but consider it a target of opportunity. Seizing the Lyonesse Brethren in Thebes is our primary aim."

"Understood, Colonel."

"Torma, out." He glanced at Vinh. "It's your show, Major. I'm merely the passenger who'll bear the blame if things go sideways, no more. Take the time you need. Afterward, we can discuss options at leisure."

"It won't take long, sir. We're not going in against heavy opposition. Land a platoon along with your ship, surround the priory, and enter. I doubt anyone will fight back, which leaves separating the Lyonesse folks from any locals who might be working with them." Vinh glanced at Ardrix. "Sister?"

"A simple task. Our basic training has not changed much over the centuries. I expect we can recognize each other because of it. If any try to hide, I'll find them."

"What if they resist, Colonel?"

Ardrix raised a hand.

"They won't. If I know my kind, even a branch that split off two centuries ago, their curiosity will overcome their reticence. That and concern we might harm others to pressure them, but please keep the latter option in reserve until I say so."

"As you say, Sister. Should we arrange our arrival for a specific time?"

"They'll likely keep the same canonical hours as we, which means they'll be abed after compline, except for those working the night shift, and that, at least in our houses, is twenty-one hundred hours. So perhaps close to midnight local time would be good."

Vinh frowned.

"What is compline?"

"We observe several services a day, and compline is the one where Brethren gather in the Chapter House one last time before bed."

"Which means they'll all be together. Perhaps we could determine when it's twenty-one hundred hours local in Thebes and strike at that time."

Ardrix seemed taken aback by the suggestion they invade a priory of the Order, even the old one, during a sacred service.

"Look, Sister. Anything that makes our task easier means fewer chances of folks getting hurt." When she nodded, he said, "May I suggest we reopen the link with *Repulse* and see if they can pinpoint both the Chapter House's location and confirm the local time?"

**

"After the excitement of attempting to vanish, this is a bit anticlimactic," Fenrir remarked as he joined Rianne at the taffrail. "Although I can't remember the last time I was this soaked with sweat. Give me the breeze of the open sea over this stuffy, still air."

"No arguments here. Still, it could be worse. The local version of insects could have developed a taste for humans and be eating us alive right now."

"True. Any idea how long we should hide?"

Rianne gave him a helpless shrug.

"I discussed it with Horam earlier, and we really don't know. It depends on how persistent they are. If they're genuinely interested in us, their sensors will continuously watch the Saqqara Sea, which means they might well catch us leaving this inlet."

"Did you warn your superiors in Thebes yet?"

"I tried this morning but couldn't raise them. Shortwave radio works best at night. But that's our other dilemma. Using the transmitter could give us away."

A humorless smile crossed Fenrir's lips.

"Caught between the devil and the deep blue sea, as we sailors say."

"If the intent of these Hegemony people is seizing anyone from Lyonesse, then either Thebes or Horam and I must stay free, so we can warn Lyonesse when the next supply ship arrives. Sure, it would be better if we could warn Thebes so they might hide, even if it means Horam and I surrender ourselves. Unfortunately, if we start transmitting and Thebes can't pick up our signal, everyone might be in jeopardy, and we must inform Lyonesse via the next supply ship."

"Again, you're assuming ill intent, Sister." Fenrir sounded a tad exasperated.

"Lyonesse learned to lean on the side of paranoia long ago, and for a good reason. If another space-faring polity now knows about our existence, it is vital, on an existential level, that Lyonesse be warned. Either the Brethren in Thebes or we must perform that sacred duty."

"If the Hegemony comes for the Brethren in Thebes, the entire republic will know and warn your supply ship crew."

Horam, who'd caught Fenrir's last line, came up the aft stairs.

"Our Lyonesse Marines can seize a target at night without the civilians in the area being any the wiser, Captain. It would be prudent if we assume the Hegemony can do the same, seeing how we're probably both descended from the old Imperial Armed Services. The Marines back in the day were no slouches, especially Pathfinders like my old outfit."

"I gather you're speaking from experience."

The Friar nodded.

"On a planet like this one, they'll go in after dark when the locals can't see what's happening, and tomorrow morning, poof, the Brethren are gone with no one the wiser." He turned to Rianne. "And that means we would be the only ones left who can warn our people, which makes staying free even more imperative. No more attempts at contacting the priory via shortwave."

"I've made the same conclusion. Now, all we can do is pray they don't find us."

"Should they visit Thebes tonight, then perhaps while their attention is elsewhere, we might sneak out of here and head further north, skirting the coast. Tell me, captain, is there a way of transforming this ship into a two-master without breaking it?"

Fenrir shook his head.

"No. Only a shipyard can remove a lower mast safely. We've taken down the topmasts to lower her silhouette, and that's everything we can do."

"Is there a way of disguising, say, the mizzen mast and make it look like anything but? I'm thinking our visitors might not be well versed on sailing ships in general and totally ignorant of the ones used on Hatshepsut. We can be sure Crimple told them *Aswan*

Trader was three-masted, and that means they'll have programmed their intelligence data filtering program to disregard anything with less or more than three." Horam snapped his fingers. "That's it! Can you rig the foremast's lower spar so it looks like a fourth mast?"

"Sure. We can make it seem so from a distance or to an untrained eye, but we can't actually rig it with sails."

"Since we'll be running under engine power, it won't matter." Horam glanced up at the sky. "Best if we can do that and leave this place before dark, say around last light. Sensors in orbit are marvelous things. They can spot a fly on a bald man's dome from four hundred kilometers up, but they're only as good as the artificial or human intelligence interpreting the data they collect. A four-masted ship emerging from the islands at dusk might fool said intelligence long enough if they used three masts as a primary search parameter."

Fenrir contemplated the Friar for a few heartbeats before shrugging.

"I'm not sure I understand everything you said. But spending the night out at sea instead of here makes complete and utter sense. Fine. Let's turn *Aswan Trader* into a ghost whose four masts are too unbelievably truncated for any real Theban sailor."

"We're not dealing with Theban sailors, Captain, but off-worlders in faster-than-light starships. They don't know a barquentine from a schooner from a ketch. It's a matter of creating an illusion."

After a curt nod, Fenrir called out orders and soon watched his crew create a believable fourth mast from the foremast's main spar. When it was done, he and Friar Horam took the Stirling engine-powered launch and circled *Aswan Trader* so they could inspect the transformation from a distance.

After they scrambled up the side ladder, leaving the launch afloat to pull *Aswan Trader* out of the inlet once the sun dropped below the islands' jagged peaks, Horam nodded at his colleagues.

"In the dark, even studying it through a millimetric sensor, I'm sure I'd be hard-pressed to make her as a disguised three-master. Perception is everything, and from the far end of the inlet, if I didn't know the extra mast hard up against the engine stack was fake, I'd take it for real."

"And now, we should pray our fuel reserves will get us back where we can head into the open ocean under a full press of sails and no off-worlders nosing about."

"The Almighty will provide, Captain."

"And I'm counting on you four Brethren to make sure he does." A half-mocking smile briefly relaxed his tense features. "Our escape might convince me I should consider something other than the nihilism of my forebears."

"Faith isn't transactional, but you will know when you find it."

— 31 —

Crevan Torma's three shuttles, guided by the Task Force Kruzenshtern ships orbiting Hatshepsut at intervals such that one could always cover the landing party, had dropped to a few hundred meters above a black ocean shimmering with millions of pinpricks. The light from the planet's moons and the stars reflecting off waves created a whole new universe, one changing by the second, and soon, the distant lights of Thebes on the horizon joined it.

No one spoke aboard his craft since lifting off from Aksum. Keter spent most of his time napping while Ardrix meditated. Torma simply stared at the map on the display showing their position, airspeed, and time to target and let his mind drift as it sifted through what they learned. One thing was for sure, no matter how the Ruling Council reacted once the task force returned with old Order Brethren from Lyonesse, nothing would ever be the same in the Wyvern Hegemony. Two centuries of slumber would end with the realization they were not alone.

Petty Officer Klaasen's voice yanked him out of his reverie.

"The target is in sight, sir. Would you like it on the passenger compartment display?"

"Please."

The map vanished, showing several one and two-story stone buildings whose windows were ablaze with light. The shuttle's sensors, capable of piercing the night, picked up every little detail, including the large, flat area in back where they would land shortly.

"An old Order house," Ardrix, who'd emerged from her trance, said in a low tone. "Interesting how strange it feels to see something we thought wiped out during the Great Scouring."

The priory's size on the display didn't change, though they were nearing at high speed.

"There." Ardrix pointed at a building with tall narrow windows. "That's the Chapter House, just as we thought. The design hasn't changed, not for us, and not for them. Since it's only lit after dark when the Brethren assemble, we timed it well."

"Five minutes, Colonel," Klaasen called out. "I'm reducing airspeed now. *Reprisal* has eyes on us and is recording."

The last few moments passed in a flash and the gentle change of the dropship's motion from horizontal to vertical as it descended caught Torma by surprise. Seconds later, so did the soft thud when their skids touched down on the compacted earth. The side displays showed both Special Forces shuttles landing on either side of them, and he unfastened his restraints, imitated by Ardrix. On this occasion, they didn't wait for Major Vinh to secure the area. There would be no time for niceties.

Torma and Ardrix loped down their craft's aft ramp the moment it touched the ground and headed for the Chapter House, surrounded by a platoon of Ground Forces troopers. The latter moved silently through the warm night air, like ghosts whose chameleon armor made them almost invisible to the naked eye.

None in the landing party wore any insignia that might identify them as members of the Wyvern Hegemony military and security forces, just in case. Ardrix didn't even sport her usual Void Reborn Orb, and her uniform looked almost like Torma's.

As they approached the door, Torma and Ardrix gave each other one last questioning glance while the sound of voices rising in plainchant reached their ears. What they did next would irreversibly alter the destiny of not only the Wyvern Hegemony but that of Lyonesse, Hatshepsut, and possibly even humanity in general. The two space-faring splinters of an empire fractured into a thousand shards long ago, meeting for the first time on this primitive world, and what does one of them do? Abduct representatives of the other. Not the most auspicious beginning, but Torma couldn't come up with any other course of action that didn't reveal the Hegemony's existence to a potential competitor, if not foe.

For a fraction of a second, he felt a stab of doubt twist his gut.

Ardrix, in her unaccountably weird way, must have sensed his hesitation because she briefly touched his arm and said, in a whisper, "We cannot let them learn more than is necessary about us, Crevan. The Hegemony's entire future might be at stake."

Torma, who felt his sense of resolve harden once more, grasped the door handle, twisted, and pushed. The carved wooden pane swung inward without a sound, releasing the plainchant into the night. He and Ardrix stepped inside, followed by a dozen troopers who fanned out along the walls.

In the few seconds before their invasion registered with the Brethren holding compline, Torma absently noted the Chapter House interior seemed little different from that of the New Draconis Abbey, albeit in miniature form. Polished wood pews, tall, stained glass windows, glow globes floating overhead, and an atmosphere of calm, perhaps even of sanctity, everything registered in the space of a heartbeat.

When he saw the other doors covered by Major Vinh's troopers and two dozen pairs of eyes staring at him, Torma said, "Pardon the intrusion, but we're looking for Brethren from Lyonesse."

The woman standing on the raised platform speared him with eyes of cold fury.

"I will not pardon your intrusion, and I do not know about this Lyonesse, now begone before you face eternal damnation."

Ardrix gave Hermina a smile devoid of feeling as she thrust her thoughts through the latter's mental barriers.

"Lying, Sister? How unbecoming a prioress of the old Order. I'm disappointed."

Hermina recoiled as if struck across the face by an open hand.

"You're a wild talent," she said in a raspy voice tainted by genuine fear. "A powerful one."

"No. I'm a Sister of the Void. But from what I sense, I'm an improvement over the old Order Brethren." Ardrix turned her gaze on Torma. "She's the leader of the Lyonesse Brethren, the prioress of this place."

Ardrix then scanned the room and pointed out seven more off-worlders who stared at her with an air of confusion after she touched their minds with no attempt at subtlety.

"The remaining sixteen are locals, still developing their talents."

Torma hadn't expected Hatshepsut-born Brethren at the priory and was momentarily at a loss. He met Ardrix's eyes, and the decision came almost at once. He turned to Major Vinh.

"Take the ones designated as off-worlders and shackle the others. They're staying. Someone will find them in the morning, no doubt."

Hermina reared up. "How dare—"

"Silence!" Torma's shout echoed off the stone walls. "You will not speak. Comply, and you won't get hurt. Resist, and you'll choose your fate."

Under the menace of unmistakably lethal plasma carbines, none of the Brethren, Lyonesse-born or local, made any show of disobedience. But Hermina kept her eyes on Ardrix almost the entire time until a pair of troopers prodded her to follow the others out into the night. Once they were strapped into the command dropship's aft seats, hands manacled in front of them while an astonished Jan Keter watched in silence, Torma and Ardrix climbed aboard.

"You're from this Hegemony, aren't you?" Hermina hissed, "and you, Sister, are an abomination cursed by the Almighty."

Both Torma and Ardrix ignored them as they took their own seats at the front of the passenger compartment while the aft ramp rose in preparation for takeoff.

"Why won't you answer?" Hermina demanded in an imperious tone.

Without turning around, Torma replied, "In good time. Now stay silent until I give you permission to speak."

"Best do as he orders," Keter said in a low tone pitched for Hermina's ears. "He and the Sister are the most fearsome humans I ever met."

Torma had many questions for Ardrix and much to discuss with her. However, it would wait until they were in the privacy of their suite aboard *Repulse*. Fortunately, their new prisoners took Keter's suggestion to heart and didn't speak during the flight, nor did any of them say a word when Major Vinh's troopers escorted them off the shuttle and to the ship's brig.

Torma and Ardrix's first destination was the flag conference room, where Commodore Watanabe and his chief of staff waited for them. After listening to Torma's verbal report, Watanabe sat back and frowned.

"A shame there were witnesses to your raid. But killing them out of hand would have been just as bad as wiping out Mazaber."

"Indeed, sir, though none of us wore insignia, mentioned names, or otherwise left those witnesses with any clues to our identity. However, once aboard the shuttle, their prioress asked if we were from the Hegemony."

Watanabe sat up.

"How could she know our origin?"

"The Brethren who visited Mazaber must have some means of communicating with the priory and reported after speaking with Crimple. That they didn't expect us in Thebes means those aboard the sailing vessel could be unaware of our presence on this world. But since they could easily have spotted our shuttles approaching Mazaber and identified them, I doubt that's the case. Doubly so because we can't find the ship, meaning they somehow hid it, a sure sign they made us for what we are. The other possibilities might be difficulties communicating consistently, which on a world with no infrastructure isn't surprising, or they've gone silent so we can't track them, which reinforces the idea they're hiding from our sensors."

"Each of our ships searches the area whenever it's overhead, both the sea and the westernmost part of the Saqqara Islands, but so far, no one spotted a three-masted sailing ship. Which makes me wonder how long we should keep looking. We've already been away from home for many long weeks and accomplished our goal. In fact, bringing back eight Brethren from Lyonesse goes well beyond what we'd hoped for or could have imagined. But it's your call."

Torma, suddenly overcome by the fatigue of a long, eventful day, gave him a weary shrug.

"Unless we sterilize Hatshepsut in the old imperial style and murder countless innocents, knowledge of the Hegemony's existence can't be erased. I assume the Lyonesse missionaries are resupplied regularly, which means the next ship that visits will find out about us, just as we found out about them. But at this moment, no one knows about our capabilities, intentions, strength, or anything that might be militarily useful, not even the location of our home system, since neither we nor Keter before us ever used the word Wyvern. The locally recruited Brethren we left behind didn't see our shuttles and can only describe our persons. The Brethren on the sailing ship will have seen nothing more than those same shuttles from a considerable distance, and although they might return and question Crimple again, they'll still not learn much."

"So, we leave?"

Torma nodded.

"Yes, sir. I recommend we return home. Sister Ardrix and I will interview our involuntary guests during the trip and prepare a comprehensive report on Lyonesse, something our superiors can use to shake up the Ruling Council."

"Out of curiosity, what will you do with your guests once we're home?"

"Release them into Archimandrite Bolack's care, I suppose." He glanced at Ardrix. "What do you think?"

"No question about it. They may be old Order, but they're still Void Sisters and Friars, our Brethren."

A mocking smile touched Torma's lips.

"Even though the prioress called you an abomination?"

"After two hundred years of separate evolution, we will certainly discover doctrinal differences." Ardrix paused for a few seconds. "I know *Repulse*'s brig is as comfortable as jails get, but if there's a block of vacant cabins that can be secured, we might do well to give them quarters more suited for guests than prisoners. It could make interviewing them easier. They'll be as curious about us as we are about them."

Watanabe gestured at his chief of staff.

"Why don't you speak with the first officer and see what's available."

"At once, sir." He stood and left the room.

"And you two, go rest. It's been a long day. I'll see that we break out of orbit without delay and head home."

"Yes, sir." Both climbed to their feet, and Torma saluted. "With your permission?"

"Dismissed."

— 32 —

Commander Jecks' day cabin intercom chimed softly. He put down his book, a printed version of one of his favorite historical accounts, one covering the years immediately before the empire's creation from the dying corpse of the old Commonwealth and tapped his desktop.

"Captain, here."

"CIC, sir. The intruders are breaking out of orbit."

"Finally. We stay under current conditions until they go FTL. Make sure we track their course just before they jump. We need to find out which wormhole they'll likely take out of this system."

"Aye, aye, sir."

Suddenly, Jecks found his interest in the book gone while renewed worry about the Lyonesse Brethren on Hatshepsut took over his thoughts. The entire crew spent the next few hours impatiently waiting for the intruders to reach the hyperlimit and vanish. At around the expected time, Jecks headed for the CIC and took the command chair from *Serenity*'s combat systems officer.

The sensor chief's report seemed almost anticlimactic when he announced unknown vessels were gone.

"What's their heading?"

"Wormhole Hatshepsut Two, Captain."

Jecks sat back and stroked his chin with his right hand.

"That one eventually leads into the Wyvern Sector. I wonder…" He touched his chair's controls. "Bridge, this is the captain, up systems and get to Hatshepsut as fast as possible."

"Aye, aye, sir," the first officer replied with such immediacy that Jecks understood he'd been waiting for the order. "Up systems and best speed for Hatshepsut."

An almost painful sense of urgency now gripped Jecks, and no doubt everyone else aboard the Void Ship. He made a point of returning to his quarters rather than stewing in the CIC or on the bridge. But that merely hid his impatience from *Serenity*'s crew, until, a few hours later…

"Captain, this is the bridge. We're within hailing distance."

"Then, by all means, see if you can rouse them from their torpor. It's what? Past sunrise in Thebes?"

"Aye, aye. I'm transmitting on the priory frequency now."

**

None in *Aswan Trader* caught more than the odd nap as the now four-masted barquentine crept out to sea, clearing the shoals surrounding the Saqqaras before turning north and resuming her journey. Every hour, on the hour, one of the Brethren turned on the shortwave radio and listened for any message from Thebes, in the vain hope of hearing encouraging news.

When Rianne took over radio watch during the hour of the wolf, while *Aswan Trader* slipped over a sea shimmering with a million stars now that both moons had set, she settled on a pile of sails from the mizzen mast stored beneath the taffrail. Whether they were being hunted or whether she and Horam imagined the whole thing seemed immaterial. Rianne simply wanted news from her Brethren but the airwaves remained stubbornly silent. Then, unexpectedly, the radio lit up with a familiar crackle, startling her and everyone within earshot.

"Priory, Priory, Priory, this is *Serenity*, do you copy?"

It was the usual message, on a loop that would continue automatically until someone on the ground answered. The only thing that changed from time to time was the Void Ship's name. Rianne listened, growing tenser by the minute, until she realized the Thebes Priory wouldn't or, more likely, couldn't answer.

Yet if *Serenity* was close enough to risk calling the priory, it could only mean the Hegemony expedition was either gone or was hidden so well one of the Lyonesse Navy's most advanced ships couldn't find it. Rianne was willing to bet on the former. She raised the set and activated the transmitter function.

"*Serenity*, *Serenity*, *Serenity*, this is Priory Detachment aboard the Theban merchant ship *Aswan Trader*. Do you copy?"

Several seconds passed, then, "Priory Detachment, this is *Serenity*, identify yourself."

"Two Lyonesse and two Hatshepsut Brethren on a detached mission, Sister Rianne speaking. Since you're on this channel, does it mean the Hegemony expedition left?"

More seconds than before passed, then another voice came through the speaker.

"This is Al Jecks, the commanding officer, Sister. We met about eighteen months ago if I recall correctly. What the hell happened?"

"You recall correctly, and I wish I knew."

"When we dropped out of FTL, we found five warships in orbit, apparently derived from old imperial designs and definitely not part of the Lyonesse Navy. We remained at the hyperlimit and observed until they went FTL outbound a few hours ago. Thebes isn't answering our hails, though long-range scans show nothing abnormal at the priory. Power emissions are within the usual range."

Rianne let out a bitter laugh.

"Do you have time for a long story, Captain? Because I can tell you a doozy, and I fear our Brethren probably left this star system aboard those ships against their will."

"Give me the complete story, Sister. If I go home without every little niggling fact in my possession, HQ won't be happy, and an unhappy HQ means less than desirable assignments once my tour in command of *Serenity* is over, so speak away."

"While I do that, can you track our position? It would be helpful if you picked us up with one of your shuttles. Sailing back to Thebes in *Aswan Trader* will take longer than you can afford, and if something happened in Thebes, we should be there as soon as possible."

"Will do." Another pause. "So, what's the story from your end?"

By this time, most off-duty crew members were within earshot of Rianne, along with Horam, Alcide, and Lilith, alerted by her unusually loud voice at this time of night, in the hours between the deepest of dark and the first spark of dawn when those aboard found sleep impossible.

Rianne recounted everything from the day Fenrir admitted trading Lyonesse medical supplies for railguns of unknown origin to their sailing out of a Saqqara Islands fjord under engine power, disguised as a four-master, the previous evening.

"Heck of a situation, Sister. Defense Force HQ will whelp a whole new sum of fears when they hear about this. Hang on." A pause. "We picked up your transmitter's coordinates. A shuttle will meet up with your ship in about ninety minutes, give or take. In the meantime, I'm sending another with the supplies to Thebes. My landing party officer will take charge until your arrival, if necessary."

"Thank you, Captain. Let's hope their transmitter is suffering from a malfunction." But even as Rianne spoke those words, she understood they voiced a forlorn hope. If the Thebes Priory wasn't responding, it could only be because the Lyonesse Brethren were no longer there.

"Hope is a fine thing, Sister, but realism is an even finer one. We should find out within the hour. Anything else?"

"Nothing that can't wait until your folks pick us up."

"In that case, *Serenity*, out."

Rianne looked up at Horam, standing with Fenrir a respectful distance from her, Alcide and Lilith at their sides. The Friar, wearing a sad expression, slowly shook his head. Though the furthest thing from a pessimist, he clearly figured if *Serenity*'s powerful transmitter couldn't light up the priory's duty office, it was because there was no one left who could hear the signal.

"How will they pick you up?" Fenrir asked. "Your spacecraft can't land on my deck."

Rianne tucked the radio away and shrugged.

"They'll probably take us off one by one via a rescue line while hovering above our windward side."

"Which means by the time we touch Thebes, whatever is destined to happen will have done so." Fenrir let out an exasperated sigh. "You lot giving us glimpses of what once was and will be at some time in the nebulous future is rather exasperating, you realize that?"

"We do. But it can't be helped. Even the Republic of Thebes can't go from sailing ships to faster-than-light travel in the space of a few years, not without the sort of social disruption that might destroy it."

"So you insist." Fenrir didn't bother hiding his skepticism.

"Mind you," Horam said, "recent events will likely change the timetable. Suppose the Almighty has decided on Hatshepsut as the interface between the mysterious Hegemony and our Republic of Lyonesse? In that case, you could find your fortunes changing faster than expected and perhaps faster than you might wish."

"A pessimistic Friar. Our fortunes are changing already."

An amused grin split Horam's features.

"Realistic, Captain. Sure, I'm a man of the Almighty, but that doesn't mean I'm not also a man of our galaxy. Trust me on this. Things change slowly until they change all at once. Been there, seen that. It doesn't work out well a lot of the time." Horam turned to Rianne. "I suggest we gather our bags and keep them on deck, ready for departure. I'll bring one of the fabricators for *Serenity*, if Captain Fenrir would be kind enough to lend me a large carryall. He can see that the other two reach the priory after he docks."

**

Just under ninety minutes later, as the first crack of dawn painted the eastern sky a delicate pink, Rianne was proved right when a sleek, unmarked aircraft appeared over the horizon behind them. It closed in and came to a hover on the ship's windward side, aft ramp open horizontally with a boom sticking out above it. Within moments, a harness on the end of a line appeared at the boom's tip and began to descend.

Horam, gaff in hand, caught the harness when it came within reach and pulled it down.

"Lilith, you're up first."

The young Sister, looking composed and without fear, travel bag tightly gripped in one hand, allowed Horam to secure the harness around her. He stepped back and raised both hands above his head, the signal that the shuttle's loadmaster could hoist her up. Then, in quick succession, he sent up Alcide and Rianne before stepping into the harness along with all his luggage.

Just before making the signal, Horam came to attention and faced Captain Fenrir.

"Permission to disembark, sir?"

"Granted. See you in Thebes."

"Godspeed and fair sailing, Captain."

"Good luck."

With that, Horam raised his arms, and his feet left the deck. Moments after he vanished into the craft, its boom withdrew, the aft ramp rose, and it peeled off to port, gaining altitude before turning east, toward Thebes.

"What's the word, Tuek?" Horam asked when the co-pilot, a Navy petty officer first class he'd known for years, stuck his head into the passenger compartment to check on them.

"The word is that you and Rianne are the only Lyonesse Brethren left on this planet. The supply shuttle landed just before we caught up with your ship. Goons in full fighting order invaded the Chapter House during compline last night, rounded up Sister Hermina and the others, tied up the local Brethren with plastic field manacles, and vanished into the night. Apparently, a Sister of the Void wearing a military uniform was among them. She pointed out the Lyonessers with unerring precision."

A look of anguish overcame Rianne's usual aura of tranquillity.

"That's what we feared would happen. The people who kidnapped them likely belong to something known as the Hegemony."

"Then it explains the five warships with that distinctly old empire design. They were in orbit when *Serenity* dropped out of FTL at the hyperlimit. We loitered, running silent until they left on a course for the wormhole terminus leading into the Wyvern Sector. Your Brethren must be aboard."

Horam patted Rianne on the shoulder.

"I guess that makes you the prioress until Hermina is back or head office sends a replacement."

She turned her head to give him a sad smile. "And it makes you the interim chief administrator."

The big Friar let out a disconsolate sigh.

"I guess this cloud has no silver lining." He reached into the borrowed bag and pulled out the Hegemony-made fabricator. "Here you go, Tuek, something for the analysts back home."

— 33 —

They landed beside the cargo shuttle an hour later, on the same spot where the previous evening, three craft set down to abduct the Lyonesse Brethren. Upon entering the Chapter House, Rianne and Horam found *Serenity*'s second officer, Lieutenant Gunther Voronov, along with a chief and two petty officers, all of them armed and wearing dark blue battledress uniform with Lyonesse Navy insignia. They were finishing interviews of the Hatshepsut Brethren who'd witnessed the kidnapping, so they could form as clear a picture as possible of the abductors.

The second officer stood the moment he spotted her.

"Sister Rianne. Or should I say, Prioress Rianne?"

"It doesn't matter much right now, does it, Gunther? What did you learn?"

"Very little. Your people here lack experience with modern military equipment, so details are sparse. Two dozen were equipped with armor, helmets, and visors that hid the face. They carried firearms, but of what sort is unknown. Two more, including the apparent leader, a man, and the one who called herself a Sister of the Void, wore no armor or helmets, though both carried small arms in hip holsters. None of them wore insignia, at least not that your folks could identify."

He reached into a tunic pocket and retrieved a strip of black plastic.

"The intruders used these quick restraints to tie them up hand and foot. Impossible to wiggle out of but easily cut with a knife or scissors. Everyone cooperated, so there were no injuries."

"What about the shuttles?"

"No one saw them. We're offloading your supplies right now, with the help of Friar Metrobius' apprentice, Friar Tati. Captain Jecks wishes to speak with you as soon as you can. Sooner rather than later would be better. He'd like to reach the first subspace relay as quickly as possible so we can warn Lyonesse, and that's over two dozen wormhole transits from here."

"Yotai, right?" Horam asked.

"We pushed them a little further out since you left Lyonesse, all the way to Isabella, Parth, and Mykonos."

"The Navy will need to push harder and link us in. There's someone else roaming the wormhole network, and since they kidnapped our people, we must assume they're not our friends. Worse yet, they found out about Lyonesse and will no doubt squeeze their captives for information."

Voronov nodded.

"Agreed, and I'm sure HQ will make the same conclusion the moment they hear about this. But let's put you on a link with Captain Jecks first."

He led Rianne and Horam to the supply shuttle and installed them in the flight deck jump seats before opening a link with *Serenity*. Jecks' anxious features appeared in a matter of seconds.

"My friends, what terrible news. I gather Gunther brought you up to speed?"

"He did," Rianne replied. "As did the co-pilot of the shuttle that retrieved us from *Aswan Trader*. Our Brethren are in the Almighty's hands now, but if a Sister of the Void is among them, I think they'll be safe."

"One thing occurs to me, Captain," Horam interjected. "Since your shuttles are here, we should make a quick trip to Mazaber and speak with Crimple again, so we can be sure it was this Hegemony he spoke of when we visited him a few days ago. I'll gladly go right now if you can spare the craft we came in on."

Jecks' eyes went over the Friar's shoulder to where Voronov stood.

"You good with that, Gunther?"

"Can do, Skipper."

"It's a rough spot, so I would appreciate some muscle, but considering the circumstances, we can set down right on the beach near Crimple's godown. A quick in-and-out, so to speak."

As they landed on the shingle fronting Mazaber a little over an hour later, Horam questioned his sanity in volunteering for a mission on a fallen world. Why did he ever give up the ability to crisscross a planet at supersonic speeds for the maddeningly sedate pace of a sailing ship? He mentally shrugged as he unfastened his seat restraints while the bosun's mates responsible for his security cautiously exited via the shuttle's aft ramp, carbines at the ready.

When the petty officer in charge gave him the okay signal, Horam walked out into the last of the morning sunshine and noticed countless eyes watching them from a safe distance, wondering what devilment was now afoot.

He found Crimple at his usual spot behind the counter, frowning at the commotion. When he recognized the Friar, Crimple made a sound Horam decided was of disgust.

"I should have known one of you damned off-worlders would be back. If I believed in the Almighty and the Infinite Void, I'd damn the lot of you. I suppose being godless has its disadvantages. What now?"

"Those off-world visitors yesterday. Did they say who they were?" When Crimple made to speak, Horam added, "No negotiations, no bribes. Answer and we'll be gone within minutes. Play stupid games with my friends and me, and I will make sure you win stupid prizes."

Crimple studied Horam for several heartbeats before shrugging.

"Fine. They said they came from the Hegemony and didn't look much different from the goons with you right now. Other than the one who calls himself Colonel Torma and the strange Sister of the Void, they had armor, weapons, the whole warlike getup, but no badges. They even brought Jan Keter with them but didn't offer any information, nor did I ask. A man needs to know when he should keep his curiosity in check. But Keter gave me the impression they weren't nice people."

Horam inclined his head.

"Thank you, Mister Crimple. Enjoy the rest of your day."

"That's it?" He sounded incredulous.

"You answered my question. I need nothing more. Goodbye."

With that, Horam turned on his heels and left the godown along with his security escort. They were back in the air within minutes, leaving a city the Friar hoped never to visit again behind them.

Horam figured Hatshepsut had accidentally become the contact point between two civilizations, survivors of Dendera's Retribution Fleet, who'd known nothing about each other until now. And the first act of the one was seizing citizens of the other against their will. A bad omen if he ever saw one.

**

"Will you be okay even though there are only two of you? I doubt your Order's Head Abbess would assign blame if you came home with us."

Rianne smiled at Jecks' image on the cargo shuttle's main flight deck display.

"Two of us born on Lyonesse, along with thirty-two born on Hatshepsut — the sixteen who were in the Chapter House last night and sixteen more serving the communities on the other islands. Yes, Horam and I will work double and triple shifts for a while, and we'll be relying on healers whose training isn't quite finished yet, but we'll persevere. I would simply ask that the Lyonesse Abbey send us reinforcements as quickly as possible."

"I'll make sure to pass on your request the moment we're within range of the nearest subspace relay. With any luck, the government will consider it a top priority and make sure the Navy sends out the next available Void Ship without waiting for the regular rotation."

"Thank you. And now, Horam and I must pay President Granat a visit and inform him what happened."

Jecks frowned.

"Will that cause you problems?"

Rianne's features briefly took on a dismissive expression.

"Nothing we can't handle. The Thebans are becoming more and more dependent on our teaching and technology. They won't do anything that might harm their only source of both. At least not until the Hegemony shows up with a better offer. But since we don't know where they hail from, hopefully, our government will speed up the reunification process, at least as far as this place is concerned. We can use all the Brethren and Defense Force personnel we can get."

"Another point for my report. Thanks. If there's nothing else, I'll say goodbye until our next visit. Take care and stay safe."

"You as well, Captain."

"*Serenity*, out."

The last two Lyonesse Brethren on Hatshepsut shook hands with Lieutenant Voronov and left the cargo shuttle, now empty of everything but the crew and the security detail. They stood at the edge of the flat area and watched the craft lift off, both lost in thought. Once they were only tiny dots in a heartbreakingly clear, blue sky, Rianne nudged Horam.

"Come on, Chief Administrator. A quick bite in the refectory and then President Granat. No doubt rumors are already reaching his ears, so there's no time to delay. He dislikes being kept in the dark when it concerns happenings in his republic, and this is a major event for everyone."

"Yes, Prioress."

"Don't sound so glum."

Horam snorted.

"Do I seem like someone at ease in the corridors of power? I'm just an old Marine noncom turned mystic."

"You'll do fine as chief administrator. Besides, I'm no more thrilled than you are at shouldering the political and diplomatic responsibilities for this mission."

"I know I'll do fine, which means I'll be stuck with the job." He grinned at her as they walked to the priory's dining hall. "And so will you. The Mother House won't send a new command team into an established situation unless they consider us unfit, which is unlikely to happen once Al Jecks sends in his report. Whether we want it or not, this is now our responsibility, our house, and our mission. Let's just do the best we can for our friends."

She gave him a light tap on the arm with the back of her hand.

"Look at you acting all grown up and leader-like."

"Some are destined for greatness; some have greatness thrust upon them. For my sins, I'm one of the latter, and I know when the Almighty is giving me a sign." A crooked grin split Horam's features. "Best I do my duty, right?"

PART III – PHOENIX RISING

34

"Good morning, Sister. You'll be glad to hear our guests are now lodged two per cabin with private heads in a section of unused spare quarters aft of officer country, with a fifth cabin turned common room, secured behind an armored bulkhead. It usually houses extra staff when the flag officer in command brings a full complement, which the commodore didn't. The main galley will deliver meals, and they can access a segregated entertainment database which contains nothing that might reveal more about us than we want for the moment."

Torma, who'd been up for the last two hours, entered their suite looking like a man who'd just enjoyed a fine breakfast in the wardroom. Ardrix, preparing for her morning yoga session after a frugal meal taken in their suite, looked up at him with approving eyes.

"Excellent. They'll be more likely to engage with us in congenial surroundings. When would you start?"

"I think we should leave them stew until we enter the wormhole. They'll be familiar with the sensation of crossing the event horizon and know we're no longer in the Hatshepsut system and that their fate is now entirely in our hands."

"Agreed."

"In the meantime, I've made sure they were issued with toiletries and two changes of clothing from the ship's stores, unmarked Hegemony Navy shipboard uniforms. If their sense of hygiene is the same as ours, by the time we reach Hegemony space, they'll be outwardly indistinguishable from everyone else aboard. Their original clothing will not come back from the ship's laundry, of course. They'll simply receive extra from stores as compensation."

"I suggest you do return their clothes, if for no other reason than simple hospitality, which they will notice, and which will affect their attitude." Ardrix adopted her favorite asana, eyes closed, and smiled. "Though their minds are weaker than those of the Void Reborn who work for the State Security Commission, they remain worthy of respect. Subjecting them to our usual non-intrusive methods should work better than brute mental force, depersonalization, and other usual tactics. Judging by the prioress' reaction when we interrupted compline, intrusive and insensitive behavior on our part will probably destroy any possibility of cooperation. Besides, they are surely as curious about us as we about them and will eventually succumb to that curiosity. We must merely stay patient."

"Very well. Points taken and noted. We'll do it the way you suggest. Since they won't be going home any time soon, there's no risk to the Hegemony in revealing information about us." He paused. "Though we'll also keep the lure of repatriation in our back pocket."

"Of course."

Ardrix's tone hinted that she would prefer if he stopped talking and let her perform her morning devotions. After a moment of hesitation, he removed his tunic, kicked off his boots, and joined her on the mat for his own meditation exercises. However, he adopted the lotus position rather than her more complex posture.

But Torma found no peace. His thoughts remained in turmoil at the enormity of their actions. He couldn't imagine what awaited them on Wyvern once they produced old Order Brethren from another human star system which not only retained FTL travel but was recolonizing parts of the former empire.

The brief transition out of hyperspace at the wormhole terminus registered distantly, as did the ship crossing the event horizon moments before Torma emerged from his light trance. He unfolded his limbs and stood, imitated by Ardrix moments later.

"Shall we introduce ourselves to our guests?" She asked. "If you'll give me a few minutes, I would rather wear the Order's robes than a uniform for this occasion."

He smiled at her. "An excellent idea."

Ardrix acknowledged the compliment with a nod and vanished into her cabin, light of foot as always when in yoga attire. She reappeared shortly after that in black, monastic robes with the Phoenix Orb pinned to her breast. The transformation from Commission officer to Sister of the Void Reborn momentarily took Torma aback, even though he'd spent almost every waking moment in her company over the past few months. And it wasn't just outward appearance. Ardrix's aura, invisible though it might be, was much different, or so his comparatively dull mind perceived.

"I'm ready."

Torma led them aft of officer country to a locked door piercing one of *Repulse*'s structural bulkheads. It had what seemed like a hastily mounted security panel on its left, with a display showing the empty corridor beyond. Ardrix found the view of open cabin doors interesting, as if their captives wanted no barriers between each other.

"Ready?"

She nodded.

"For every task, there is a beginning, a first step, and though it seems the hardest of them, it is the most important."

He gave her a questioning look.

"Scripture?"

"A saying passed down over the centuries. The founder of our Order, Jackson Thorn, apparently coined it." She nodded at the display. "The founder of both our Orders."

Torma touched the screen, and they heard mechanical latches withdraw. Then the door swung inward. He crossed the threshold, followed by Ardrix, and the door slammed shut behind them. No startled faces appeared in the open doorways, wondering about the noise, and their first stop was the common room, immediately to the right of the entrance. There, they found the eight old Order Brethren seated around a table, cup in hand, staring at them.

The one Ardrix identified as the prioress studied her and Torma with overt disdain.

"Finally, the head jailers. Those robes suit you better than a military uniform, Sister, though I don't recognize the strange orb you wear. Not that either makes you any less of an abomination before the Almighty."

Both Torma and Ardrix pointedly ignored her.

"My name is Crevan Torma, and I'm a colonel in the Wyvern Hegemony's Guards Corps. And if you're wondering whether we come from the old imperial capital, the answer is yes. Wyvern and a few of its neighbors survived the Great Scouring intact enough to retain the capability for faster-than-light travel."

He paused and looked for a reaction to his revelation but saw nothing.

"I work for the State Security Commission, which deals with non-military threats to the Hegemony's security. This is Sister Ardrix of the Order of the Void Reborn. She belongs to the New Draconis Abbey and works for my organization." None of the Lyonesse Brethren so much as blinked. "You've no doubt felt our ship, the cruiser *Repulse*, cross a wormhole's event horizon a short time ago. It means we are no longer in the Hatshepsut system. You'll be guests of the Hegemony government and the Order of the Void Reborn for an indeterminate length of time. Now, if you could please name yourselves."

Still no reaction. Fine, Torma and Ardrix could play this game all day long. They'd done it often enough. He pointed at Hermina.

"You're obviously the prioress. Would you prefer Ardrix to rummage through your mind and find your name?"

"She wouldn't dare."

Hermina spat out the words with such venom, Torma struggled to refrain from an amused smile.

"Then let's be reasonable. You realize we left two of yours on Hatshepsut, unharmed, and did not damage your priory so that your work among the Thebans will continue. We didn't even take samples of your equipment, though we scanned the priory extensively."

The eldest of the four Friars let out a mocking chuckle.

"You left our two colleagues behind because you couldn't find their ship, and we have only your word that the priory remains undamaged."

"Then your prioress should touch my mind to see if I lie. Since we use Sisters as truth-sayers, surely yours possess the same talent."

Hermina's eyes narrowed for a few seconds.

"He's not lying. Or at least not entirely."

"True, we couldn't find the ship, but I decided we'd leave them alone and return home rather than spend days searching."

She nodded.

"Okay, Colonel Torma. We've established you're not a complete monster, but you're consorting with an abomination, and no amount of honesty will wash away a stain of such magnitude."

"Then tell me, prioress who won't speak her name, why do you call Sister Ardrix an abomination?"

"Because she entered my mind without my permission. That is one of the worst sins imaginable, a violation of the soul that should never be committed in the service of the Almighty."

The vehemence of her words struck Torma and Ardrix as strange and the latter looked away, seemingly lost in thought for a few moments.

When she glanced at Hermina again, Ardrix asked, "Please allow me to speculate, Prioress. Is it possible your version of the Order experienced an event, perhaps sometime after the empire's collapse, that made entering another's mind without permission such a strong taboo?"

"Got it in one, Abomination. Our abbey took in a strong wild talent a few decades after the Retribution Fleet passed through the Coalsack Sector; a man shipwrecked on Yotai. A passing Void Ship picked him up. Our strongest teachers at the time developed his abilities, and he became a Friar, one with a potential for greatness. He may even have become the first abbot in the Order's history. But he turned to the side of darkness, entering the minds of others and manipulating them in the furtherance of political changes that would have destroyed Lyonesse. He ended up murdering several people with his mind, including our abbess at the time, before he was, in turn, destroyed. Ever since, we've been trained to consider the very idea of entering another's mind uninvited, unless it's essential for the individual's immediate survival, as anathema."

"I see," Ardrix replied in a thoughtful tone. "Based on the records saved from destruction, the old Order of the Void at the time of the collapse had no such ingrained interdiction. Nor did our reborn Order experience anything that would call for it. In fact, we consider entering minds without permission normal in the pursuance of our duties to keep the Hegemony and its citizens safe. The old Order allowed Sisters to enter minds without permission for routine medical purposes rather than just in extremis."

"And we saw where that led. But I know one thing, *Sister*. From the evidence before me, your Order of the Void Reborn is in no form or fashion related to what you call the old Order, let alone ours, which is the sole true Order of the Void."

Torma smiled at her.

"Excellent, and now that we know why you insist on insulting Sister Ardrix even though she follows the precepts of the Void as evolved by her branch, how about you introduce yourselves? We're curious about you and Lyonesse, and I'm sure you're equally curious about us. You answer our questions; we will answer yours."

"And risk Lyonesse's safety?" The old Friar gave him a look of scorn. "Perish the thought. A society that abducts people instead of introducing themselves peacefully and who use a perverted version of humanity's oldest monastic order to mind rape others in the name of security is not one I would entrust with the slightest bit of knowledge."

"So, names are a matter of state security on Lyonesse? How strange." No one could miss the mockery behind Torma's words. "Do you address each other by numbers or function?"

"Hermina," the prioress snapped. "I am Sister Hermina, Prioress of Hatshepsut."

She exhaled slowly, then glanced at her Brethren and said, in a resigned tone, "Tell him your names and your responsibilities at the priory. Perhaps then they'll leave us alone."

Each introduced him or herself in turn, stating their responsibilities in the priory, though the stony expressions remained. Once the last one finished speaking, Torma inclined his head.

"Thank you. I will not insult your intelligence by promising none of what we learn from you might be used to harm Lyonesse because I neither exercise control over the Hegemony government, nor can I predict the future, but—"

Friar Metrobius let out a dismissive grunt.

"You'll learn nothing more from us, period, so problem solved."

"Fair enough." Torma glanced at Ardrix. "In that case, we will leave you alone."

Both bowed their head formally, turned on their heels, and left.

Once back in their quarters, Ardrix said, "They had their mental shields at full strength. Not enough to keep me out, but even the Friars would have noticed any unwanted intrusion. I, therefore, couldn't get a sense of their feelings."

"Shall we turn on the surveillance sensors and watch them for a while?"

She thought about it for a moment, then shook her head.

"They're probably expecting us to do so and will tailor their behavior accordingly. And no matter how well trained you are, they'll confirm we're watching based on questions or comments you might make, and that won't help us."

"And how will we overcome their ingrained aversion to you?"

"If they implanted the taboo during conditioning — we receive a form of it as well, by the way, just with different interdictions — there is no way they'll ever consider me anything other than an abomination. It means you'll do the talking. Perhaps you should even see them alone, at least for the first few weeks, until you build some sort of rapport."

"A good idea."

**

"Do you think they're listening to us?" Friar Basam asked once Torma and Ardrix left what Hermina was already calling their gilded cage.

"I would if I were them," Metrobius replied. "We might enjoy what looks like officers' quarters, but we're still prisoners. And in a society where Sisters of the Void work for what sounds very much like a political police organization, covert surveillance must be as common as dandruff."

Hermina made a face.

"In that case, we might as well not worry about it. You know what subjects are out of bounds. As for the rest, let them enjoy their voyeurism."

"Will we exchange information?"

She nodded.

"Provided I judge there's no risk of harming Lyonesse. I'm curious about them and their evolution since the empire's collapse. If we ever make it home, they'll want to know as much as possible."

Metrobius shook his head.

"I never thought we'd become an unofficial arm of the Defense Force Intelligence Agency, yet here we are."

Hermina patted his arm. "We've always been in the intelligence gathering game, my old friend, but until now, we didn't face a potentially hostile power capable of threatening all we hold dear."

— 35 —

"Good morning." Torma stuck his head into the common room where the Lyonesse Brethren enjoyed a cup of tea after morning devotions and breakfast. "May I join you?"

"You're the jailer," Hermina replied. "And this is your jail. Do as you please."

"I thought I'd tell you a bit about how the Hegemony came to be, and if the Almighty so moves you, perhaps you can tell me how Lyonesse got its start."

"A bit of story time?" Friar Metrobius examined Torma with a gimlet eye. "I suppose there's nothing else on our agenda."

Torma pointed at the tea urn, delivered by *Repulse*'s wardroom steward that very morning.

"May I?"

"Good Lord, man. Enough with the fake politeness." Metrobius didn't bother hiding his irritation.

Hermina put a hand on the friar's arm.

"He's not faking. Our captor is a genuinely polite man, and he no doubt regrets abducting us." She glanced at Torma. "I suppose the abomination is watching via the security system?"

"Sister Ardrix is in sickbay, helping the ship's healers clean and do the inventory."

His answer seemed to catch Hermina by surprise.

"She may work with me, but she remains a servant of the Almighty and a Sister of the Order, someone who dedicated her life to selflessly helping others."

One of her eyes narrowed, and she let out an almost imperceptible snort.

"The theological debates we'll enjoy with your Void Reborn Brethren should be fascinating. Too bad I'm not a theologian at heart."

Torma couldn't quite tell if she was being sarcastic or not. He chose to believe the latter.

"Neither am I. While I believe in the Almighty and learned a few mind discipline techniques from Ardrix, I couldn't begin to debate the nature of the Infinite Void."

"Go fetch yourself a cup of tea and join us. Sorry that we can't offer you coffee, which I understand from your wardroom steward is the preferred drink. We tried the legendary stuff yesterday. Coffee plants don't grow on Lyonesse, and the last stocks ran out long before we were born. Sadly, we found it horrible."

"I suppose it's an acquired taste, and you probably lost it long ago. Don't worry, tea is a common beverage in the Hegemony as well, so you won't miss out."

Hermina gave him a strange smile. "I'm finding you more interesting than I expected."

Since there was no possible answer that didn't sound immodest, Torma picked up a mug adorned with *Repulse*'s crest, a golden razor-beaked raptor native to Wyvern, with raised wings, standing on a rock above the motto 'Who touches me is broken.' He filled it from the urn, then took the sole empty seat at the round table.

"May I assume you're familiar with the last days of the old empire, Dendera's Retribution Fleet, and the Great Scouring?"

Hermina nodded.

"In exquisite detail. Fortunately, the Retribution Fleet didn't come any closer to Lyonesse than Micarat, five wormhole transits away. Our ships went out in the following quarter-century looking for salvage and rescuing any Void Brethren who survived. They saw the results. I trust the Almighty has ensured Dendera's rotten soul will suffer torment for eternity."

Torma raised his mug.

"A sentiment everyone in the Wyvern Hegemony shares because we barely escaped the fate of just about every other human world except for Lyonesse. Our ancestors witnessed the ultimate battle that ended the Ruggero Dynasty and the empire. It left an indelible scar which still resonates to this day and explains why we are the way we are, our Order of the Void Reborn included."

"So, what happened?" Metrobius asked with an unexpected tinge of interest in his tone.

"When Dendera sent out the Retribution Fleet, against the advice of the General Staff, she kept a reinforced 1st Fleet to guard Wyvern. In this case, reinforced meant two-and-a-half times the size of a normal fleet. The admiral commanding sent battle groups to the far end of the stable wormholes connecting Wyvern with the rest of the galaxy in the Torrinos, Dordogne, and Arcadia star systems. That way, he wouldn't be caught napping by rebel forces intent on sacking the capital. Those three and Wyvern now form the Hegemony."

Torma took a sip of tea.

"According to the historical records, pretty much everyone in the 1st Fleet was revolted when stories of the Retribution Fleet's depredations filtered back through the communications nodes. The admiral in command decided, along with his fellow flag officers, that enough was enough. They would remove Dendera and stop the madness, but he wanted it done without destroying what remained of the imperial government and scarring the four star systems under his protection. It meant he spent time building a cabal within the Navy that could overwhelm Dendera's personal bodyguards. A few weeks, no more. But somehow, she got wind of it and recalled the Retribution Fleet, which by then was scattered across several sectors. That might be why it didn't go beyond Micarat, thereby sparing Lyonesse.

"What followed were three set-piece fights between the battle groups guarding the wormhole termini in the Torrinos, Dordogne, and Arcadia systems and Retribution Fleet elements answering Dendera's call. The casualties were terrible on both sides, though minuscule compared to what the Retribution Fleet inflicted on its victims. The battlegroups protecting the Dordogne and Arcadia ends of the Wyvern wormholes were essentially rendered combat ineffective. Enough ships made it through to decimate the formations in the Wyvern system. Humanity never saw so many starships lost in so short a time in its entire history."

Torma paused and shook his head, a grim expression on his face.

"It could have gone either way. A few more ships on the Retribution Fleet's side, and they would have ended the 1st Fleet's hopes of victory. In despair, the latter's commander ordered Draconis, the capital, evacuated within the hour, counting on the fact Dendera would consider the threat hollow and never comply. Once the sixty minutes were up, he ordered a kinetic strike that destroyed the city, killing Dendera and her entourage, the

Empress' Bodyguard Regiment, as well as those in the Armed Services General Staff still loyal to her. In effect, he removed the imperial government in one fell swoop."

"A few years too late," Hermina remarked in a tart tone.

Torma nodded.

"As you say, Prioress. But it was what it was."

"What about the capital's civilian population?" Metrobius asked.

"By that time, Draconis was a forbidden city. If you weren't a member of the imperial government, you couldn't enter. Dendera's paranoia, you see. Anyway, after that, the surviving 1st Fleet admirals, and those on the ground who'd fled Dendera's service during the battles in the four star systems, came together and formed a military government to prevent anarchy. In due course, they founded the Hegemony, built a replacement capital, New Draconis, and swore the Oath of Reunification.

"Then, their successors, content with absolute power over what they believed were the only worlds that survived reasonably intact, established a system of government whose sole purpose was preserving the status quo so that the last light of interstellar civilization didn't fade out. We've been in stasis ever since. Until that is, a merchant named Jan Keter, chartered by parties unknown, set out on an illegal trip into the wormhole network. He reached Hatshepsut and brought back artifacts of undeniably recent manufacture by a human civilization with advanced technology. Some of those artifacts bore what our Order of the Void identified as abbey markings, but from one they couldn't place, L slash L."

"Lannion Abbey on Lyonesse. Our Mother House."

Torma inclined his head by way of thanks.

"And that's when a group of senior officers in the Hegemony Guards Corps decided it was time we took a peek at the wider galaxy, but without informing our rulers. They would surely have buried the information Sister Ardrix and I dug up, lest knowledge of others besides ourselves disturb the long-standing social peace. You see, we've believed ourselves the sole heirs of humanity's past for generations. And that encapsulates our story. I've arranged for access to the ship's historical database if you're interested in us and our system of government."

He drained his tea.

"I won't ask for a quid pro quo, but I'd enjoy hearing about how Lyonesse survived the empire's collapse and thrived enough to strike out and help fallen worlds rebuild."

Hermina nodded at Metrobius.

"You're our historian. How about you go ahead?"

"Sure, but before I do that, can I ask two questions? The first is about the insignia on your upper arms. Is that a stylized phoenix, by any chance?"

"It is. The Hegemony's first Ruling Council adopted it as our state symbol, and it is on the crests of the Navy, the Ground Forces, and in my case, the State Security Commission."

"As in reborn from the ashes?" Metrobius stroked his white beard. "Not a bad heraldic choice. My second question concerns your usage of the name Guards Corps. Our historical records tell us the Guards Corps replaced the Army during the first Ruggero emperor's reign. Apparently, there was no love lost between it and the other two services, the Marines in particular. So if your Hegemony's founders put an end to the Ruggeros, how is it your armed forces kept the name?"

"A somewhat controversial issue at the time, according to our records. Your forebears probably missed the fact that in her final few years, Dendera made the whole 1st Fleet part of the Imperial Guards Corps so it would answer to her directly rather than the Navy's Supreme Commander. As command-and-control problems went during the empire's last days, this was apparently one of the more egregious examples. At the same time, there no longer were any Imperial Marine Corps units in the Wyvern Sector, only Guards Ground Forces, because so many of the former's regiments mutinied against the Crown.

"When the dust settled after the Battle of Wyvern, all that remained were the Guards 1st Fleet and the Guards Ground Forces on the Hegemony's four inhabited planets. The latter weren't interested in abandoning their title. At the same time, the 1st Fleet admirals were keen on quickly painting a patina of legitimacy over their junta as a way of keeping a traumatized citizenry quiescent. And they decided that patina would come from claiming themselves guardians of the empire's heritage until a legitimate sovereign appeared, which is why we call our head of state the Regent. No one questions it anymore."

Metrobius nodded.

"Fascinating. I gather your population is still quiescent?"

"To a large extent. Those who buck the long-standing social contract, obey the government in return for living in an orderly and safe society, become a problem for my branch of the Guards Corps."

"Right. The police state in action. So, let's see. I suppose the story starts a few years before the Great Scouring with a starship captain called Jonas Morane, who fled the battle of Toboso with the Imperial 197th Battle Group's remnants rather than surrender or fight to the death. He'd formulated a strange plan, that of building a vault on Lyonesse to preserve humanity's accumulated knowledge as a way of short-circuiting the long night of barbarism and thereby recreate interstellar civilization much faster. Along the way, he picked up survivors of the Order of the Void, fleeing Admiral Pendrick Zahar's pogrom in the Coalsack, and a battalion of Marines stranded on a doomed world..."

When Metrobius fell silent after describing the events that led to the Republic of Lyonesse's formation, Torma said, "That is utterly fascinating. Jonas Morane sounds like one hell of a visionary, the sort who, if he'd been on the imperial throne, would have ensured another thousand years of peace."

"He was our most beloved president. There's a statue of him and our first *Summus Abbatissa*, Sister Gwenneth, standing back-to-back, on Lannion's main square. They are our republic's two founders and most devoted protectors, who shepherded Lyonesse through its tumultuous first decades and set government policy for the ages."

Torma couldn't help but notice the reverence in Metrobius' voice, and he inclined his head.

"Thank you, Friar."

"So," Hermina asked, "did you record that?"

"No. When I said we wouldn't use surveillance on your quarters, I meant it. But I'm blessed with a quasi-eidetic memory and will transcribe what I heard when I return to my quarters."

She let out a soft snort. "That quasi-eidetic memory must come in handy for a political police officer."

"It does. Criminals can't fool me with any sort of ease." He stood. "Thank you for your forbearance. If you're agreeable, I'll join you again tomorrow, and you can ask me any questions you want."

Back in the quarters he shared with Ardrix, Torma kicked off his boots and removed his tunic. The hour he'd spent with the Lyonesse Brethren took a lot out of him for some strange reason.

After recording what he'd learned, Torma unrolled the meditation mat, adopted the lotus position, and closed his eyes.

Ardrix found him deep in a trance half an hour later and noiselessly settled on the mat as well. She figured that if he felt the need for mental cleansing this early in the day, it could only mean Hermina and her colleagues had probed his mind's defenses, though Torma wouldn't have noticed.

So much for Hermina calling Ardrix an abomination. But then, hypocrisy wasn't just a secular failing. All humans were guilty of that sin regularly, Void Brethren included.

— 36 —

"Are you out of your mind?" Major General Ishani Robbins glared at the image of Crevan Torma on her office display. "Bringing back prisoners from Hatshepsut?"

Torma had opened an encrypted link between *Repulse* and the Commission headquarters shortly after Task Force Kruzenshtern entered orbit around Wyvern after one last FTL jump from the wormhole terminus. Unencumbered by stops to scan former imperial worlds and outposts, their return trip took little more than half as long as the outbound voyage.

But even so, both Torma and Ardrix became, if not friendly with the Lyonesse Brethren, then reasonably familiar. Curiosity was indeed driving them to exchange information about each other's respective worlds, histories, and versions of the Order.

"They're living proof the Navy sent an unauthorized expedition beyond the Hegemony sphere," she continued, "and with our active participation. Where do you intend to stash them? In our cells? Or maybe you should simply shove them out the airlock now."

"Not our cells, General," Torma shook his head, "and I can guarantee even suggesting the idea of spacing them will destroy the good rapport we've built with the Navy on the Commission's behalf. They don't take kindly to cold-blooded murder, which is why the town of Mazaber still stands, and the ship carrying the remaining two Void Brethren still sails. We've been treating the Lyonesse folks like involuntary guests, not prisoners, by giving them comfortable quarters, the same food as the crew, and entertainment database access. Our interactions are a voluntary exchange of information between equals. They're not exactly our friends at this point, but we owe them guest rights. Once you and I are done here, Ardrix will call Archimandrite Bolack and arrange accommodations at an out-of-the-way priory. I'm sure his theologians will be keen on comparing doctrinal differences between the original Void and the Void Reborn."

"You take a lot on yourself, Crevan. What if Admiral Benes or I disagree with your plans?"

"You can discipline or fire me and see what happens."

She frowned at his tone more than his words.

"Was that a threat?"

He shook his head.

"No, General. Merely a statement of fact. Commodore Watanabe will refuse any order to harm the Lyonesse folks, and Ardrix would make sure you face Archimandrite Bolack's wrath if you arrange for someone else to kill them."

Robbins raised a hand in surrender.

"Stand down, Colonel. I was simply checking to see how far you've committed yourself. This will upset the Hegemony's political balance in ways we can't even predict."

"I should certainly hope so. Lyonesse has been re-colonizing former imperial worlds in the Coalsack Sector for almost half a century, complete with naval outposts, ground forces garrisons, orbital platforms, subspace radio relays, wormhole control forts, the works. They swore their own version of our Oath of Reunification at about the same time we did, but unlike us, they're acting on it."

"Your so-called guests told you that? Did Ardrix plunge into their minds, or did they defect?"

"As I said, we exchanged information. Lyonesse has spent the last two hundred years convinced it was the only surviving FTL-capable star system left in this part of the galaxy. Proof of our existence shattered our guests' deepest-held assumptions and beliefs, as proof of their existence has and will continue to shatter ours." He shrugged. "Mind you, it took a while. They consider Ardrix an abomination because she's not conditioned against entering another mind unbidden."

"And they'll live with members of the Void Reborn?"

"Again, curiosity is the primary driving force. They finally interacted with Ardrix and now understand she's part of a tiny minority among the Void Reborn, that most of the Sisters can't force their way into another's mind. And there's the theological aspect." Torma chuckled. "I can't help wonder whether the Lyonesse Brethren are entertaining notions of leading the Void Reborn back into the old Order."

"Bolack will probably entertain the same notions, but in reverse." Robbins let out a soft grunt. "In any case, what's done is done. Get them hidden away. I'll set up a meeting with Admiral Benes and Johannes Godfrey so you can give them the same briefing. They can decide on next steps. Mind you, Commodore

Watanabe is probably speaking with one or both at this very moment."

"If he is, it's only to submit the fictitious patrol report, so he can account for the consumption of supplies and fuel. Watanabe made it clear he would not discuss events with anyone and make sure none of his people do, while Major Vinh's troopers are used to never speaking about missions, not even with their chief of operations. Therefore, briefing flag officers from both combatant services on the results of an unauthorized mission is my job and mine only. However, there's not much time if we plan on staying ahead of the story. Even though the task force is disbanding, and its personnel are sworn to secrecy, rumors will circulate within days. These things always do."

A smirk twisted Robbins' lips.

"Don't I know it. Be warned, Nero Cabreras will likely buttonhole you the moment he hears you're back. He's been snooping around my office during your absence, and I don't think he bought the story about fostering more operational integration between the Navy and the Commission."

"Duly noted."

"Welcome home, Crevan. I'm glad everybody is safe. We'll speak again once you're on the ground. Robbins, out."

Her image faded from the workstation's display, and Torma let out a long exhalation while giving Ardrix a wry smile.

"Now the hazardous work begins. Regimes like ours have a history of shooting the messenger."

She smiled back.

"They'll need an army for this job because, the way I see it, there are a lot of messengers. Shall I call the Archimandrite and let him know he'll be hosting throwbacks still stunned that we're the sort of heretics who allow males as head of priories, abbeys, and the Order itself?"

"Enjoy the call."

To Ardrix's surprise, Bolack promptly answered himself rather than let the friar acting as his executive assistant do so.

"Welcome home, Sister. General Robbins just let me know in a very cryptic way I should expect your call momentarily. I understand you brought back tremendous news."

"We did. You recall the double L abbey markings on the medical instruments?"

"How could I forget?"

"The Lannion Abbey on Lyonesse, a house of the old Order, made them."

"Good heavens! And where is this Lyonesse?"

"At the end of a wormhole cul-de-sac on the distant outskirts of the Coalsack Sector. Survivors of the Great Purge established a new house there in the years before Dendera unleashed the Retribution Fleet, which didn't visit Lyonesse, by the way. The Lannion Abbey took in thousands of Brethren rescued from across the Coalsack and adjoining sectors. Eventually, it took on the title of Mother House, figuring Lindisfarne no longer existed, which is quite likely. In the last few decades, working with the Republic of Lyonesse government, they've sent out dozens of missions to reclaim former imperial worlds. They help locals recover lost knowledge and technology and prepare them for reunification under Lyonesse's banner. Hatshepsut is the newest and most distant from Lyonesse, established three years ago."

Bolack let out a low whistle.

"How extraordinary. And you've met these old Order Brethren?"

"We brought eight of the ten back with us as involuntary guests. The other two were in hiding at the time. Since this expedition was unauthorized, we cannot parade them around, nor can we keep them in the Commission's cells. Colonel Torma would like our Order to receive them in one of our priories on Wyvern, and I was thinking Grenfell. It gets no secular visitors, the Brethren there are contemplatives who never leave the grounds, and it's still within reasonable aircar distance from New Draconis. I'm sure our Order's theologians and historians will be keen on interviewing our guests to their hearts' content."

"Done. Can a shuttle from *Repulse* fly them directly there?"

"Of course."

"Let me warn the prioress. I assume I'll see you in person within the day, so you can brief me on the expedition?" Bolack paused and glanced to one side. "I received an invitation from Admiral Benes for a meeting at Navy HQ tomorrow morning. May I assume there's a relation with your expedition?"

"That is likely the briefing Colonel Torma, and I will be giving. Admiral Godfrey and General Robbins should also be in attendance. Perhaps even a few others who helped organize our trip, such as General Sarkis."

"Then I shall welcome you home in person tomorrow. Was there anything else?"

"No."

"Until the morning. Bolack, out."

Ardrix glanced over her workstation display at Torma.

"The Grenfell Priory it is."

"I received a message from General Robbins. We're staying aboard *Repulse* until tomorrow's meeting at Navy HQ. The shuttle will take us directly to the HQ landing pad. Our guests will stay here until afterward."

She gave him a knowing nod.

"In case Benes decides that we can't risk letting them live."

"There's nothing in his background that might suggest he's the type who'd commit an atrocity, but this is the most unusual situation in the Hegemony's history."

"You sound worried."

Torma chuckled.

"I am worried. We've come home with a shipload of extremely uncomfortable truths which will upend the paradigm that has governed us for two centuries. Historically, one of three things happens when such a paradigm is shown as false. The government in place sees the light and changes course; it refuses to see the light and successfully punishes those who dare upset the established order, or it tries to punish those who dare, triggering a coup d'état which removes the government in place. The latter two, not unsurprisingly, can trigger civil unrest, perhaps even a rebellion or an outright revolution. Those never end well."

Ardrix grimaced. "Something like the chain of events which ended the Ruggero Dynasty and the old empire."

Torma tapped an extended index finger against his nose.

"Precisely. However we handle this, we must make sure it doesn't end in another collapse. And now, I should warn our guests and make the transportation arrangements."

**

The next morning, Torma and Ardrix, bags in hand, reported to the hangar deck where *Repulse*'s pinnace piloted by Petty Officer Klaasen, waited for them. They landed on the Navy HQ roof less than an hour later, under a glowering sky that promised a deluge before the morning was over.

The moment they stepped out, a lieutenant senior grade came through the enclosed stairhead's door and walked toward them.

He wore an aide-de-camp's knotted gold cord over the left shoulder, but judging by his worn features, he was probably a former chief petty officer commissioned from the ranks. Since old chiefs usually weren't given dog robber duties, those being reserved for young, up-and-coming Academy graduates, Torma figured he worked for Godfrey, and his actual job didn't involve catering to a flag officer's official needs.

He halted and raised his hand in salute.

"Welcome home, sir. And you, Sister. My name is Krennek, and I'm on Admiral Godfrey's staff. He and the rest of the attendees are assembling in the secure conference room. We can leave your bags in his office on the way there."

Torma returned the salute, then gestured at the stairhead.

"Lead on."

He took one last look back before the door closed behind him and saw the pinnace lift off. He felt a brief and somewhat strange sensation of loss, as if its departure marked the end of an adventure among people who made him feel like a proper officer and not a political policeman in a Guards uniform. People he now considered comrades in arms, if not necessarily close friends.

By the time Krennek ushered them into the secure conference room, several seats were occupied by people Torma didn't know. Besides Benes, Godfrey, Robbins, General Sarkis, and Archimandrite Bolack, there was the chief of Ground Forces Intelligence and three middle-aged civilians wearing obviously expensive business suits. Senior bureaucrats who were part of the network, perhaps. They gave him the impression of being Chancellery secretaries, the sort who ran the machinery of government from the shadows.

"Colonel Torma and Sister Ardrix," Krennek announced.

Benes smiled at them.

"Welcome back. I understand the mission was successful beyond anyone's expectations. So successful, in fact, that we face several hard decisions." He gestured at a pair of empty chairs on his right. "Please sit."

They did so while Krennek busied himself at a discreet control panel by the wall-sized display. After a few moments, he turned around and nodded once.

"We are protected from any and all attempts at eavesdropping, sir."

"In that case, Colonel, please go ahead."

— 37 —

When Torma fell silent over an hour later, he felt curiously buoyed rather than exhausted. The men and women around the table had listened intently, eyes on him or on Ardrix whenever she took over telling part of the tale, though none interrupted with a question or comment, which was unusual with flag officers in his experience.

Rear Admiral Johannes Godfrey was the first to speak.

"History has a way of reaching out and touching you in the most unusual ways. That ghost fleet you found, Rear Admiral Leung's 211th Battlegroup, according to the logs Commodore Watanabe's people recovered, could have changed the Battle of Wyvern's outcome and handed Dendera one last victory, had its crews not mutinied. Leung was a well-known loyalist back in his day. Had he reached Wyvern, the Hegemony would never have been born because the rebellious admirals who founded it would be dead, and Wyvern devastated in retaliation. We'd be worse off than the unfortunates on Hatshepsut, and Lyonesse would have eventually owned all human worlds."

"History also has a habit of repeating itself," Benes' tone combined thoughtfulness and worry. "What shall we do with Colonel Torma's findings, the Lyonesse Brethren he brought back, and news of another human polity absorbing former imperial worlds? Technically, we are already in rebellion against a Ruling Council whose greatest fear is losing its absolute control over the Hegemony, its mandate of the Infinite Void, if you're of a mystical bent."

"And yet that control is more illusion than fact," Archimandrite Bolack said. "Otherwise, General Robbins, Colonel Torma, and the rest of the State Security Commission wouldn't face more work than they can handle. If you look closely enough, you might wonder whether the Hegemony keeps on existing in its current form out of sheer habit."

Benes tapped the tabletop with his fingertips.

"That sheer habit will end soon if it hasn't already. The question now is, how do we approach the Regent? Our dear Vigdis is also a creature of habit, as are the service chiefs and the Consuls. The idea of bestirring themselves because of a potential and still distant threat won't hold much appeal. Not if it means diverting funds from the entitlement spending that keeps the citizenry fat, dumb, and happy to pay for a large naval expansion program. I won't even mention the costs of imitating Lyonesse by sending missions to former imperial star systems, where they won't be under the Council's direct thumb and might think for themselves."

"I would need more Brethren for missions of the sort Lyonesse uses, and that also means added funding," Bolack said. "And I doubt the Ruling Council would be enthusiastic about expanding the Order's size. We're just about the only thing in the Hegemony that isn't both under its control and under constant surveillance."

A grimace crossed Godfrey's face.

"We don't have many options. And those we can consider all involve bypassing the service chiefs, which will be construed as insubordination."

"Not if I act as a messenger," Bolack replied. "I'm one of the few who enjoys direct access to the Regent, can see her alone with the evidence and explain in no uncertain terms what must happen if she wishes to keep power. If she dithers or outright refuses, then you can activate the network and make sure the Ruling Council, along with the service chiefs, do nothing that might cause overt rebellion. For the sake of civil peace, any change in government policy this momentous, let alone regime change itself, must be carried out behind the scenes."

"You would do that?" Benes asked.

"Vigdis Mandus is hardly the sort who'd risk alienating me, Admiral. She may not always listen, but my person is as safe as any. Even the Regent understands that should she strike me down or order someone to do it on her behalf, the accord between the Hegemony government and the Void Reborn is nullified. And that means we will no longer preach obeisance to the regime for the greater good under the Almighty's benevolent gaze."

"Looking the gift horse straight in the mouth, what's your motivation?" One of the unnamed civilians, a narrow-faced man with a receding hairline and a prominent nose, asked.

Bolack shrugged.

"My wish to see the Hegemony fulfill its destiny, one in which the Order of the Void Reborn plays a major role."

A faintly mocking smile appeared on the civilian's lips.

"Especially now that you know you face competition guiding the human soul through the Infinite Void."

"Competition or fellowship?" Bolack returned the smile with just a hint of condescension. "The Brethren Colonel Torma and Ardrix brought back may well help to reunify not just the secular but the spiritual as well, something that should interest you immensely."

"Oh, I'm interested. There are opportunities galore for those who can seize the moment. And many in the Chancellery keep our eyes on the future, unlike those in the Wyvern Palace."

Suddenly, Torma knew who the man was — First Secretary Gelban Vermat, one of the mostly unknown bureaucrats surrounding Chancellor Conteh who, as the top civilian in the Hegemony, oversaw the government's day-to-day operations. The other two must be colleagues of his.

Bolack inclined his head.

"Of that, I have no doubt. But back to the Lyonesse Brethren. May we receive them in the Grenfell Priory?"

Benes raised his hand.

"Just one moment, if you please, Archimandrite. We've not yet decided on a course of action."

"If you plan on anything other than releasing them into my care, we might find ourselves at odds, Admiral."

"Meaning?"

Bolack didn't answer for what seemed to everyone else as an eternity. Then, he said, "For the good of the Wyvern Hegemony, you and I cannot be at odds."

None dared speak in the tense atmosphere that suddenly weighed on all present until Godfrey let out an exasperated sigh.

"Folks, we're not debating options because there are none. The Lyonesse Brethren may take up residence in the Grenfell Priory so that everyone else forgets about their existence. They are interesting but aren't a factor in the immediate decisions we face. Archimandrite Bolack offers his services as an emissary to the Regent. I think it is the most efficacious solution. Once we know how Grand Admiral Mandus reacts, we can plan the next steps. In the meantime, Task Force Kruzenshtern must disperse, its ships return to their battle groups, and the Network alerted for possible action."

The Chief of Naval Operations gave his Chief of Naval Intelligence a stern look. Not so much for his words, which were on target, but for his tone, which bordered on the insubordinate.

"Johannes is right, Admiral," Vermat said when he saw Benes' reaction. "Both about the Lyonesse people and the Archimandrite acting as an emissary. I would add just one suggestion. Colonel Torma and Sister Ardrix should go with him to the Palace."

"Why?"

"A twofold purpose, as subject matter experts and targets should the Regent feel an uncontrollable need to shoot the messenger." Vermat pointedly did not glance at Torma or Ardrix, both of whom showed no emotions whatsoever. "Best we give her rage an immediate target that isn't named Bolack. Guards colonels and Sisters of the Order, on the other hand, are eminently disposable."

Neither could tell whether Vermat was serious. The senior civilian echelons of the Hegemony government were just as ruthless as their military superiors. And just as self-interested.

"Very well." Benes turned his gaze on Torma. "Colonel, when we're done here, Lieutenant Krennek will take you to the secure communications room. There, you'll call Commodore Watanabe and pass on my order that the Lyonesse Brethren be landed at the Grenfell Priory and that he then disbands Task Force Kruzenshtern."

"Yes, sir." The easy way in which Benes gave him orders, even though he belonged to a different branch of the service and his own superior was in the room, supported Torma's belief the CNO was, if not the head of the Network, then one of its top leaders.

"Then, you and Sister Ardrix will be at Archimandrite Bolack's disposal. Consider yourselves confined to quarters for security reasons. As far as the rest of the universe is concerned, you're still detached from the State Security Commission and under sealed orders. That means no visiting your offices or leaving your quarters for any other reason than mealtimes in the officer's mess or the abbey's refectory. While out of your quarters, you will not engage in any conversations beyond saying hello and commenting on the weather. Is that understood?"

"Yes, sir," they replied in unison.

"I was about to suggest the same thing," General Robbins said. "Commissioner Cabreras is keen on interrogating Colonel Torma about his expedition. He doesn't believe the cover story for a single second."

Benes gave her a knowing nod.

"And he has his eyes on the Chief Commissioner's job, which means he'll use any means of ingratiating himself with the Ruling Council, so they'll support his nomination when the Conclave meets to elect Bucco's successor."

Vermat let out a snort of derision.

"Cabreras is neither ruthless nor smart enough to claw his way into the Ruling Council's private chambers. I'd be surprised if he ever becomes Chief Commissioner, for that matter."

"Does anyone wish to raise last-minute questions?" Benes let his eyes roam around the table. When all present shook their heads, he stood. "This meeting is adjourned. You may carry out your orders, Colonel."

Torma expected a few minutes with Robbins, but Benes' tone brooked no dilly-dallying. He nodded at Lieutenant Krennek and waited while the senior officers filed out of the conference room. Krennek then led them past Admiral Godfrey's office and through an empty storeroom with a second door at its far end.

"I'm sorry, Sister, but the intelligence communications node is top-secret special access, and you don't have the need to know at this moment. If you'll wait here while the Colonel speaks with *Repulse*."

She inclined her head.

"Of course."

Krennek approached the inner door and touched the jamb. Nothing happened for a few seconds, then a voice asked, "Guests?"

"Colonel Torma is entering with me. The Sister is staying put."

"Understood."

The door slid aside, revealing a small, airlock-like compartment with a further door at its far end. Krennek motioned at Torma to follow him in. The opening shut behind them and the other door vanished into the wall. Beyond was a fully staffed and equipped communications center, separate from Navy HQ's official one. Displays lined three of the four walls while half a dozen petty officers sat at lit consoles.

The lieutenant sitting at a workstation in the center of the room, presumably the duty officer, turned her throne-like chair around and faced them.

"Entertain me, Krennek. Why is a State Security Commission officer in this, Naval Intelligence's holy of holies?" Her light and breezy tone belied her words. "No disrespect intended, Colonel, but you know how it is."

Krennek gave her a wolfish grin.

"Everything shall be revealed if you give us a secure channel with *Repulse* in orbit. Commodore Watanabe personally, if you please. Colonel Torma is calling."

"Obviously, your wish is Admiral Godfrey's command." She sketched a seated bow. "Petty Officer Grieg, please link us with Commodore Watanabe in *Repulse*."

"At once, sir."

The duty officer pointed at a vacant workstation.

"Whoever wants Commodore Watanabe can sit there."

Krennek glanced at Torma and nodded. The latter slipped into the chair and waited. Almost a minute later, the workstation's display lit up with Watanabe's impassive features.

"Colonel. I trust you bear good news."

"Yes, sir. From Admiral Benes, transport our guests to the designated destination, disband the task force, and go home."

Relief mixed with curiosity crossed Watanabe's face.

"Precisely what I wanted to hear. I shall execute at once. May I infer that no further information is forthcoming?"

"That's pretty much the case, sir. It was a pleasure sailing under your command. What happens next will happen."

"To happier days, then, Colonel."

"Happier days, sir."

"Watanabe, out."

The display went dark, and Torma climbed to his feet.

"That's done. Will you be taking care of our transport, Lieutenant Krennek?"

"It's already waiting in the underground garage, sir."

— 38 —

Torma found a message waiting for him in his quarters when he returned from lunch in the officer's mess two days later. A ground car would pick him up in front of the senior officers' quarters at fourteen-hundred-hours. He should wear an impeccable service uniform with ribbons and devices. No mention of the Archimandrite or Ardrix, but he figured the instructions came from Bolack and he would see both at that time. Although they'd been apart for less than forty-eight hours, after months sharing a suite aboard a starship, Torma felt strangely bereft of her presence.

Shortly before the appointed time, he took the stairs down to the apartment block's lobby, empty at this time of day. As ordered, Torma did his best to look like a recruiting poster model in his sharp, well-fitted, silver-trimmed black uniform, with the silver crossed swords and triple diamonds of his rank on each shoulder strap. Four rows of colorful ribbons filled the space above his tunic's left breast pocket, while an enameled metal shield with the insignia of the Commission's Wyvern Group was pinned above his right breast pocket. Black trousers with silver piping on the outside seams were tucked into shiny boots that reached almost to his knees. An equally black beret, with the State Security Commission's silver phoenix, sword, and scales of justice insignia, sat at the correct angle on his head. The Regent might find fault with his very existence, but she would find no fault with his appearance.

Though he'd spent his entire adult life as a Commission officer after graduating from the Academy and becoming one of the Ruling Council's relentless enforcers, Torma felt unaccustomedly nervous at the thought of facing the Hegemony's ruler and commander-in-chief. One word from her could mean the end of his career, if not his life.

He was guilty of triggering the largest instance of mass disobedience to the Council's orders about travel beyond the Hegemony's sphere. That Bolack, Benes, and the Network would throw him and Ardrix into the maw of death should they consider it necessary was beyond doubt. If only he'd ignored the reports concerning one Jan Keter's contraband all those months ago…

The Order's ground car, a dark gray, utilitarian, rectangular box hovering on an antigrav bed, appeared around a bend at almost precisely the appointed time. Built for cargo rather than passengers, let alone an august personage such as the Archimandrite, it seemed an incongruous means of conveying him to the Palace. But then, a sleek, aerodynamic staff car like those enjoyed by the service chiefs and other notables would strike a false chord.

The Void Reborn's leader took the same vows as his Brethren and was entitled to no more amenities than those necessary for his duties. A regular abbey van with passenger seats in the aft compartment would do just fine. Torma saw nothing behind the polarized windows but knew Bolack and Ardrix, as well as the conveyance's pilot, saw him.

It stopped in front of the lobby just as Torma stepped out. The side door opened, and Bolack's deep, resonant voice invited him to climb aboard. Inside, he found the Archimandrite and Ardrix wearing the Order's formal black robes with Phoenix Orbs pinned to their breasts. Torma was slightly surprised Bolack wore nothing that distinguished him from the Friar at the controls but brushed the thought aside as he settled onto the bench seat facing aft, across from where both Brethren sat.

"A fine morning to you, Colonel."

Torma nodded formally.

"And you, sir. How are you, Ardrix?"

"I am well. It will please you to know the Lyonesse Brethren are settling in at Grenfell and studying the Void Reborn in its natural habitat with keen interest. Our people there say they feel like experimental subjects in a life-sized maze."

Torma chuckled at her choice of words. He only realized later that her little joke took some of the edge off his apprehension at meeting the Regent under the current circumstances.

"And the Grenfell people are studying them in return," Bolack said. "Though I've not heard any complaints. Now, when we're in Grand Admiral Mandus' presence, I will do the talking. Unless either she or I ask you a direct question, you shall stay silent."

"Understood."

"I will bend the truth just a bit to protect the innocent, so do not show surprise and definitely don't contradict me. Ardrix tells me you've developed a remarkable level of self-control under her guidance, Colonel. You will need every microgram of it in the next few hours."

"Yes, sir."

As they left Joint Forces Base New Draconis, the conversation devolved into small talk clearly designed as a tonic against nervousness. Torma gazed idly through the windows at the passing scenery as they drove along the capital's broad, tree-lined avenues. In contrast to the old imperial capital, New Draconis had been planned and laid out from the start as a functional rather than an inviting replacement for the city that vanished in a kinetic strike from orbit long ago.

But Torma thought the few square kilometers at its core lacked charm. Somehow, the perfect grid of thoroughfares lined by endless rows of forbidding government and corporate buildings clad in pinkish-gray granite, relieved only here and there by statuary, tiny parks, and clumps of vegetation struck him as a shade too brutal. The lack of pedestrians that might add color on a day rendered gloomy by thick, dark clouds didn't help. Only cars moved about, mostly expensive, as befitted those who toiled in the Government Precinct.

Finally, the van turned onto the optimistically named, though relatively short, Avenue of the Stars connecting the Chancellery and the Wyvern Palace. Large monuments to the Hegemony's founders and, ironically, the Oath of Reunification they swore, filled the broad grassy strip between the avenue's two double lanes.

The design on which both the Chancellery and the Palace were based was deliberately austere and functional, with little that distinguished them from the rest of the government buildings, in stark contrast to their vast, overwrought, almost gaudy imperial predecessors. And yet, those who occupied the Wyvern Palace wielded the same autocratic power as the Ruggero Dynasty did, with as little consideration for ordinary people and as much viciousness for dissenters.

Then again, Torma figured the admirals who founded the Hegemony knew no other system than autocracy, and thought it would be best they kept the empire's core from collapsing like every other human star system by using an iron fist. For the good of the people, naturally, but mainly for the good of the rulers.

Their arrival at the Palace's main entrance broke through his reverie, and he stared out at the perimeter fence. Two-and-a-half meters tall, made to look like simple wrought iron, it was merely the most visible part of the security arrangements. Torma knew there were other, less visible elements, sensors, remote weapon stations capable of reaching high-altitude aircraft as well as deal with ground targets, and much more which ordinary visitors couldn't spot.

The van stopped at the security station, where a pair of smartly attired troopers from the Wyvern Regiment, the Regent's personal security force, checked their credentials, compared their biometrics with those on file, and cleared them with the duty officer. As they entered the visitor's parking lot behind the Palace, a Navy captain wearing the gold knotted cord of an aide-de-camp over his right shoulder, denoting he served the Regent, emerged from the back door, and waited until the van came to a halt.

Bolack climbed out first, as befitted his lofty rank in the Hegemony's hierarchy, and the captain saluted with parade-ground precision.

"Welcome back to the Wyvern Palace, sir. It's always a pleasure."

"Thank you, Captain. I trust you're well?"

"Yes, sir." He glanced at Torma and Ardrix as they joined the Archimandrite.

"Good morning to you, Colonel, Sister."

Torma gave him a polite nod.

"Captain."

"If you'll follow me. The Regent is expecting you."

Torma had never been inside the Wyvern Palace and was happy to discover its interior was as utilitarian and sober as its exterior, or at least the corridors they took seemed so. The floors were of polished stone, the white walls decorated with portraits of past rulers and images of the Hegemony's naval and military might, and what little furniture he saw was of similar quality to that found in any officers' mess.

They arrived at an unmarked door, its appearance no different from the others he'd seen, and the aide rapped his knuckles against the panel three times. Seconds later, a strong woman's voice on the other side bade them enter. The door slid aside silently, and the aide stepped forward.

"Archimandrite Bolack, Colonel Crevan Torma, and Sister Ardrix, sir." Then he took one pace to the right and ushered them in.

Torma had seen Grand Admiral Vigdis Mandus, Regent of the Wyvern Hegemony before, but not this close and not in her private office, a large, airy space with plenty of light streaming through tall windows. Somehow, he was relieved that the furniture and decorations were in keeping with what he'd seen so far. No ostentation, let alone the sybaritic luxury of an imperial ruler.

Mandus, as per tradition, wore a simple, high-collared black Guards Corps uniform, without the rank insignia or the gold braid of a flag officer. The only difference between hers and that of an ordinary spacer were the undress ribbons above the left breast pocket and a commanding officer's wreathed star above the right.

Elected by a Conclave of three and four-star flag officers and their civilian counterparts from the Chancellery and serving for a single nine-year term, Mandus was in her seventies. However, her delicately sculpted face, surrounded by short platinum hair, could have been that of someone twenty years younger.

Pale blue eyes devoid of emotion studied her visitors as she stood to greet them in front of her desk, and Torma realized the commander-in-chief of the Hegemony's armed forces, as well as its absolute ruler, was his height, though more slender.

She shook hands with Bolack, bowed her head at Ardrix in greeting, and returned Torma's stiff salute with a formal nod before waving them to a settee grouping around a low table.

"Please sit. I confess I'm a tad bemused at seeing a colonel from the State Security Commission in your company, Archimandrite. Did you fall into dangerous company, or is the Order considering an expansion of its work supporting police investigations?"

A chuckling Bolack settled on the sofa to the right of Mandus' chair while Torma and Ardrix took the one across from him.

"The colonel and Ardrix work together at the Commission and are subject matter experts on the issue at hand, Regent. But if the Commission wants more help from us, I'm always ready for new challenges."

"I see. Can I offer you coffee, tea, or something else?" When all three shook their heads, she glanced at the aide and nodded once. He vanished through another door, leaving them to continue in private. "Now, what is this urgent matter?"

— 39 —

"What would you say if I stated we are not the only ones who survived the empire's collapse, that there is another human society in the galaxy capable of faster-than-light travel and whose technological prowess might actually surpass ours?"

Mandus gave Bolack an amused smile which, Torma noted, didn't reach her eyes.

"I'd wonder whether you've been spending too much time in your abbey's distillery."

"Word has come of an entity calling itself the Republic of Lyonesse, which, not coincidentally, is centered on the Lyonesse star system, a wormhole cul-de-sac at the far end of the Coalsack Sector. It escaped the empire's collapse through the foresight of an Imperial Navy officer who collected everything Lyonesse might need to remain a star-faring society. He also gathered thousands of Order of the Void Brethren, the old Order, you understand, to help preserve knowledge of the past and of advanced technology.

These Brethren are now spreading across the former empire's sphere, establishing missions in advance of Lyonesse claiming those star systems for her own."

An air of sheer incredulity crossed Mandus' finely-shaped features.

"And you found out about this how?"

Then, surprising them, she snapped her fingers and pointed at Torma.

"Oh, that's right, through you and Task Force Kruzenshtern, correct, Colonel? And you, Sister?" Their visible astonishment drew a peal of cruel laughter from the Regent. "You didn't think it would stay a secret for long, now did you? Spacers talk, they talk a lot, and some don't think about operational security when they talk. I heard about it through certain backchannels I can still access, even though I'm no longer in the immediate chain of command. I thought this visit would concern the expedition to Hatshepsut."

She leaned forward. "Should I ask if you planned on telling me the truth or were you going to spin a web of lies that would cover this mutinous expedition beyond the Hegemony's sphere?"

"What I said so far is the truth, Regent." Butter wouldn't melt in Bolack's mouth.

She gave him a hard look but knew arguing would be just as useless as threatening the leader of the Hegemony's official faith.

"Give me one good reason I shouldn't order Colonel Torma, Sister Ardrix, and everyone involved in this treasonous cabal arrested and executed for crimes against the Hegemony?"

Bolack's tone, when he replied, was tinged with mild amusement.

"I think you'd find rounding up and executing the crews of five Navy starships rather difficult. It might cause a real mutiny. Not to mention discontent among the senior ranks of the Guards Corps, both naval and ground at such a way of handling what is, for all intents and purposes, an existential crisis."

She stared at him for a few seconds like a venomous snake intent on striking its prey.

"Why are you the messenger, Archimandrite? And who in the Guards Corps helped organize the expedition?"

"The first should be obvious. As head of the Order of the Void Reborn, I enjoy direct access to you. I also have a keen interest in the matter since the old Order not only survived but thrives in a way the Void Reborn cannot because the Hegemony will not expand its rule. And if the Void Reborn is overtaken by the old Order, then I fear for the Hegemony's future."

Mandus waved away his response.

"Fears of hypothetical religious rivalry is hardly an excuse for this."

"Then consider the reasons it was done without your approval or the Ruling Council's oversight. If Task Force Kruzenshtern discovered nothing that might threaten the Hegemony's future, then no more need be said about the matter. But that was not the case, which is why I am here with those who know the most about the situation."

"So?"

"To answer your second question, those who helped were in the Conclave that elected you Regent, which means they know you well. Many likely even voted for your elevation."

"In that case, why not ask first?"

Bolack shrugged.

"Despite your views on the matter, I consider it a foregone conclusion the Ruling Council would have refused to allow the expedition and ordered that the evidence Colonel Torma collected be suppressed. Too many in high places prefer isolation in our own little corner of the galaxy. It's not only safer but more lucrative and with less effort."

"For a man of faith, you possess such an insultingly small amount in me, the one charged with the Hegemony's security and its future."

"And yet, here we are, asking for forgiveness rather than permission because in this case, I fear the former will be more easily granted than the latter would have been."

"Then you fear wrong." Her fingers danced on the arm of her chair. "You, I cannot touch, Archimandrite. But the two who are ultimately responsible for this gross violation of the Ruling Council's prerogatives…"

Torma successfully kept an impassive expression and knew Ardrix did as well without glancing at her.

"You'll order these two fine servants of the Hegemony arrested and tried for treason? Why? They did what was necessary because they feared for our security."

Mandus scoffed.

"I can't allow a senior State Security Commission officer to blatantly disregard government policy. That would only encourage more to second guess those set above them, and on that path lies anarchy, the sort capable of destroying us."

One of the office doors opened, and four armed troopers wearing the Wyvern Regiment's insignia entered. The lieutenant in charge saluted.

"You summoned us, sir?"

Mandus pointed at Torma and Ardrix.

"Arrest them on charges of treason and hold them in complete isolation in the regimental cells. No contact with anyone absent my authority, and that includes members of the Ruling Council."

"Yes, Regent." The lieutenant turned toward them. "Please stand and place your hands on the top of your heads."

"Now see here—" Bolack half stood.

Mandus raised a restraining hand.

"Even though Sister Ardrix belongs to the Void Reborn, this is now out of your hands, Archimandrite. Please tell those who hide behind your robes that their days are numbered, not for violating Council policy, but for hiding something this momentous from the Hegemony's legal rulers. This meeting is over."

She stood, imitated by Bolack, while the troopers chivvied Torma and Ardrix out of her office.

"I'm disappointed in you, Archimandrite. Of all the ways this could have played out, you chose the worst. The Council and I will decide how we deal with this information, no one else, and we will not be stampeded by anyone anxious to profit from it."

Bolack inclined his head.

"As you wish. But it would be a mistake if you ignored this new reality in favor of a comfortable, though untenable status quo."

"Is that a threat?"

"No, Regent. A warning from history. Goodbye."

With that, he turned on his heels and walked past Mandus' aide, standing by the open door, and made his way back to where the abbey van waited.

**

"Her informants don't know about the Lyonesse Brethren tucked away in Grenfell Priory? Or is she deliberately ignoring their existence?"

Rear Admiral Godfrey gave Archimandrite Bolack a dubious look as they and Major General Robbins strolled through the abbey orchard shortly before the evening meal that same day. Bolack had invited them to dine with him after leaving the Wyvern Palace, so he could update them on the afternoon's events.

"The first could well mean the Network isn't betrayed, and what we see here is just another example of informal backchannels working overtime. As to the second possibility, who knows what's brewing in her devious mind."

"She made no mention of them, but Vigdis Mandus is nobody's fool. She doesn't give away that which she can barter." Bolack shrugged. "We might still be compromised, and she's merely giving us the rope her executioners will eventually use. Do you know anything about Colonel Torma's and Ardrix's fate, General?"

"According to *my* backchannels," Robbins said, "they're under something more like house arrest in apartment suites kept vacant for high-ranking detainees in the Wyvern Regiment's garrison."

Godfrey let out an amused chuckle.

"She's hedging her bets. Shoving Torma and Ardrix into the Commission's dungeons would irreparably damage them in the eyes of others and incur not only the Archimandrite's anger but that of the high-ranking officers who sponsored the Hatshepsut expedition."

"Our Regent is good at triangulation, which is why she now sits in the Wyvern Palace. I just hope they know better than to interrogate them. Crevan Torma has been conditioned, and Sisters of Void who work for the Commission are beyond anyone's ability. Though I wonder what message she's sending with the arrests."

Bolack made a dubious face.

"I suppose Vigdis is telling the admirals and generals any wrong moves on the Lyonesse matter will result in more arrests. I'm afraid First Secretary Vermat was right. Colonels and Sisters are expendable under the present circumstances, though I hope the Regent and her counselors won't realize that just yet. Otherwise, she may get the idea of executing them to make a point."

"It wouldn't be the first time a Regent and his or her Ruling Council felt a tinge of worry at losing their absolute grip on power because of unexpected events and lashed out in ways that annoyed the Conclave. Thankfully, whenever it was time to replace either before their terms ended, it happened peacefully, at least in as far as outside observers could tell."

Godfrey glanced at his companions.

"And finding out about a rival already reuniting human worlds is about as unexpected as it gets. Can you imagine the fear of losing control by sending missions and colonists beyond our star systems? Large, interstellar polities are, by definition, decentralized, which was what allowed the various viceroys to rebel so successfully against the Ruggero Dynasty."

"Do you think we did her wrong?" Robbins asked. "That we should have asked permission for Task Force Kruzenshtern's mission instead of seeking forgiveness now that we were found out?"

Godfrey shook his head.

"The answer would have been insufficient evidence, permission denied, under the tried-and-true principle practiced by authoritarian regimes throughout history. If you suppress knowledge about something, then it doesn't exist."

Bolack let out a bark of laughter.

"Until everyone sees that it does."

"And that's when regimes collapse, often in an orgy of violence. No, we did the right thing for our people, though probably not for our rulers or our system of government. But if it means

Colonel Torma and Sister Ardrix must pay the ultimate price, then so be it."

"Rather cold-blooded of you, Johannes. Those two are patriots who willingly went beyond the call of duty and, at our orders, broke the very rules they enforce."

"Agreed, but you can't say I'm wrong."

Robbins let out a soft grunt. "No, I can't."

"What happens now?" Bolack asked as they turned back toward the abbey proper.

"That depends on her next move, which must happen within the next eighteen to twenty-four hours," Godfrey replied. "She can't wait much longer before control over events slips through her fingers. In fact, I wouldn't be surprised if she's summoned the Ruling Council for a late-night sitting."

Robbins gave him a sly smile. "Meaning you know she's summoned them."

He nodded. "I wish I could sit in on that meeting. It should be quite the performance by dear Vigdis."

"You mean you've not planted surveillance gear in the Regent's conference room?"

"Tried and failed. Her close protection people are rather good at keeping the Wyvern Palace clean. I've been luckier with the Chancellery, but the intelligence we gather isn't particularly useful. Gossip, on the other hand…" He winked at Robbins. "By the way, whatever happened with the hapless merchant captain who triggered this?"

"He's learning the ways of the Void at an isolated priory on the other side of the planet. It was that or my cells and a date with the executioner. No one will look for him there."

Godfrey let out a delighted burst of laughter. "Serves him right."

40

"How is it none of you knew five of our ships, along with a company of Special Forces operators and a detachment from the State Security Commission, left the Hegemony for months on an expedition to the Hatshepsut star system?"

Grand Admiral Vigdis Mandus, Commander-in-Chief and Regent of the Wyvern Hegemony, paced back and forth behind her chair at the head of the conference table as she vented her spleen. Without warning, she stopped and gave the three service chiefs a venomous glare.

"Are you not in control of your branches?"

"That's a bit unfair, Regent," Admiral Marco VanReeth, Commander, Hegemony Guards Navy replied in a measured tone. "You know we rely on our chiefs of operations for the day-to-day running of the services. Our duties on the Ruling Council absorb much of our time. It simply takes the three of them to form a little cabal, and we're none the wiser."

"I can assure you my deputy was wholly unaware," Chief Commissioner Cameron Bucco said, "and so was the commander of the Wyvern Group, General Cabreras. This was cooked up at lower levels in my branch."

"Be that as it may."

Mandus resumed pacing under the eight Council members' guarded eyes. Five were present in the flesh, the service chiefs, the Chancellor, and the Consul ruling Wyvern, and three, the Consuls of the Torrinos, Dordogne, and Arcadia star systems via subspace radio. The latter hadn't said a word, both because they weren't directly involved and because the delay in transmission quickly became irritating. Even with powerful subspace relays in geosynchronous orbit above the four planetary capitals and interstellar relays between the four systems, it was hardly instantaneous. And the Regent seemed irritated enough.

"It's clear both the Navy and Ground Forces operations chiefs were involved. There's no way around that. Which leaves us with the question of what next? Conspiring to violate the laws this Council has decreed in the interests of state security is a serious matter. Civilians who do so receive the harshest of penalties, including death."

"Only if they're not well connected," Chancellor Elrod Conteh muttered.

"What was that?"

"Nothing, Regent."

She glared at him for a few seconds, then let her eyes roam around the table and across the three displays at its far end.

"The way I see it, we have two options. One, we bury the whole matter, execute Torma and Ardrix, replace the Navy and Ground Forces operations chiefs and those who directly helped them, including Commodore Watanabe and the five starship captains, along with the officer commanding the Special Forces company. Then, Chief Commissioner Bucco conducts a thorough purge of the Guards Corps ranks, starting with his own service, because we obviously face a core of dissenters who do not respect this Council or its authority."

Bucco nodded.

"We're due for a serious purge anyhow. There's too much laxity in the senior ranks."

"Including the Commission, it seems." Mandus gave him a hard stare. "Don't become overly enthusiastic at the thought of shooting your own people, Cameron."

"Regent."

He and his seven colleagues might form a Ruling Council with Mandus at its head, but she wielded the ultimate instrument of absolute control, the Wyvern Regiment. Not only was it under her personal control, but it acted as a military police unit that could easily counterbalance the Commission in and around the capital if necessary.

The Regent personally selected its commanding officer for unbreakable loyalty to the Hegemony's supreme office above anything else. He or she would defy anyone of higher rank other than the Regent, with force if necessary.

"Our second option is to get ahead of the matter. Accept Task Force Kruzenshtern's findings and make them our own by saying we approved the expedition. Then, announce Lyonesse's existence and plan our own expansion using similar means. I'm sure Archimandrite Bolack can scrape up Void missions to seed our first colonies beyond the four home star systems."

Admiral VanReeth glanced at Bucco.

"Can the Commission scrape up enough teams to make sure those missions don't threaten our security by their activities on planets we can't effectively control? Teams that don't show this Colonel Torma's unfortunate tendencies I mean."

Bucco gave VanReeth a dirty look.

"The Commission serves the state and will do what it requires."

"Enough!" The word cracked like a whip above the Council members present in the flesh. Those at the far end of a subspace link flinched a little while later. "Two options and no leeway, my friends and colleagues. What is the safest path for the Hegemony?"

"Bury the matter," Bucco replied without hesitation. "News that after two centuries of believing we were the last survivors, it seems there's not only another but one who's seizing former imperial star systems, will destabilize the current order. And that is the road to ruin."

"For whom?" Chancellor Conteh asked.

"What do you mean?"

"Precisely what I asked. Who will be ruined by acknowledging we are not the sole survivors?"

"I'm with Cameron on this," General Kristianne Farrah, Commander, Hegemony Guards Ground Forces, said before Bucco could answer Conteh's question. "We can't acknowledge the existence of a rival outdoing us until we have his full measure and can show the people we will become the sole heir of the fallen empire. Anything less means unrest and upheaval. After almost two hundred years of peace and stability, we cannot afford a breakdown of the social contract."

Mandus turned to the Commander of the Guards Corps Navy. "Marco?"

"I'm with my fellow service chiefs, Regent."

"Chancellor?"

"I'd still like to hear Chief Commissioner Bucco explain for whom not burying this issue is the road to ruin?"

A faint sneer briefly crossed Bucco's face.

"Surely you get my meaning."

"Of course, I do, though I'd rather hear you say it. But since you won't, please allow me. The knowledge we've held back for two centuries, comfortable with our illusion of absolute control over four planets, while another surviving chunk of the empire is slowly reunifying human worlds, can ruin our very system of government. And with it, those of us around this table, the members of the Conclave who elected us, and elites who profit from the way we've run things for so long."

"Illusion?" A frown creased Bucco's forehead. "My dear Chancellor, it's not an illusion if the people believe it to be real. And after all this time, none would tempt fate by pushing the boundaries."

"Yet many already are, such as the people behind this merchant's voyage beyond our sphere. How many others escaped your notice altogether? I tell you, we've been riding a dangerous beast for generations, and it's hungry. We must stay ahead of the news, whatever the consequences or that beast will surely devour us. Our denying the truth because we find it inconvenient will end in disaster. That which cannot go on forever will not go on forever. And ignoring the galaxy at large because we've become ossified is something that cannot go on."

Mandus studied Conteh with greater interest than ever before.

"Why are you so passionate about the subject, Chancellor? I've never heard you talk about the need for change. Our system works. The worlds in our care remained safe since Dendera's defeat. Why upset everything? Sure, we can't deny reality, but we can adjust to it slowly, without saying anything about Lyonesse or even intimating someone else is reunifying humanity. That way, our current system of government will survive."

Conteh chuckled.

"It might survive the annexation of three, four, or even ten star systems. But as Dendera proved, absolute control over a thousand star systems, home to countless worlds, non-planetary habitats, and unregistered colonies, is impossible. I won't even mention control over traffic through the entire wormhole network and the unimaginable vastness of interstellar space. We should face reality right here, right now, and adapt. If that means changing how we govern the Hegemony, then so be it. Yes, I can give you a long list of those who will strenuously object and perhaps even sabotage our efforts. They've become the closest thing to the old imperial aristocracy, a caste for whom any change to the system of government means loss of power, influence, wealth, or all three. And that includes a fair number of Conclave members." Conteh turned to Bucco. "But I'm sure the Commission can rouse itself to finally arrest saboteurs who are part of the upper crust, even though they've been quite literally getting away with murder for longer than anyone can remember."

"Careful, Chancellor," Bucco growled.

"Instead of executing him, why not promote the colonel who triggered this? He strikes me as rather fearless and unimpressed by rank, even though I've never met him."

Mandus rapped the tabletop with her knuckles.

"Back to the debate at hand. The three service chiefs favor burying the entire story and presumably purging their organizations, the two going hand in hand. Let's just be sure what a purge implies. It means I will execute the most senior officers involved. We can't just force them out and watch as they build an underground opposition network."

Admiral VanReeth shrugged.

"I'm good with that. Sandor Benes has been eying my job with undue interest. He's the sort who might just engineer my removal."

"No love lost there," Chancellor Conteh said to no one in particular.

"Benes wasn't my pick, and he's been scheming behind my back from day one."

Mandus turned to General Farrah.

"Are you just as unhappy with your second-in-command?"

"No." She shook her head. "We've always worked well together, and I wouldn't want him executed over this."

"Suppression means to purge. Are you changing your mind?" When Farrah didn't immediately reply, Mandus resumed pacing. "Admiral VanReeth is for suppression; Chancellor Conteh is for releasing the news and changing the way government does business, and General Farrah has joined the ranks of the undecided. Consuls, what say you?"

The rulers of the Hegemony's star systems, retired admirals or generals elected by the Conclave for nine-year terms, ran their worlds almost like medieval fiefs. And it was an open secret that Consuls, along with their deputies and secretaries, left the post much wealthier than they were before taking it up. As such, they had a vested interest in the current system, and Mandus fully expected they would voice support for suppression.

"Wyvern?"

"I'm worried about the idea of a purge, Regent. It would generate a lot of discontent within the Guards Corps, especially if that purge includes those who took part in the Hatshepsut expedition. There's no way of keeping it hidden from the rest of the armed forces. Worse yet, Sandor Benes has a strong following in the Navy." He glanced at VanReeth. "I can still count on friends in various places, Marco, and most would rather see him in your seat. Sorry, but that's the reality at the more junior flag officer levels and below. I'm convinced suppression won't work, and the fact we tried will only make matters more fraught with peril for the government. What is it they say since time immemorial? The coverup is always worse than the scandal? I'm with Chancellor Conteh on this. Acknowledge, adapt, and move forward."

"Dordogne?"

She waited for the usual transmission delay, first for her question to reach the Consul, then for her answer, eyes on the relevant display.

"We're caught between the devil and the deep blue sea, Regent, and damned either way. News of this magnitude will come out, if not tomorrow or the day after, then next month. Five starship crews will make sure of it, especially if we purge Gatam Watanabe. He's another Sandor Benes, with a loyal following among the Navy's officers. I'd rather not be hanged by the neck from the nearest lamppost by enraged spacers because mutiny will be a real concern if we don't limit a purge to the most senior people.

"I vote no to suppression. Let's focus our energies on a managed release of information and plan to carry out the Oath of Reunification. Even among those who might not, at first, be favorable, the general reaction might surprise us. There's a lot of opportunity in a growing Navy, revived exploration, and especially colonization. The worlds between Hatshepsut and the Hegemony are ours for the taking. I'll bet if we ask the Conclave in a plenary session, we'll obtain a majority vote to get on with expansion before Lyonesse wipes us out. And that's all I have to say on the matter."

Chancellor Conteh clapped his hands in a slow, measured beat.

"Bravo. Someone who truly gets it."

Mandus ignored him and turned her eyes on the next display. "Arcadia?"

Again, a delay before the reply came across the subspace net.

"My gut tells me this is a no-win situation. Keeping news of Lyonesse from the Hegemony's people would place us on the wrong side of history. I'm with Dordogne. Let's seize the opportunities. There should be plenty of riches for everyone out there. Count my vote as a no to suppression."

"That's three against two, with one abstention. Torrinos?"

"I'll make the Consuls' response unanimous, Regent. Suppression wouldn't do our credibility any favors, and a purge would see us replaced wholesale without Conclave intervention."

Mandus nodded once.

"Four in favor. I'll add my vote and make it five. The debate is over. Before we discuss how to handle the situation, it might be prudent if I take a few minutes and inform the Archimandrite. Who knows what mischief is brewing across New Draconis in the expectation we would move against those involved for defying this Council? A five-minute break, everyone."

Shortly afterward, Mandus settled behind her desk, alone in the office, and opened an encrypted link with the Archimandrite's office in the New Draconis Abbey. He answered within seconds, an expectant air on his face.

"And?"

"We're good. Surprisingly, the four Consuls agreed, absolving me of the need to force the issue, but I'm disappointed in the service chiefs. Two blood-thirsty bastards in favor of a purge and one waffling general who somehow reached four stars in the Ground Forces without facing a hard decision."

Bolack nodded.

"Then you know who needs replacing. I'm not surprised, however. The Consuls are nearer to the people, especially those with wealth. They know which path will keep them in power and riches, and it isn't the one that might trigger a revolt."

"Thank you for trusting me with this, Archimandrite, even if you waited until Task Force Kruzenshtern left the Torrinos system on a course for Hatshepsut."

He inclined his head.

"When faced with such an existential decision, I knew you would make the right choice, provided you had time to think about it."

"Call it enlightened self-interest. I enjoy my job and would rather not be hauled out of the Wyvern Palace by enraged Guards Corps officers or overthrown by the Conclave."

"I admire your self-awareness." He smiled at her. "When will you release Colonel Torma and Sister Ardrix?"

"As soon as we're done here. But they must stay silent until I unveil my plan of action."

"Then see that they're delivered straight to the abbey. They can join the Lyonesse Brethren at the Grenfell Priory."

"Whom I should enjoy meeting as soon as possible." She sighed. "Just make sure no one ever finds out you've been keeping me apprised of Task Force Kruzenshtern's expedition, for both our sakes. This must forever be known as the night Vigdis Mandus stared down inertia and reaffirmed the Oath of Reunification. Those involved would not react well if they knew we've been manipulating events."

— 41 —

When Mandus, wearing a grim expression, returned to the conference room and took her seat at the head of the table, Admiral VanReeth rose.

"Regent, during your absence, we discussed options."

She cocked an eyebrow at him.

"Did you now. Clearly, you'd like to lay them out before me, so please, go ahead."

"The idea of wholesale suppression is off the table. Fine. But few heard the name Lyonesse and are aware it's expanding across the Coalsack and neighboring sectors. We know who they are and can swear them to secrecy in return for a prominent place in our own expansion plans. That way, we keep control of the story. Yes, we sent an expedition to Hatshepsut as a way of defining an expansion corridor now that we, the Hegemony's Ruling Council, determined the time has come for enacting the Oath of Reunification. Without public worry about another polity taking away what many consider our birthright, we can manage recolonization at our pace. And not coincidentally, we would make sure certain elements in our society who might otherwise wish for full suppression see they have a stake in supporting the new policy."

Mandus let out an amused snort.

"In other words, contracts for ships, colonization packages, and the like would go to the right people. And they, in turn, will do what is necessary, so this government persists no matter what."

"While this government enforces social peace so the right people can do what is necessary and see that we meet Lyonesse on our terms."

"In other words, the same old graft, only on a larger scale," Chancellor Conteh said in a sardonic tone.

VanReeth turned a hard eye on him.

"Would you rather face unrest?"

"Of course not. I merely deplore the fact our political status quo rests on keeping the wealthy happy and the citizenry under both tight control and a smothering blanket of entitlements that kills any drive for change. It wasn't always so in the centuries before the Ruggero Dynasty perverted a perfectly functioning, quasi-republican system under a Crown with defined powers who stayed above petty politics. Oh, the wealthy had their fingers in every pie, but at the star system level mostly, which limited the damage."

"Pardon me, Chancellor, but has anyone ever mentioned your love of ancient history can be trying at times?"

"My wife reminds me every day, Admiral." Conteh winked at VanReeth, then turned to Mandus. "Notwithstanding my comments, the Admiral's proposal is sound. As much as I'd like to eliminate graft, we can't do so in one fell swoop, and the Almighty knows how far the privileged will go to preserve their privilege. Better we use it as a way of expanding the Hegemony. Structural changes will follow in due course, though not as fast as some, such as I, would like."

"If the Chancellor agrees, that means it's unanimous. We suppress intelligence about Lyonesse but announce Task Force Kruzenshtern was our first move in enacting the Oath of Reunification."

Everyone around the table nodded, as did the three off-world Consuls a short time later.

"Then a press release tomorrow morning announcing the success of Kruzenshtern's expedition meets with everyone's approval?"

More nods.

"Admiral VanReeth, you have the rest of the night to make sure no utters the name Lyonesse until we say so. Fortunately, as I understand, only Commodore Watanabe and a few Kruzenshtern personnel know the full story. If ever word gets out before we're ready, we will run a disinformation campaign that paints it as an unsubstantiated rumor, but something we will check out in due course."

"Yes, Regent."

"What about Colonel Torma and Sister Ardrix?" Chief Commissioner Bucco asked. "They're ground zero of this whole debacle."

"Both will help further our plan in due course. And no, I won't discuss what it is until we deal with the immediate fallout. In the meantime, I've arranged for their temporary disappearance from mainstream society, so no one can question them about their knowledge of this matter, and that includes you, Chief Commissioner, and anyone else in the State Security

Commission. Consider them temporarily part of the Wyvern Regiment and under my personal command for all intents and purposes."

Bucco inclined his head.

"Understood, Regent."

But Mandus could hear resentment in his tone.

"Then we're done here for the moment. It's late, and we have a lot of work ahead of us. Thank you, everyone."

With that, she swept out of the room as the displays went dark and the members present in the flesh stood, lost in thought. All save Chancellor Conteh called their aides on the way to the underground parking lot.

Conteh, who enjoyed walking between the Wyvern Palace and the Chancellery since it was a mere one kilometer, nothing for a man in decent physical condition, let himself out via the side door and arrived at his office even before the service chiefs reached theirs. As arranged, First Secretary Vermat waited patiently in the antechamber, reading from a tablet, coffee cup in hand. He made as if to stand, and Conteh waved him down before taking a seat.

"And?"

"Vigdis convinced them they should accept reality, make the Kruzenshtern expedition their idea, and announce the start of a recolonization program, but without mentioning Lyonesse. Those few who know about it will be told silence on the subject is a good career move. In other words, we obtained most of what we wanted. It might take a few years, perhaps even a few decades longer than if Lyonesse's existence was made public now, but military rule will end in due course. The admirals and generals will inevitably come back under civilian control because they'll be too busy spearheading the Hegemony's expansion and adapting to a radically different outlook than the one that has governed us since the empire's downfall. You and I may not see that day, at least not in our current roles, but it's coming."

Conteh allowed himself a sigh of contentment as Vermat put down his cup.

"Excellent news, sir. I confess I was doubtful when you came up with the plan of sending out fishing expeditions in the hopes one of them would bring back something that could shake the Council out of its torpor. It took almost five years, but Jan Keter hit the motherlode. Anonymously denouncing him to Crevan Torma when we found out what he discovered was a piece of genius, by the way."

Conteh smiled at his first secretary and de facto Deputy Chancellor.

"Torma was the right man at the right time, but I can't take credit for thinking of him. That was the Archimandrite's doing, based on what he knew from his people in the Commission. Wheels within wheels, Gelban. I do hope Keter's still alive and well, by the way. I'd hate to think our sole successful dupe died because of this."

"He's under the Order's protection, tucked away in one of their houses and undergoing a Friar's training." A frown crossed Vermat's face. "Wait a minute, sir. Was the Archimandrite in on the fishing expedition scheme?"

"No. I simply asked whether one of his people worked with a senior officer known for doggedness, who didn't fear his superiors and focused on doing the right thing. I don't doubt he eventually suspected a connection with Keter's illegal travels but was so captivated by the mystery and the possibilities for his Order that he didn't breathe a word to anyone."

"Wasn't it risky?"

Conteh shook his head.

"He's motivated by self-interest, just like the rest of us. Besides, if anyone asked, I'd simply have said Keter came to my attention via a backchannel, and I wanted his case investigated by a senior officer who wouldn't bury it out of political expediency."

"We do love our backchannels." Vermat chuckled. "What happens next?"

"Considering the hour, we go home, sleep and come back in the morning. Other than that, it depends on Vigdis." Conteh climbed to his feet. "Good night, Gelban."

"Good night, sir."

Vermat didn't leave right away. He strolled over to the nearest window and gazed out at the sleeping city. Come tomorrow, everything would change, one way or the other. Either Mandus officially announced a recolonization and naval expansion plan like none before and to hell with those who'll howl at the dismantling of the status quo, or there would be a coup d'état ousting the entire Council and replacing it with a junta. Since a coup would have made him acting Chancellor, Vermat privately acknowledged slightly mixed feelings at the missed opportunity. But better this than blood in the streets. Besides, Conteh was a decent man and a fine administrator. He didn't deserve arrest at gunpoint, especially since his views coincided with those of the Network. Wheels within wheels, indeed.

**

General Cameron Bucco and Admiral Marco VanReeth met at the former's residence after exchanging a few quiet words on the way to the Wyvern Palace garage. As head of the Hegemony's powerful paramilitary police, Bucco ensured his property was the most secure spot on the planet where no one could overhear conversations or observe those within. If someone were watching, he or she would see VanReeth's staff car enter the grounds but not discover anything more.

Once in Bucco's study, whiskey glass in hand, they settled into comfortable chairs facing each other across a low table.

"I found Vigdis surprisingly eager to disrupt the status quo," VanReeth remarked after taking a sip. "And in such a hurried manner. It's as if she has another agenda. You'd think a prudent Regent would take her time and study every possibility, perhaps even consult with relevant people outside government before shaking up the masses with news we were heading back into the galaxy. Watanabe and his ships returned what? Less than ninety-six hours ago, and Bolack didn't bring word until this morning. Did you ever know her capable of making momentous decisions so quickly?"

Bucco shook his head.

"No, and I agree, there has to be something else behind her unusual behavior. It's almost as if Vigdis was aware of Task Force Kruzenshtern's expedition from the start."

"Could she and Bolack be cooking up something we won't like?"

"Without a doubt. Then, there's her making Torma and Sister Ardrix vanish right after Bolack's visit. What better way of removing them from circulation than arrest by the Wyvern Regiment." Bucco tasted his drink, then smacked his lips. "Good stuff. It's a shame we can't tap into the Regent's private conversations without leaving a trace. I'd pay good money to know what she and Bolack discussed during our break tonight. Those two have been in cahoots for a long time."

"So, they're scheming. But to what end?"

"I can make a few guesses." Another sip. "The most obvious is Vigdis seeing a way of increasing her power with Bolack's help by springing the news on everyone and grabbing what she can in the turmoil. Without a constitution or a supreme court, the only thing that stops her from disbanding the Council and becoming Regent for life is two hundred years of accepted protocol and procedures and, ultimately, the Guards Corps. However, she owns the Wyvern Regiment, and I'm sure sentiment in the Navy and the Ground Forces will be such that anyone perceived as impeding her call for expanding the Guards and recolonizing former imperial worlds will be deemed an enemy of the state. In effect, Vigdis could be making a bid for the imperial Crown under the blessing of the Almighty via his servant Archimandrite Bolack. Historically, it's always been a tiny step between Regent and Sovereign."

VanReeth nodded thoughtfully. "Plausible. Extremely plausible, if worrisome. Vigdis always was ambitious, which is why she's one of the youngest admirals whoever became Regent."

Bucco let out an amused chuckle.

"Do I hear jealousy in your voice, Marco?"

"My commission predates hers by two years, and we received our fourth star at the same time. I should be Regent in her stead, but she outmaneuvered me with her predecessor and the Conclave."

"And if she seizes absolute power, you'll never get the chance." Bucco fell silent for a bit, eyes on his glass. "Did you ever hear of an obscure prophecy uttered by a mystical Sister shortly after the Hegemony's birth concerning the reunification of human worlds? Jessica was her name, I believe."

"No. What manner of nonsense is that?"

A shrug.

"Void nonsense. I came across it years ago when I was digging into religious matters during an investigation. The Order suppressed the prophecy almost from day one due to the political implications at a delicate time in our history. I can still recall the wording, however. *When both halves of that which was split asunder merge once more under a new, glorious Crown, humanity will fulfill its destiny in the Infinite Void.* Apparently, she uttered a lot of obscure rubbish like that. I doubt many of the Brethren remember her name, but it wouldn't surprise me if the records of her visions were passed down from Archimandrite to Archimandrite. They do like their mysticism, and this is just the stuff that'll give them a frisson."

"No matter what's driving Vigdis and Bolack, we face a problem. If she's intent on sidelining the Council and the Conclave, then we must do something."

Bucco gave his colleague a sardonic smile.

"I'm open to proposals because I can't think of anything that'll stop her now. She timed it much too well for any real pushback, and if the Navy and Ground Forces chiefs of operations were involved in the Kruzenshtern expedition from day one, the Council is effectively helpless. Should it reach that point, my folks will obey the Regent before they obey me, and they definitely won't take up arms against the rest of the Guards Corps, let alone the Wyvern Regiment."

"Don't you use professional assassins?"

"Sure, but once Vigdis makes her announcement in a few hours, the ball will start rolling, and then, even if one of my people takes her out, it'll be too late. Someone else will seize power and carry on with the plan. Your man Sandor Benes, perhaps."

"Why can't one of us seize power?" VanReeth took a healthy slug of his drink and sat back, scowling.

"I can't because no one will accept a Commission officer as Regent. You won't because the moment Vigdis falls to an assassin, the rest of us will fall victim to a coup d'état."

"How do you know that?"

"Because logic dictates that if Vigdis had opted for suppression, we would shortly have found ourselves in cells or dead, perhaps caught in the crossfire between the Wyvern Regiment and enough rebellious Guards Corps units to wipe it out. Please don't tell me you didn't figure out Benes and his cabal wouldn't stand by idly once my folks start executing senior officers. They made their plans well before the task force came back."

"Which leaves us where?"

"Damned if I know."

— 42 —

Torma and Ardrix didn't speak a word during their strange trip aboard a Wyvern Regiment staff car straight from the detention apartments to the abbey. But once they climbed out in the abbey's quadrangle and the vehicle sped away, Torma gave her a questioning look.

"Any idea what this is about? If we're here, it must be the Archimandrite's doing, though it's pretty late in the evening for services."

"Compline is long gone, and everyone except for the duty staff is asleep. Just be happy we don't observe Midnight Offices." She shrugged. "I know as much as you do, which is nothing."

At that moment, an aircar appeared from the direction of the abbey's motor pool. It glided to a halt beside them, and the passenger compartment doors opened.

"Come in," Archimandrite Bolack's voice commanded.

They obeyed and settled on a bench facing him. But the doors didn't close, nor did the car drive off. Instead, Bolack studied them for a few heartbeats.

"The Ruling Council has voted in favor of revealing Task Force Kruzenshtern's mission and owning it for the greater good of the Hegemony, but without mentioning Lyonesse's existence. However, much work needs doing in a short time frame to minimize social disruption. Meanwhile, you're joining the Lyonesse Brethren at the Grenfell Priory, where you'll be sheltered from anyone who might plan on circumventing the Regent and her actions."

A frown creased Torma's forehead.

"You mean she's on our side?"

"Vigdis Mandus is on the side which will do the least damage to the Hegemony and its chances for a prosperous future, and that's acknowledging we've been asleep for two centuries. You will play a role in this, but for now, you must vanish so that she may act without fear her opponents might nab you." Surprising them, Bolack climbed out of the car. He stuck his head in. "A late-night trip isn't for everyone, but it is necessary. Enjoy the priory."

The doors closed, and their car moved off at a sedate speed, leaving the lights of the New Draconis Abbey behind them before lifting off into the starry night.

Torma and Ardrix glanced at each other.

"Whatever I was expecting, this isn't it," he said. "Earlier today, Mandus seemed ready to see us shot for treason. Now, she's on the side of progress? Something isn't right."

"Knowing the Archimandrite, I'd say everything is right. Plans within plans, Crevan. The Order mastered that skill long before the Ruggero Dynasty ascended the imperial throne."

"Which Order?"

An angelic smile lifted the corners of her lips.

"We are both children of the same Infinite Void. If the Almighty wills it, we will become one again in due time."

The flight to the Grenfell Priory took much less time than it would if they'd traveled on the surface. But it was still closer to dawn than compline by the time they landed in its courtyard, where a sleepy Friar, roused by the Mother House, guided them down. He led his unexpected guests to tiny, individual cells in the dormitory and shuffled off without ever speaking a word.

The gentle chimes of Matins, shortly after dawn, came much too early for Torma, and not being of the faith, let alone the Order, he simply turned over and tried to fall asleep again. A smiling Ardrix poked her head in his cell an hour later, looking and sounding as fresh as someone who'd enjoyed an eight-hour night.

"If you're interested in breakfast, now would be a good time. I'd consider it a personal favor if you wore the robes provided instead of your uniform. This is a contemplative house and disturbing the Brethren's peace with evidence of a less than saintly world beyond its walls would be rude."

Torma nodded as he sat up.

"For you, anything. Besides, I don't much feel like a colonel of the State Security Commission right now. Not after spending time in the custody of the Wyvern Regiment, even though they treated us with due courtesy and respect once we left the Palace. Something breaks when your own side arrests you after years of loyal service, even though you're released several hours later without so much as an explanation, let alone an apology."

"It was an act, Crevan, of that I'm sure. Knowing the Archimandrite, he might even have told Mandus everything once Task Force Kruzenshtern was beyond recall."

"The Wyvern Regiment troopers certainly didn't think it was an act when they hauled us out of the Regent's office." He stood, clad only in his underclothes, and reached for a black Friar's robe hanging on the wall beside his uniform. "Why would Bolack inform the Regent while we were still outbound?"

"So she could come to grips with the idea that our old ways were over for good, no matter what we found on Hatshepsut, and do so without pressure from the other Ruling Council members? It's better than surprising her upon our return. Our Archimandrite is a wise and canny man, Crevan. Since he's virtually untouchable, he's the only one who could bring her the news without causing a crisis."

Ardrix gave Torma a critical once-over after he settled the robes around his shoulders.

"You almost seem like a real Friar. Keep in mind that he and the Regent are pursuing their own agendas, but they know it's best if those agendas don't contradict each other at the very least. What they are is not clear, but we can make informed guesses."

"Power. It's always the primary driver. Keeping a grip on power and expanding that grip without losing control has driven Ruling Councils for ages. I suppose in Bolack's case, it's getting the upper hand on a rival whose doctrines vary from yours, especially as it concerns the subordinate role of men in their version of the Order. Although he didn't know the latter until we returned."

Ardrix chivvied him out of his cell.

"But our records tell us how the old Order functioned, and he would have consulted them when we first suspected it survived, and that was well before our departure."

They joined a line of Brethren entering the refectory just as the first light of day painted the craggy mountaintops around them a delicate pink. Grenfell was at the bottom of a narrow alpine valley, beside a running stream and a country road, both of which appeared at one end and vanished at the other. The priory's cluster of one and two-story stone buildings dating back to the empire's happier days were the only evidence of habitation for dozens of kilometers, and the nearest town was almost an hour away by ground car.

As they crossed the quadrangle, Torma took several deep breaths, reveling in a chill morning air filled with the clean, spicy scent of the native coniferous trees carpeting the lower slopes. For reasons that escaped him, he suddenly felt a little lighter of spirit, as if there was something about Grenfell capable of soothing troubled minds. Perhaps it was why the Order used this as their house for contemplatives, who wished a life far from the secular world.

Once inside, they saw the Lyonesse Brethren, breakfast trays in hand, settle around a table in the furthest corner, and after Torma and Ardrix picked up their food, they made a beeline for it. Hermina watched them approach with a wry smile, and when he glanced at the vacant chairs with a question in his eyes, she nodded.

"You come across much better in robes than in uniform, Colonel," she said by way of greeting as they sat. "Are you taking vows?"

"We are here for the same reason as you, to hide far from hostile eyes. Blending in is part of it. Our head of state was apprised of your republic's existence, though not you specifically, yesterday by Archimandrite Bolack, who took us along with him. And her reaction was harsh. She ordered Ardrix and me arrested and placed in detention until late last evening when the Archimandrite saw us delivered here by aircar. Things are probably stirring in the capital, and someone wanted us where we couldn't answer questions that should stay unanswered for the moment." Torma nodded at his companion. "Ardrix has her own theories as to what is transpiring."

"Things are probably in a tizzy back home as well," Hermina replied. "The supply ship should have come through by now and hightailed it back the moment its captain spoke with Rianne and Horam. But our leaders won't arrest the messenger, nor will our people face an existential crisis."

"And ours will?"

Hermina turned her eyes on Ardrix.

"If my understanding of your government system is correct, the idea there are humans with advanced technology freely spreading across former imperial worlds will likely trigger cognitive dissonance. Not least because Hegemony citizens have lived for generations under autocratic rule supposedly for the good of humanity's last surviving civilization."

The latter nodded once.

"I agree. Which is why our leaders must handle this with utmost delicacy."

"And can they?"

Torma made a face.

"Our system is brittle and ossified. It won't handle wholesale change well, I'm afraid."

"The fact you were arrested and then stashed away here certainly doesn't speak of a regime that handles paradigm shifts. Our republic's government will do much better, I think, and won't shoot the messenger, not even figuratively."

He swallowed a spoonful of porridge, then shrugged.

"We're still alive and free, even though we've been asked to lie low. And that's certainly for an excellent reason. I trust the head of the Void Reborn in this matter. He's one of the good guys."

Hermina let out a soft snort.

"I still can't believe your lot lets men run the show. It almost happened on Lyonesse and would have meant disaster for both the republic and the recolonization effort."

"Different place, different needs, different outcomes, Prioress." Ardrix gave her a brief smile. "It works for us and has been since the empire's collapse, so who can say our path is wrong?"

"Granted."

"In the aftermath of the Great Scouring, many who would not otherwise have postulated found refuge in the Order and that changed the balance between men and women. Since then, on average, the Archimandrites have been half Friars, half Sisters, as have the abbots and abbesses, and the priors and prioresses."

It was Hermina's turn to smile this time.

"How very egalitarian of you. Do your Friars possess as strong a talent as the Sisters?"

"Not on average, no, though a few are fairly remarkable. But we don't pick the top leaders based only on that. We also consider other factors, and in the Archimandrite's case, the ability to navigate political currents and eddies and make the Order indispensable. The Hegemony government is based on absolute power and control over all things and brooks no rivals. Were we not useful to it, we would have been suppressed us long ago, leaving our society bereft of spiritual guidance and without a shred of hope, so we've adapted over the years."

"I see. Another fascinating glimpse into a civilization that went down the wrong path." Hermina's tone was as dry as a bone and, if not tinged with scorn, then with a hint of disdain. However, Torma and Ardrix were by now inured to it and ignored her pointed comments.

"Keep in mind Wyvern was ground zero for the fall of the empire. The admirals defeated Dendera by a slim margin and barely saved this world along with three others. That sort of thing leaves a multi-generation scar on the human psyche. I'll take you to visit the site of the old imperial capital eventually, a place which still echoes with anguish and death two centuries later. Perhaps then you'll understand why our civilization took this path. We didn't enjoy the luxury of refuge at the far end of a distant wormhole cul-de-sac, one which escaped the ravages of the Great Scouring. It meant our forebears had no choice but take every measure they believed necessary for survival."

Friar Metrobius let out an amused chuckle.

"She's got you there, Hermina."

"Whether those measures are still necessary," Ardrix continued, "I cannot say, but discovering you will change us, just as it will change Lyonesse. How is something only the Almighty can answer. The Void giveth, the Void taketh away."

The Lyonesse Brethren gave the ancient response in unison. "Blessed be the Void."

"See, you're not that different from each other," Torma said, grinning. "And as for Archimandrite Bolack, I'm sure you'll meet him sooner rather than later. Perhaps in the next few days. Then you can judge for yourself."

— 43 —

Later that morning, an announcement over the public address system shattered Grenfell Priory's silence. All within its walls were summoned to the Chapter House at eleven-thirty for a special announcement by Archimandrite Bolack's order. Ardrix and Torma, who were wandering around the perimeter in silence, glanced at each other.

"That is highly unusual," the former said. "Normally, announcements are made immediately after one of the regular services or during communal meals."

"Which means, I sincerely hope, that things are on the verge of moving very fast."

Shortly before the appointed time, they joined a throng of Brethren, Void Reborn and Lyonesse, at the Chapter House entrance. Because he was a visitor, Torma slipped into one of the upper pews along with Hermina and her colleagues while Ardrix joined the others. At eleven-thirty precisely, just as the prioress and the chief administrator took their chairs on the dais, a large display over the entrance came to life with the image of a lectern flanked by Hegemony flags and backed by the banners of the Guards Corps' three branches. The pulpit itself was decorated with the phoenix, sword, and stars emblem of the Wyvern Hegemony. Moments later, Regent Vigdis Mandus, wearing her unadorned black uniform, appeared on the display and walked up to the lectern. She looked straight into the video pickup.

"Citizens of the Hegemony, greetings. It is with great pleasure and pride that I stand before you to announce the return of the first successful expedition beyond the Hegemony sphere by our courageous Navy. Task Force Kruzenshtern, under Commodore Gatam Watanabe's command, carried out the reconnaissance of one of the main wormhole network branches leading to former imperial sectors beyond our own. During that trip, they discovered several worlds still inhabited by humans but whose civilizations collapsed. As a result, the Ruling Council and I decree that the Hegemony will go forth into what was once the human empire and recolonize those worlds so they may join us in rebuilding and erasing the scars left by the Great Scouring. We will therefore embark on a substantial naval expansion program, increase our Ground Forces, and invite the Order of the Void Reborn to increase is numbers so it can minister to those who will soon become our fellow citizens."

She paused, chin raised in a regal bearing, eyes looking straight into the video pickup. Whether it was by some clever technical design or merely his imagination at work, Torma felt as if she was addressing him directly, and he wondered if anyone else got the same eerie impression.

"Our ancestors swore the Oath of Reunification long ago. Today, I order every branch of the Hegemony government to execute it. The first inhabited world that will rejoin humanity across the stars shall be Santa Theresa, which is connected to Torrinos via two wormhole transits. Our initial reconnaissance will leave Wyvern in six weeks and the first colonization mission in six months. After a long slumber, we will finally mend that which was rent asunder and reunite our species under the banner of the Hegemony."

Torma felt Metrobius, sitting next to him, tense up, though he and the rest of the Lyonesse Brethren didn't say a word.

"Thank you, and may the Almighty in the Infinite Void watch over you always."

The display went dark, and though Torma heard the rustling of robes as Brethren turned to each other in astonishment, none broke the customary silence. The prioress stood.

"You may return to your customary activities."

Ardrix rejoined him as they filed out, a smile of quiet satisfaction on her narrow face.

"Our travels were not in vain."

"No, but let's give this time to play out. The Regent's speech just now was merely the opening salvo. She'll likely face plenty of opposition from those who fear diluting the state's power through expansion will carry a cost they cannot bear, and many of them can sabotage her efforts by using the government's habitual inertia. They've had almost two centuries of practice."

"What will happen with us?" She led him back on the perimeter path so they could avoid the Lyonesse Brethren, who seemed stunned by the announcement.

"I couldn't say, but our returning to Commission duty might not be the greatest idea at the moment. Those at the highest levels will know our role in the matter by now, and no one wants a pair of investigators who presume to go so far beyond their remit that they travel countless light-years through the wormhole network."

"Not even General Robbins?"

Torma shrugged.

"She may not have a choice in the matter, depending on how Chief Commissioner Bucco reacted. We might as well enjoy the peace and quiet here, where our Commission colleagues won't tread for fear of the Archimandrite's wrath."

"In that case, shall we meditate while walking? It will help us digest these events which, using your expression, are now moving extremely fast."

**

Two days later, Torma, Ardrix, and the prioress stood on one side of the quadrangle and watched the same abbey aircar that brought them to Grenfell land with Archimandrite Bolack aboard. They were warned about his arrival by the prioress less than five minutes earlier, meaning he hadn't announced his visit for what Torma suspected were security reasons. The situation in New Draconis must be tense indeed, but then Bolack was likely in the eye of the storm, supporting Mandus in her nascent attempt at pushing the Hegemony in a new direction.

After a gentle landing under the driver's deft control, the side door opened, and Bolack climbed out. He spotted them and broke into a broad smile.

"You'd enjoy the stir back in the capital, my friends. It hasn't been this lively in living memory. Everyone wonders what everyone else is thinking or planning; the Regent is casting about for trustworthy people who can spearhead the colonization effort;

rumors say the Navy is in a leadership crisis and your service, Colonel, isn't far behind."

"Welcome to Grenfell," the prioress bowed her head, imitated by Torma and Ardrix.

"Always a pleasure. This is my favorite house. Such peace. I shall keep myself from disturbing it, but I must speak with your guests, these two and the ones from Lyonesse."

"Of course. I've set aside an office for your discussion with Colonel Torma and Sister Ardrix. The Lyonesse Brethren will meet you in the refectory afterward."

"Very gracious of you."

The prioress inclined her head again, then indicated the administration building's open front door.

"If you'll follow me."

She led them through a part of the building Torma hadn't visited before, but Bolack seemed in perfectly familiar territory. After ushering them into a sparsely furnished room — desk, four chairs, and a credenza — the prioress left, closing the door behind her. Bolack gestured at the chairs and, instead of settling behind the desk, turned his to face them so that they sat in a tiny circle, knees almost touching.

"New Draconis is in utter turmoil. The Regent has upended so many iron rice bowls with her announcement, you'd think the End of Days is nigh. There are few senior people in government she can trust besides the Chancellor and his people, Vice Admiral Benes and Lieutenant General Sarkis and their people, and perhaps you two."

"And you, sir?" Torma asked.

"The Regent and I have always enjoyed a relationship of mutual trust, Colonel."

"That, I don't doubt."

"I see a question in your eyes. Ask it."

Torma hesitated for a second or two.

"Did you inform her of the Task Force Kruzenshtern expedition before we returned? Perhaps shortly after we vanished from Hegemony space? Her reaction in our presence seemed a little strange."

"You mean the arrests?" Bolack chuckled. "That was for your own protection. Yes, I told Vigdis Mandus about the Hatshepsut mystery once Kruzenshtern was beyond recall. At first, she was furious, but after weeks of thinking it over and long conversations with me, she finally acknowledged there could only be one workable path to secure the Hegemony's future."

"So that day in her office, it was an act."

Bolack nodded.

"I'd given her a thorough briefing the day before. However, I then played my role as a messenger for Benes and his colleagues so no one would find out she already knew everything they did. As far as everyone involved is concerned, Regent Mandus heard about Hatshepsut and Lyonesse for the first time that afternoon and faced a momentous decision. But she'd already decided long ago at that point and just needed the Council's, if not approval, then grudging acceptance. Yet, it meant you needed to disappear so no one could ask awkward questions while she forced the Council's hand."

A smirk lit up Torma's solemn features.

"Admirably devious, both you and the Regent, sir, and I mean that as a compliment. I've dealt with slippery customers of every sort in my career, but this is on a whole new level."

The Archimandrite let out an amused chuckle.

"I'll take the compliment, but in truth, it was more a case of seizing the opportunity. Many of us fear for the Hegemony's future if we don't shake off our torpor, and we'd been seeking something dramatic that might do so for years, so thank you for your diligence in pursuing Jan Keter's case."

He bestowed a benevolent smile on them.

"Since the Regent can only rely on a few senior officials and must leave Benes and Sarkis in their respective posts because both services face rapid expansion over the coming years, she will create a fourth branch of the Guards Corps. It shall be known as the Guards Colonial Service, whose supreme commander will not become a member of the Ruling Council and thus will not be appointed by the Conclave like the other service chiefs."

Torma gave Bolack a knowing look.

"That will shelter the incumbent from day-to-day Hegemony politics so he or she can concentrate on the mission. Slick. I like the idea. Make the Navy and the Ground Forces generate ships and troops for the Colonial Service. What about the Commission?"

Bolack's smile took on a tinge of mischief.

"That's where you come in. The Colonial Service will have an Inspector General Branch whose personnel will be drawn from the Commission. However, the IG will not report to the Chief Commissioner but to both the Regent and the Colonial Service's supreme commander."

When he saw Torma's expression, Bolack let out a bark of laughter.

"This didn't pop into the Regent's brain overnight, Colonel. She and I developed a long-range plan over the last few months. Part of the upset in New Draconis is because some people are figuring that out and believe she deliberately sandbagged the Council, the Conclave, and everyone who's been profiting from the status quo. Which, of course, is true. The decree creating a Colonial Service upset even those who stand behind her, such as Admiral Benes and General Sarkis, but they'll come around, I'm sure, if only because they'd rather keep their jobs."

"With the help of your silver tongue, no doubt, sir."

"I do enjoy good relationships will all the players in this drama."

"One might almost think you've been orchestrating the whole affair."

Bolack snorted in a most non-monastic manner.

"The Almighty forbid, but no. Still, I live by the motto that victories result from opportunities clearly seen and swiftly seized. Your discovering the Lyonesse-manufactured goods among Jan Keter's cargo gave the impetus. But back to the Colonial Service. I recommended you become its first IG, with Sister Ardrix as the Order's senior representative in the inspectorate general. Your career in the Commission is essentially over anyhow, and limited though it may be, you have the most experience with humans beyond the Hegemony's sphere. Oh, and it comes with a promotion to brigadier general."

Torma and Ardrix exchanged a glance.

"I suppose I have no choice."

"You always have choices, Colonel. You can become a brigadier general and play an instrumental role in ensuring the changes you unleashed help rather than harm the Hegemony. Or you can stand on the sidelines, carrying out increasingly futile investigations until you retire as a colonel. Neither the Chief Commissioner nor your Group commander will ever trust you again, and there's only so much General Robbins can do."

"I'd already figured that out, sir. Who will head the Colonial Service?"

"Rear Admiral Johannes Godfrey, on promotion to vice admiral. If everything goes well and the service prospers, he'll receive his fourth star, and you could be in line for a second one."

Torma thought for a moment, then nodded.

"Makes sense. Godfrey takes a broad view of things, knows where skeletons are buried, and is skilled enough to navigate the worst of the New Draconis shoals. But most importantly, he believes in acting on the Oath of Reunification instead of simply mouthing platitudes. I think I can work for him."

"As do I," Ardrix said.

"Good. You'll stay here for now. Showing up in the capital at this juncture would be a distraction the Regent and her team doesn't need. Use your time in these peaceful surroundings to learn from Ardrix. The skills she can teach will stand you in good stead over the coming months and years." Bolack climbed to his feet, swiftly imitated by Torma and Ardrix. "If one of you would be so kind as to warn the prioress that I'm ready for our Lyonesse Brethren?"

Ardrix bowed her head.

"I'll go."

She vanished down the corridor while Bolack and Torma followed at a more leisurely pace.

"I guess the old saying that things happen slowly until they happen all at once applies to the current situation in spades," Torma remarked as they stepped back out into the late morning sun.

"Certainly, but that was the only way we could succeed. Giving the naysayers on the Council time to regroup and form a front against the Regent would have meant failure. Now that they're cowed into cooperation and a sizeable plurality of the Conclave support the Regent's call for action, she can deal with the more intractable and less overt opposition." Bolack stopped to look at Torma. "One of your biggest jobs as Colonial Service IG initially will be looking for the latter who'll no doubt try their hand at sabotaging its efforts."

"Then I'll want a final say on who from the Commission I get, in case General Bucco sends me the lazy, the incompetent, the venal, and his very own spies."

"That goes without saying. Admiral Godfrey will also be allowed his pick from the other services and the civilian bureaucracy, at least for the senior ranks." Bolack spotted Ardrix at the Chapter House door, right hand raised in signal. "Ah, our guests are assembled. I shall speak with them alone if you don't mind."

"This is your house, sir." Torma inclined his head. "May the Almighty keep you."

"And you."

— 44 —

Archimandrite Bolack found Hermina and her flock sitting around a corner table, waiting for him. He entered and stopped a respectful number of paces from them, then bowed his head. All eight stood without a word and faced him.

"My name is Bolack, and I head the Order of the Void Reborn. Though I regret the circumstances that brought you to Wyvern, I hope you've been made welcome here."

"We have. I'm Hermina, Prioress of Hatshepsut." She also bowed her head and then introduced her companions, who greeted Bolack with the same respect as they would their *Summus Abbatissa*.

Bolack gestured at the table.

"May I join you?"

"Do we have a choice?"

"Of course. If you don't wish to speak with me, I shall leave."

Hermina locked eyes with him, then shrugged.

"Your house, your rules. Please take a seat."

Bolack dropped into one of the vacant chairs and looked around the table, meeting eight pairs of eyes that gave no hint as to their owners' thoughts.

"Colonel Torma and Sister Ardrix briefed me on everything you told them and everything they told you. I find it fascinating how we went down separate yet parallel paths, both leading to the Almighty in the Infinite Void."

"Except your path takes Void Reborn into the heart of secular affairs while ours learned at great expense the dangers of doing so. And that's without mentioning abominations like Ardrix, something we've also learned to avoid at a high cost. Oh, I know." Hermina raised her hand as if waving away an unvoiced reply from Bolack. "Different circumstances, different times, different needs. Yet the Almighty is an absolute, and so are our vows of service."

"I can't argue with you on that point, Prioress. The Almighty is indeed an absolute but will forgive our ways because we either took part in secular affairs or would have watched our Order die out in the Hegemony. That would have left the people with no spiritual guidance and little hope for a better future, not to mention our traditional teaching and healing works would have disappeared."

"Fine words, but things changed since the collapse. I doubt there's a need for your involvement in politics, let alone policing nowadays."

"I'm not so sure. We continue to be a moderating influence on an autocratic regime which, if left unchecked, would turn the Hegemony into something worse than the Ruggero Dynasty's empire. But other than that, we're not terribly different, you and us. Based on what you told Colonel Torma and Sister Ardrix, we believe in the same things, work with the community in the same ways, and offer succor where it's needed."

Once again, Hermina stared at him for a few seconds before replying.

"I will confess that the Sisters and Friars of this priory, the services, the scriptures, your adherence to the Rule, and everything else that makes Grenfell a House of the Order of the Void differ in no discernible way from how we live back home. The most visible distinction is your orb, but I suppose using a phoenix as a symbol of the Order Reborn is apt. Of course, a different version of the same mythical bird is also used by your government, which doesn't quite make you outwardly independent of the secular powers." A bitter smile crossed her lips. "And now you'll be sending Void Reborn missions to reclaim fallen worlds, just like we do, and prepare them for Hegemony control."

Bolack nodded.

"We either leave our four star systems and re-enter the wider galaxy, or our society will crumble. Perhaps not as violently as the empire did, but with the same end result and with countless millions dead before their time. Stasis always leads to decline and eventual collapse."

"And so, we once again find ourselves with competing interstellar polities, each seeking the upper hand as the sole legitimate heir of our species' patrimony. Considering the Hegemony's aggressiveness, that cannot end well."

"Aggressiveness?" The Archimandrite's eyebrows shot up. "Did anything you saw or heard give you the idea we were more warlike than your own people?"

Hermina let out a bark of grim laughter.

"Your Hegemony is a military dictatorship, and history teaches us such regimes are always prone to solving problems, be they internal or external, through force. Yes, you're by definition more warlike than our republic, which is built on consensus between the government and the people. What do you think will happen when our respective navies meet in a star system such as Hatshepsut, with each commander claiming it for his or her people?"

"They'll negotiate? Or refer the matter back to their government?"

"That's what ours would do, provided yours doesn't open fire first. Can you say the same?" A faint smirk briefly crossed Hermina's face, and Bolack understood she was gently goading him.

"If the commander is under orders to withdraw rather than risk a deadly confrontation, and why wouldn't he or she be, then yes. The Hegemony may be a dictatorship in everything but name. However, neither our leaders nor our military personnel are foolhardy and itching for a fight. Remember, we still bear the intergenerational scars of the last genocidal war. Besides, the galaxy is huge, and the number of human star systems languishing since the empire's collapse is so great that by the time we face each other, we'll both have devised ways of avoiding the errors of the past."

"So you hope." She eyed him speculatively. "And when will you return us to Hatshepsut? Or will we stay your captives for the rest of our lives? Perhaps you might consider that freeing us will go a long way in regaining our government's goodwill and building the foundations for more friendly relationships as we each pursue our vision of reuniting humanity. Besides, we've told you everything we ever will about Lyonesse. Not even an abomination like Ardrix can wring more from us."

"She may be an abomination in your eyes, but her work with the Commission saves lives. Yes, she will enter minds uninvited, but only in the course of her duties. She cannot do so in any other situation thanks to the conditioning our most powerful talents undergo." He shrugged. "But I won't argue the point with you. I understand where you're coming from, and I respect that. Perhaps, during your stay with us, we could explore that difference of outlook further. We are eager to learn about your evolution since your forerunners settled on Lyonesse during the last years of Dendera's reign. Perhaps we'll find that our path needs adjusting so we can more closely match yours."

"Start with Ardrix and her like. That'll go a long way." Another pause. "And if you're thinking about a merger, then you must fix the issue of men as head of the Order, abbeys, and priories."

He gave her an amused smile.

"Or you might relax restrictions and make the best use of the people available, regardless of gender. In any case, I just wanted to meet you and introduce myself, not enter into a debate over our minuscule differences. If you wish, I'll answer questions at this point." He met each of the Lyonesse Brethren's eyes in turn once more. When no one took him up on the offer, he said, "Thank you for your time. We will speak again. Meanwhile, I'll explore returning you to Hatshepsut now that our government has dropped restrictions on official travel beyond the Hegemony's sphere. Perhaps we can charter a hardy merchant captain."

A smirk spread across Hermina's face.

"Isn't that how we ended up as your involuntary guests in the first place?"

"True, but this time, said captain would travel with the government's permission." He stood, imitated by the others.

"We won't hold our breaths. Your government will balk at releasing us after everything we learned about you."

"Perhaps, which is why I make no promises, but I'll try. And even if I receive permission, it might take a while." Bolack bowed his head. "Enjoy the rest of your day."

Then he swept out of the refectory.

"Not quite what I expected," Metrobius said.

"Why?"

"I'm not sure. Bolack reminds me of no one quite so much as the Order's Chief Administrator back home, Friar Odabo."

"Don't get sympathetic with our captors, Metrobius," Hermina warned. "But you're right. There are a few minor points of resemblance."

"Including a talent for managing expectations." The Friar sighed. "We're never getting home, are we?"

"Probably not. It's best if we consider ourselves on a mission to guide the Void Reborn back into the fold."

**

After the prioress, Torma, and Ardrix saw him off, Bolack settled in the back of the aircar, his forehead creased in thought. He couldn't see Mandus ever allowing the Lyonesse Brethren off Wyvern. Based on Torma's account, the folks on Hatshepsut knew people from something called the Hegemony visited and took eight of the ten Lyonesse Friars and Sisters with them, but nothing more. Mandus would likely want the Hegemony's identity, never mind everything that Hermina and her flock learned, kept from the Lyonesse government for as long as possible so the first wave of expansion could be carried out unhindered.

His personal communicator, one provided by Admiral Godfrey and using the sort of encryption proof even from the Commission's best, chimed for attention. He retrieved it from a pocket hidden inside his voluminous black robes.

"Bolack."

"Godfrey, here. Where are you?"

"I just left Grenfell Priory after visiting Torma, Ardrix, and our guests."

"Could you divert to Navy HQ, please, and land on the roof? Admiral VanReeth and General Bucco are demanding the Conclave come together and vote on the Regent's decrees forming the Colonial Service, calling them illegitimate as they were issued without the Council's legal support."

Bolack frowned.

"The Conclave's sole reason is electing the Council members. It has no say on policy."

"They're looking for a way of invalidating her actions, something they can point at and say she should no longer serve as Regent. I think they fear the Council's end as the supreme governing body is nigh."

"I suppose it's one last desperate attempt to wrest power from Vigdis."

"Perhaps, but I'm seeing signs of support for their actions from outside government, interests who didn't enjoy being caught flat-footed with announcements that drastically change the balance of power."

"Will enough Conclave members respond to get a quorum?"

"That depends on how many have patrons pushing them. Ishani Robbins is trying to find out, but she's proceeding cautiously. Her own superior, Commissioner Cabreras, hasn't declared his views, though it's well known he wants the top job, and if this attempt at stopping Mandus fails, it might well become vacant." Godfrey fell silent for a moment. "This is interesting. I just received word the Regent quietly placed the Wyvern Regiment on full alert."

"Really? I can't remember that ever happening."

"You wouldn't. The last time was during Guillermo Toshida's term as Regent when you and I were mere toddlers. It didn't end well for the cabal of disgruntled senior officers intent on overthrowing him. Half of the Council was in on it. By the time things settled down, the three services were under new chiefs and Wyvern a new Consul. The previous incumbents vanished into unmarked graves. I wonder whether the Wyvern Regiment's intelligence analysts suspect VanReeth and Bucco are doing more than just agitating for an ad hoc Conclave meeting. They're damn good at sniffing out threats to the Regent. This new development makes it even more imperative you land at Navy HQ."

"I shall join you as fast as possible. Was there anything else?"

"No. Godfrey, out."

Bolack sat back, staring at the communicator in his right hand. Why were some people so concerned about personal power when the future of the Hegemony was at stake? It couldn't be simple greed, but then, the pathological urge to enrich oneself was always reliably the source of so much political turmoil throughout history.

Yet more important matters were at stake, such as Sister Jessica's prophecy that the two halves of what was rent asunder will reunite. If it comes to pass, then the new union of human star systems must happen under the Hegemony's banner and the Void Reborn's Phoenix Orb.

The old Order, with its outdated views, its strange scruples, and its refusal to use the abilities of all Friars and Sisters to the utmost couldn't be the way of the future.

No, that future belonged to the Void Reborn, and if it must, his Order would have no problems weaponizing powerful minds, such as Ardrix's.

**

"What did you think of the Archimandrite?" Torma and Ardrix met Hermina halfway around the priory's walking meditation circuit not long after Bolack's aircar vanished over the mountaintops, and all three stopped by common accord.

"I'm sure you don't want to hear my impression, Colonel."

"Strangely enough, I do."

A faint air of annoyance crossed her face.

"He's intelligent, with a stronger mind than I expected in a Friar. Definitely not one to trifle with. But he's a politician as well, and that isn't what you want in a monastic."

"Why do you call him a politician?"

A bitter smile twisted her lips.

"Because he can equivocate and manipulate with the best of them rather than speak the Almighty's naked truth openly. Enjoy the rest of your day."

And with that, Hermina walked away.

Torma and Ardrix looked at each other in surprise.

"She's not wrong, you know," the latter finally said.

45

As Bolack's aircar flew over New Draconis, he looked down, searching for signs of what might have put the Wyvern Regiment on full alert, but saw nothing. The city seemed as quiet as always on a weekday morning because it was devoted to government business, which mainly happened indoors.

Godfrey's aide, Lieutenant Krennek, met him on the Navy HQ roof and led him down to Admiral Benes' office, where he and Godfrey waited. Both wore an extra star on the collar since Bolack saw them a few days earlier.

"I gather congratulations are in order?" He joined them around the low table by settling into one of the deep, leather-covered chairs.

"For everyone, Archimandrite." Benes winked at him.

"What do you mean?"

"The Wyvern Regiment is on high alert because Grand Admiral Mandus is unilaterally changing the composition of the

Hegemony's executive branch. You might note that I now wear a fourth star. Admiral VanReeth has been relieved of his duties, along with Generals Bucco and Farrah. The Wyvern Palace has just announced they are retiring effective at midnight tonight, after long and honorable careers, so that a new slate can take over and implement the Oath. I now command the Navy, General Sarkis the Ground Forces, and General Cabreras yes, Nero Cabreras of all people, the Commission for State Security. However, none of us are members of the Ruling Council because Grand Admiral Mandus, Regent of the Hegemony and its absolute ruler, abolished it. But the four Consuls stay in place, as does the Chancellor."

"She abolished the Ruling Council?" Bolack sounded incredulous. "Can she do that?"

"Sure. No one ever bothered drawing up a constitution that spells out how the Hegemony is governed. The only reason no previous Regent made a bid for change was because of inertia and the lack of Guards Corps support to carry out what is in effect a coup against the established order. Task Force Kruzenshtern's return has changed everything. Both the Navy and the Ground Forces are vibrating with enthusiasm at the notion of expanding back into the former empire's domains and won't countenance any reticence. Since the Ruling Council, or at least part of it, didn't show the same enthusiasm, Mandus used the occasion for a shakeup."

"A necessary one," Godfrey said. "The current structure would have impeded the build-up of our forces and the recolonization effort due to excessive centralization of power and decision making."

"As a result, the Regent centralizes power even more in her own hands?" Bolack raised a skeptical eyebrow.

"Not quite." Benes' mysterious smile widened. "For the next while, until the Conclave aligns itself with the new reality, a triumvirate made up of the Regent, the Chancellor, and you will run the Hegemony."

"Me?" Bolack sat up, astonishment writ large on his face.

"Sure. Vigdis represents the military part of our state, Conteh, the civilian part, and you, the religious part. Think about it. The people, by and large, trust the Order. As its leader and a major voice in secular as well as religious affairs, your membership in the triumvirate will lend the new structure greater legitimacy in the eyes of the public than the Ruling Council enjoyed."

"I didn't know she was contemplating such a move."

Godfrey chuckled.

"It's been in the works since before Kruzenshtern's return. That's the beauty of compartmentalization. You worked with her to change the Hegemony's path should Torma and company come back bearing evidence of another star-faring polity, unbeknownst to us. Meanwhile, we worked with her to get rid of the Ruling Council, which bears most of the responsibility for our long societal stasis, unbeknown to you. The Almighty only knows what she plotted with the Chancellor, but she most assuredly did since he's one of the triumvirs." Godfrey let out a contented sigh. "Getting rid of the Council has been a long time coming. Without it, we can finally push through the first genuine change in almost two hundred years."

"Vigdis Mandus is full of surprises. Who would think she'd abolish the Council on top of everything else?" Bolack shook his head.

"Anyone who saw the naked ambition hiding behind her stone-cold competence. I'm not a fan of the great man or woman theory, but Vigdis is indeed the right person at the right time. I can only shudder at how things would have unfolded if VanReeth were the Regent instead. We dodged a bullet when she won the election."

"What about the Conclave?"

"For now, it stays and elects the Regent and the Chancellor. The Archimandrite, of course, will be elected by the Brethren of the Order as before. But the Conclave's role will change as we expand. Right now, Mandus needs to centralize power in her hands so she can push through her decrees and make recolonizing former imperial worlds happen. Yet as we expand, power will by necessity flow downward. It wouldn't surprise me if the Conclave, initially designed as a militaristic version of a senate with limited powers, becomes a true legislature. Something with the powers of the one which existed in the empire's early days."

"And then, hopefully," Benes said, "when we finally meet the Republic of Lyonesse head-on, it will be as equals, if not with us as superiors because the alternative is unthinkable."

Bolack opened his mouth to reply when Benes' communicator chimed. The latter retrieved it from his tunic pocket and glanced at its screen.

"The Regent. Wait one." He thumbed the controls, then placed it on the low table. "Benes here, sir. Admiral Godfrey and Archimandrite Bolack are with me and I have you on speaker."

"Good morning, Gentlemen. I'm calling to give you an update. VanReeth, Farrah, and Bucco are under house arrest, so they can't dispute my announcement they retired voluntarily. Troopers from the Wyvern Regiment are guarding them. I set the trap to test Nero Cabreras, so we'll soon know whether he's driven by ambition or ideology. Can you transport the Archimandrite to the Wyvern Palace in half an hour?"

"Yes, sir."

"Good. The Chancellor is coming over as well. We will make the public announcement together at noon, and that should cut short anything the opposition could be plotting. Without a Council, all those political grifters no longer have a window into the upper echelons of government."

"How did the Consuls take the news?" Godfrey asked.

"With more equanimity than I expected, but I made it clear the first sign of opposition on anyone's part means early retirement, at gunpoint if necessary. I doubt they're happy they now report to a triumvirate instead of sitting on a Ruling Council, but there's little they can do. Oh, and I'd like to shed the Regent title. Our ancestors adopted it because the incumbent was supposed to be a military stand-in for the true sovereign that will come and heal the damage caused by the Ruggero Dynasty. But there's no true sovereign coming, and our head of state isn't a mere stand-in sitting at the head of a Council of equals anymore. I'm open to suggestions."

"If I may," Bolack said. "The Republic of Lyonesse is headed by a president elected by a senate whose members are elected by eligible citizens. Since our founders designed the Conclave as something with a senate's power to appoint a ruler, why not call our highest office president as well? It makes for a neat break with the past."

Benes raised his hand. "Seconded."

"And me," Godfrey added. "President, Chancellor, and Archimandrite, the Hegemony's new executive team. It scans. Perhaps your next move is wearing civilian clothes, sir."

"One step at a time, Admiral," Mandus growled. "I wouldn't want any Conclave members thinking I've become ripe for the picking."

"With the Wyvern Regiment, which you should re-title the Presidential Guard Regiment, by the way, looking out for your welfare, I can't think of a single flag officer who'd try. Besides, most are excited at the opportunities for promotion and preferment in an expanding Hegemony, their patrons be damned."

"Okay. Enough. I'll think it over and discuss the matter with Chancellor Conteh momentarily. If he agrees with Archimandrite Bolack, then President Mandus I shall become when I announce that I've dissolved the Ruling Council in favor of a more progressive and forward-thinking executive." A pause. "Archimandrite, I shall see you at the Palace. Mandus, out."

"The speed of events makes one's head spin," Bolack remarked as Benes retrieved his communicator.

"Things barely move until everything happens at once. A piece of wisdom that survived every human calamity and is still applicable today. What did Torma say about becoming my inspector general?"

Bolack chuckled. "His exact words were 'I suppose I have no choice' if you'll believe it."

"That's him alright. I would suspect someone too eager for the job of hiding a personal agenda. And Ardrix?"

"She'll do as the Order commands, but I think the appointment pleased her. Our Ardrix hides an unquenchable curiosity behind that demure appearance. I suppose it comes from having a strong will along with a well-developed talent. In any case, she's yours until you tire of her or she tires of the assignment."

"Which could be years."

"Probably. Ardrix is one of those who wouldn't be in the Order except for her extraordinarily powerful talent, so don't be surprised if she prefers adventure over worship."

A sardonic grin tugged at Benes' lips. "Does Torma know that?"

**

Newly minted Brigadier General Crevan Torma examined his reflection in the mirror of his freshly assigned flag officer quarters on Joint Forces Base New Draconis. The silver star on either side of his tunic's collar opening, along with a general's silver braid decorating his black uniform, felt unreal, as did the Guards Colonial Service badge on his sleeves. The design wasn't much older than his promotion orders and featured the Hegemony's phoenix, sword, and stars insignia inside the Colonial Service's emblem, a compass rose pointing outward in every direction.

He'd received his promotion from President Mandus' hands in the Wyvern Palace the day before, under the benevolent gaze of Vice Admiral Johannes Godfrey and the amused eyes of Ardrix, the Colonial Service's leading Sister of the Void Reborn. Bolack was searching for a new title, something that would convey her status as equal to a prioress, but so far couldn't come up with anything that passed muster among the Order's senior Brethren.

"Why not keep it simple and call her Leading Sister of the Colonial Service?" He muttered to himself. "That's the problem with theologians. They're always arguing about how many angels can dance on the head of a pin."

Today was his first day of duty as the newest branch's inspector general, which suited him fine. He'd been as surprised as anyone at hearing the President appointed Nero Cabreras Chief Commissioner for State Security. When he remarked on the fact, his new commanding officer merely smiled and said Cabreras passed Mandus' test with flying colors but wouldn't elaborate beyond a cryptic statement to the effect that personal ambition beats ideology ninety-nine times out of a hundred. However, seeing Ishani Robbins take Cabreras' place as the Wyvern Group commander pleased him.

Torma made his way to the Wyvern Palace's Blue Annex, a free-standing two-story office building within the security perimeter. It was where Godfrey was setting up the Colonial Service's temporary HQ, close to the President and inaccessible to the grifters who would inevitably clamor for a piece of the action. They'd started soon after Mandus' announcement the previous week and only backed away after Cabreras threatened them with charges of harassing government officials, a serious crime under Hegemony law.

The Commission's new chief also quietly spread the word that the era of influence peddling, graft, and corruption was over. Guilty parties, however, wouldn't face execution or a long sentence in the Hegemony's penal system but permanent exile as involuntary colonists on the worlds opened for resettlement. Whether it was working, Torma couldn't tell, but he'd likely find out once the deportations began and the guilty parties became his problem.

The Wyvern Palace's rear guard post let him through without fuss, his biometrics having already been entered into the security system. He parked in front of the Blue Annex in the spot marked 'Inspector General' and climbed out, eyes taking in his surroundings. If nothing else told the entire Hegemony that President Mandus wasn't taking half measures with recolonizing the former empire, then placing her new Colonial Service HQ on her back step did.

Torma found Godfrey, Ewing Saleh, now wearing a commodore's star as chief of staff, Lieutenant Commander

Krennek, and Sister Ardrix in the admiral's office, enjoying a cup of coffee.

"Ah, Crevan?" Godfrey waved him in. "The general officer's uniform suits you. Serve yourself."

He pointed at a coffee urn on the sideboard. When Torma had done so, Godfrey raised his cup.

"To the Colonial Service, my friends. May we reunite our species under the Hegemony banner before Lyonesse does so under hers."

— 46 —

Lannion
Republic of Lyonesse
Coalsack Sector

"Admiral, please come in and sit." President Aurelia Hecht, a tall, lean, dark-haired woman in her late sixties, wearing a warm, welcoming smile, rose from behind her ornate desk to greet Admiral Farrin Norum.

The Lyonesse Defense Force's Supreme Commander was an old Defense Force Academy classmate from longer ago than either would admit. She nodded at her aide, who stepped back into the corridor, closing the doors behind him.

"Martin said you needed to see me urgently."

"Indeed, Madame President."

"It's just the two of us right now, Farrin. There's no one within earshot who'll be scandalized by overt familiarity." She gestured at the settee group by the window overlooking the Haven River. "What's up?"

"We received an encrypted report from the Void Ship *Serenity* an hour ago over the subspace net. She was within hailing distance of the new Parth relay at the time of transmission, on her way home from Hatshepsut."

"The newest of our Void missions. Is it well? Did they encounter problems?"

Norum nodded.

"You could say so." He gestured at the presidential office's primary display. "May I?"

"Sure."

He reached into his tunic pocket, withdrew his service issue communicator, and linked it with the Government House network. Moments later, the display came to life, showing starships orbiting a planet.

"That, Aurelia, is Hatshepsut, and those are not from the Lyonesse Navy."

A gasp escaped the normally staid Hecht's lips.

"What in the name of the Infinite Void are they?"

"Two cruisers, two frigates, and a transport whose designs clearly evolved from the old empire's naval architecture. Their lines resemble those of Ruggero era warships enough that it makes us one hundred percent sure."

"Oh, dear. I hope you embargoed this information."

"Yes, and the only folks who handled *Serenity*'s report deal with top-secret special access intelligence all the time. It'll stay embargoed until you say differently. But the story gets worse."

Hecht let out a sigh.

"Of course, it does."

"As best we can tell from what *Serenity* pieced together, they belong to something called the Hegemony, a polity which has maintained roughly pre-collapse level technology. They abducted eight of the ten Lyonesse Brethren from the Hatshepsut Priory during compline service. The other two were at sea aboard a sailing vessel at the time and escaped." Norum went on to relate Rianne and Horam's adventures, as recounted by Captain Al Jecks. "The two are now running a priory staffed only with locals apart from themselves. They'll need reinforcements from the Lyonesse Abbey as soon as possible, so work on bringing the Republic of Thebes into the industrial age doesn't falter."

"Whatever is necessary once I make this public knowledge." A grimace briefly twisted Hecht's finely sculpted feature. "Or perhaps not. This Hegemony now knows we exist and will probably learn quite a bit from their prisoners. Including, I fear, our long-range plan of establishing Void missions on fallen worlds, followed by military outposts once a given planet has attained the minimum required technological level to offer basic support."

"And Hatshepsut is still twenty or thirty years away from entering our military sphere. We should decide whether we reinforce the place at once and make it the gateway into Lyonesse space from wherever this Hegemony holds sway or whether we should withdraw the mission. One risks a clash with the Hegemony. The other will erase three years of work and abandon a key star system. Letting our current mission wither on the vine isn't a choice I'd consider. Besides, I'm not sure the Head Abbess will send another group of Brethren if there's no longer a definite schedule for our establishing military control of Hatshepsut."

Hecht allowed herself an un-presidential snort.

"Withdrawing from a major wormhole nexus like Hatshepsut will cause a political crisis, as well you know. Jonas Morane established the grand plan to reunite humanity almost two hundred years ago, and so far, we've been keeping faith with his vision and his overarching timetable. Most people would consider a step back just short of blasphemy, especially if it's because of an unknown Hegemony which might be just as far from Hatshepsut as we are. After all, that expedition was there to discover who was distributing advanced tech on a mostly pre-industrial world. They are surely as surprised, worried, and disturbed as we are."

"But they took eight of our best citizens, volunteer missionaries whose breadth of knowledge and experience gives them insight into most facets of the republic, and we know merely what the last two Brethren on Hatshepsut and *Serenity* picked up."

When she opened her mouth to reply, Norum held up his hand.

"Before you say it, Aurelia, no, we can't send reconnaissance expeditions into the wormhole network past Hatshepsut just yet. The Void Ships are already over-tasked and operating at the very limits of their effective range, and we cannot afford a squadron of regular units gone for months at a time. The Hegemony sent a force capable of fighting off anything they might meet on a mere chase for information. That should tell you something. Besides, with the number of wormhole branches leading into the rest of the old empire from Hatshepsut, it'll most likely turn into a snipe hunt."

She contemplated her old friend in silence for a few moments, then nodded.

"Fair enough. I was a naval officer longer than I've been a politician, so I understand the constraints only too well. What advice will you present to the Secretary of Defense when you let him know about this?"

Norum wasn't surprised that she figured he hadn't yet spoken with his nominal civilian superior. Secretary of Defense was the most critical cabinet position and second in the line of succession after the vice president. Only one SecDef ever became the republic's chief executive after both president and vice president were incapacitated, which was in the republic's early years. But the defense job was widely seen as the best way of gaining the sort of profile, and track record demanded of presidential candidates. As such, it attracted the ambitious and politically connected. The days when the position almost automatically went to a retired Defense Force supreme commander were long gone.

Though the current incumbent was no worse and no better than average, he was a career politician. In both Hecht's and Norum's opinion, he displayed a politician's almost unconscious habit of triangulating so he could draw the most advantage from any situation. Since *Serenity*'s subspace message would shake the Republic of Lyonesse to its very core, it was precisely the sort of thing he shouldn't find out about before the president did. Or the rest of the cabinet, for that matter.

"Let me rephrase that," Hecht, who'd been thinking along the same lines as Norum, said. "What advice will you present to the cabinet when I call it together late this afternoon so you can brief everyone at once?"

"You plan on including Sister Gwendolyn, I hope? She should find out along with the other top decision-makers."

"Oh, I wouldn't dare forget our *Summus Abbatissa*."

Though not a member of the administration, the Void's chief abbess attended cabinet meetings whenever decisions or discussions would touch on her Order.

"Then my advice is skip garrisoning Parth for now and send the ships, orbitals, and troops destined for it to Hatshepsut. Suppose the Hegemony returns and finds vessels more advanced than theirs, orbital defense platforms, forts along with traffic control buoys at each wormhole terminus, and a battalion of Marines on the ground. In that case, they might think twice about being hostile. Then, we can demand they return our mission's Brethren. We'll just keep controlling entry into the republic's part of that wormhole branch via Takeshi. The Hatshepsut garrison will simply have to adopt an all-around defensive posture and become an island in the wormhole network."

Hecht smiled.

"That's what I wanted to hear. Although you'll likely find opposition around the cabinet table because this will be a massive disruption in the plan and leave what? Two inhabited and three sterile star systems between our most advanced garrison in that branch of the network and the republic's secure sphere? I can give you the names of the objectors right now."

"I think I know them already. My argument will be simple. The inhabited planets have Void missions on them, so it's not as if there's a break in continuity on that axis of advance." Norum grinned at her. "Besides, you're in favor, I'm sure the vice president won't demur, and our dear SecDef, after seeing which way the wind blows at both ends of the cabinet table, will back me up. This is one of those history-changing events where everyone will be desperate to end up on the winning side."

"Will there be enough time between now and sixteen hundred hours for a comparison between the Hegemony ship design with Imperial Navy roots and our own home-grown naval architecture, based on *Serenity*'s passive scans?"

"My intelligence folks are already on it. I'll have something solid for the cabinet meeting."

She gave him a wry smile.

"You always were a step ahead of me, even at the Academy."

"And yet you made flag officer before I did."

"The luck of the draw." She glanced at the time. "I think it's best if I call the vice president and see if he has time to join us. He'll be less annoyed with me if he finds out now rather than this afternoon."

"A good idea."

The vice president, another career politician, wasn't Hecht's pick. Presidents and vice presidents were elected separately by the senate and chosen for a variety of reasons. Mostly the relationships were good, but wise presidents took pains to make sure they didn't cause resentment, even for minor things.

To Norum's surprise, Vice President Derik Juska proposed moving up the garrisoning timetable once he absorbed the briefing. No political triangulating there.

"Any idea where they might come from?" He asked.

"Nothing concrete, but my gut reaction and that of the intelligence folks who read the message was Wyvern. It would make sense that Wyvern escaped the Retribution Fleet's depredations, no matter the rumors that were circulating at the time. And perhaps a few of the surrounding star systems escaped too. That part of the empire had a solid industrial and technological base, capable of rebuilding if the damage wasn't overly severe. Besides, Dendera wouldn't vaporize her own nest, and I'm sure the Imperial High Command at the time valued their skins more than their personal oaths to a loathsome sovereign."

"Funny how we thought we were alone, the sole guardians of humanity's accumulated knowledge, and yet there was another who probably thought they were also alone. And now, after two centuries apart, we finally meet in the Hatshepsut system of all places." Juska shook his head. "The Almighty moves in mysterious ways. Let's hope we can reunite peacefully, notwithstanding their abduction of our citizens. Otherwise, it might have been for naught."

Hecht smiled at her vice president.

"Always the pessimist."

"Realist, Madame President. I try to see the universe as it is, not as it should be, and won't shy from admitting this news shocks me to the core. And it will make for an exciting cabinet meeting."

"Will anyone object to our claiming Hatshepsut immediately, without telling the locals, let alone ask for their opinion on being made part of the republic, and then fortifying it against any attempts at Hegemony adventurism?"

Juska let out a bark of laughter.

"Half of them will cry bloody murder on principle. Not because we propose annexing a star system so distant from our current sphere. But because we plan on doing so without consulting its inhabitants, thereby violating one of the basic tenets of the reunification plan laid out by Jonas Morane, consent of the governed. A good thing we can get this going without salving the purists' wounded souls. But expect a hue and cry from the senate in due course. Not that they'll try to remove you from office over the matter, but there will be plenty of public posturing and chest-beating for the voters' sake."

"Fine by me. In the meantime, Admiral Norum can get on with it. The next time a Hegemony battle group shows up in the Hatshepsut system, I want it met by our own forces. Whether that will be peacefully or not is up to them. We certainly won't open fire first, even though we're currently the aggrieved party."

"That's what I would suggest," Norum said. "Once we've secured Hatshepsut and established a naval base, we can run reconnaissance missions through the wormhole network between it and every system in the Wyvern Sector, if we so wish. That will allow us to confirm whether a few of them not only survived but thrived."

"Make it so, Admiral."

Norum inclined his head.

"Yes, Madame President."

Ashes of Empire continues with
Imperial Ghosts

About the Author

Eric Thomson is the pen name of a retired Canadian soldier who spent more time in uniform than he expected, both in the Regular Army and the Army Reserve. He spent his Regular Army career in the Infantry and his Reserve service in the Armoured Corps. He worked as an information technology specialist for several years before retiring to become a full-time author.

Eric has been a voracious reader of science fiction, military fiction, and history all his life. Several years ago, he put fingers to keyboard and started writing his own military sci-fi, with a definite space opera slant, using many of his own experiences as a soldier for inspiration.

When he is not writing fiction, Eric indulges in his other passions: photography, hiking, and scuba diving, all of which he shares with his wife.

Join Eric Thomson at http://www.thomsonfiction.ca/

Scan to visit the site.

Where you will find news about upcoming books and more information about the universe in which his heroes fight for humanity's survival.

Read his blog at https://ericthomsonblog.wordpress.com/

Or join his reader forum at https://forum.thomsonfiction.ca/

If you enjoyed this book, please consider leaving a review on Goodreads or with your favorite online retailer to help others discover it.

Also by Eric Thomson

Siobhan Dunmoore
No Honor in Death (Siobhan Dunmoore Book 1)
The Path of Duty (Siobhan Dunmoore Book 2)
Like Stars in Heaven (Siobhan Dunmoore Book 3)
Victory's Bright Dawn (Siobhan Dunmoore Book 4)
Without Mercy (Siobhan Dunmoore Book 5)
When the Guns Roar (Siobhan Dunmoore Book 6)

Decker's War
Death Comes But Once (Decker's War Book 1)
Cold Comfort (Decker's War Book 2)
Fatal Blade (Decker's War Book 3)
Howling Stars (Decker's War Book 4)
Black Sword (Decker's War Book 5)
No Remorse (Decker's War Book 6)
Hard Strike (Decker's War Book 7)

Constabulary Casefiles
The Warrior's Knife – Case #1
A Colonial Murder – Case #2

Ashes of Empire
Imperial Sunset (Ashes of Empire #1)
Imperial Twilight (Ashes of Empire #2)
Imperial Night (Ashes of Empire #3)
Imperial Echoes (Ashes of Empire #4)

Ghost Squadron
We Dare (Ghost Squadron No. 1)
Deadly Intent (Ghost Squadron No. 2)

Made in the USA
Las Vegas, NV
06 November 2024